The Kingpin of Camelot

A Kinda Fairytale

Cassandra Gannon

Text copyright © 2017 Cassandra Gannon
Cover Image copyright © 2017 Cassandra Gannon
All Rights Reserved

Published by Star Turtle Publishing
www.starturtlepublishing.com

Visit Cassandra Gannon at starturtlepublishing.com or on the Star Turtle Publishing Facebook page for news on upcoming books and promotions!

Email Star Turtle Publishing directly:
starturtlepublishing@gmail.com

We'd love to hear from you!

Also by Cassandra Gannon

The Elemental Phases Series
Warrior from the Shadowland
Guardian of the Earth House
Exile in the Water Kingdom
Treasure of the Fire Kingdom
Queen of the Magnetland
Magic of the Wood House
Coming Soon: *Destiny of the Time House*

A Kinda Fairytale Series
Wicked Ugly Bad
Beast in Shining Armor
The Kingpin of Camelot
Best Knight Ever
Coming Soon: *Happily Ever Witch*

Other Books
Love in the Time of Zombies
Not Another Vampire Book
Vampire Charming
Cowboy from the Future
Once Upon a Caveman
Ghost Walk

You may also enjoy books by Cassandra's sister, Elizabeth Gannon.

The Consortium of Chaos series
Yesterday's Heroes
The Son of Sun and Sand
The Guy Your Friends Warned You About
Electrical Hazard

The Only Fish in the Sea
Not Currently Evil

The Mad Scientist's Guide to Dating
Broke and Famous

<u>*Other books*</u>
The Snow Queen
Travels with a Fairytale Monster
Nobody Likes Fairytale Pirates
Captive of a Fairytale Barbarian

Foreword

There is a contract in this book, which is often cited by the characters. At the beginning of each chapter there is a pertinent clause from it, which should be more than sufficient for you to follow along. (Trust me. It's not that complicated.) In case you'd like to read the entire contract in order, though, I have included all its clauses at the end of the book. Personally, I would not read the whole contract first, as it contains spoilers, but that is up to you. It's there if you need it for reference, want a bit extra, or just feel like spoiling yourself. Happy reading, my friends!

For Toby
Irrefutable proof that you can indeed buy love
...And it only costs $55 at the local pound.

Prologue

Avalon
Three Days Ago

Avalon Pendragon wanted her daddy.

Her mommy was locked up in the dungeon, and her house was full of mean people, and the Scarecrow kept yelling at her, and she just wanted her daddy to come and make everything okay.

Since that wasn't happening today, she comforted herself with her drawings. Avalon liked to draw. Her mommy said she was the best artist in the whole world and had set up a special place for her, on the western terrace of the palace, where she could create her masterpieces in the open air. Usually, Avalon used her crayons to color flowers and dolphins and the rocking-horseflies in the garden. But lately all her pictures featured a mighty queen with an eyepatch and wings, who would sweep down to get rid of all the mean people forever. Avalon liked those pictures.

"Now isn't the time to obfuscate." The Scarecrow paced around the veranda, trying to hide the fact that he hated her under his phony smile.

It was a gloomy day, a cold breeze cutting across the kingdom. From the terrace, Avi could see straight down the hill to the foggy forest and then to Mount Baden far in the distance. All of it was dreary. Avalon missed the sun, but it would stay away until Camelot was happy again.

"We need to identify where the wand is located and it's incumbent on you to relay the information forthwith." The Scarecrow nodded like she was supposed to know what all of that meant. "It's *imperative* that you cooperate, Princess Avalon."

Of all the people in the world, the Scarecrow was her least favorite. Not just because he was ugly and talked funny, but because he was the meanest of them all.

He *was* ugly, though.

His head was made of burlap, with painted features that somehow moved, and a wide-brimmed felt hat. He dressed in a long coat made up of different patches of fabric all sewn together. Avalon had heard someone say that each square had been ripped from the clothing of his victims. That was just icky, because some of them still had blood stains on them.

Most gross of all, of course, were the birds. The Scarecrow's body was made of straw and kindling, his arms "comprised" of many branches that he could "articulate" like "appendages." Those were the words Avalon had heard him using to describe his weird finger-y sticks, anyhow. The Scarecrow liked to use big words when he talked. She wasn't always sure what they all meant, but she kinda thought that was the point of him using them. To make everybody think they were dumber than him.

As if the bundles of wooden twigs he used as hands weren't creepy enough, inside his torso and limbs lived dozens of blackbirds. They nested in the hay and sticks, always ready to do his bidding.

Avalon liked animals, but she was terrified of those birds. She wasn't even sure they *were* birds. Sometimes she felt like they were pieces of the Scarecrow himself that he could send flying out of his body to peck out his enemies' eyes and noses. Avalon never knew where they would be and it was scary.

In Camelot, there were all kinds of people. Human-sized mice, and giants, and pixies, and fish who could talk... Avalon respected them all as unique beings. Her mommy said it was important to treat everybody equal. But the Scarecrow was different. Wrong. Inside of him there was nothing but birds and meanness. She didn't want to talk to him.

"Are you heeding this discussion?" He prompted when she didn't answer. "Avalon, *concentrate*. You must confess to where the wand is located. If you relinquish it to me, you can have Guinevere back." He crouched down in front of the small table where she was coloring and tried a big, fake smile. "Isn't that what you desire? Your mother returned to you? You need to help me in my undertaking, if we're going to make that fond dream a reality."

Avalon didn't like to look at him. It disturbed her to watch his dirty coat move as the birds shifted under the patchwork fabric. "You're a bad person." She told him, because it was wrong to lie. "I'm not helping you."

His painted-on eyes narrowed and he forgot he was pretending to be her friend. "I'm not Bad. *You're* Bad. You and your Bad kind have polluted this kingdom long enough with your villainy. Soon enough, all of you will be expunged from Camelot."

Avalon wasn't sure what "expunged" meant, but it sounded mean. "My mommy and daddy are going to stop you from hurting everyone." She knew that was true, so why didn't he? It was clear to her that the Scarecrow wasn't nearly as smart as he pretended.

"Your father is dead!" He shouted and his birds restlessly fluttered in agitation. "Killed by your murderous mother in this very house!" He pointed upward, towards the balcony where King Arthur had fallen the year before.

Avalon finally met his eyes, shocked that he could believe such a lie. "My daddy isn't dead." She said with absolute confidence.

The Scarecrow hesitated, as if her certainty confused him. "Of course, he's dead. I beheld his corpse with my own eyes. It's interred in the royal tomb."

Avalon tilted her head, studying him for a long moment. "No," she finally decided and went back to her drawing, "you're wrong."

The Scarecrow's lips tightened. They were painted to look like stitches in the burlap. "I grow weary of your obstructionism." Reaching over with his twig-fingers, he grabbed all the crayons from her.

Avalon sent him an angry glare. "Those are mine!"

"No more coloring for you, until I receive the information that I seek." He glowered down at the drawing she was working on. "And that is one fucking hideous picture."

Avalon gasped in outrage. It was a *beautiful* picture and cursing was a no-no.

"I realize now that I've been too lax in my interactions with you *and* your mother." He snapped. "Perhaps you'd like to spend some time in the dungeon yourself." He seized Avalon by the arm, dragging her inside. "See if *that* refreshes your memory."

Avalon allowed herself to be tugged along. Not that she had much of a choice, since he was so much bigger than her. But if the Scarecrow was taking her to see her mommy, then he was forcing her to go just where she wanted to be, anyhow. Avalon loved her mommy more than anyone and missed her desperately.

She didn't fight at all, as he propelled her past the castle's fancy rooms, towards the stairs she was never supposed to play on. They were made of heavy stones and led down, down, down into the lowest level of the house.

Avalon squinted into the darkness looming below her, her heart pounding. "You shouldn't do this." She warned him quietly, because everybody deserved one last chance to fix their behavior.

Her mommy always said that when Avalon was breaking the rules. "One last chance to fix your behavior, Avi, and then you're going to be in *big* trouble." If you were smart, like Avalon, at that point you stopped being naughty and made better choices. If Mommy said you were in big trouble, something horrible could happen. Like losing your dessert, or having to cut playtime short, or even an early bedtime.

The Scarecrow wasn't nearly so smart as her, though. He ignored Avalon's advice and began lugging her down the cold steps. "It's about time you and your mother comprehended who's ruling this kingdom, now. Once I marry her, you'll learn to obey me and show some respect for your betters, you Bad little..."

And then he was gone.

One second he was shouting at her, his twiggy hand crushing her wrist. The next he was flailing down the stairs, into the blackness of the dungeon. It all happened very fast. Avalon felt someone yanking her away from the Scarecrow's grip and lifting her off the ground.

"Don't watch, Avi." Mommy said.

At almost the same time, the Scarecrow was shouting in alarm and careening backwards. Avalon obediently closed her eyes, like her mommy said, but she still heard his body thumping down the steps. The disgusting birds squawked with panic.

Mommy had pushed him and his nasty flock down the stairs.

Mommy always kept her safe from the mean people.

Avalon peeked upward and wasn't surprised at all that her mother was invisible. The cloak was one of their favorite magical objects. Usually, Mommy got it out during games of hide-and-seek.

She beamed happily. "Hi, Mommy! Are we going to play, now?"

"Absolutely we are. And it's going to be very fun. We're going to be super-duper quiet, so no one can find us."

The cloak swirled around Avalon and she became invisible, too. Inside the folds of the enchanted fabric she could finally see her mommy and she didn't look so good. Being locked in the dungeon for days and days must have been sad for her. She was hurt and covered in dirt and way thinner, now.

Avalon blinked up at her, her eyes filling with tears. This didn't seem like a fun game, at all. "You okay, Mommy?"

"I'm fine, baby. Are *you* okay?" She scanned Avalon from head to toe. "Did anyone hurt you?"

"No." Avalon shook her head. "But I don't like it here, anymore. I want my daddy."

Mommy sighed, like she was tired. "I need you to be very, very quiet, alright?" She made a "shhh!" sound and carried Avalon back upstairs. "We have to escape without anyone noticing." At the top of the steps, she hesitated and cautiously looked around. There were several of the King's Men stationed about, but they couldn't see Avi or her mommy inside the cloak.

Mommy carefully edged around them, heading for the terrace. It was the closest way out. "I wish we could steal a horse, but I don't see how we can get into the stables without someone noticing." She whispered. "So, we're going to hop over the railing in your art area and run as fast as we can towards the woods."

"I like running."

"Good. Don't *stop* running. You keep going until we're in the trees. We just need to put some distance between…"

The Scarecrow's angry bellow cut her off. "Find them!" He screamed, charging up the steps in a furious rush. It was super hard to kill a person who wasn't a person, but at least Mommy had hurt him. All his stuffing was askew, making him look lumpy and messed up. Straw and feathers poked out every which way. "Locate that bitch and her evil whelp or I'll have all of your heads!"

Mommy flattened her body to the wall, holding Avalon against her. Avalon squeezed her eyes shut, trying to make herself as small as possible.

"How did Guinevere get free of the dungeon?" Sir Percival demanded, hot on his heels. He was almost as mean as the Scarecrow.

"I don't know. It was too dark on the stairs to even see her. She must have had assistance. She's not clever enough to outmaneuver me herself." The Scarecrow sounded mad. "Is there anyone still inhabiting the palace who could remain loyal to her?"

"No, sire. We disposed of all the Bad servants long ago and the Good folk who replaced them know better than to cross you."

"Where's Galahad? Could he be back?"

Percival scowled at the name. "I'm not sure, sire. No one's seen him since King Arthur had him banished, because of his betrayal and his… *attachment* to the queen."

"Find him." The Scarecrow spat out. "In the meantime, I want Guinevere back and locked in chains immediately. Seal the doors and ensure she can't leave the property." He issued orders to random soldiers as he walked, pointing at them. "Cut off all her access points. Alert the perimeter guards. If Gwen escapes, she could locate the wand and ruin us!"

"Even if she gets out of the castle, the bitch won't have anywhere to go." Sir Percival assured him. They were so close now, Avalon was surprised they couldn't hear her breathing. "No Good folk in the kingdom will support her, as long as she insists that Bad brat is Arthur's heir."

Mommy's hand came up to cradle the back of Avalon's head, shielding her from danger. Mommy was the best person in the world. She protected Avi. But Daddy wasn't there, so who protected Mommy? Avalon hugged her tight, scared they would be found and her mother would be taken away, again.

Luckily, the Scarecrow and his men walked right past them.

"And someone make sure Arthur's really dead!" The Scarecrow bellowed to nobody in particular as he stormed by.

Avalon breathed a sigh of relief as they headed down the hall, their weapons drawn.

"Fucking bastards." Mommy muttered.

"You shouldn't curse, Mommy. It's a no-no."

"Sorry, baby." Mommy hitched Avalon up on her hip, not sounding very sorry. She hurried towards the terrace, barely squeezing through the door before one of the guards slammed it shut. "What a pretty picture!" Avalon's art was still sitting on the small table and Mommy nodded to the sketch of the flying lady as they hurried by. "That just might be your very best drawing, yet."

Avalon bobbed her head, pleased that her work was appreciated. "Lyrssa's brave. Like you, Mommy."

"Like *us*, baby. You and I are going to be very brave together." She swung them both over the low railing, dropping into the flower garden below. Rocking-horseflies buzzed. Those were Avalon's favorite and they made her feel a little bit better.

Mommy paused by a statue of Arthur's father, kicking it over with her foot.

Avalon winced as the boring clay bust of King Uther shattered into a million pieces. "Why'd you do that?"

"I hid something under here that we might need." She grabbed a small rolled up package from beneath the base of the ruined memorial, keeping one arm locked around Avalon. "A present from Galahad."

Avalon smiled. "I love Gal *and* I love presents."

"I love him, too." Mommy sighed again, 'cause she missed him a lot. "We'll see him soon. I promise."

"We should find him."

"We will, but not today. Today, we're running to the forest and we're not stopping until we're safe in the trees, remember?"

Avalon nodded, trying to be brave like her mommy said, but she was still afraid. "Then where are we going to go?"

"I'm not sure." Mommy kissed the top of her head. "We'll figure it out when we get there, won't we?"

Avalon popped her thumb into her mouth. Things that made sense to her usually didn't make sense to other people. She'd figured that out a long time ago. Arthur used to get real mad when she'd tell him stuff and the Scarecrow called her names. Mommy would listen, though. She always listened, especially when it was important.

"Mommy?"

"Yes, Avi?"

"I want my daddy."

Chapter One

This Contract is entered into by Guinevere Pendragon and Midas (no last name given) willingly and knowingly. Each party wishes to define their rights and obligations under the arrangement herein discussed and attest that they fully understand all its terms, conditions, clauses, and caveats. The purpose of this Contract is to ensure there will be no misunderstanding in the future and to facilitate a smooth and profitable partnership.

Clause 1- General Purpose of Contract

Gold could buy many things.

Palaces. Armies. Women. Just about anything a man could want, really.

But gold couldn't buy class.

At least, that's what everyone told him. All his life, Midas had been trying to prove them wrong. He refused to accept that there was anything in existence that he couldn't purchase.

Class was proving to be an elusive item on his shopping list, though. He'd tried to acquire it in a thousand different ways and he'd still come up empty. Maybe it *was* hopeless. Maybe class was just an innate quality that some people were born with and most people weren't. That possibility never seemed as frustratingly true as when he saw Arthur's wife entered the ballroom.

She was shivering and soaking wet from the rain. Her dress was so worn that it was falling apart. Her body was frail, her pale hair a bedraggled mess around her colorless face. In her arms, she carried a small girl who couldn't have been more than five. Quite frankly, Guinevere Pendragon looked as if she'd just walked straight through hell itself, carrying her daughter on her hip.

And somehow she was still the only woman in the room.

All around Midas, the finely-dressed guests at the party transformed. Their lavish clothes and priceless jewelry became gaudy. Their artful, cutting laughter suddenly seemed grating. Their carefully made up faces now looked overblown and fake. Next to Guinevere, all the illusions they had crafted for themselves fell away and revealed the common tin under their gilded surfaces.

Imitations would always look like imitations when you set them next to the genuine article. When you compared them to the best.

From his perch on the balcony, Midas' golden eyes sited on Guinevere and he saw what he could never have. He had more money than he could ever spend and enough power to change the course of history, but he didn't possess what this tiny woman wore like perfume.

Class.

His detractors were right. Midas could try and fake it, but his efforts no doubt looked just as artificial as the rest of the partygoers'. In that moment, he saw the truth. You couldn't bullshit class. Couldn't pick it up like a new language. Couldn't bibbity-bob it into existence with a fairy godmother. It was quite simply bred in the bone. Guinevere had it and he wanted it.

And if she was coming to Midas, she must want something from him, too.

Satisfaction filled him. He'd been right, too. Everything was for sale, if you offered the right price. *Everything.* Midas believed that with a fervor other men reserved for God and kingdom. If he couldn't buy class itself, he'd simply own someone who possessed it. It amounted to the same thing.

Every day, people showed up at his custom-designed castle to pay homage and beg favors. Guinevere might be royalty, but she was no different in that respect. He could already tell. She needed something desperately or she would've stayed far away.

They'd certainly never met before. Arthur would roll over in his tomb before he'd let his pristine bride within a mile of the Kingpin. Their dearly departed ruler was quoted as calling Midas a "violent predator who lured innocents into his evil clutches." It was all right there in the trial transcripts, along with other memorably colorful phrases such as "upstart commoner," "mindless gorilla" and "tawdry, feral animal."

The "tawdry" part was just a low-blow, in Midas' opinion, but the jury sure had liked it.

In any case, classy noblewomen and their sleeping daughters usually stayed far, far away from Midas and his home. Especially with the Round Table about to begin. The guests at his bacchanalia were the worst the kingdom had to offer. Soulless predators in the sometimes *literal* sense of the words. A lady like Guinevere would never willingly walk through his front door.

Not unless she was completely out of options.

Two of the ogres Midas employed as guards moved in,

wanting to know Guinevere's business at the party. Midas had to stop himself from interfering as they loomed over her. His instincts told him to stalk down there and clear her path. The feeling was so strong that his free palm tightened on the banister in front of him, the leather glove clenching around the gold railing. He forced himself to wait and see what she'd do.

Clearly, his men planned to toss Gwen out on her sweet little ass. Just as clearly, she didn't plan to leave. Midas expected tears or pleading. Instead the woman squared her shoulders and faced them down, ready for a fight.

His head tilted at the show of strength.

Interesting.

"What the hell is *she* doing here?" Jill Hill demanded, coming up beside him. "How dare she show her fucking face at this party!"

Midas didn't even glance in Jill's direction. "You know the queen?" Somehow he doubted it. They didn't exactly run in the same social circles. Jill operated the most exclusive "gentleman's club" in Camelot and Guinevere... did whatever the hell royalty did with their frivolous lives. Attend tea parties maybe?

Jill tossed back her long red hair, arranging her body to show off her ample curves to best advantage. "No, darling. I knew *Arthur*."

Ah, that made more sense. Jill was attracted to powerful men and no one had been more powerful than the king. Until he fell four stories onto that cobblestone patio, anyway. That was one battle not even their fearless leader could win.

"I never met the man." Midas said mildly. "Unless you count my trial."

He detested Arthur, alive or dead. In addition to the whole "tawdry, feral animal" remark, the king had done everything in his power to ruin Midas. God, you'd think Midas was the only villain in Camelot, the way that jackass had railed against him. If Midas was the kind of guy to hold a grudge, he'd be *especially* pissed over the six months he'd spent in prison thanks to Arthur's vendetta. Also the whole "sending men to murder him" thing. That hadn't been fun.

And what kind of pretentious dickhead actually used the word "tawdry," anyway?

"Well, Arthur was fabulous." Jill assured him, tears welling at the thought of their lost ruler. "Practically a saint. He deserved so much better than that damn ice queen. Gwen is totally heartless!"

Midas made a noncommittal sound. People said he was heartless, too, so he wasn't about to hold that against the girl. And was it his imagination or were Guinevere's breasts the absolute perfect size? A dozen plastic surgeries could never replicate the natural, elegant shape of them. This woman had simply been born the best.

"Their marriage certainly wasn't a love match." Jill continued. "Just some prophesized union pushed on Arthur by the wizards. Especially by Gwen's nut-ball father. Her lineage is all any man would ever want from her."

"No. It's not." The attraction she held for Midas had nothing to do with her social status. Guinevere could have been raised in a barnyard and she still would have been fascinating. Even someone as stupid as Arthur must have appreciated the beauty of this woman.

Jill ignored his opinion. "Arthur and Guinevere were both totally free to see other people." She shook her head, like she was an expert on marriage. Which she *was*, given her clientele. "That's the way it is with Good folk. They always say 'I do' for political standing, rather than waiting for their True Love. Especially when there's a royal marriage on the line."

Midas kept his eyes on Guinevere. She didn't look like the type to screw around on her husband, but Jill had a point. It was impossible to underestimate what Good folk were capable of. Besides, everyone knew Arthur wasn't Gwen's True Love. Maybe she saw that as a loophole in their marriage contract. Smart people always took advantage of the fine print, after all. Midas had certainly heard rumors about her infidelity.

Lots of rumors. Everyone had.

"They say that little girl isn't even Arthur's." Jill continued. "How could she be? She was born Bad. What are the odds of two Good parents having a Bad baby?"

"It happens." Midas knew that better than most. That bologna sandwich flashed through his mind and he shook it away.

"Well, Arthur wasn't convinced. Neither was I. We discussed *all* their marital problems." She sighed, feeling sorry for the dead king and the countless ways that he'd suffered. "He needed more than just a warm body from me. He needed a real friend. A partner."

Midas glanced at her from the corner of his eye.

"We used to talk a lot!" Jill insisted, sensing his skepticism. "People like to talk to me after sex. You know that. Well, not *personally*, since you're all," she held up her hands and pointedly waved her fingers, "afflicted."

"Cursed." Midas corrected, not taking offense.

"Whatever. Point is, people like to fuck and talk. Usually in that order. With Arthur it was more than that, though. He *respected* me." Jill dabbed at her eyes. "We were so happy, until that bitch murdered him."

That rumor was an incontrovertible fact according to half the Good folk in the kingdom. Few of them wanted to believe the Once and Future Asshole got drunk and tumbled over a railing. It was far more comforting to whisper that his heartless queen was behind it.

"My only consolation is the Scarecrow is making her pay for her crimes." Jill ranted. "He's going to take *everything* from that cold-blooded monster."

Midas kept his attention on Guinevere, who was still arguing with his guards. She hitched her child farther up her hip and didn't back down from the eight-foot ogres glowering at her. Did cold-blooded monsters hold their sleeping daughters so carefully?

"Gwen's coming to beg for help, you know." Jill fairly spat out the words. "To defeat the Scarecrow, she needs someone powerful on her side and that's *you*. But, you can't get involved in this." She shook her head. "The Scarecrow is leaving you alone *right now*, but you're Bad. If you draw too much attention..." She trailed off and lowered her voice. "I know enough about the Scarecrow's plans for our kind to know they aren't plans that you want to be a part of."

Midas didn't doubt that for a second. The Scarecrow never bothered to hide his hatred of Bad folk. His "plans" no doubt involved all of them being transported to labor camps or vanishing into rabbit holes.

"If you offer Gwen any sort of sanctuary, you'll piss off the Scarecrow and he'll come after *you*." Jill added, just in case Midas hadn't reasoned that out for himself. "These days, the best option for us is to keep our heads down and our mouths shut."

"I've never been much good at blending in." Midas took a sip of champagne from his ornate glass. Every inch of it was decorated with gold and engraved with intricate designs. It had cost a fortune. The very best crystal money could buy.

"Gwen has got nothing left to offer." Jill stressed. "No money, no power... There's *nothing* in this for you."

"Of course there's something in it for me." He kept his tone bored, even as he memorized every move Guinevere made. "I'm about to own a queen."

Jill stared at Midas like he was out of his mind. Maybe he was.

"You can't be serious." She finally sputtered. "*That's* what this is about? Getting that bitch into bed? Since when do you care about sex, Midas? You've never even slept with *me*." Apparently, she viewed that as conclusive proof that he was celibate. "Is this some kind of revenge, because she was Arthur's wife?"

"No." It was about Midas refusing to settle for inferior belongings.

Jill didn't like that simple answer. "You can't... *collect* Gwen Pendragon like you do your damn paintings and horses and books. You can't just buy the Queen of Camelot!"

"I can buy anything."

Jill made a frustrated sound at the finality of his tone. "That girl is poison and I'm not standing anywhere close to you when the fallout starts." Her eyes were furious and betrayed. "Don't come whining to me when this blows up in your face." She went stalking off in an offended huff. "I swear to God, you're usually smarter than this, Midas."

Jill was at least partially right. It was a terrible idea to back the underdog in the battle for Camelot's throne. Midas knew that. The Scarecrow was too powerful and he had the support of the kingdom's Good folk. Gwen was going to lose this war. The smart play would be to keep out of her messy little life.

But no one could warn Midas away from what he wanted and he wanted the best.

It was a hopeless stance for someone like him to take. There were two kinds of people in the world: Those born Good and those born Bad. Laws made sure Good folk were always on top. People like Guinevere lived their lives insulated from people like Midas, safe behind their protective walls. Bad folk were nothing but a disposable underclass. Wolves and witches and ugly stepsisters never got "the best" of anything. Society made sure of that. If a villain like Midas wanted to possess something of real value, he had to *take* it.

...Unless, of course, something of real value came marching straight into his home and saved him the trouble of stealing it for himself.

Guinevere pushed past the guards and the two ogres seemed unable to stop her. Her jaw set at a determined angle, she looked around, trying to spot someone. Midas braced himself. He knew what was about to happen. Maybe he'd known from the minute he first saw her enter the ballroom and felt the magnetic pull of their connection. Blue eyes, the exact color of Vivien's enchanted lake, looked up at him...

> And for the first time in his life, Midas belonged somewhere.
> Oh God.
> He'd found her.

Incredible amounts of lust and possession and fear and triumph roared through him, all mixing together so it was impossible to tell for sure what he was feeling. So many conflicting emotions hit him so fast that it left him disoriented. This woman could upend his whole life. He saw it so clearly. She could take *everything* from him. For one wild second, he even debated letting her go. Turning her away before she left him alone on a porch, with nothing at all.

No.

Midas shook off the idea as soon as it formed. *No.* He could do this. Of course he could. They key was not to panic. It was no different than any other deal. He wanted what she had and so he'd buy it. Anything could be bought. He just needed to stay in control and not let Guinevere see how much he was willing to pay.

Anything. Jesus, he would pay anything.

Guinevere marched straight for him, like she expected the crowd to move out of her way. ...Which they did. Partly because they didn't want water dripped all over their expensive clothes and partly because Guinevere Pendragon possessed an innate air of authority.

Still, it was good to see at least *one* of his men wasn't intimidated by a tiny blonde girl. His most loyal guard, Trystan, stalked towards her with an inscrutable expression on his inscrutable face. Trystan never worried about his wardrobe being ruined by a little water.

...Or a little blood and entrails.

The man wore the simple garments of his vanquished people, refusing to don anything else. That choice was fine with Midas. No one employed a gryphon for their sartorial sense. It was mainly just for their "killing people" skills. Trystan could do whatever he wished, because Trystan was the best warrior in Camelot and the one person in the world Midas trusted. When you had the best on your payroll, you let them work without a lot of micromanaging. It just made sense.

Still, Midas could handle the woman without any help from his fanatically protective bodyguard. He waved Trystan back, ignoring the gryphon's characteristic frown, and headed down the steps so he could meet Guinevere at the bottom. There was something to be said for making your opponents come to you, but he didn't want her to climb the stairs with the child in her arms. She didn't look strong enough to make the trip.

"Queen Guinevere. Welcome." Midas said quietly, coming to a stop in front of her.

He always spoke quietly. Given his massive build and harsh

features, bellowing at people would have been redundant. They were generally terrified enough. As an added bonus, it helped to mask his Celliwig accent. To his ear, the lower-class cadence never quite went away, no matter how much he tried to mask it. Still, it was a miracle that his voice sounded even semi-normal, given the pounding in his ears.

The woman smelled like gingerbread, damn it. That was just fighting dirty.

Guinevere's expression lost some of its do-or-die intensity when she realized he wasn't going to immediately kick her out. Whatever welcome she'd anticipated, his polite greeting obviously wasn't it. God only knew what kind of stories Arthur had told her about Midas. Hell, most of them were probably true.

"It's a pleasure to finally meet you." He murmured, when she just blinked up at him. "I feel as if it's been a long time coming."

Too fucking long. His eyes drank her in, desire nearly dropping him to his knees. She was beautiful in the understated, timeless way of pearls, and lace and white roses. Beautiful in a way that couldn't be created with the right makeup or enhanced with designer clothes, because it was part of her very bones. Class was so obvious when you had it right in front of you.

Whatever she'd been facing recently had taken a toll, though. Up close, he could see the exhaustion in Guinevere's lovely eyes. Luckily, Midas was a master at separating business from his personal feelings, so he barely felt his heart breaking, at all. He was *sure* of that.

When he was in prison, the psychiatrists had gravely diagnosed that Midas was incapable of distinguishing right from wrong. Therefore, he couldn't *possibly* know that it was wrong to take advantage of this woman when she was at her weakest. If Guinevere was tired and out of options, he could strike a better deal with her. That was all that mattered. As long as he stayed in control, Midas could have everything and give nothing. That was the goal in every business transaction. Right and wrong were immaterial.

He was very, very sure of that.

Damn it, he wanted to feed her something. She looked too thin.

Gwen still didn't say anything. Instead, her gaze traveled up and down his body, taking in his colossal size. She didn't even reach his shoulder, so he wasn't surprised when her grip tightened on the child and she nervously gulped.

"Can I get you anything?" Midas pressed, afraid she would

turn around and flee for the door. She looked befuddled to be standing in front of the most notorious gangster in Camelot, even though she was the one who'd sought him out. What could he say to make her stay? "Maybe some food?" She was clearly half-starved. He really wanted to *insist* that she eat something, but he had a feeling it would just piss her off. Pride was wrapped around her like a mantle.

Guinevere gave her head a quick shake, regaining her composure. "No. Thank you." Her voice sounded like liquid class, the fancy accent smooth as the finest silks. "I'm sorry to arrive unannounced. I didn't know you were having a party. I'm not dressed... um..." her gaze drifted over Midas' purple, pinstriped, sharkskin tuxedo as if it fascinated her, "...as *vibrantly* as the rest of you."

"You look fine." Midas assured her and it was the greatest understatement ever uttered in the history of the world. The woman was wearing rags and still outshone everyone else in the room. A flawless diamond set next to rhinestones.

"Thank you." Guinevere said again and took a deep breath, getting back on track. For someone who appeared as delicate as a glass slipper, she was definitely a fighter. That was so... interesting. She squared her shoulders, ready for the next battle. "I'd like to speak with you." She said in a firmer voice. "About business."

"What kind of business...?"

A loud commotion at the door interrupted his question. Midas' head snapped up as a half-dozen of Camelot's most elite knights pushed their way into his home. Oh for God's sake. If they thought he'd keep up his exorbitant bribes when they interrupted him during the most important meeting of his life...

His annoyance over an ill-timed shake-down was cut off as Guinevere let out an audible gasp. She took a tiny step backward, closer to Midas, her hand coming up to rest protectively on her daughter's blonde hair. Gwen's back was nearly touching his front, the damp hem of her tattered dress sloshing against his two-toned shoes.

Oh.

Midas was so used to being the most wanted person in the room that it hadn't even occurred to him that the soldiers weren't there for him. They were there for the queen.

Wearing glistening armor and angry expressions, they began shoving past the guests and heading towards Guinevere. Since most of the attendees had prices on their heads, the knights' presence put a bit of a damper on the festive atmosphere. A stampede of Baddies bolted for the doors and windows, doing a not-so-small fortune worth of damage to the furnishings in their rush.

Midas barely noticed. "I take it this is the 'business' you'd like to speak to me about?" He asked Guinevere in a calm tone.

She shot him a quick look over her shoulder, as if startled to see him standing directly behind her. She must not have realized that she'd shifted so close, because her eyes widened in surprise. Midas arched a brow, expecting her to jump back and stammer out excuses. No Good folk wanted to stand near the Kingpin of Camelot.

Instead of jerking away, though, Gwen leaned in even closer. That perfect lake-blue gaze met his, earnest and clear, and Midas forgot how to breathe.

"The King's Men are here to arrest me." She whispered fiercely. Both of her thin arms were wrapped around her child, as if someone might try to steal the little girl away. Given the current mood of Camelot, it wasn't such a farfetched idea. "I'm a fugitive, now."

"Well, you're certainly at the right party, then." He assured her, his gaze memorizing every shiny strand of her shiny hair. He had never wanted to touch anything so much. Inside his gloves, his fingers ached to feel the softness.

Gwen didn't appear to notice his distraction. Luminous eyes darted back to gauge the knights' approach. "It's my fault they're here. I'm sorry. I didn't think they were so close behind me. I swear. But, don't worry. I can handle this." Determination lit her patrician face. "Just... don't worry."

"I'll try not to."

She missed his sarcasm. He could see her brain working, running scenarios. The woman clearly had a "Damn the torpedoes!" streak, because she wasn't going to back down from the heavily-armed force headed towards her. "It'll be alright." She took a deep breath and looked up at him, again. "I'll make sure they don't hurt you."

That was either adorable or insane. Midas wasn't sure which. Before he could make up his mind, she was handing him her sleeping daughter.

"Here. Watch Avalon for a second." She ordered. "Do *not* let her go."

"What? Wait..."

But she didn't wait and Midas was too shocked to do anything but grasp the girl when Gwen passed her to him. He'd never held a child before. She was too light. Too delicate. Shit! He tried to keep his fingers away from her tiny body, afraid his curse would kill her. The leather gloves he wore *should* protect her, but what if they somehow didn't?

"You need to take her back." He said a little desperately.

Guinevere ignored him.

The child made an irritated sound at his awkward handling, blue eyes opening to peer at him in confusion. Midas cringed, afraid to even move, and waited for her to scream bloody murder. His face looked far more like the monster under the bed than any storybook hero.

The mud and blood and brutality of Celliwig were in his very DNA. He had the harsh profile of a thug who'd battled his way up from the worst part of the worst village in Camelot, because that's exactly what he'd done. No one would ever mistake him for someone Good. He was too big and ugly and hard to be anything but a villain. Compared to Arthur's aristocratic blondness, Midas' hulking presence would terrify the child. Hell, he terrified most adults.

Apparently, the girl wasn't awake enough to notice she was in the grasp of a notorious mobster, though. The Princess of Camelot stared up at his harsh features for a beat and then gave him a sleepy smile. One teeny hand moved so it was fisted around the lapel of his expensive jacket, holding on tight. Less than a second later, she was back to sleep, her head innocently nestled on his shoulder.

Midas blinked.

"Guinevere Pendragon!" Percival had been named Captain of the King's Men after Galahad was banished and he used his new position like a club. He had brown hair, overly-bronzed armor, and a perpetual sneer that he aimed at everyone he found unworthy. ...Which was *everyone*. "In the name of the Scarecrow, you are hereby under arrest. Surrender yourself to Camelot's justice and you will be treated fairly by his royal highness."

"If anyone's guilty here, it's *you*, Percival." Guinevere snapped. "You swore to serve this kingdom. Instead, you're helping a lunatic seize control and threaten all of us. Do you *really* think I'm going to let that happen?"

She stood directly in front of Midas and the child like she planned to... what? Protect them? Was he losing his mind or was this really happening? Midas looked over at Trystan, to see if he was the only one witnessing this crazy woman and her crazy daughter and all their craziness.

Trystan's gaze stayed on Guinevere, scanning her for ulterior motives. Clearly, he already regarded her as a bigger threat than Percival. Conclusive proof that gryphons weren't the mindless savages that people thought.

"The Scarecrow is going to purify Camelot!" Percival roared

at Guinevere. "You may have fooled poor Galahad, ruining him with your licentious wiles, but I see right through you. Hand over the wand. If you don't, you'll die along with the evil creatures you love so much."

"You take one more step towards my daughter and you'll see which of us dies."

The fierceness of Guinevere's tone surprised Midas. She sounded like she really meant that. He looked down at the child in his arms, trying to make sense of it. This girl was Bad. He'd never known any Good folk to give a damn about a Bad folk, mother or not.

"You're on the wrong side of history, Guinevere." Percival's eyes glowed with the crazed light of a true zealot. "The Bad folk are as dead as the gryphons, now." He glowered pointedly at Trystan. "They're all genetic mistakes, being wiped out by time and God and better men."

Trystan watched him without expression.

Gwen wasn't so reserved. "You're an idiot, Percival. You always have been."

"I'm *right!*" He insisted passionately. "You're either with your own kind, a part of the Good and honorable future. ...Or you're standing with the Bad folk, in the dirty, shadowed past." He jerked his chin at Midas and the dozing kindergartener like they were garbage that someone had forgotten to throw out. "Which is it going to be? Us or them?"

From the sodden folds of her dress, Gwen pulled out a handgun and pointed it at him. "Take one goddamn guess, asshole."

And then the Queen of Camelot shot Sir Percival right there in the ballroom.

Midas' eyebrows shot up. Well, that was interesting.

Even Trystan blinked and it took a lot to surprise someone born without emotions.

Sadly, while Guinevere was proving to be a lady of many and varied talents, she didn't have much of an aim. Midas blamed Arthur. The King of the Idiots had outlawed guns, back when he was just a prince. Not because he cared about preventing violence, but because he felt swords looked more "majestic" for his soldiers. Therefore, *all* guns had to go. It made no sense for everyone to have better weapons than the King's Men, after all. The result was that people in Camelot did not know how to shoot and Gwen was no exception.

The bullet missed Percival's head, imbedding itself into his armored shoulder. He gave a bellow of pain and surprise, stumbling backwards. His hand came up to grasp at his wounded arm, blood trickling between his fingers. A witch-practitioner could have him healed in no time, but he was still acting like a pussy about it. Furious eyes flashed back to Gwen, glinting with hate. "You fucking *bitch!*"

"Next one goes through your traitorous heart." She warned, not lowering her weapon.

That would be a much harder injury to heal, so Midas was all for it.

The other knights gaped at the scene, unsure of what to do when their commander was getting his ass kicked by a small woman in a tattered peach dress. Presumably, they'd been sent to collect Guinevere for the Scarecrow, not to engage her in combat. The whole dumbass lot of them were better at posing with sabers at state dinners than participating in gunfights.

They looked lost as to their next step.

Amusing as the spectacle was to watch, Midas had had enough. He moved forward, before Guinevere killed any of the tin-canned idiots. It seemed like the kind of thing that would bother a lady, even an interesting one. "Percival, get the hell out of my house." Midas commanded in a tone no Bad folk ever used when speaking to the Good. "You're bleeding on my carpet and it was handwoven by pixies. Do you have any idea how long it takes them to weave rugs with their tiny little hands? Costs a fortune."

Guinevere's lips parted in astonishment, like she'd forgotten Midas was capable of speech. She glanced up at him, big blue eyes wide and hopeful.

Percival's scowl got even deeper. "You're usually smarter than this, Kingpin." He snapped, unconsciously echoing Jill's words. "The Scarecrow gave us orders to leave you alone... *for now*. Unless you want to be labeled an enemy of the crown, just hand over the woman and her devil-spawn."

"No."

Percival and Gwen both stared at Midas for a beat, not knowing what to make of the flat denial. A lot of times people looked at him that way when he responded to their questions. They always seemed to want elaboration, when the answer was simple and clear.

"No?" Percival sputtered. "What do you mean 'no'? You can't just say 'no' to soldiers of the realm, you uppity bastard!"

"Well, I just did." Midas passed the child back to Gwen and stepped in front of them both. "They're staying and you're leaving. Now."

"I'm not going fucking anywhere without *her!*" Percival jabbed a finger at Guinevere.

"Yes, you are." Trystan and the ogres were already moving

in to enforce his orders. No one could doubt the outcome of the fight. Not even Percival. "It's time for you to go."

Gwen held her daughter tightly, still gazing up at Midas in something like wonder. He was surprised, too. Who could have predicted that the Kingpin of Camelot would ever protect a damsel in distress from a knight in shining armor?

Not that Gwen *needed* much protection. The gun was still in her hand.

The woman was just endlessly interesting.

"Think long and hard about this, Midas." Percival warned, because he was clever enough not to want a physical fight, but too much of an idiot to think of a better verbal response. "You might win today, but there will be a bigger battle coming tomorrow. The Scarecrow can make things very uncomfortable for you. *He's* in control of the kingdom now."

"If he has control, why is he so desperate to get his hands on Queen Guinevere?"

"She's not the queen anymore!"

"Except she *is*." Midas didn't give a rat's ass about politics, but he very *certainly* cared about the Scarecrow and his followers attacking this woman. "I don't recognize that usurping dickhead or his piss-ant authority." He arched a brow. "And I'm not the only one. That's why you're after this woman, right? Because there are quite a few Bad folk who won't support your new regime. Who will back her and the child, if there's a war."

"We don't *need* your support." Percival hissed. "By the time we're through, you won't be able to inflict your villainy on the rest of us. Every damn one of you will finally know your place."

"Oh, I know my place. It's right here in the house *I* built, on the land *I* own, at the party *I'm* hosting. And you weren't fucking invited." Midas looked over at his towering bodyguard. "Trystan? Kindly have the men escort Percival off of my property. He was just leaving."

Trystan wasn't much for talking. Or subtlety. He just pulled his double-bladed axe free and spun it in his hand. The rest of Midas' men took the hint and reached for their own weapons. Midas believed in hiring lots and lots of armed killers to guard his parties. He was entertaining criminals, after all. Who the hell knew what they might try?

The Scarecrow's flunkies froze, weighing their options. None of them were great. The King's Men were outnumbered three to one. Hell, Trystan could have been alone with the knights and *still* outnumber them.

The wings alone were an advantage.

With no other options, Percival stepped back, grasping his wounded shoulder. "This isn't over." He snarled, trite to the last. "I told the Scarecrow to take care of you long ago, Midas. You've always been a stupid, vulgar brute. And *that's* how you'll be treated." He turned on his heel, gesturing for his men to follow, and went striding out of Midas' home.

For the moment, anyway.

Midas had no doubt that they'd be back. He needed more guards. And weapons. And supplies. ...And girly things, since Guinevere was going to stay with him for the foreseeable future. Where else could she go? Gwen and the child clearly weren't safe on their own.

That fact made everything easier for Midas, actually. For all intents and purposes, the queen and her daughter were shipwrecked in his home. But, they'd no doubt need frilly pillows and flowery skirts and all kinds of mysterious feminine items to comfortably adapt. They both seemed very small and dainty. They'd need stuff he didn't have, so he'd just have to get it for them.

Time to buy out Camelot's weapons depots and dress shops.

Guinevere released a long breath as the knights slammed the door behind them. "You made them leave." She whispered. "No one has *ever* defeated the King's Men, but you frightened them away in -- like-- two seconds. That was incredible. You were... incredible." She smiled as if he'd just impressed the hell out of her.

As if he was a hero instead of a tawdry feral animal.

It felt pretty fucking amazing.

"Well, you shot their captain in my ballroom." Midas reminded her, uncomfortable with how damn pleased he was with her obvious admiration. "I believe that kick-started the process."

"Yes, but I didn't have enough bullets for all of them." She explained blithely. "Actually, I've had this gun hidden in the palace gardens for months, buried under a statue of Arthur's odious father." She glanced down at the weapon with the vaguely unsettled expression of someone who'd never really held a gun before. "I'm kind of shocked it worked, at all."

Midas stifled a wince at that news. Definitely a "damn the torpedoes" kind of girl.

"So, thank you for helping us." She finished sincerely. "Thank you *so much*."

"It was my pleasure." Midas swept a gloved hand towards

his office. "Why don't we go in here and talk about business?"

Guinevere nodded and followed him towards the elaborate double doors, like she wasn't worried about being locked in a room with the Kingpin of Camelot. The woman should've been warned about blindly trusting Bad men, but Midas certainly wasn't fool enough to do it.

"You plan to be alone in a room with that girl when she's still armed?" Trystan demanded in his people's language. From his tone, it was clear that he thought Midas was the one blindly trusting somebody and he didn't like it.

Midas was used to his attitude. Trystan believed that everyone born without wings was an idiot.

Midas held the door so Guinevere could enter and met Trystan's eyes. "I'll be fine." He assured him in the gryphons' dialect. It wasn't a particularly lyrical language, but, since most gryphons were long dead, only a handful of people still spoke it. That came in handy when you wanted to communicate privately. "The queen is half my size."

"Arthur was bigger than her, too." Trystan agreed with a credible amount of sarcasm for someone so utterly humorless. "Right up until the moment he was significantly shortened by an impact with the pavement."

"I promise not to visit any tall balconies with her. Just make sure the soldiers don't double-back on us." Midas fixed Trystan with a warning look, because it was always a bright idea to be explicit when you dealt with a paranoid, arrogant, trained assassin who carried an arsenal everywhere he went. "This woman is mine."

"Since when? She only just arrived."

"Since *now*. Do nothing to frighten her."

"Have you missed the last few moments? Be concerned about the violence she might inflict on *you*, not what I might do to *her*. She is a remorseless killer. Believe me. I know the breed well. You should let her people take her away and save yourself the trouble."

Midas ignored that analysis. "*Ha'na*, Trystan." Gryphons were born without emotions, but that word was sacrosanct.

Trystan hesitated. "You're sure?"

Midas nodded. He'd never been more sure of anything. "No matter what happens, *don't hurt her*."

Midas paid Trystan a great deal of money to act as a bodyguard, but the man wasn't exactly a traditional employee. He only bothered to follow directions when he agreed with them and he basically considered Midas a teenager with poor impulse control.

Despite his misgivings, though, Trystan wouldn't hack Gwen to pieces if he understood the truth.

Sure enough, Trystan relented with a sigh. "She is your woman." He agreed, grudgingly. "But, claiming her is ill-advised, even for you and you have *many* stupid ideas. She is dangerous."

Midas ignored the (no doubt accurate) naysaying. He could no more have stayed away from Guinevere than he could have stopped the sun from setting behind Mount Baden each night. Midas followed Gwen into the office and shut both doors, sealing them in.

...And he was finally alone with his True Love.

Chapter Two

Full disclosure need not be given on matters that happened before parties met, do not pertain to the other party, and/or do not violate any other clauses in this agreement.
Especially if those matters regard Arthur Pendragon.

Clause 8- Privacy and Disclosure

Possession and relief hummed through Midas, once he had the woman trapped in his private sanctum.

Guinevere's gaze scanned around the interior of the room. Like the rest of his home, it was decorated in the most expensive, lavish furnishings in Camelot. Massive pillars lined the muraled walls, layers of silk curtains dripped from the stained-glass windows, and a desk the size of a small kingdom dominated the center. No palace in the world could match its opulence.

It was the best.

"This is quite… large." Gwen said cautiously, her gaze on the frescoed ceiling and the two-ton chandelier. The multi-colored crystals dangling from it were as big as bowling balls. To Midas' way of thinking, bigger was always better.

"Thank you." He took a seat on his chair, which had a twelve foot high back and was made of wood from four separate species of extinct trees. "Lay your child down and have a seat. You must be exhausted."

She hesitated, putting the gun back in her pocket as she looked around. Her gaze scanned the overstuffed sofas. All of them were covered in exotic leathers from the remotest lands. All of them had cost a fortune. "Um… We're very wet."

Of course they were. Camelot was always gray and rainy. It had been like that for years, but overly dramatic Arthur supporters swore that the land itself was mourning its lost ruler. Others insisted that the blue sky would only return when Camelot finally had a *true* king. Someone worthy, who was more interested in justice than Uther or Arthur had been. No matter the cause, the foggy, dreary weather seemed far too harsh for beings as delicate as Guinevere and her daughter.

"Maybe you should put a blanket down first?" She continued. "Or..."

Midas cut her off. "It's fine." He could always buy more couches, but queens were a far rarer commodity. "Please." He picked up a remote control and clicked on his two-story high fireplace, in case she was cold. The mantle was made of yellow bricks. Damn Munchkins had charged him an outrageous amount for each and every one, but they were the best.

Guinevere gave him an odd look and then hesitantly placed her daughter on the thick cushions. She brushed the girl's hair back from her face with a gentle hand. Gwen was clearly attached to her child. A *Bad* child.

Why?

Midas frowned in confusion. He genuinely didn't understand it. Good parents never gave a damn about their Bad offspring. It was the way of the world. Maybe her affection was an act. Or maybe Gwen tolerated her because they looked alike. Both of them were blonde, with elegant features, lake-blue eyes, and long bones.

Avalon. That was the girl's name. Arthur's only child.

Allegedly.

The girl's paternity didn't much matter to Midas. He had every intention of having Gwen in his home, so it appeared Avalon would be staying with him, too. He frowned. What he knew about children was... nothing.

Absolutely nothing.

"I'm sorry to arrive unannounced, like this." Guinevere said again, straightening up. "And for shooting Percival at your party. As I said, I knew he was following me, but I didn't know he was so close. I didn't mean to ruin your evening."

"You haven't ruined it. Believe me. What kind of business did you want to discuss?"

She crossed the massive expanse of room to sit in the monumental chair across from him. The damn thing nearly swallowed her, but she still managed to arrange herself like she was about to hold court. "Well, maybe you've heard, but the Scarecrow is trying to steal my kingdom."

"I've heard."

"He wants me to marry him."

That Midas *hadn't* heard. His eyes narrowed. Anyone who knew him would have been shocked by the small display of anger. "Somehow I don't see you as a happy couple. The man is made of birds, isn't he? The smell alone must be off-putting."

"The Scarecrow will never be my husband." The words were cold and certain. "But he wants me to put the sheen of legitimacy on his coup. Whoever marries me will be the king."

"Yes." Midas had read Camelot's constitution, just to get an idea of all the laws he broke. One of the more obscure regulations concerned the line of succession. He'd never really considered the details closely before, but he recalled them all to the letter. Midas remembered everything he read.

"The Scarecrow is a lunatic, but he was Arthur's top adviser and he's the smartest man in the kingdom, so many Good folk are loyal to him. They're supporting his cruel ideas." She tiredly rubbed her eyes. "They won't see reason. I don't understand it."

Of course she didn't. This woman fearlessly stood against all the King's Men, armed with nothing but an antique gun. Midas studied her for a long moment, wondering how long her idealism would last in the face of reality.

"Who says the Scarecrow is the smartest man in Camelot?" He finally asked.

"Everyone. Arthur conducted a test of all the noblemen in the court. He only wanted the brightest minds by his side."

Midas made a noncommittal "umm" sound. Arthur had *certainly* needed all the help he could get when it came to ruling. Camelot was nearly bankrupt under his ham-fisted management. A kingdom was a business, after all. Arthur had run it like an irresponsible idiot, with no eye to the future.

"Of course, as I said, he only screened *Good* people... Who were men... And nobles." Guinevere made an irritated face that was really quite delightful. "I *told* Arthur that was shortsighted, but he refused to listen."

Midas did his best not to look thrilled over her criticism of Camelot's Golden Son.

"Anyway, they played a round of catur." She paused. "Have you ever played that?"

"No." Catur was a chess-like strategy game taught only to the high-born elite. They were expected to play and master it from the cradle, as part of their training to rule empires. Bad folk weren't even allowed to own one of the boards. Apparently, Gwen didn't know that and he saw no profit in telling her. "I read a book on it once, though."

She shrugged. "Well, the Scarecrow won the game, easily. Aside from Chryson, the wizard, he's the best player in the kingdom. So Arthur made him his chief councilor. Now he's moving in on the throne." She met Midas' eyes. "I'm going to make sure he loses."

"I believe you." What could ever stop such a woman?

That lake-colored gaze met his levelly, trying to decide if he really was just a tawdry, feral animal or something more. Thinking it over one last time before she told him why the hell she was sitting in his office. Midas waited, while she mentally weighed him, afraid to even move for fear of ruining his chances with her.

"I need your help." Guinevere said after a long pause.

...And Midas released a breath he hadn't even been aware he was holding. Whatever it was she'd been looking for, she'd apparently seen it in him. He had no idea how that was possible, but he wasn't about to question his good fortune.

"You are the only person with the resources and power to fight the Scarecrow." Guinevere continued. "He might be brilliant at political maneuvering, but that's the only game he knows." She arched a brow. "You're *not* a politician. You're a criminal."

"Yes." There was no sense in lying about it.

She nodded, pleased with the simple answer, for once. "So am I, now. I'm almost-Bad."

It was cute that she thought so.

"Maybe," Midas allowed, "but I'm all the way Bad. What makes you think I won't just steal Camelot for myself?"

"You have a reputation for keeping your word."

That was true, but it still didn't explain her willingness to give herself into the "evil clutches" of a man Arthur had publically and repeatedly called a "mindless gorilla." The things her sainted husband had said in private were no doubt even *more* colorfully quotable.

"I haven't given you my word about anything." Midas reminded her.

"Not yet. But, someone told me that you're a kind, gentle, and honorable man. That I should come here and you'd help me.

Midas squinted. "Were they taking drugs at the time?" He couldn't imagine anyone sober telling her something so stupid.

"I very much doubt it." She tugged on her sleeves and smoothed a wrinkle in her ancient dress, like somehow that might help it be less hideous. She still wore Arthur's wedding band on her left hand. It glinted as she fiddled with the worn fabric.

The sight of the gold ring set Midas' teeth on edge.

"Well, no one who knows me would *ever* say that." He assured her.

She gave him an arch look, like she didn't believe that. "I'm sure you need to keep up your reputation as a villain..."

"I *am* a villain."

She kept talking. "But I know that you and I can strike a fair deal."

Ah... that was more like it. No matter what craziness brought her there, she wanted to deal and he was ready. No one could match him in business, certainly not this small, baffling woman. Midas steepled his fingers, feeling like a spider must when a butterfly was caught in his web. "I'm listening."

"Instead of marrying the Scarecrow, I will marry you." Guinevere said bluntly.

...And Midas' smug confidence in how this meeting would proceed vanished.

"What?" He blurted out, trying to catch up. It was another uncharacteristic lapse in control, but this time he didn't even notice.

Gwen didn't seem to take offence at his astonished tone. "I will marry *you*, giving *you* the king's crown."

Midas blinked.

"Legally, the throne is mine, but I need the Congress of Wizards to back me. And they *will*. My father knew them all. But the Scarecrow is going to try and stop them from supporting me. He hates the wizards. He wanted to go to the academy and they turned him down, so..."

Midas impatiently cut her off. "Go back to the part where we get married."

"Right, well, you said yourself the Bad folk will support me as queen. They're the majority of the population. And I know I can get the wizards on my side. I just need some power and money to make sure the Scarecrow doesn't stop me before I win."

"And I'm the power and money."

"Exactly! Once you have the king's crown, that son of a bitch Scarecrow will lose his only ticket to legitimacy." Somehow, she even made cursing sound classy. "*You* will be my husband. He'll have to win through open rebellion and even most of the Good folk will dislike that idea." She gave a firm nod. "*That's* the deal."

Midas tried to think.

He'd been prepared to pay a fortune just to have her at his side. This was beyond his expectations. *Way* beyond. Guinevere would no longer be Arthur's wife. She would be *Midas'*. He'd own her so completely that not even his biggest detractors could deny his claim.

Holy shit... The deal was too good to be true.

"I've thought it all through." She persisted, when he didn't respond. "I'm a very logical person. Very organized. I used to draft all my father's contracts for him, so I'm an excellent negotiator. I guarantee, this will be a good bargain for both of us."

Midas' head tilted, watching her carefully for some sign of deception. "How do you know I'm not an even bigger son of a bitch than the Scarecrow?"

"Someone told me you're not." She ran a hand through her damp hair. "Besides, nobody else will even *try* to help me contact the wizards or keep my crown." She paused. "The wizards are all sealed in the Emerald City, ignoring us, you know."

"I know." The wizards had left Camelot to its own devices years before. They were safely sealed behind their giant green walls, playing catur and writing spells.

"So typical of them to pout right through the war. They've been in a snit, ever since Arthur..." She trailed off and sighed. "Never mind. The point is, I've asked everyone I ever thought was my friend for assistance. They've all abandoned me."

He wasn't surprised. "Friends" were a product, like anything else. You had to buy them.

"Galahad would have been by my side," she continued in a wistful tone, "if Arthur hadn't banished him. He was always there for me. Truly, he was the greatest knight in the kingdom. And he *adored* Avalon. I have to find him, as soon as it's safe."

Midas' barely held back a snarl, already detesting the man.

"Anyway, I was desperate and I thought of you and I got the idea for this trade." She tugged on her sleeve and Arthur's wedding ring gleamed. "Not to brag, but I'm a very logical thinker. You give me a safe place to win my throne and I'll give you a crown. It's a fair deal."

"Who says I want a crown?" He retorted, unwilling to show just how eager he was to strike this bargain. It all seemed too damn easy. "Especially a crown to *this* kingdom. Recently, Camelot's property value has plummeted. Seems like a risky investment."

"Risky investments are the ones with the biggest payoffs."

"And the biggest *risks*. It's right there in the name."

Guinevere leaned back against the chair, rubbing at her eyes. "Look, I'm too tired to play games." She really did look exhausted.

And beautiful.

God, she was the most beautiful creature he'd ever seen. It was hard to focus on anything except how much he wanted her. He didn't give a rat's ass about Camelot, but he'd do whatever it took to have this woman. Even save this shithole kingdom, if that's what she wanted.

"I haven't slept in three days." She went on. "Let's just

bottom line this, shall we?"

"By all means."

"Good." Guinevere nodded, her expression intent in spite of her weariness. She might look like she spent her days eating bread and honey, but she really was a fighter. "I see you, Midas. I see this gigantic trying-too-hard house, and all those sycophantic guests, and these phony paintings that someone must have told you were genuine." She waved a hand at an ugly landscape that had cost him two golden geese eggs.

He frowned. "They *are* genuine."

"They're not." Her voice was ruthless, in a way he had to appreciate. "But you want them to be. You want to buy yourself some respectability, right? Prove you're not just a sleazy hoodlum, living in a nice zip code. You want the things money *can't* buy."

"Money can buy *anything*." He was more sure of that than ever. Fuck the naysayers. He was presently purchasing himself some class, a kingdom, and a True Love all in one pretty package. There was nothing in the world you couldn't acquire if you offered a high enough price.

"It *can't* buy you everything." She sounded naively certain. "But I can get the rest of it for you. In return, all you have to do is keep my daughter safe."

Midas' attention slipped back over to the child. How was she not awake, yet? He couldn't imagine sleeping so deeply. It was baffling. Did she really have so much faith in her delicate mother to look after her? Good parents never guarded their Bad offspring from the monsters of the world. Did she not know that?

Apparently not. ...And neither did Guinevere.

She followed his gaze. "Avalon needs to be protected and you're the only one in Camelot who's strong enough to do it." She said quietly.

Just that fast, Midas understood why this deal was so delightfully one sided: Because Guinevere wasn't like other Good parents. Her feelings for Avalon weren't an act or grudgingly given because the girl happened to look like her. Her love for the child was real and vast and unconditional. He could see it on her face. Gwen would strike *any* deal that provided a safe haven for her baby, even if it meant coming to the Kingpin.

This woman wasn't heartless, at all. This woman was the only truly *Good* person left in the whole dismal kingdom.

Hell, that made his bargaining position even better.

"I have to make sure my daughter's safe." Guinevere

murmured, her gaze still on Avalon. "No matter what."

Her devotion to the girl was admirable, but mystifying. "Not many people would fight so hard for a Bad folk, even if she is their own child." He knew that firsthand.

Guinevere's head snapped around, lake-blue eyes blazing with anger. "Meaning what?"

Uh-oh. Midas hesitated, afraid to say anything for fear she'd storm out. He'd just screwed up. He could tell, although he wasn't sure how. He'd been giving her a compliment.

"I don't care what the Scarecrow and his bigoted flunkies say," she continued hotly, "Good and Bad mean *nothing*. It's what's inside someone's heart that matters and my daughter has the purest heart of anyone I've ever met. People will see that, once they get to know her."

Midas' eyebrows soared. Jesus, Guinevere sounded like Scarlett Riding-Wolf, with all her Villains' Rights protests. They were both kidding themselves if they thought Good folk would *ever* willingly give Bad folk anything. It would be a fight for every inch of ground.

"If you intend for the child to rule Camelot one day, you'd better be prepared for a war." He told her honestly.

"I'm already at goddamn war!" She shouted, her face flushed with passion. "There's me and Avalon on one side and the rest of the kingdom on the other. Now, do you have a problem with my daughter being Bad? Because if you do, we can just stop this negotiation, right now."

"Of course not." He spoke carefully, unsure what kind of minefield he'd stumbled into. The child was clearly a sensitive issue. "You're both welcome in my home, for as long as you wish to stay." Avalon belonged to Guinevere and Guinevere belonged to Midas. That was all that mattered to him. "It makes no difference to me what she is. I'm Bad myself. We already established that. I'm hardly going to be prejudiced against my own kind."

She didn't seem mollified. "Avalon is *wonderful*."

"I have no doubt." He agreed dutifully. For no reason he could imagine, he found himself compelled to add: "I doubt she'll like me, though. Very few people do. Is that going to matter to you?"

"My daughter matters more than anything else in the world."

Shit.

"Well, why don't I just stay away from her, then?" He offered. It seemed like the safest course. The child couldn't be frightened of him if she didn't see him. And if she wasn't frightened of him, then Gwen wouldn't be upset with him. It was win/win all the way around.

"If that's what you want, fine. Avi will want to talk to you, at first. She's very curious, but she's used to men ignoring her. Just be patient and she'll eventually ignore you, too."

Midas frowned, not liking the way that sounded.

"Do *not* yell at her, though." Guinevere continued, her voice getting harder. "That's not even a point of negotiation. Do *not* hit her. Don't be cruel to her or I will make you suffer..."

"I wouldn't harm a little girl." Midas interrupted, annoyed for the first time.

She glowered at him. "I'm serious, Midas."

"So am I. *I won't hurt her*." It was a vow. "You have my word. I just want you to understand that I'm not good with children." At least, he didn't think he was. He'd never actually spoken to one. "Don't expect us to bond."

Gwen frowned, measuring him, again. This time she wasn't sure she liked what she saw. "This might not work." She blurted out. "Maybe we should just stop."

Shit, shit, *shit*.

She couldn't leave. Not when he'd just found her.

"I will keep the child safe." Midas tried, desperate to appease her. "But, I'll probably scare your daughter if I talk to her. That's all I'm trying to say. I'm big and Bad and..."

She cut him off. "Do you like rocking-horseflies?"

"What?"

"Rocking-horseflies. Do you like them?"

Midas hesitated. "I love them." He said, wondering why this was important to her, but willing to go along with it. "I built my garden just to attract them." It was his way to make amends.

She exhaled like that meaningless fact reassured her. Somehow he'd just passed another test, but it had been a very near miss. "Thank God. For a minute I wondered if I was wrong about coming to you."

Midas' tension eased, seeing that she intended to remain in his home.

"Okay." She cleared her throat. "You just ignore Avalon, then. Don't talk to her and everything will be fine."

That's what Midas had wanted, but it still felt like a rejection. Who could blame any woman for keeping her baby away from a tawdry, feral animal, though? "Yes." He agreed quietly. "I'll ignore her. Just tell me what kind of toys and clothes she needs, so I can buy them first."

"You don't have to buy Avalon toys, Midas."

"But, she needs toys." He argued, unable to help himself. Children liked toys. At least he remembered yearning for them, when he was a boy. Watching the other kids play with balls or toy soldiers and wishing he had one of his own. He glanced at the little girl, dissatisfied with the idea that she would experience any kind of deprivation. "I don't see the harm in buying her a doll. It will bring her comfort." When he was young, before his parents left, he'd slept with a sock stuffed with sawdust, just so he'd have something to hold at night. It had made him feel safe in the darkness.

Gwen chewed her lower lip, her desire to make her daughter happy warring with her pride. "I guess one doll wouldn't hurt. We had to leave everything behind. I can pay you back for it, after I'm queen again."

Midas somehow restrained himself from rolling his eyes, unwilling to even argue over something so ridiculous. He could buy every doll in existence and barely notice it on his counting house statements. "We'll discuss the reimbursement issue later."

"Okay." Gwen nodded, like it was settled. "Thanks for being so generous."

Midas shrugged. Buying things was easy. Maybe if he bought them enough, Gwen and her daughter would be happy with him and decide to stay. No price was too high to have the best.

"And just so you know, I can be a very good wife." Gwen continued, back to selling him on her plan. "Marriage is kind of lackluster. To be honest, I wouldn't try it again, if I had another option. But I'm used to it, so I'll do a good job." She tilted her head. "Have you ever been married?"

"No."

"Well, overall, it's just so..." she shrugged, like she couldn't think of a better way to describe it, "*lackluster.*"

"Lackluster." He repeated. "Interesting."

She hesitated, like it suddenly occurred to her that "lackluster" wasn't the best adjective to use in convincing him holy wedded bliss was a terrific idea. "But I mean, I'm *still* a very good wife. Really. I'm very skilled at running a castle and I make a wonderful pecan pie."

The woman said the damnedest things. "I don't know... Now, you've got me thinking I might prefer a single life." He mused, still not willing to show her his enthusiasm for this bargain. "I do enjoy pie, but I already hire people to do my housekeeping. I'm not a man whose life lacks luster." He gestured to the gilded furnishings around him.

"But our marriage isn't a *real* marriage." She backpedaled. "It's a *fake* marriage."

Midas' eyes narrowed. "A fake marriage?" He didn't like that phrasing.

"Well, it would be a legal wedding and all, but it's primarily a *business deal*. We won't have all the messy, illogical problems of an *actual* couple. It will be so much simpler. We can negotiate all the points of the Contract, so there are no surprises."

"With you, I have a feeling there will be endless surprises." Every word out of her mouth was unexpected.

"We can negotiate that part, too." Guinevere clearly loved drafting deals. She'd tack on all the provisos he wanted. "We'll put it right in the Contract."

"Are you going to write an *actual* contract for us?"

"Just a little one, with the basic stuff outlined. It's all very logical. I'll specify no more than three surprises a day. That's fair." She lowered her voice, just in case Avalon could hear. "And I am *excellent* at turning a blind eye to... um... whatever other activities you want to engage in. Really. Your affairs can be completely your own."

She wasn't talking about his business affairs. "You don't care if I fuck other women?" He summed up just to watch her jaw drop at the coarse phrasing. She'd better get used to cursing, if she planned to "fake" marry him. Midas' vocabulary had been developed in the sleaziest parts of the kingdom and he doubted he could clean it up now.

"I'm merely saying that we can have separate lives." Gwen sputtered.

Clearly, this was her roundabout way of telling him she didn't want to share a bed. Huge surprise. "How much do you know about me, Guinevere?" He held up his palms. "About my curse?"

"Um..." Her eyes went to his shrouded fingers and stayed there. "I guess just the usual rumors..." She trailed off nervously when he began stripping off the black leather gloves.

"It's not a rumor. When my hands touch something living, it turns to gold. Animals. Plants. People. It's irreversible. One brush of my fingers and they become twenty-four karat, all the way through."

To prove his point, he plucked the borogrove blossom from his tuxedo jacket and dropped it to the desk top. The delicate red petals were solid metal before they even stopped falling. The flower clanged heavily against the wooden surface, frozen forever.

Guinevere couldn't seem to look away from it.

"Now, do you *really* think," Midas continued calmly, "that I sleep with many women?"

Midas already knew he and Guinevere would never so much as kiss. She wouldn't want to (obviously) and it seemed like a terrible idea to reveal just how important she was to him. It was no secret that Baddies were pretty much helpless in the face of their True Loves.

Everyone was born with a True Love. Their other half, who they'd been made to share their lives with. Bad folk usually knew their True Love on sight. And, unlike many Good folks, they were fanatically possessive and protective of their mates. To them, the connection was soul-deep, right from the beginning.

On the other hand, Good folk couldn't identify their True Love until they'd slept with them. Even when they *did* know, their feelings seemed far shallower. Gwen was in the dark about their connection. Midas wanted to keep it that way. If she discovered the truth, she'd just use it against him. Why wouldn't she?

Everyone was looking for an advantage.

Guinevere didn't *have* to strike a deal with Midas, at all. He was going to keep her safe regardless. Anything else would go against every instinct in his body. Which meant he wasn't telling her jack-shit about their True Love match. Once she knew, she'd take the protection he offered and leave him with nothing. There was no *way* he was giving her that kind of power. Keeping control was the key. Midas was a businessman and this was just like any other deal.

Except his heart was pounding out of his chest, just from looking at her.

Guinevere considered the revelations about his golden touch for a long moment. "How did it happen?" She finally asked.

"I didn't read the fine print of a contract."

"Can it be cured?"

"No."

She studied him for a beat, processing that. "But, it's just your hands?"

Once again, Midas was caught off guard. "What?"

"Just your hands turn people to gold? The rest of your body can touch... things?"

He frowned. "Yes, it's just my hands and, as long as I keep the gloves on, I can live fairly normally. Still, few women would want to take the chance."

Guinevere snorted. "Oh, I'll bet it's not *that* difficult for you to find companionship."

"I don't pay for sex." He assured her, assuming that's what she meant and not taking offense. There was no sense in being angry about the truth. Money was the only attraction he held for women. It hadn't taken him long to figure that out.

Guinevere was wrong, though. He'd buy anything else, but he'd preferred to be alone rather than have someone *pretend* to want him. Midas couldn't abide imitations. He was even planning to get rid of that ugly landscape she said was a fake. No *way* could he tolerate some insincere bedmate. Just the idea annoyed him.

He'd have nothing at all before he settled for less than the best.

Lake-blue eyes blinked like Guinevere was surprised by his words. "No, I didn't mean *that*. I meant you probably have a lot of girlfriends, because you're so attractive."

Midas' eyebrows shot up. No one had ever called him "attractive" before, mostly because he *wasn't* attractive. He'd never be mistaken for a handsome prince who honorably defended fair maidens. Midas was far more likely to be the barbarian at the gate, threatening to burn down the whole fucking town if his demands weren't met.

Gwen's cheeks turned pink under his incredulous stare. "Sorry. Crap. That just kinda slipped out." She cleared her throat nervously. "Sometimes I can be --um-- slightly too direct. My father called it 'a little bit brash around the edges.' It's --like-- something comes into my head and I just," she shrugged, "say it."

"I see."

"I didn't mean to make you uncomfortable. Sometimes I make people uncomfortable. Are you feeling uncomfortable?"

"I'll survive."

"I was just saying that I'm sure a lot of women want to sleep with you." She continued blithely. "You're much more appealing than I even expected."

"Thank you." He cleared his throat, wondering if he'd ever had a weirder conversation. "Well, if I need sex, my appealing self can find it elsewhere, then." He would *never* sleep with another woman. He knew that. Now that he'd met Gwen, everyone else was second best. There was no sense in explaining that, though. It would just give her more power. "We don't need to consummate our arrangement." Midas put his gloves back on. "Satisfied?"

"Yes, it's *very* reassuring to know you could kill me if we shake hands." There was a bite to her tone now, like she was irritated.

He had no idea why. He'd just agreed with her.

"I'll leave you alone." Midas reiterated, in case she still wasn't convinced of his sincerity. "You have my word. So, unless *you* want to seduce *me*, I think you're safe." He arched a brow. "Obviously, if you have physical needs you'd like me to assist with, we can negotiate that into the Contract."

She rolled her eyes at the sarcasm.

"And if it makes you feel any better, I haven't *accidently* killed anyone in years." He paused and figured they might as well put all their cards out on the table. "Speaking of which, you might be okay with me cheating on you, but I am *not* okay with you cheating on me. You can underline that in our Contract. All you'll end up with is a golden statue of the unlucky guy."

Her lips compressed. "So, you've heard rumors about me, too? That I was unfaithful to my husband?"

"Yes."

"And you believe them?'

"I don't care what you did with Arthur. Just don't do it with me."

Guinevere snorted, as if he'd said something epically stupid. "Don't worry. I'm hardly in the mood to date." She crossed her arms over her chest, the sleeves of her peach dress inadvertently tugging away from her hands. "Sex is even more lackluster than marriage. Truthfully, I'm over the entire idea of romance. It's impractical, illogical, and unpredictable."

"Very true." Look at what True Love was doing to him. Twenty minutes with the girl and he was ready to start a war. Still, her pragmatism was a good sign. The last thing Midas needed was a lot of phony sentimentality from her.

Gwen pursed her lips. "You're not worried about having an heir?"

"No, I'd be a terrible father. I barely had one myself, so I'm completely unprepared for the job. Like you said, I'm a criminal. You want to kill the Scarecrow, I'll help you. Raising a child, though...?" He shook his head. "I have very little to offer."

"I haven't really worked out the specifics of how to kill the Scarecrow, actually. I'm not sure what weapons are effective on a man made of hay."

"Fire." Midas suggested. Years of toiling as a stable boy told him that a lit match worked just fine to destroy straw.

Gwen brightened for a moment. "That's what I was thinking! I was going to use an invisibility cloak to help me sneak up on him and give it a try, but I waited too long. They locked me up in the dungeon."

A dark rage moved within him. "The dungeon?" His eyes slipped down to her wrists and he realized that was why she kept fiddling with her sleeves. To hide the bruises that encircled her pale skin.

Son of a *bitch*.

Gwen followed his gaze and sighed. "It took a while to pop the manacles open." She admitted. "I finally had to use the underwire from my bra to pick the lock."

It took everything in Midas not to lower his eyes to her perfect breasts. "Resourceful." He managed to get out.

"Thank you." She smiled at the compliment. "I used the invisibility cloak to help me escape. I had it on me, but they didn't see it, because it was --you know-- invisible. Then I grabbed Avalon and the gun and ran. My father had a home close by, so I know this area. I could avoid the search parties. It took me a few days, but I made it here."

"To me." It wasn't a statement so much as a purr.

"To you." She chewed her lower lip. "So... What do you think? About the deal to marry me, I mean. Will you agree to it?"

"Yes."

Her lips parted in shock at the instant reply. "You'll *agree* to this arrangement?" Gwen clarified, like she might have misheard him. "Really?"

"Yes." Nothing in this world or any other could keep Midas from his True Love.

"And you'll protect Avalon?" She persisted. "That needs to be a clause in our Contract. No matter what happens, you have to make sure Avi's safe. I have your word on that?"

"You have my word that I'll protect *both* of you."

"Alright then." She studied him closely. "Do you want to add any clauses of your own?"

"No."

Blonde eyebrows compressed, as if she disapproved. "Well, you *should*. What if I try to slip in something underhanded? You need to be prepared."

"I'm sure you'll give me fair terms." This woman wouldn't be able to pull off anything "underhanded" if her life depended on it. She was the bluntest creature he'd ever met. "You've driven a hard bargain, but I'm convinced we've reached a fair compromise. Let's just move onto the next step." His only concern was getting her to say "I do" as quickly as possible.

"You need to be careful about contracts, Midas. You said

yourself, it's how you got cursed." Apparently, his decades of professional villainy weren't enough to convince her he was able to take care of himself. She looked concerned for him. "Tell you what, I'll go over *everything* with you before we sign. Contracts can be complicated."

"That's very thoughtful of you." Midas gave up trying to understand the woman. He balanced the receiver between his shoulder and ear, busily dialing. "In the meantime, I'll just summon a wizard to perform the wedding ceremony."

That shifted her attention. "You mean you want to get married, right *now?*"

"Do you see a reason to wait?"

"No, but..."

"Neither do I." He wanted her name next to his on a long and formal marriage scroll, so she couldn't escape him without one hell of a fight. That was the only contract he cared about at the moment. If he waited, she might realize that he was getting the *far* better deal and try to escape. Midas needed to make this happen *now*.

Guinevere let out a long breath, still confused. "Why was this so simple?" She asked, her big blue eyes clouded with exhaustion and something like relief. "I thought it would take ages to convince you. Why are you agreeing to this mess so quickly?"

"You're just one hell of a negotiator."

Chapter Three

The Contract can be voided for any of the following reasons: Abuse, lies, excessive drinking and/or drug use, unseemly behavior around Avalon, general incompatibility, misuse of magic, breaking any clauses in the Contract, and/or a judgment by one or both parties that the agreement is no longer in the best interest of them, their dependents, or the Kingdom of Camelot for any reason whatsoever, even if it is not specifically listed above.

It can also be terminated in case of the discovery of Midas' True Love.

Clause 11- Reasons for Nullification and/or Termination of Marriage

It only took Gwen about thirty minutes to realize that the Kingpin of Camelot was a terrible businessman.

Like *really* terrible.

For a professional gangster, he was astonishingly, terrifyingly, hopelessly trusting. Gwen had sat across from him in appalled silence, as he signed whatever she put in front of him. Midas hadn't seemed interested in negotiating *anything*. He impatiently accepted whatever deal she proposed, initialing all the spots she indicated on the Contract.

"You should be more careful about what you sign." She'd informed him for the tenth time, hoping he listened to her damn good advice. "I could be trying to rip you off, you know."

"I doubt you'd be *repeatedly* warning me of the possibility, if that was your plan." He'd murmured and she had the feeling he was amused by her lecturing.

It would've annoyed Gwen that he somehow thought *she* was being the silly one, except... Shit. It was really, really hard to be annoyed with someone so really, *really* attractive.

Midas wasn't handsome. With golden-colored eyes framed with thick lashes and dark hair that brushed his wide shoulders, he was too damn fearsome to ever be considered something so beige and innocuous. Nothing could break this man. He seemed big enough and strong enough and confident enough to fight monsters with his bare hands.

...Hands that were covered in black leather gloves.

Every horrible rumor she'd ever heard about his curse had flickered through her mind, but they did nothing to dampen his appeal. The pheromones Midas gave off clouded her better judgement.

"You're very big and scary." Gwen had continued, clearing her throat and trying to focus. "I'm not arguing that. And it's clearly gotten you this far in your business. People are intimidated by your reputation." She'd regarded him gravely. "But that won't always be enough. One day, someone will see that it's all just... exaggeration. Like I have."

"Uh-huh." His gaze had stayed on the Contract, reading each word.

"I'm certainly not telling you to change. I would hate for you to become cynical and hardened, like me. It's *wonderful* that you've retained your innocence."

Midas' eyes had flicked up to her, like that heartfelt assurance confused him. Then he'd honest-to-God looked over his shoulder to see if she was talking to someone else.

"But, this is a dangerous world." She'd pressed on, wanting to help him. "You only see the best in people. You think fairness and justice will always win. Galahad is the same way."

"Is he?" The words were quiet.

"Oh yes. And look where it got him? Banished!" It still hurt her to think about it. "You're an honorable man, Midas, but so many others *aren't*. You simply can't be so trusting."

"I'll keep that in mind." He'd returned to reading through the long list of reasons they could end the Contract.

Gwen had sighed in dismay. He just wasn't taking the situation seriously. She'd mentally readjusted her plans to deal with the fact that she would have to protect Midas from himself. It would be difficult, but it was her responsibility to keep him safe, now.

One black brow arched as he'd scanned the Contract's Termination Clause. "What if one of us finds their True Love?" He'd asked conversationally. "That's not explicitly noted here as a reason to break up."

"You can't be serious."

He'd glanced at her again, his golden eyes thoughtful. They were the exact color of old coins. "You don't think that's a possibility?"

"No, I don't." She'd said frankly. "True Love is a children's story."

Of course, Midas hadn't believed that, either. Gwen wasn't sure how she could read him so well, since he didn't say anything or

50

even shift his expression, but she'd sensed his bone-deep conviction that some perfect girl was going to show up and sweep him off his feet. She'd made her voice as gentle as possible so she didn't crush his dreams, even as she tried to get him to see the truth. The man clearly possessed a sensitive soul under the fearsome exterior.

"Midas, be practical. Do you *really* think you'll just look up one day and see Miss Right walking towards you?"

"Yes."

He had a tendency to answer questions with a simple "yes" or "no." If you wanted him to elaborate or explain, you had to be a little pushy. Luckily, Gwen was *a lot* pushy.

"*Really?*" She'd pushed. "Not a doubt in your mind?"

"No." His face had stayed serious and certain. "I absolutely believe that I have a True Love and that she'll find me."

His utter assurance that some mythical woman was coming to save him from their marriage had annoyed Gwen. "Fine." She'd reluctantly added his "True Love" nonsense to Clause 11- "Reasons for Nullification and/or Termination of Marriage," so it was explicit. What did it matter? On the off chance he wasn't crazy, they might as well prepare for that eventuality, too. Contracts were all that stood between order and chaos. "If you find your one-and-only, you can back out of our deal immediately. Satisfied?"

"I'm sure that will come in handy." His eyes returned to the fine print.

For some reason, as Gwen watched him read every word on every page, she hadn't been able to let the True Love thing go. Midas might be terminally romantic, but he was also smart. He'd signed whatever she asked, but he made sure he *understood* every clause. Most of his ideas and comments had been incredibly astute. She'd wanted him to see reason about this nonsense.

"As you can see, Clause 7 allows us to lead separate lives, just as I promised." She'd pointed to Clause 7- "Separate Lives and Other Relationships," watched him closely. "So, that's another obstacle out of your way. You can date and sleep with whomever you like. Total freedom. I won't even be involved."

"I don't mind if you're involved." Midas had murmured.

He wanted to --what?-- *discuss* his mistresses with her? Not even Arthur had done *that*. "Sure." Gwen had said anyway and her fingers had drummed on his desktop. "If you want to talk to me about your love life, that's... great. I'm hoping we can be friends. Maybe I can give you some advice."

Like, for instance, don't discuss your slutty girlfriends with your wife. Not that she was his *real* wife, of course. It was just a business deal.

"But, if you leave me, you won't be King of Camelot, anymore." She'd heard herself tell him. "That will probably put a kink in your big plans. I mean are you really going to give up the crown for True Love?"

"I will when she asks me to." He'd shrugged like it was inevitable. "And she will."

Gwen's teeth had ground together at his blind devotion to some imaginary girl. How could such a bright man be so frivolous?

The whole concept of True Love was a terrible idea. Why would you want to leave so much to blind fate? Much better to approach things logically. All she'd ever wanted was to find the Right Man. Someone she connected with. Someone who understood her. Someone compatible. Someone... *right*. Mystio-physiological screenings for True Love didn't matter to Gwen. She didn't care about destiny or epic romance or blood tests that proved a magical bond. She just wanted someone:

1) She could trust
2) Who loved Avalon
3) Who wanted to be with her as much as she wanted to be with him

Her father had assured her she'd find such a man, but Gwen wasn't so sure. Why was such a simple, practical list so difficult to fulfill?

"Well, I don't believe in True Love." She'd reiterated. "People say I'm heartless, but I'm really just rational."

"Rationally speaking, you don't have to believe in oxygen... but you still need to breathe it." He'd said obliquely and initialed Clause 11- "Reasons for Nullification and/or Termination of Marriage," just like he had all the others.

In the end, he'd gone along with every single thing she'd wanted. His size and reputation might fool everyone else into thinking he was a tough businessman, but nothing could be farther from the truth. It was a miracle people didn't take advantage of him night and day, given his kindhearted temperament. Gwen had a feeling he would have signed over a kidney, if she'd pushed hard enough.

She'd let out a long breath, watching Midas sign his name along the bottom of the Contract. Done. Gwen had snatched it up before he could change his mind, scrawling her own name next to his massive signature.

It was actually done!

Instantly, her mood had soared and she'd sent him a shining smile. Midas was legally hers and she was on her way to getting her kingdom back.

"I did it." She'd told him, blurting out the words before she considered them. That was typical for Gwen. Whatever was in her head, somehow came out of her mouth.

"Almost." He'd stood up, not looking nearly as relieved as she felt. "We still need to get through the wedding."

And that was how Gwen found herself getting married again. Only this time, there were no magical doves dropping rainbow-colored rice from the sky as a fancy-dressed wizard conducted the ceremony. Instead there was a dozing officiant, paid an obscene amount of money by Midas, who was still wearing his pajamas, stank of whiskey, and slurred his way through half the vows.

There was no music from the world-renown Bremen Band or fifty-six attendants from the most prosperous families in Camelot, either. Instead there was Avalon asleep on the couch, a gryphon who looked like he disapproved of the world in general and *really* disapproved of Gwen in particular, and whatever random guests from his ruined party that Midas could corral as witnesses.

And there was certainly no handsome prince promising to become her husband 'til death do they part and move her into his elegant castle. Instead, there was a criminal --a mobster, by all accounts-- who favored incredibly tacky suits over shining armor.

No matter how you looked at it, this wedding was far more enjoyable than her last one.

"I do." Midas' voice was dark and certain as agreed to marry her.

They were still standing in his office, where atrocious taste apparently went to die. Whoever decorated it had spared no expense to make it the tackiest room outside of a brothel. Gwen wasn't sure why she didn't hate the garish space, but, for some reason, it seemed... comfortable. Far more so than the refined, impersonal, beige furnishings of Arthur's palace. No one who lived there was allowed to move so much as a chair without a committee reviewing the exact placement of the pillows.

Midas' house, for all its overblown madness, was a home.

Still, Gwen couldn't help but notice there wasn't a single candid photograph or family portrait anywhere in sight. That seemed strange. Did he have no relatives? No one who he spent holidays with or sent him pictures of their kids? Apparently not. Maybe that was why Midas was desperately trying to fill his mansion with things.

Maybe he had no people to share his life with and so he made do with objects.

"Um --hold on-- I don't seem to... We seemed to have missed the part with the... uhhhh..." The wizard took ten minutes to say a simple sentence with all his rambling and stuttering. Since he wasn't sealed in the Emerald City with the others of his kind, she could only imagine he was at the bottom rungs of the profession. She'd never met him and she knew all the great wizards in Camelot. "Your last name?" He blinked at Midas. "Do you have a last name?"

"No."

"No?"

"No."

Gwen spared Midas a quick look. His lack of a last name had been a pain in the ass when she drafted the Contract and she was still irritated by it. "Why *don't* you have a last name?" She demanded, when it became obvious he only planned to give that one syllable reply. "Yes," and "no" seemed to be his favorite things to say. Sometimes he'd mutter "fucking hell" under his breath, but only used it when he was feeling positively verbose.

"I don't have a last name, because last names are a way to link you to a family and I don't have a family." He kept his attention on the wizard. "Continue."

The wizard gulped. "Okay, um... Do you have uhhhhh?" He made a vague gesture with his hand, trying to recall the word in his tired (and probably drunk) state. "The things that go on the fingers...? Rings!" It came to him with a triumphant exclamation. "Do you have rings?"

"We can skip that part." Gwen told him before Midas could answer. There was no time for jewelry shopping, for God's sake. She needed to get this over with, before her groom backed out. Having the signed Contract relieved quite a bit of her worry, but it was always a good idea to make sure all the loose ends were tied up in a deal. "Just keep going."

Midas glanced down at her hand, where Arthur's ring still gleamed, and didn't say a word.

"Okay." The wizard gave his head a shake, trying to stay awake, and peered down at his scroll. "Do you, Guinevere *Pendragon*," he stressed her last name, "take this man...?" He stopped, like a new thought had just occurred to him. "Hey, Guinevere Pendragon is the... um... queen's name." He tried to focus on Gwen, his face scrunching up in concentration. "You kind of --a little bit, kind of-- look like her, too."

"Oh for Lyrssa's sake..." Trystan, the gryphon, muttered randomly from the sidelines. "Is this really what passes for a mating ceremony among your people, Midas? No wonder this kingdom is in ruins. The words you use to pledge yourselves are so hollow that you need to echo them from the mouths of idiots."

Gwen slanted him a glare. The gryphon glared back. Clearly, the two of them were not destined to be best friends. Or *second* best friends, as Avalon liked to say.

Trystan was a mountain of a man, with the face of a fallen angel and tawny-colored hair that he wore tied back in a long braid. He was, objectively speaking, beautiful. But, it was hard to even look at his stunning features, because her eyes kept going to the damaged wings that fell behind his shoulders like a shroud. She wasn't sure what had caused the vicious scars that crisscrossed the white feathers, but brutal fighting seemed a good guess.

"We didn't have time to write our own vows." She snapped in annoyance.

"Possibly, because you just met." Trystan agreed sarcastically. How did someone born without emotions manage to deliver sarcasm so well? "Isn't there a part of this hollow ritual when onlookers can object? Because I object to this fucking terrible idea."

Midas rolled his eyes, like he was used to his guard's insubordination. "Shut up or leave."

"Yeah, you should leave, Trystan." Dower put in. "I can't *believe* he let you be Best Man instead of me. The Kingpin is having enough problems keeping this shit-show going without you swearing your way through his girl's vows." He glanced at Midas. "Hey, is she a hostage or something? Is that how you talked her into this?"

"You shut up, too." Gwen ordered.

Dower was a wolf, a species that was barely above gryphons on the socially acceptable scale. In his human form, Dower was a burly, bearded man in a sleeveless shirt and camouflaged cargo pants. Gwen wasn't sure why he'd come to Midas' party or hung around to attend the ceremony. Maybe he just wanted the free champagne. He was sprawled in a zebra-striped chair, his leg tossed up over one arm, drinking from a gaudy crystal flute.

Midas shot Dower a warning look from the corner of his eye. "I agree with Guinevere. Now would be a good time for you to forever hold your peace." He said quietly and then focused on Trystan. "*Ha'na.*" He snapped. Whatever the word meant, it sounded important.

"It is my duty to protect you, even from yourself." Trystan's voice wasn't the least bit repentant. It sounded like it came from another age, where warriors fought with claws and clubs and teeth for what they believed in. "*Ha'na* or no, allowing yourself to be strong-armed into this madness is a *fucking terrible idea*."

"Do you honestly think I'd allow myself to be strong-armed by Gwen or anyone else?"

"Yes." Trystan intoned.

Gwen silently agreed. She'd *completely* strong-armed Midas into marriage. In a way, it was nice that someone else saw that. Even if it did put her plan into jeopardy, she liked the idea that Trystan was looking out for her innocent groom. No one else was.

Thankfully, though, Midas ignored Trystan's logic. He said something in the gryphons' language, which sounded inflexible.

"She doesn't know that." Trystan retorted in the common tongue. "The woman will use you for what she needs and then discard you. All her kind are the same."

Midas' jaw ticked. "Anyone who isn't happy with my wedding or my bride," he told the room at large, in an ominously calm voice, "can leave now." His head snapped around as the wizard gratefully started for the door. "Except *you*. Keep going with the vows."

"I won't hurt Midas." Gwen told Trystan in a grudging tone. "In fact, the Contract guarantees that I'll keep him safe." She glanced up at Midas. "Doesn't it say that?"

"Yes. Clause 6, I believe. 'Partnership Responsibilities of Guinevere Pendragon.'"

Gwen smiled, impressed with his memory.

"Your honorless people sign many contracts and write many laws." Trystan intoned. "Then they break them all and do as they wish."

"I have never broken a contract in my life!" Gwen objected hotly.

God, the man was such a jerk. She was trying to be nice, but he was making it super hard not to hate him.

Except --damn it!-- the gryphon stood between the rest of the villains in the room and Avalon. When he'd walked in, Midas had said, "Guard the child above all else" and Trystan had taken position directly in front of her. No one and nothing was getting past that man to harm Avi. There wasn't a doubt in Gwen's mind. She was having a hard time hating anyone who protected her poor trusting groom *and* her baby.

No matter how annoying the big, winged jerk was.

"Is this wedding some kind of plan to takeover Camelot?" Dower asked Midas, still trying to figure it out. "Because, I hate this dump!" He smiled, which was really just a baring of teeth. "I'll help ya ask Letty for soldiers, if you make me Best Man. She *loves* me. Her and that pussy Marrok are controlling the Enchanted Forest, now. There's an ass-ton of Bad folk living there. I doubt any of them like the Scarecrow. Maybe you could hire 'em."

There was only one "Letty" in charge of the Enchanted Forest and she was the most famous Villains' Rights crusader in existence. Gwen whirled around to face Midas, distracted from not hating Trystan. "You know Scarlett Riding-Wolf?"

"Of course. The woman is annoyingly involved in everything these days."

"Well, I don't know her. Not personally. But she's doing *amazing* work." Guinevere's beloved daughter was Bad. Anyone working to ensure that Avalon lived in a world where she was treated fairly was a hero in Gwen's eyes. "I want Camelot to have equality for Bad folk, just like the Four Kingdoms. That's my number one priority as queen."

Midas shot her a skeptical look. "Your number one priority should be fiscal solvency. Arthur racked up more debts than any king in history, according to the palace budget reports."

"You read the palace budget reports?" Not even Gwen read those endless spreadsheets, if she could help it. Why bother? Even when she read them, she didn't understand the numbers.

"I read everything that impacts my life and business." Midas said mildly. "And believe me, your books are a mess."

She believed him. "They're *our* books, now. You're the king, so you can deal with the budget. Problem solved. I'll focus on Villains' Rights and the environment and things that *matter*. You do the boring stuff."

Midas' eyebrows climbed.

"Well, it's not boring stuff to *you*, right?" She defended. "You like money. Have fun sorting it all out. I was always better at contracts than math."

"*You're* the king now?" Trystan snorted. "Lyrssa help us all."

"Stop trying to make it all about *you*, Midas." Dower objected, as if Midas had somehow taken his spotlight. "We *all* know that do-Gooding do-Gooder, Scarlett." He gestured around the room to the other villains. "Hell, most of us were in the WUB Club together." He paused for Gwen's benefit. "That's the Wicked, Ugly and Bad Mental Health Treatment Center and Maximum Security Prison."

"I know." She kept her eyes on Midas. "I remember the night you escaped."

It was the same night Arthur died.

"Some of us escaped more awesomely than others. I got out with the Tuesday share circle." Dower bragged. "I heard Midas nearly got blasted with the sleeping potion gas. Had to crawl out through the garbage chute."

That was clearly not a memory Midas treasured. His eyes narrowed at Dower, who smirked.

"Nothing blew up." Miss Muffet, the Arachnid Queen, corrected in a long-suffering tone. She would have been pretty, if it wasn't for the millions of spiders running along her arms and neck. The whole army of them shifted and skittered every time she moved. It was just... unsanitary. Midas should really have his home exterminated after she left. "Letty took a chainsaw to the cafeteria. *That's* what got us out."

"It was dragons." Hansel and Gretel, the conjoined twins, interjected in perfect unison. Everything they said was in perfect unison. It was even creepier than their creepy little lederhosen.

"That was when *Trevelyan* escaped. He was the only dragon in the WUB Club. Like one of the only dragons *anywhere* really. Why are the hottest species always the ones closest to extinction?" Miss Muffet adopted a wistful, reminiscing expression. "God*damn*, he was hot. I would have traded half my spiders to get his evil ass into bed."

Dower banged a fist against the arm of his fuzzy chair. "All of this is bullshit! I know how the escape went down. I was there when Marrok set the bombs. In fact, *I* set most of them. All you assholes should be *thanking* me."

Predictably enough that triggered another argument.

"If we need soldiers for this war, I can find them." Midas assured Gwen, over the shouting and death threats and spider bites.

Gwen smiled, touched that he'd said "we." "Thank you, but I can win without a battle."

Trystan scoffed at that idea, even though no one had asked for his opinion. "Seeking a bloodless victory inevitably leads to more blood. Hit your enemies hard and without remorse, woman. Kill enough of their people to take away their will to fight and end the war quickly."

Dower shot him a "holy shit!" kind of squint and stopped lobbying to become Best Man.

Gwen disregarded Trystan's homicidal attitude, still grinning at Midas. "So you escaped prison using a garbage chute?" That was very clever. "I'm surprised you fit. How did you even know where it led?"

"I didn't."

She tilted her head. "You went down a garbage chute, without knowing if it led to an incinerator or something? You could have been killed."

Trystan grunted.

"It was a possibility." Midas allowed. "At the time, though, I had nothing much to live for, anyway." He hesitated, staring down at her. "I would be more careful, now. I would make sure I escaped *and* survived, so I could protect you and the child."

Gwen studied him for a long moment and then looked back to their officiant, who appeared to have nodded off. "I do." She decided.

Midas blinked, like he couldn't believe that he'd really just heard what he'd heard.

"Huh?" The wizard jerked awake. "What?"

"I do." Gwen repeated. "I'll marry him."

"Yes, but I haven't finished with the... uh... the vows, so..."

Midas cut him off, his voice more animated than she'd ever heard it. "She already said, 'I do.' Finish this. Now."

"Ummm..."

"*Now.*"

The wizard's eyes went wide at the bellow, his words coming out in a blurred rush. "Youhavetokissthebride."

Midas' brows slammed together. "What?"

"Legally, you --um-- have to kiss the bride for the --um-- names to appear on the --um-- scroll. It's just how it...ya know... works."

Midas hesitated. "Oh." He looked uncertain for the first time since she'd met him. "Isn't there another way to...?"

"We can do it." Gwen interrupted, turning to face Midas. *Nothing* was going to stop this wedding, certainly not her groom's shyness. "Come on. It'll be simple." Then, because she was a take-charge person by nature, she stood on tiptoe and firmly pressed her lips against his.

Midas froze.

It was as if he was afraid to do anything, for fear of scaring her away. Which was ridiculous. Gwen wasn't a timid soul. It took a hell of a lot to frighten her from her path. Still, she had really only *intended* to give him a meaningless peck, so they could move on. But it quickly occurred to her that kissing this man was kind of... pleasant.

So pleasant, in fact, that her strategy of a half-second graze of their lips vanished in a cloud of surprise and excitement.

Hot damn! For the first time in her life, kissing was living up to the hype.

Still on tiptoe, Gwen caught hold of his lapel for balance and began to enjoy herself. Her mouth opened against his and Midas surrendered. His head dipped lower, his lips parting for hers. He tasted like expensive wine. Deep and complicated and intoxicating. Dazzled, Gwen drank him in. It was so much better than she'd even imagined. She'd be a total idiot to stop now.

And Midas wasn't exactly pushing her away. He made a low sound somewhere between a groan, a curse, and a snarl of lust. Whatever you wanted to call it, it turned her insides to liquid. He was enjoying the kiss, too! That observation emboldened her. Gwen leaned against him, holding nothing back. Previously, only her strapping stable boy fantasies had made her this hot. She felt a hand settle at the small of her back, clenching the fabric of her dress. Fisting it tight. Pulling her closer. God, he was so strong and kind and appealing and...

"Shit, man, how much longer is this going to last?" Dower demanded. "It's getting socially awkward here."

He might as well of dumped cold water on Gwen's head. What was she doing? Oh God! What was she *doing?* There were other people in the room! Her cheeks went bright red and she scrambled back from Midas. Holy hell! Nothing like that had ever happened to her before. She hadn't known it *could* happen.

"Sorry." She blurted out, a little appalled at herself for taking advantage of her new business partner. Midas had been so respectful of her and, in return, she'd just assaulted the poor guy in public. That wasn't part of the deal. "I'm *really* sorry." She said again and quickly tried to straighten the wrinkles out of his lapel. She'd crumpled the expensive, garishly purple material in her hands, holding on for dear life. "It was totally my fault. I hope you're not mad."

Midas stood perfectly still and let her fix his tacky jacket, not saying anything.

"The moment kind of got away from me." Gwen admitted, nervous over his silence. Then, because bluntness was just a part of her nature, she lowered her voice and added. "You really are a much better kisser than Arthur. Has anyone ever told you that?"

Midas stared down at her, breathing hard. His eyes were the exact color of mysterious coins, unearthed from some ancient city. They glowed with a totally uncivilized, totally fascinating light.

"Are you okay?" She prompted, when he just kept looking at her with that wild glint.

"Midas." Trystan said sharply. "Not yet."

Midas jolted at his name and gave his head a clearing shake, his normal expression returning. Mostly. His face was still savage when he turned to the wizard. "Finish it." He growled and somehow his quiet voice echoed throughout the room.

The wizard gulped. "I now pronounce you man and wife?" It sounded like a question, but it was enough. Their names instantly appeared on the marriage scroll, magically written in glowing ink.

They were married.

Seeing proof of their union on an official document seemed to amaze Midas. His eyes stayed fixed on their illuminated names, as if he expected them to vanish. "It's done." It sounded like he was talking to himself. "I did it." He ran a hand over his face and let out an uneven breath. "How the hell did that just happen?"

Gwen gave his arm a comforting pat. Midas looked overwhelmed and it was her fault. Her new husband was a delicate soul. She really had strong-armed him into this and then kissed him with barely any warning. It was no wonder he had no idea how he'd wound up standing next to her, with his name glinting on a marriage scroll.

"Don't worry." She consoled. "This won't be forever. We have a lot of outs under Clause 11- "Termination of Marriage." One day, we'll have the wizard tear up the marriage scroll and you'll be free, again."

Midas hesitated and looked at the scroll in the wizard's hand. A frown tugged at his brow. He said something in the gryphons' language, which Gwen didn't understand.

Trystan's response was bored and short, ending with a shrug.

"Good." Midas nodded. "Do it."

Gwen looked between them, confused.

"So, you two headed upstairs to finish the fun, Kingpin?" Dower taunted, before Gwen could demand to know what Trystan and Midas were discussing. "Might as well enjoy yourself, while you're still breathing. Historically speaking, her honeymoons don't last real long."

Gwen and Midas flashed him identical glowers.

The wizard blinked, like he was finally sobering up. "That's right. They say the queen --um-- she pushed King Arthur from that balcony." He whispered to no one in particular. "And she *is* the --uh-- queen, isn't she?"

"Don't be ridiculous." Miss Muffet waved a dismissive hand.

"She poisoned Art first and *then* tossed him off the balcony. Best way to be sure. Trust me."

"Why would she *need* poison when she had concrete to do the job?" Dower demanded.

"It was dragons." Hansel and Gretel chorused stubbornly.

"Arthur's death was an *accident*." Gwen insisted. She looked up at Midas, afraid he might listen to them and see her as a murderer. "There was an inquiry that *ruled* it an accident. Why is that so hard for everyone to accept?"

"Because you so obviously killed him." Trystan intoned.

Midas slanted a deadly look around the room. "You're all catching me in the very best mood of my life. Does anyone *really* want to change that?"

Everybody stopped talking.

Trystan rolled his eyes.

The door to the office burst open and Jill Hill came stumbling in, a drink in her hand. "I can't believe you really did it." Arthur's mistress wore a betrayed expression. "I can't believe you really married her." She'd obviously been crying. "My only consolation was that she was suffering and now you're going to save her!"

Midas frowned. "Jill..."

Gwen waved him back. "Let me handle this." She took a step towards Jill, not angry by her outburst. She'd never been jealous of the woman's relationship with Arthur. Really, all she felt was compassion. "Arthur's death was an *accident*." She said for the millionth time. "I know you don't believe that, Jill, but it's true."

"You're lying! You've been lying this whole time and everyone believes it. Even him." She pointed at Midas, on the verge of hysterical sobbing. "He's usually smart, but you've blinded him. You're going to kill him and he doesn't even see it!"

Trystan nodded, like Jill was making a lot of sense.

Gwen mentally counted to ten. "Jill, I'm not going to kill Midas. We have a legally binding Contract together. Now, I've been as kind to you as I possibly can..."

"Kind?" Jill hissed, her tears drying up. "Are you fucking kidding me?"

Gwen kept talking. "...But Arthur is gone and there's nothing either of us can do to change it. We need to move on. Both of us. Maybe we can work through this and become friends."

Jill responded to that offer by flinging herself at Gwen, manicured fingers clawing out like knives.

Gwen tried to be understanding about Jill. She knew the

other woman was grieving Arthur. It was nice that *someone* missed the asshole, she supposed. And Jill herself was a Bad folk, who ran a very popular (albeit sleazy) business. It was important for little Bad girls everywhere to see that Bad women could be successful professionals. They didn't *have* to be just wicked witches and evil stepmothers. Entrepreneurial opportunities were everywhere.

Still, enough was enough. Jill charged forward and Gwen hit her. Hard. Gwen was actually pretty good at punching people. This was the second fight she'd won. Like everything else in life, hitting people worked best if you were blunt about it. Her fist slammed out, plowing right into the other woman's mascara-stained face.

Trystan gave an approving grunt.

Jill staggered back in shock, tottering on her --really pretty-- high heels. "Wha...?"

Gwen wasn't giving her a chance to regroup. She hit Jill again, this time on the chin, because the woman was annoyingly statuesque and that was the easiest place to reach. It hurt her hand, but it did the trick. Arthur's mistress collapsed to the floor in a puddle of red silk and champagne.

Midas blinked.

"That wouldn't have happened if *I* was Best Man." Dower told the room at large.

Gwen stood over Jill, breathing hard. Crap. She'd knocked her out. Granted, all the booze Jill had downed helped, but still... Rendering another woman unconscious during the ceremony didn't seem like a very "bride" thing to do.

"I'm really not a violent person." Gwen assured her astonished groom, in case all the guns and fistfights confused him. "Things just keep happening to me."

Golden eyes flicked over to her face. "You are the most interesting woman I've ever met." He finally murmured.

That didn't sound *too* bad. Gwen wasn't completely satisfied, though. "She's going to be fine. Really." A new thought occurred to her and she scowled. "Wait, are you and Jill...?"

He didn't even let her finish the sentence. "No. Not *ever*. You have my word."

Relief flooded her, even though it was none of her business. "Good."

"Mommy?"

Gwen's head snapped around. Great. Jill's antics had woken up Avalon. She should hit that insensitive wedding crasher, again. "I'm here, Avi." She hurried over to the sofa, darting past Trystan so she could reach her daughter. "I'm right here."

Trystan watched her, not offended that she'd basically shoved him out of the way. In fact, he stepped aside so Gwen could scoop Avalon up into her arms, a thoughtful expression on his face. It was the first time he looked halfway encouraged about her.

Gwen didn't really notice. She ran a hand over Avi's soft curls. "Everything's fine." She soothed, in case the noise had frightened her. "Mommy's got you."

"Sleepy." Avalon rested her cheek against Gwen's shoulder. "Can we go to bed now?"

"Of course, sweetie." Gwen kissed her hair, boundless love filling her.

"I'll… um… have someone show you to your rooms." Midas interjected awkwardly.

All the Bad folk in the room watched Avalon like she might detonate at any moment. None of them had children. That was pretty damn clear. Dower edged backwards in his seat as if he was afraid that Avalon's blonde ringlets and dimples might be contagious.

Gwen smiled at Midas. "Thank you. I'm going to take her up to bed and we can finish talking about all this tomorrow."

He nodded. "Whatever you wish." He said, because he really was the most agreeable person in the world.

Arthur had been a total ass for throwing him in prison on whatever trumped up charges the Scarecrow had helped him concoct. All the horror stories about Midas' villainy were *clearly* lies. This man might be a gangster in the technical sense, but he was no fiend.

Why, he was a complete gentleman.

Avi blinked over at Midas without raising her head, her eyes unfocused. "Hi." She said quite clearly and then she was drifting off to sleep again. "I seen you before."

Chapter Four

**Arthur
Eighteen Months Ago**

"Oh my God." King Arthur complained to no one in particular. "I am so bored, right now."

He could feel Galahad and Guinevere exchanging long-suffering looks with each other, but he didn't really care. He was the king and he was bored and that was all that mattered. His bitch of a queen and her lapdog of a bodyguard might have nothing better to do with their boring days, but Arthur was an important man.

"I'm sorry, your majesty." The White Rabbit stammered out. "Won't be but a minute more." He checked his pocket watch, as if prepared to time this stupid experiment right down to the second. The twitchy creature was supposed to be the greatest Dark Scientist in the known world, but he was also as irritating as --well-- a hyper-active rabbit.

The whole group of royal observers were standing in the lab that Arthur had bought the little fucker, staring through the glass window at two swamp trolls. Who were doing nothing. And *had* been doing nothing, for *at least* twenty minutes. The wart-y bastards were just sitting in the middle of the sterile, white space, playing cards. It was like watching boring paint dry on a boring wall.

Arthur tilted his head back to stare up at the ceiling, groaning impatiently. "This is taking for*ever*." He whined, because nobody there understood how hard it was to be him. It was just never ending responsibility and bullshit and pressure. "I want to go to my jousting match, already." Where Jill would be waiting with a willing mouth and a lot of praise for his athletic prowess. How could anyone expect him to sit through this boring chemistry crap?

"Patience, sire." The Scarecrow soothed. His painted-on gaze stayed riveted on the trolls. "We've been anticipating this moment with much fervor. We can contain our eagerness for a few moments more, yes?"

Arthur rolled his eyes, restlessly fishing out his cellphone to check his texts. "Whatever." Maybe Jill had sent him some naked pictures or something.

"I don't like this." Gwen told Galahad, because *now* she wanted to whore around with Camelot's greatest, Goodest knight. Never let it be said that the woman didn't like variety in her bed partners. "Are we sure those men are volunteers?"

"I checked, highness." Galahad always called Gwen by her title, but his voice was filled with familiarity and warmth. They were so definitely screwing each other, it was a wonder they didn't just video tape it and sell copies to the whole court. "The two trolls did indeed agree to take part in the experiment. They were not forced into this. They're actually very good friends, who are being well-compensated." He smiled. "They were both heartened by your concern for them, by the way."

Arthur made a face at the Prick's spineless pandering. Galahad was the one man in Camelot more handsome than Arthur, which meant he was a *total* prick. Even his toothbrush-ad of a smile was prick-ish.

Gwen beamed up at Galahad, like the Prick had just single-handedly found Atlantis. "Thank you, Gal. I knew I could count on you to ensure they were safe." She patted his muscular arm and stared into the lab for another endless number of boring seconds. "This *is* kind of ridiculous, though." She finally admitted. "I hate to agree with Arthur, but it's taking forever. I'm supposed to have a board meeting for that Lilliputian charity thing…"

"And I have to go to my jousting match!" Arthur interrupted loudly. "Why is your stuff always more important than mine, huh? *I'm* the king."

Galahad's purpley-blue eyes narrowed in Arthur's direction, because the Prick was always on *her* side. Everyone was on Gwen's side. *Arthur* was the king, but no one ever cared about *his* side. They wanted *her* to run the damn kingdom.

Even Arthur's own father had told him to shut up and let Gwen handle things. Those had been the old fart's final words of advice, in fact, before he left to fight the gryphon on another one of the Looking Glass Campaigns.

While I'm gone, shut up and let the woman run the kingdom. I'd like it to still be standing when I get back.

Of course Uther hadn't come back. Arthur's father had died fighting the winged monsters, a victim of their barbaric nature. Those lawless savages had sent back his body in pieces, painted with primitive markings and skinned alive. It wasn't hard to understand why Uther had been so intent on wiping their entire cave-dwelling race from existence. It was the only thing Arthur and his father had ever agreed on, in fact.

Gryphons all deserved to die.

Luckily, most of them already *had*. Good always triumphed over Bad.

Once Uther was gone, though, Arthur had ignored his insulting order to let Gwen rule and taken over the kingdom himself. Why shouldn't he? He was born for the job. Ordained by God. Somehow things kept going wrong for him, though. No matter what Arthur did, he still had nothing to show for it. He was *king* now, but he was stuck with an unfaithful wife, a bastard daughter, and a kingdom that seemed to be crumbling all around him.

Once Dark Science got up and running, he would show them all.

He would do what his father couldn't and exterminate the few remaining gryphon. He would force everyone to bend to his will. He would make sure Avalon was dealt with, and Gwen learned her place, and get rid of Galahad, once and for all.

No one was ever going to disrespect him, again.

Gwen flashed Arthur a look of total contempt. "I'm *agreeing* with you, you big, dumb idiot. This is taking too long. We can't stand here all day and..."

"It's happening!" The White Rabbit burst out. "Look!" Inside the lab the two swamp trolls had risen to their feet, blank expressions on their faces. It was like they were no longer present inside their bodies, their eyes just glassy marbles in their green faces.

"*What's* happening?" Arthur demanded, kind of creeped out by the trolls' stillness. "They're just standing there. Is this what I've been paying you to do? Get Baddies to stand in a room and look stupid? I could get that done for free."

Gwen slanted him another disgusted look.

"These two trolls are Bad, sire." The White Rabbit adjusted his bowtie. "Yes indeedy. Very, very Bad. But thanks to Dark Science, we're about to fix them right up. I've given them a shot of my new formula, you see. Under its influence, they'll have to follow any command a Good folk gives them. Anything at all."

"Anything?" Arthur's mind went to some delightfully dirty places. "So, if... say.... a really hot, really evil fairy took this formula, she'd have to do *anything* I asked?" Well, hell! This was turning out to be a great investment, after all. Arthur started to grin. "Why do we have ugly trolls to experiment on, then? We should have some ladies!"

Galahad caught hold of Gwen's wrist, like he expected her to do something violent to Arthur. Which was probably a good guess. The woman was a total bitch.

The Rabbit smiled proudly, buck-teeth jutting. "Oh we'll be doing far more than just getting lap-dances from wicked strippers, sire. I'm going to use my formula to turn Bad folks Good! Just as you asked. For your daughter."

Oh yeah... Arthur *had* asked that.

He'd been drunk at the time, but it was still an awesome idea.

He didn't hate *all* Bad folk. Jill was Bad, after all. But there was no getting around the fact that Bad folk were just... less. Fixing them was necessary. A gift to the world. Especially, if the formula fixed *Avalon*. God, he detested her. If this stuff actually worked, that little harpy could start taking it with her milk and cookies at bedtime. Maybe then Arthur would stop hearing about her fucking "daddy."

"What?" Gwen's head whipped around, not even considering the awesomeness of the idea. "*That's* what this is about?!" Blazing eyes narrowed at Arthur. "You think you can turn my daughter into some kind of laboratory rat? Is that your plan?"

"If you want to pass that delusional brat off as mine, we're going to have to fix her somehow." Arthur argued, angry that suddenly *he* was the villain here. The child always started the problems, not him. "I asked the Rabbit to look into some formulas to cure Avalon's Baddness and he's done it."

"There is nothing wrong with Avalon, you son of a bitch!"

"Of course there is! She's *evil*." Arthur slapped a hand across his forehead, demonstrating the utter stupidity of Gwen's stupid objections. He never should have married such an idiot. "She was born Bad. But if the Rabbit tells her she's *Good*, she'll turn Good." Or something. He wasn't really sure how it worked, but it was certainly worth a shot. "Then she won't be such an embarrassment."

"You're a fucking monster!"

"It's a *medical procedure!*"

Gwen went for him again, Galahad holding her back. "I will see you dead in the ground, before I allow you to touch her." She raged. "And you fucking *know* it, so this is all a waste of time."

"She just threatened me!" Arthur yelped at Galahad. "You're supposed to be Captain of the King's Men. Are you going to let her threaten me?"

"I serve the queen." Galahad said flatly. "And the princess." He gripped Gwen tightly, as if to both calm her down and join them together as a unit.

Arthur's eyes narrowed. Galahad shielded Guinevere and Avalon from any kind of punishment and it pissed him off. He really was the greatest knight in Camelot, so Arthur wasn't dumb enough to fight him outright. One of these days, though, he would find a way to get rid of the Prick. Because of the Prick's perfect reputation and inexplicable popularity, Arthur couldn't deal with Galahad as effectively as he'd like, but he'd make sure the Prick suffered.

Arthur didn't care if Guinevere fucked around, but he was damn sick of being made a laughingstock by her choices in lovers. You'd think she would have learned her lesson after the last time, but it seemed like she needed to be taught again.

"Waste of time?" The Scarecrow scoffed, ignoring the byplay. "You think small, Queen Guinevere. This formula is our path to glory. The Rabbit just explained that it will compel Bad folk to do our bidding. We'll soon have an obedient, unstoppable army at our disposal, just as the king commanded."

"Right!" Arthur nodded, because *finally* someone was making sense. "An army to fight the gryphons and anyone else who disrespects me. Just like I commanded." Another drunken, *awesome* idea. Arthur did all of his best thinking when he was loaded.

Gwen frowned like she didn't understand. "An army? What are you…?"

"Watch." The Scarecrow cut her off by leaning over the microphone. "Kill each other." He ordered, so his voice could be heard inside the lab.

The two trolls instantly turned on one another. They might have once been friends, but now they were doing their very best to rip each other limb from limb. Snarling like animals, they attacked with a terrible, brutal ferocity. Blood and teeth flew. Guttural screaming and the sounds of blows landing on flash. Someone's finger got bit off.

Actually, it was kind of disgusting.

Arthur wrinkled his nose in distaste. He only liked sports with horses.

"Stop!" Gwen gasped, her lips parted in horror. "Oh my God! *No*. Galahad, do something!"

The Scarecrow smiled and ignored her cries, his gaze locked on the carnage. "Behold the future of Camelot."

Chapter Five

Midas (no last name given) will do his best to protect Avalon Pendragon (a minor). He will *attempt to* use appropriate language when around her (emphasis his) and refrain from exposing her to unsavory elements. He will provide a suitable bodyguard. He will not harm Avalon Pendragon, endanger her, deliberately hurt her feelings, allow her to be injured by a failure of action on his part, interfere with her upbringing, or instigate unnecessary conversations.

When possible, he will simply ignore her.

Clause 3- Care and Protection of Avalon Pendragon (a minor)

"This is a really pretty house, Mommy. Do you think it's bigger than the palace?"

"I think it might be." Gwen squinted against the shine as she looked around their incredibly gaudy surroundings. "Our host likes everything... big."

And gilded.

Truthfully, it seemed like Midas had purchased two of everything in the world and then stuffed it all in his house, regardless of whether or not it matched anything else. The clash of patterns and mishmash of overblown styles should have been a nightmare, but Gwen was having a hard time not smiling every time she looked around her.

"How many people live here?" Avi wanted to know.

"I think just Midas and his servants."

Gwen helped Avalon down the huge, sweeping staircase. It was wide enough for at least two carriages to travel up it side-by-side and she was pretty sure the bannister was made of solid gold. Now, that really *was* a bit much. She was willing to concede that a man of Midas' size probably needed a spacious house, if he was going to fit his shoulders through doorways and avoid hitting his head on the ceiling. Still, he simply had *way* too much money, if he spent it on twenty-four karat railings. Couldn't he think of anything better to do with his fortune?

Apparently not.

That was actually kind of sad.

"And us now." Avi beamed. "*We's* live here, Mommy. This is *our* house."

"Well, we're *staying* here." Gwen temporized, not willing to promise more than that.

"I like this house." Avalon persisted, still admiring Midas' bedazzled home. "I's okay right here, until my daddy builds me a ballet studio with wallpaper that sings and my very own swing set!"

Gwen looked at the ceiling and prayed for patience.

She stopped at the bottom of the stairs and adjusted her daughter's extremely frilly outfit. Avalon had picked it out herself, so it was a cupcake-y nightmare of pink, sparkles, and more pink. Avi, like Midas, always believed that more was better.

New clothes had been waiting for them this morning. A *lot* of clothes. And handbags and books and several computers and a mountain of fashion dolls. Last night, she and Midas had agreed on *one* doll and somehow Avalon now had fifty-three. Plus every video game, building block, art set, jump rope, stuffed animal, and miniature tea service ever manufactured.

The man had literally bought out a toy store.

He'd left her a bill for the massive haul, so it all adhered to Clause 9- "Partnership Responsibilities of Midas (no last name given)." He'd even attached a pleasant note, saying she could pay him back at her leisure. Gwen wasn't fooled. The figure typed at the bottom of the invoice was so ridiculously low that Avalon could have afforded it with the change from her six new (pre-filled) piggy banks. Midas was cooking the books on their expenses. He was just *incredibly* impractical.

...And incredibly charming.

He'd bought Avi toys. That caused all kinds of warm and tender feelings inside of Gwen, which she was trying to ignore. The last thing she needed was to have any sort of warm and tender feelings towards the unexpectedly marshmallow-y Kingpin of Camelot.

This was just *business*, after all

She needed to remain on guard. Midas might be her husband, but their marriage was fake. He wasn't really on their side. He was on *his* side. When push came to shove, she and Avalon would only have each other.

"Do you remember what we talked about, Avi?" She prompted, willing the girl to pay attention for once. Her daughter was always drifting between reality and whatever she saw in her own head.

Avalon's eyes rolled. "Yeeeesssss." She drew out the word,

tired of all the reminders to watch what she said to Midas.

For the time being, Gwen would have been far happier to keep Midas and Avi apart, but there was no way that was going to happen. Hopefully, Midas really would ignore the little girl.

Hopefully, Avalon would *let* him.

"You're *not* going to tell him about your daddy, right?" Gwen continued. "In fact, you're going to be very, very quiet and not say *anything*." She made a production of holding her finger to her lips and lowering her voice to a dramatic whisper. Avalon liked games. Maybe if she made keeping quiet into a spy mission, Avi would want to play. "We don't want to tell him things he won't understand."

Avalon wasn't falling for it. All the experts agreed, she was exceptionally bright. Her vocabulary and logic skills were frustratingly advanced for her age. And there was no reasoning with her, once she decided on something. Her little brows drew together. "I can't lie, Mommy. It would be wrong."

Gwen's eyes closed for a beat, blaming Merlyn for this. "Telling the truth is always the right thing, sweetie." She took a deep breath and smoothed a hand over Avalon's hair. "I'm so proud that you know that."

Avalon nodded, pleased with herself.

"Of *course,* you don't have to lie." Although, it would really, really help. "But Midas is very busy, just like Arthur used to be. He doesn't have a lot time for either one of us, right now. This is all new to him. You mustn't bother him."

"There he is." Avalon whispered suddenly. All her attention was focused on Midas as he came striding into the room.

Guinevere's thoughts skidded to a halt, her eyes nearly as big as her daughter's.

Shit. He was still the most attractive man she'd ever seen. If she didn't know better, she'd swear it was some kind of spell messing with her mind.

"Good morning." He said mildly.

"Uh-huh." It was the best response she could muster.

Was she staring? It felt like she was staring. A low hum of electrical current went buzzing through her whenever he was nearby. She'd never been so drawn to anyone. And, unlike Midas, Gwen sucked at hiding her thoughts. She'd already kissed the poor man and called him handsome during their business negotiations. God only knew what she'd come up with next.

The probability for personal humiliation loomed larger by the minute.

"You got the clothes." Midas scanned Guinevere up and down, taking in her simple sapphire-colored sweater and jeans. It felt like a trail of fire followed his gaze, her body heating in response. Being so close to him left her tingly, inside and out.

As usual, his face stayed utterly impassive, but she sensed something surprised him. Maybe it was the fact nothing she wore twinkled or clashed. Midas was dressed in a white pinstriped suit and a dizzyingly checkered tie, which Avalon no doubt wholeheartedly approved of. Gwen could only imagine that the outfit was custom-made. Surely no company would mass-produce such incredibly... *distinctive* clothing.

And how in the hell did he manage to look so good in it?

"How do you look so good in that?" He asked as if reading her mind. Even his lyrical accent was a turn on, although she wasn't sure what village it might be from. "It has got to be the least expensive outfit I bought you."

"It's also the most practical outfit you bought me." Gwen had no idea where he thought she was going that required sixteen sequined ball gowns. "We're headed to war, not to a cotillion." She shook her head in exasperation. "And, by the way, that bill you gave me is preposterously low."

He shrugged, not even pretending to look guilty. "I'm a very savvy shopper."

She crossed her arms over her chest, reminding herself to stay strong in the face of his marshmallow-ness. "You don't need to buy us things, Midas."

He hesitated and she could tell he didn't agree. "I only got the basic necessities."

"You bought a four-foot tall robotic teddy bear that plays golf."

"All children need one of those. The shop clerk assured me it's educational."

Meanwhile, for the first time in her life, Avi was feeling shy. She eased behind Gwen, gaping up at Midas. "He's bigger than I thought he'd be, Mommy." She whispered loudly. "Like a giant."

That assessment wasn't far off. "He's just an ordinary person, sweetie." Gwen said anyway. "So, you wanted to talk to me?" She prompted, giving Midas a determined look. She could lecture him on his spending habits later. Right now, she needed to get this meeting over with fast, before Avalon recovered her nerve and said something damning.

"Yes, I needed your input on... um..." Midas trailed off, his gaze landing on Avalon, for the first time. His eyes met hers and his head tilted slightly, like he was fascinated.

Avalon stared back, just as spellbound.

For an endless moment, they studied each other, like they were trying to figure out a puzzle. Whatever they saw in each other's faces, it apparently captivated them both.

Guinevere put her arm down to ease Avalon farther behind her. "You needed my input on what?" She persisted, her attention on Midas.

Midas shot her a quick frown, not missing the fact that she was shielding her daughter from him. "I told you, I'm not going to harm the child." He reminded her stiffly.

"You also told me you were going to i-g-n-o-r-e her. We *agreed* on it, remember? It's in Clause 3 of the Contract- 'Care and Protection of Avalon Pendragon.'"

He didn't like that reminder. "I know what Clause 3 says. But, I've yet to utter a single word to her, so I've upheld my..."

"Hi." Avalon interrupted, gathering her courage to peek out from behind Gwen.

Midas refocused on her so fast and with such amazement you'd think a table had started talking. It was almost comical. "Ummm..." His gaze flicked to Gwen, like he wasn't sure how he was supposed to respond to the greeting.

Guinevere sighed. There was no way to avoid the introduction. Avalon was too curious about Midas to stay away from him. Maybe he'd do something obnoxious and disappointing soon, so Avi could move on. "This is my daughter, Avalon Pendragon, Princess of Camelot." She reluctantly muttered. "Avi, this is Midas, Mommy's new... uh...."

"Husband." Midas interjected in that quietly inflexible voice of his. The man always sounded like he was in complete control of himself and the rest of existence. "I'm your *husband,* Guinevere."

Gwen flashed him a sharp look, which he ignored.

Instead, Midas inclined his head at Avalon, like he was meeting a far older dignitary. "How do you do, Princess?" He said very formally, proving that he really didn't spend much time with children. "It's a pleasure to meet you."

Avalon regarded Midas nervously. "I seen you before." She announced, her thumb in her mouth.

Gwen squeezed her eyes shut, braced for disaster.

Midas still looked disconcerted to be speaking with someone so small. "You said that last night, too. Do you mean when Percival and his men came to the party?"

"No. Before. Lots of times."

"On TV?" If she didn't know better, Gwen would've sworn that Midas winced. "You saw me on the news?" He guessed, as if flashing back to his well-documented and colorful history with law enforcement.

Avalon's thumb stayed in her mouth. "Arthur said you're Bad, just like me."

Gwen mentally cursed her dead husband for his continuous and unrelenting stupidity. "Avi, Arthur sometimes didn't think before he spoke." Or think *at all*, really. It was why she'd done her best to keep Avalon far away from him.

"You're *not* like me." Midas said at the same time, his eyes on Avalon. "Anyone can see that we're not the same kind of Bad."

Gwen's head tilted, struck by the vehemence of his remark. "Good and Bad don't mean nearly as much as people think they do." She told him quietly. "I always tell Avalon that and I'll tell you, too: Good and Bad are just labels. It's our actions that determine who we are."

He sent her another one of those unreadable looks through his lashes.

Damn it, why did he have to have such incredibly long lashes? It was unfair.

Avalon was regaining her confidence. She nodded, blonde curls bouncing. "We's exactly the same and that makes me happy, 'cause now we can be best friends."

Midas hesitated, like he'd never heard the words before. "Best... friends? Wait, who?"

"You and me." Her tone was now completely sure. "We's best friends. I's seen it."

"Oh." Midas processed that ambiguous announcement for a beat and then seemed to give up on making sense of it. Instead, against all odds, his mouth twitched upward. "Well, thank you for telling me."

"You's welcome."

The cruel edges of his lips softened further, warming his whole face. "It's excellent news, I must admit. I never had a best friend before and I *do* enjoy having the best."

Uh-oh...

Gwen braced herself against the impact of his small smile. Midas might never be handsome, but he was something a hell of a lot more interesting and it was nothing but trouble. To make matters worse, he was visibly delighted by Avalon. First the toys and now *this*. It was surprisingly wonderful to see someone else enchanted by her daughter. Something melted inside of Gwen at his amused expression. Something that hinted at all kinds of problems.

No.

No, no, no, no, no.

She shook her head, trying to block out the feeling. *No*. She had to stay logical. Avalon and Midas bonding was the *last* thing she needed, right now. If Avi decided to share any of her ideas with Midas, he might kick them out and then they'd be totally screwed.

"Avi..." She said warningly, before this madness could go any farther. "What did we talk about?"

Avalon hesitated, trying to remember. "Don't bother him?" She finally guessed.

"That's right. Just leave Midas be. He's very busy."

Because he seemed incapable of doing anything even slightly predictable, Midas took offence at that instruction. "I'm not *that* busy."

The man was being plenty obnoxious, but not in a useful way. "Clause 3..."

He cut her off. "Clause 3 doesn't explicitly say I have to i-g-n-o-r-e her when the child *herself* initiates the conversation. Contractually, she can talk to me, if she wishes."

Gwen flashed him a "shut up" look, which he refused to acknowledge. Damn it, he was right about the wording on Clause 3, too. That pissed her off.

"See, Mommy? He says it's okay to bother him. We's best friends, now."

Gwen arched a brow at her daughter and that was all it took.

Avalon pouted for a second, before giving in. "Fine." She glanced back at Midas and lowered her voice to a stage-whisper. "I'm not supposed to talk to you, 'cause you don't have time for me and Mommy. Just like Arthur."

Midas' eyes sharpened.

Gwen was sure her cheeks were flaming. "I'm sorry." She'd (mostly) averted disaster for now, but it was like walking a tightrope. Midas was too clever, while Avalon had no filter and *a lot* of damning information in her head. "This is all very confusing for her."

The *polite* thing would be for Midas to agree with that very obvious subject change. Instead, he disregarded her excuse, his gaze on Avalon. "Your father didn't spend much time with you before he died?"

"My daddy's not dead." Avalon scoffed, as if Midas was being ridiculous.

"Not dead?" Midas almost looked concerned. "Arthur's alive?"

"He's *not* alive." Gwen insisted loudly, knowing this was a catastrophic topic.

Sure enough, at the very same moment, Avalon exclaimed, "Oh, *Arthur's* not my daddy. Arthur's just Arthur. My *daddy* is my daddy."

Shit. Gwen dropped her forehead into her hand.

"I see." Midas' eyes gleamed like gold. "Well, I beg your pardon, then. I must have been misinformed."

Avalon nodded, mollified. "It's okay. Lots of people gets it mixed up."

Guinevere rubbed her temples in frustration. "Avalon, *Arthur* was your father." She repeated those words at least ten times a day.

As usual, Avi ignored them. She smiled up at Midas, like they were having the most pleasant chat in the world.

Midas' expression revealed nothing. "Well, regardless, I'm not Arthur." He said after a long pause. "So I have lots of time for you *and* your mother."

Avalon clapped her hands, delighted with every bit of that quiet statement.

Midas blinked under the force of her grin.

"Avi and I will be fine on our own." Gwen stressed, terrified of the idea of Midas spending "lots of time" with Avalon. God only knew what information she'd let slip. "I'm going to win this war very soon. In the meantime, *your* only job is to keep her safe, Midas."

"And I will."

He snapped his fingers and two hulking guards stalked up from out of nowhere. They were ogres and didn't worry Gwen, at all. Her attention was on the other man she'd just spotted hovering in the shadows. Trystan.

"Shit." She muttered, still not liking the guy.

"Cursing is a no-no, Mommy." Avalon lectured.

"Sorry, baby." Guinevere's attention stayed on the gryphon.

So did Avalon's. "Hi." She chirped at him, like he wasn't the size of a glacier and armed to the teeth. "I'm Avi. I live here now." She looked him over with obvious interest. "You got big wings. I's like wings. They make you fly!"

Trystan's head tilted, considering that information. "You are far smarter than most of your kind." He decided.

"I know! We can be friends. He's my *best* friend." She pointed at Midas. "You can be my *second* best friend." She looked up at Gwen and beamed. "They's you best friends, too!"

"Thank you, baby. But I don't think we should bother Trystan, either..."

"Children do not bother me." Trystan interrupted. "It's adults I can't stand."

Gwen was surprisingly reassured by that flat statement. Gryphons might have no emotions and a well-earned reputation as merciless savages, but they'd always been ferociously protective of children. All children. During the Looking Glass Campaigns, their people had regularly taken in orphans from both sides of the conflict. It was one of the reasons there were so few gryphons left alive.

Arthur's father, King Uther, had targeted the gryphons' offspring, stealing them away, knowing the gryphons would fight to the death to get them back, again. Hell, his brutal tactics had even extended to the children of his own people, torturing them to draw the gryphons out. Like his son, Uther had been a real dick.

"She is innocent." Trystan told Gwen, like he was reading her mind. "The innocent belong to all who would care for them. I do not blame babies for the crimes of their fathers and grandfathers. ...Or mothers."

Gwen made a face at him.

"Trystan." Midas said warningly. "*Ha'na.*"

The gryphon subsided with a sigh that suggested Midas was the stupidest man alive.

"What does *ha'na* mean?" Gwen asked, because they kept saying it.

"Take the princess to the stables." Midas instructed the ogres, as if he didn't hear her question. "Let her pick out a horse."

Oh for God's sake... Next he'd be buying her a circus. Gwen debated banging her head against the garishly painted wall. "She doesn't need a horse, Midas."

"All children need a pet." He glanced at his new "best friend." "Do you like horses?"

Avalon nodded and spread her arms out. "Especially big ones!"

Midas made a sound of agreement, apparently impressed with her perception. "Bigger is always better." He concurred and glanced at the guards. "Let her pick out a big one."

Gwen's eyes widened at the idea of her daughter leaving her

sight. Midas' palace was a literal fortress, but still... "Is that safe?"

Trystan arched a brow as if the question landed somewhere between insulting and amusing. "Is *anything* in this accursed kingdom safe?"

Touché.

"There is no one Trystan can't defeat in a fight." Midas assured her and there was certainly no reason to doubt him. "He's the most dangerous man in Camelot. I promise you, so long as he's with your daughter, she'll be protected."

Trystan gave an arrogant shrug of agreement.

Gwen chewed on her lower lip and leaned closer to Midas. "Are you sure your dangerous guard isn't dangerous to *us?*"

"If Trystan wanted us dead, we'd already be dead."

Well, that was sure heartening.

"It's okay, Mommy." Avalon was already skipping towards the door. "Trystan is my second best friend. He isn't mean. I'd know if he was."

Midas and Trystan both squinted slightly, as if trying to figure out what that meant. With Avalon, it was a fairly common expression for people to wear.

Gwen barely noticed. She took a deep breath and finally nodded consent. Avalon couldn't spend her life wrapped in cotton. Gwen didn't want that for her. She wanted her to play outside and have the freedom to visit horses. It was why she'd made this deal with Midas in the first place. To make sure her daughter had a childhood. The Scarecrow couldn't harm Avalon if she was under Midas' care. Gwen wouldn't have come here, if she didn't totally believe that.

...But it was still damn hard not to hover over her twenty-four hours a day.

"Just make sure all your guards understand how ruthless the Scarecrow can be." She whispered at Midas, so Avalon couldn't overhear. "Please."

Midas looked at the men. "Kill anyone who gets within twenty feet of the princess." He said in way of an answer. "Then track down and kill their families."

The two ogres saluted, falling into formation around Avi as she went dashing outside into the dreary day like it was the brightest sunlight. One of them was already carrying a tiny pink jacket and polka dot scarf for her, the (completely bogus) price tags still attached. Ogres were always great for anticipating needs and following orders without question. It was why they were such popular choices for bodyguards and hired muscle.

Gryphons didn't have the same reputation for reliability.

"I am *extremely* mean." Trystan told Midas, just in case he was inclined to believe Avalon's pronouncement. "Ask anyone who's ever met me. Especially the dead ones."

"I know. I've seen you building your résumé firsthand, remember?"

Gwen kept her eyes on Trystan, still totally unmoved by his physical beauty. He was remarkably handsome, but Arthur had been handsome, too, and look where *that* had gotten them.

"My daughter is *everything* to me." She informed Trystan in her most serious voice. She knew the gryphon wouldn't hurt Avalon, for a variety of reasons. But it was better to cover all the bases. If there was ever a time to be blunt, this was it. "If anything happens to her, I will blame *you*. And by 'blame,' I mean I will do my best to rip your wings off and burn them right in front of you."

Midas seemed amused by the threat.

"No one will touch the child." Everything Trystan said sounded like a blood vow. Old fashioned and steeped in moral certainty. "Midas says she is now my top priority, so I'll protect her." One brow arched. "*And* him."

"Protect Midas? From me, I suppose you mean."

"From you."

Midas sighed and said something to Trystan in the gryphons' language, which Gwen didn't understand. She had a feeling it was a warning to leave her alone, though.

Sure enough, Trystan flashed him an unreadable look. "You take too many chances with your safety."

Despite herself, Gwen couldn't help but agree with that assessment. "Actually, he has a point, Midas. You shouldn't be so trusting. Heartless people like us," she waved a hand between herself and Trystan, "could take advantage of you and you wouldn't even know it."

Trystan grunted, but he didn't argue. And he obviously enjoyed arguing about *everything,* so that was kind of a triumph.

Midas decided to pick up the slack for him. "I'll be fine on *my* own, too." His tone suggested that she was being crazy, probably because he was head of a criminal empire and he thought that made him invulnerable. Which was absurd reasoning. The man was apparently brilliant at his job, but that didn't mean he wasn't also a bit naïve. It just meant he was lucky. "I've been taking care of myself since I was nine years old."

Gwen frowned, wondering why he'd been on his own as a

little boy. "Well, it can't hurt to have people looking out for you, can it? We'll both be fine alone, but we can be *better* if we cooperate. You help me and I help you. That's how our relationship works. It's all outlined in Clause 12 of the Contract- "Respect and Cooperation Between Partners.'"

Midas stared at her. "You believe we have a relationship?" He finally asked, as if that's all he got out of her inspirational speech.

Trystan shook his head in emotionless exasperation. "He will not hear your pretty words, woman. I have warned him about his sentimentality too many times to count and behold where he stands today: Starting a war to impress a female, who would no doubt bed him, anyway."

"Fucking hell." Midas muttered, pinching the bridge of his nose. "Why did I ever save your life, Trystan?"

"No, no, no." Gwen blurted out at the same time. "This is a *business* deal."

Trystan ignored them both. "Thankfully, I have taken on the responsibility of guarding Midas and the child, so they will survive." He shrugged as if he was the only logical man in a land turned upside-down. "Once I begin a task, I do not fail."

Gwen decided to focus on *that* comment. "Well, this might be a difficult challenge even for you. Avalon has *a lot* of enemies. Percival and his men could come back…"

"If those puny boys from last night are the most fearsome warriors your enemies can muster, then you have nothing to worry about."

"The King's Men are the most elite soldiers in the realm!"

Trystan scoffed outright at that news. "Given the state of this pathetic hellhole, I'm sure that's true. Everyone here is weak and small. With a bit of training, the child could defeat them by herself." His eyes narrowed, as if thinking that over. "I'll begin training her this afternoon."

With that, he went striding off after the ogres. Unstoppable and arrogant and *extremely* mean.

Gwen shook her head, unable to believe she'd just kind of hired a gryphon to be Avalon's nanny. "He's *not* training my daughter to kill people. Was he serious about that?"

"Probably. Gryphons aren't really known for their comedy skills. And they train all their children to be warriors, pretty much from birth." Midas held up a palm before she could protest. "Is it such a bad idea for the child to learn how to defend herself?"

"*I* can defend her!"

"What if you're not there?" Midas retorted. "You can't be around every minute of her life. Gryphons are the greatest fighters who ever lived. If their numbers had been higher, they'd rule this kingdom and every other, today."

That was probably true. At least ten of King Uther's conscripts had died for every gryphon who fell. Unfortunately for Trystan's people, they'd been outnumbered *hundreds* to one, so it didn't much matter.

"Let Trystan give the child a few self-defense lessons." Midas continued. "It can only help her be safer. I'll speak to him before he buys her a lance or teaches her to skin her enemies."

Gwen considered that logic and sighed, because he had a point. "I wish I *could* be with her every minute. I don't like it when Avi's out of my sight."

"I *will* guard her for you, Gwen." It was a vow.

That feeling of tenderness swelled again. He really was the kindest man. "Thank you." She reached out to touch the sleeve of his jacket. "You have no idea what she means to me."

Midas glanced down at her hand, as if surprised by the contact. His gaze seemed to linger on Arthur's wedding band for a long moment. Then, he cleared his throat. "Anyway, I wanted to discuss your plans for the day. I need to talk to you about what sort of war strategies you're…"

Gwen cut him off. "I have to go out."

Midas paused. "Go out?" He repeated with no particular inflection.

"Yes, but I'll be back before dinner." She expected him to press her for specifics, which would be awkward, because she didn't want to lie. "Kind of a private matter, from… a while ago. Can we talk about whatever you want to talk about when I return?"

Instead of demanding answers, Midas just nodded. "Of course."

Gwen frowned at the easy agreement. "Really? That's it?"

"I read the Contract." Midas smiled politely. "Clause 8- 'Privacy and Disclosure,' says that we don't need to provide full disclosure about matters that happened before we met, that do not pertain to the other party, and/or that do not violate any other clauses in our agreement. Also, Clause 9- 'Partnership Responsibilities of Midas,' gives you command of the offensive and charge over *all* strategic planning." He even added extra emphasis to the word. "So, you don't have to share anything you don't want to."

The Contract *did* say all of that. Word for word, actually.

Even the "extra emphasis" part. He must have memorized it, just from reading it through the previous night. The man really was startlingly intelligent. And he seemed very sanguine about her keeping secrets. Gwen squinted, trying to figure out why. Did he just not care? Was he just incredibly understanding?

...Or was he up to something himself?

She didn't believe for a moment that he was plotting against her or anything, but six years of marriage to Arthur had taught her some things. Such as, when your husband doesn't care if you're around, it's usually because he's planning to go visit his girlfriend.

Clause 7-"Separate Lives and Other Relationships" said Midas could date whoever he liked and for sure he'd memorized *that* part of the Contract, too. Gwen had written the damn thing, but, now that he was actually planning to date somebody else, desperation filled her and she didn't stop to analyze why. Midas being with another woman was wrong. She needed to stop him.

"You should come with me." She blurted out.

He paused as if that offer surprised him. "I thought it was a private matter."

"It is. But I guess you could come, just so you don't ask too many questions. Or interfere. Or try to stop me. Or touch anything."

Midas studied her for a long moment. "Let me just get my coat."

Chapter Six

Parties will keep their respective last names. Or lack thereof.

Clause 2- Change of Names

Midas had been planning to follow his mysterious bride on her mysterious errand, obviously. The woman had more enemies than Midas had gold and he had an unlimited amount of gold. Letting her wander around the countryside alone was a terrible idea. One way or another, he would have ensured that she was protected. Still, it made things so much easier when she'd simply invited him along.

Why the hell had she done that?

He wanted to ask, but he wasn't sure he'd like the answer.

Guinevere walked through the gnarled trees, the mist drifting around her like a veil. The weather was gray, as usual, grieving for Arthur. It grew more and more melancholy as they traveled deeper into the woods. Midas couldn't imagine why Gwen wanted to tour a swamp in the drizzling rain. Given how delicate she seemed, it would be a miracle if she didn't simultaneously catch pneumonia and dysentery.

"I love it here." She said happily, as if she didn't notice they were standing in the middle of a stagnant marsh. "It's always different, but it's always the same."

He felt his mouth curve a bit. There were worse things to have than a wife who didn't notice ugliness. Especially when you looked like Midas.

Careful not to touch her skin, he reached over to adjust the collar of her practical houndstooth coat. He didn't want her to be cold. She'd fastened the buttons wrong and it was adorable. *She* was adorable. Midas had bought her many jackets, made of everything from jub-jub bird feathers to the downy fleece of a yeti, but she'd picked the simplest one available to wear on this journey.

And she looked perfect in it. Classic and classy and perfect.

Blonde tresses cascaded over his glove, distracting him from her collar. Sunshine against black leather. His fingers lingered for a beat, tangled in her amazing hair. Mesmerized...

Guinevere glanced up at him and Midas yanked his hand back.

"Sorry." He blurted out.

Midas could barely remember what it felt like to really touch anything. He'd been wearing gloves for twenty years. Even before he'd been cursed, though, he'd never touched *anything* as soft as his wife's hair. He knew that without a doubt. Christ, he would have gladly traded everything he owned to feel the glittering strands against his actual flesh.

"It's okay." Gwen smiled at him, like she hadn't minded his touch.

Confused by her lack of irritation, Midas cleared his throat. "Are we nearly to wherever it is we're going?"

"Almost." She hesitated. "Remember not to interfere once we get there, okay? Promise me. Don't do anything, or touch anything, or stop *me* from doing anything or touching anything. It's important that you let me handle this."

Midas nodded, his gaze on her shiny curls, again. Their color was brighter than gold.

One day in Gwen's company and he was already realizing that their relationship was going to be more complicated than he'd anticipated. He wanted her desperately and Midas was a man accustomed to getting what he wanted. Even if some miracle occurred and he convinced her to want him back, it wouldn't make a difference, though. Sex would reveal they were True Loves, so that was out.

Forever.

The whole situation was going to be hell. Plus, the ground was spongy beneath his feet, reminding him of Celliwig's endless acres of mud. That did nothing to improve his mood.

Neither did the idiots trailing after them in the fog.

Midas glanced into the underbrush, keeping his body in between Gwen and the soldiers. Percival's men were following them. Four of them, by the sound of it. The morons were attempting to be stealthy, but it was hard to sneak around when you were wearing sixty pounds of armor. Since they weren't attacking, Midas could only assume that they hoped Gwen led them somewhere before they struck.

He'd considered alerting her to their presence. It was probably the "right" thing to do. If he did that, though, she would stop her plan and march over to confront them. No, not stop. *Postpone*. Whatever she was plotting, she'd keep on plotting it, only next time Midas might not be there to ensure she was okay.

Gwen's safety meant more to him than trying to figure out what was "right." After all, his prison psychiatrists had decided he was incapable of telling right from wrong. Rather than debate an issue he was apparently unable to understand, it seemed wiser to kill the men threatening Gwen *now*.

He just hoped to kill them without his wife noticing. A stack of dead bodies would be a terrible way to start a honeymoon, when your bride thought you were "kind" and "gentle."

"It's just up here." Guinevere walked faster, her boots crunching on the overgrown path. It looked as if no one had ever come this way before, but she seemed to know where she was going and he didn't argue. "Not everyone can even see it, but this place is very special."

Midas glanced around the depressing forest. "Okay." He said, not wanting to hurt her feelings.

"I was raised here." Guinevere told him. "It was our vacation house. My father owned all of this, as far as you can see." She waved a hand around the forgotten landscape. "He left it in trust to Avalon, before she was even born. Not that I think it's a good idea to let her come here, right now. It could be dangerous."

Midas couldn't argue with that. These woods were ominous as hell. One day, though, he was sure that Avalon would love the strange place as much as her mother did. The two of them seemed remarkably alike.

Tiny and sweet, Avalon was like an alien species. She'd smiled at Midas and said they could be best friends. He couldn't explain that, but he found it... pleasant. He no longer wished simply to ignore her. Arthur might not have wanted a child that wasn't biologically his around, but Midas was coming to like the idea. Avalon interested him.

Especially her claims that Arthur wasn't her daddy.

"Our main house was much grander, but this was the place my father came when he wanted to relax." Gwen continued. "It's quiet here. Merlyn couldn't think when too many people were around. All their thoughts and feelings and futures would crowd in on him."

Merlyn. Her father.

The wizard's name was still whispered in respect and he'd been dead for nearly six years. It was one more reason that Guinevere didn't belong with Midas. She was Arthur's widow, the Queen of Camelot, the daughter of the greatest sorcerer in history, the best mother he'd ever seen, and Good straight down to her sparkling clean soul. Gwen could do far, *far* better than a tawdry, feral animal.

Fuck.

"There it is." Gwen pointed to a pile of debris that didn't look like it had been an actual dwelling for centuries.

Midas squinted at it. At what point did a house stop being a house and become something that had *once been* a house? He wasn't sure, but he knew that this particular place had long since crossed that line.

Gwen glanced from the haphazardly piled stones to Midas. "Do you see it?" She asked intently.

Midas frowned. Not wanting to disappoint her, he looked towards the building and wondered what the hell he was supposed to see beyond squalor. For a long moment there was nothing ...and then Midas began to feel the latent magic in the air. Sense the power that cloaked the home. The edges of the stones shimmered and his mouth parted in wonder.

"Jesus." He whispered.

Merlyn had enspelled the house to trick all those who did not look deeply enough. If Midas concentrated, he could see that the abandoned ruin was really just a gauzy overlay obscuring reality. Beneath the magic, the actual house --the building Gwen's father had constructed-- was a miniature castle, surrounded by a wide moat. Its shining façade was entirely intact, Merlyn's banner still flying from a tall tower.

It was magical.

Midas drew in a deep breath, overwhelmed and yet not surprised by the small palace. Of *course* Gwen would have stepped right out of a storybook. Where else could such a woman have grown up?

"It's beautiful." He murmured and meant it.

She sent him another smile. "Not everyone thinks so. Not everyone sees." Her eyes glowed with warmth. "I knew *you* would, though."

That was a compliment. He could tell by her tone and it was the first compliment he ever remembered receiving. He wasn't sure how he was supposed to respond.

"Galahad's the only other person I've ever brought here and even *he* had trouble peering through the magic. That surprised me, because he's wonderful at everything. But he was so apologetic about it, that it was kind of funny."

Midas' mood darkened again. Every time she spoke of Galahad, he heard the affection and admiration in her voice. There wasn't a doubt in Midas' mind that the only reason she'd come to him for help was because her knight in shining armor was inconveniently banished. If Galahad ever showed up to offer her aid, Gwen would be rushing out Midas' door and right into his shining-armor-clad arms.

Hopefully, Arthur had been smart enough to send the wonderful bastard far, far away.

"Just... don't touch anything." Gwen reiterated, not bothered by his lack of an answer. "Whether you see it or not, *don't touch it*. It could be dangerous. Just leave it all to me." With that, as if she was just too excited to wait any longer, she bounded towards the enchanted castle.

Midas smiled despite himself, amused by her enthusiasm.

One of the soldiers was apparently just as eager. He burst from the forest, running forward with his sword extended. Percival's brain-trust wasn't much for strategic thinking. Midas moved sideways, so the imbecile charged right past him. The knight must have decided to do away with Midas while Gwen was distracted, so he'd have a clear shot at her afterwards.

It wasn't the best plan.

As the man thundered by, it was shockingly simple to reach out and grab the sword. The razor-sharp edge didn't do any damage to his palm. The curse made sure that Midas' hands were always protected. He knew that without question, because he'd tried hacking them off in an effort to cure his golden touch and it didn't work. They were indestructible.

He wrenched the sword right out of the man's grasp, his fingers wrapped tightly around the blade.

The guard kept running for a few paces and then staggered to a stop, surprised that he'd overshot his target and lost his weapon. He turned, an astonished look on his face. Maybe he'd expected Midas to fight fair. Maybe that was what a knight would do.

Truthfully, Midas didn't give a fuck.

He stepped forward, flipping the sword around in his hand and stabbing it right between the armored plates on the man's chest. His other palm came up to clamp over the bastard's mouth, so he couldn't cry out.

"If you want to try and kill me," he said quietly, as the man gurgled in shock, "don't do it with my wife around. It pisses me off." He gave one quick twist of the blade, making sure the man was dead.

Pitiful.

"Coming, Midas?" Guinevere called, without turning around.

"Coming." Midas tossed the body into the underbrush at the side of the road, so she wouldn't see it on their way out. The rest of the King's Men would be spread out, waiting for openings to attack.

Hopefully, they'd all be considerate enough to die quietly. He was in no hurry to spoil Gwen's fun

...Or dispel her illusions about his honorable nature.

Midas walked up the path after his wife, wincing a bit as the mud ruined his handmade shoes. He hated mud. It sucked you down and stuck to your skin and stained your clothes. His whole life, he'd been trying to wash it off and he still never seemed to come clean. Sighing in annoyance, he headed across the drawbridge and through the arched door of the miniature castle. He wiped his shoes before he entered, but he could still see the dirt marring them. As soon as he got home, he was going to throw them away and buy a new pair.

Gwen was already disappearing up the curving staircase. "This way!"

Another one of the King's Men came at him, swinging a saber at Midas' head. Midas jumped back to avoid decapitation. "Oh for fuck's sake..."

"Everything okay?" Guinevere called from upstairs.

"It's fine." Midas ducked another blow from the sword and slammed his foot into the other man's leg.

The knight was encased in armor, so the impact didn't do much damage, but it did knock him off balance. The smaller man collapsed to one knee, his arm coming out to steady himself on the wall. "Bad folk will never win." He snarled. "Give us the woman and we'll allow you to live."

Midas arched a brow. "No." Casually, he shoved the guy backwards. That was all it took. His assailant toppled over, flailing around like an upside down turtle unable to right himself.

Growing up, brawling on the streets for food, Midas learned absolutely nothing about gentlemanly conduct. ...But he *had* learned how to win. If the King's Men spent more time fighting and less time signing autographs, they might have discovered that armor was great for impressing the ladies at court, but it kind of sucked when it came to a fistfight.

Midas seized his would-be assassin by the helmet strap and dragged him out the door again, before Gwen heard his swearing and threats.

"There's nothing you can do that will stop what's coming." The man raged. "Good folk are the future of Camelot!"

"You won't be *in* the future, so what do you care?" Midas tipped the dickhead into the moat without giving him a chance to sputter out a response. The weight of the armor made swimming impossible and water slurped him down with a greedy splash.

"Midas?" Gwen shouted. "Where are you?"

"By the moat."

"The moat?" Gwen sounded alarmed. "Don't get too close. George is in there."

"George...?"

Even as he said the word, a gigantic monster was swimming beneath him, drawn by movement in the water. Midas' eyebrows soared as the beast rushed directly under the drawbridge, tentacles sweeping the depths of the moat. He couldn't get a clear view of it, but he had the distinct impression of an octopus-like creature with a parrot's beak and black spikes on its slimy skin.

"He's just a baby." Gwen continued loudly. "I thought of releasing him into the ocean, so he could have more room, but he only has three arms." She sounded sad for the gigantic sea serpent. "He's practically helpless! In the wild, he'd be gobbled up in no time. Fortunately, kraken make wonderful pets, just so you don't touch them."

An ominous swarm of bubbles exploded to the surface, telling Midas that Gwen's helpless baby had found an armored-coated snack.

"Don't worry. I'm not going to touch George." He shook his head in exasperation. A pet kraken. Fucking hell.

Exasperated, Midas went back inside and immediately muttered a curse. Another of the King's Men had come in from a different direction. He was already racing upstairs, towards the sound of Gwen's voice, his gaze fanatically determined.

Son of a bitch.

Midas' eyes narrowed and he headed after him, leaping over the banister in silent pursuit. It was one thing to try and kill *him*. Obviously, he didn't like it, but he could handle it with, he thought, an admirable degree of restraint. *Nobody* went after Guinevere, though. Not unless they wanted to see the fucking "violent predator" Arthur had raged against in court.

Midas reached the man halfway up the steps, yanking him to a halt on the landing. The guy gave a squawk of alarm as Midas seized him from behind. He attempted to wrestle his sword free of its scabbard, but it was no use. Midas took him down faster than George devouring the last knight. He spun the smaller man around and hefted him up by the throat, so his feet didn't even touch the ground.

The guy gave a strangled gurgle, clawing for air.

"Midas, are you okay?" Guinevere shouted from above them. "I heard something crash."

"I'm fine, Gwen."

"Well, it's not safe for you to be wandering around alone. Come up here, so I can keep an eye on you."

Midas didn't know whether to be irritated or charmed by her insistence that she needed to look after him. "I'll be right there, kitten." The endearment slipped out without him even noticing. He kept his eyes on his captive and lowered his voice. "Explain why you're coming after my wife." He ordered softly. "And, for your sake, it had better be one goddamn compelling reason."

"Not going to… harm her." The guard wheezed, still trying to pry Midas' fingers from his windpipe. "The Scarecrow wants… his woman alive."

"The woman is *mine* and I don't fucking share." Midas reached over to unlatch the landing's stained-glass window with his free hand.

The guy's face was going purple, but he remained defiant. "Kill me… if you want… villain." He choked out. "The Scarecrow… will just keep coming… *forever*… until he has her."

"Not forever. Just until I kill him, too."

Midas pitched the bastard out a second story window. It had taken an extra moment to *open* the window, so as not to break the delicate pattern of flowers worked into the multicolored glass, but it had been worth it. Gwen wouldn't like it if he harmed her father's home. This way was just as effective, with no property damage. He watched dispassionately as the soldier hit the bank of the moat with a reverberating clang of metal against rocks and bone.

Instantly, three tentacles slithered out of the water to pull the body under the murky surface. George was still hungry.

"Are you *sure* you didn't hear something?" Gwen asked, appearing over the edge of the balcony.

Midas tilted his head, listening. "I don't hear anything, *now*." He told her truthfully and trotted up the remainder of the stairs.

She accepted that with a nod and headed down the hall. "Just don't touch anything. There are more animals around here and not all of them are friendly. They kind of have the run of the house, these days."

Well, that was great news. Midas sighed and followed her into a random room. "Are you sure that kraken is getting enough to eat? I think maybe it wants some meat."

"Kraken are herbivores. George eats the algae in the moat. It's very nutritious."

"Uh-huh." Midas made a mental note to bring the creature

some steaks or something. George was clearly sick of his vegetarian diet. "Can I ask what we're doing here, Gwen?"

"We're searching for clues." She started rooting through a bedroom closet. From the furnishings, Midas guessed that it was Merlyn's room. Everything was oversized and masculine.

"Clues to what?" He stood half in the doorway and half in the room, so he could scan for more uninvited company of either the armed maniac or wild animal varieties.

Gwen sent him a sideways look, like she was debating how much to tell him. Midas waited, allowing himself to be weighed by those lake-blue eyes.

"Clues to the location of my father's magic wand." She finally said and Midas realized that he'd somehow passed another test with her. Hell if he knew how that kept happening, but he wasn't about to question his luck.

"Is this the wand that Percival was after last night?"

"Yes. I've been searching for it for months now." She gave up on the closet and crawled under the bed tossing out mismatched shoes and an animal that looked like a chicken with scales. The hideous creature gave an angry chirp at being disturbed and waddled away, dragging a reptilian tail behind it. "Before he died, Merlyn videotaped a message for me, saying that he hid his wand someplace."

"Why?"

"So I could have it if I ever needed it, but no one else could find it. He told me it was in the very last place he'd want to look."

"Who's 'he'?"

"Arthur, I assume. But where would Arthur not want to look? I've tried all the libraries. That was my first guess." She made a face. "So typical of my father to be vague. Did I mention he remembered things in reverse?"

"No, you didn't. That sounds... complicated."

"Complicated?" She scoffed, like that was a massive understatement. "Everything that had already happened, he forgot. He only remembered what hadn't happened *yet*. He would be sad when he first met someone, because he knew it would be the last time he ever saw them. He'd plan for events that we'd attended yesterday and talk about tomorrow in the past tense. It was impossible to keep up." She paused, a grin crossing her face, like she was recalling all the chaos her father had caused. "He was marvelous."

Midas had no idea what it would be like to have a "marvelous" parent. Looking at Gwen, though, he caught a glimpse of it and it warmed something inside of him. "I'm glad you were happy."

92

He said quietly. His own childhood had been so bleak. So empty. He would never want that for her. Gwen deserved to be surrounded by love.

"That was my mother." Gwen pointed to a portrait of a blonde haired woman in a wedding dress.

Midas tilted his head to study the picture. "She's lovely." She looked like Guinevere so how could she be anything else?

"She died giving birth to me. My whole life, it was just me and Merlyn. Until Arthur, anyway." Gwen paused, her expression growing darker. "He and Merlyn had some... differences."

Midas made a noncommittal sound and decided he was a hundred percent on *Merlyn's* side of the dispute.

"Merlyn knew that, one day, Avalon would be born." Gwen explained. "He knew how much I'd love her and how important she'd be, but he was *not* Arthur's biggest fan. He was the head of the Wizard's Congress. Rather than give Arthur any spells, he decided to just *stop* doing magic."

"That's why the wizards locked themselves in the Emerald City?"

"Exactly." She sighed. "Anyway, Merlyn left his wand somewhere and said I'd be able to find it when I needed it. Except, I need it *now* and I can't find it."

"And now the Scarecrow is looking for it, too." That wasn't good news.

"He wants to stop me from stopping him. It won't work." She stood up, dusting the dirt from her hands. "I will *never* let him carry out his monstrous plans." Gwen began yanking drawers from the dresser. A flurry of half-spider/half-dachshund looking animals came skittering out of the bureau, as she tossed aside old clothing.

Midas would have kept asking questions, but there was a small sound in the hall. "Excuse me for a moment." He stepped out, closing the door behind him, sealing her safely in her father's room.

"What are you doing?" Gwen demanded through the cheerfully painted wood. "Don't touch anything."

Midas ignored that, his eyes scanning around for the source of the noise. It only took him a heartbeat to know that the fourth guard was hiding in the next room. Jesus. He rolled his eyes towards the ceiling. These jackasses would last about twenty minutes in Celliwig.

He absently took his jacket off and crumpled it in his fist, trying not to think about the unicorn-thread fabric he was ruining. Instead, he counted down from ten.

At seven, the door to the next room cracked open, the other man too impatient to wait any longer. At six, Midas grasped the knob, yanking it forward while the guard was still holding the other side. The guy stumbled forward, off balance. At five, Midas slammed it back, so the door smashed into the soldier's head and knocked him down. By four, he'd prowled into the room and stuffed the ball of fabric over the lower half of the man's face so he couldn't cry out. At three, the genius tried to stab Midas with a knife that had been strapped to his belt. He ended up slicing Midas' arm. By two, Midas was leaning over him, wrestling the blade away.

And, at one, he snapped the man's neck between his large hands.

Shit.

Midas sat back and examined the wound on his forearm. Blood seeped from it, several drops hitting the dead body. That had been a clumsy fight, but no matter. It would heal. He stood up, shrugging his wrinkled jacket back on to hide the gash in his shirt sleeve. The last thing he wanted was Gwen asking how he'd been injured. Not that she'd care, overly much, but it would raise all kinds of questions about…

A bloodthirsty growl interrupted his thoughts.

Midas' head whipped around, coming face-to-face with the most grotesque creature he'd ever seen. It was hideous, with the body of a hyena and the head of a monkey. It looked like the two species had been split down the middle and sewn back together. Badly. Its fur was a patchy mix of tawny spots and laboratory tattoos.

Someone had *made* this thing.

Why?

The nameless animal slowly advanced on him, snarling like a demon from a horror movie. Yellow teeth, the size of human fingers, dripped with saliva and foam. Its too-round, too-intelligent eyes stayed fixed on him, like it was just as puzzled to see Midas standing there. The two of them stared at each other for an endless moment.

"Midas?" Gwen called, breaking the spell.

The mutated whatzit suddenly leapt at him, its claws extended.

Midas bolted backwards into the hall, slamming the door behind him. Almost instantly, he heard the animal impact the wood, shaking the whole house. Fuck. A second slower and it would have gotten him. Some skin-crawling combination of angry monkey screams and hyena yowls sounded from inside the room, quickly followed by the unmistakable noise of the creature devouring the knight's body.

Midas winced.

"I think you're touching things." Gwen accused from behind him.

He spun around to look at her. "There's some kind of... *something* in that room."

"Oh. That's just the monkena. I call him Henry."

"Why is *Henry* staying in your guest room?"

She wrinkled her nose. "Because he likes it in there. Believe me, I've tried to get him into the basement, but he just won't live anyplace else. I think he likes the view."

Midas pinched the bridge of his nose and rephrased. "Where did all these weird animals come from, Gwen?"

"I brought them here." She admitted reluctantly. "There are hundreds of empty acres for them to live on, plus the house. The whole place is enspelled, so it self-cleans and they have food. It seemed like the safest place for them."

"Safe from what?

"Dark Science."

"What the hell is that?"

She chewed her lower lip. "When Merlyn refused to use spells to help him win his wars, Arthur tried science. You have to understand, Arthur lived with the legacy of his father, the hero of the Looking Glass Campaigns. He wanted to prove himself in some epic battle."

"King Uther was a genocidal maniac."

"But he was also his father and Arthur wanted to measure up." She paused. "Also, I think he was drunk. Arthur had the worst ideas when he was drinking."

Fucking hell.

"Anyway, Arthur hired scientists to create weapons that were *better* than magic. Without the built-in boundaries that keep us safe. Before long, their experiments became... twisted. Dark. You can't artificially create something natural. There are always consequences."

Not killing Arthur himself really was Midas' biggest regret. It just became clearer every day.

"Now, the Scarecrow is pushing Dark Science farther than ever. Doing ghastly things, thanks to the White Rabbit, his conscienceless stooge. My father's wand is the only thing that can stop this madness. His magic will destroy Dark Science, once and for all. It *has* to. The monkena is one of that evil bunny's *better* experiments. You should see the firebird." Gwen sniffed. "I just feel terrible about poor Harriet"

He was probably going to regret asking, but... "What's a firebird?"

"Oh, Harriet's half-bird, half-fire. Her feathers are *literally* burning. I have to keep her locked in the tower." Gwen pointed towards the ceiling and the stone turret beyond. "It's fireproof. Otherwise, all of Camelot would be ablaze. It's not fair, because she's *so* sweet. She follows me around like a puppy."

Good God.

"I tried to let Harriet nest in the trees outside, but she started a forest fire." Gwen held up a palm, like she wanted to forestall his *pretty fucking obvious* concerns. "Just a small one. I'm hoping I can train her to control the flames." The firebird was clearly Gwen's favorite monster-y pet. "I bought her a dog whistle, so we can practice. So far, Harriet's not getting it, though. But she *does* come when she's called. Isn't that cute?"

"Adorable." The woman was going to give him a heart attack before their first anniversary. "Let's rewind to the part where you brought all the fiery, tentacled animals *here*."

"Well, when we..." She broke off and started again. "When *I* saw what was happening in the lab, I decided to stop it. I broke all the animals out and did my best to destroy the White Rabbit's research. I set him behind for a while, but it wasn't enough." She sighed. "Anyway, after I saved them, I hid the animals here. It seemed like the best choice."

"Did it? Did it *really?*"

"Well, I know it's not perfect, but this is just temporary." She ran a hand through her hair. "Before the Scarecrow stole everything from me, I thought that I could --I don't know-- hire someone to take care of them in a sanctuary or something. Obviously, that's kind of taking a backseat, because of being locked in a dungeon and getting married and the war."

"Obviously."

"That's why I told you to stay close to me, while we're here. It can be dangerous around the animals, unless you're used to dealing with life-threatening situations."

"Which *you* are and *I'm* not?" He translated, incredulously.

"Of course." She laid a hand on his uninjured arm, like she had some tragic news to relay. "You probably don't want to hear this, but you're not the most street-smart man in Camelot. I know you have a job as a gangster, but you're kind of a little bit naïve. Plus, you keep touching things."

"I did *not* touch..." Midas broke off as a hoard of mice raced by. Only, somehow, it was just *one* mouse. It looked as if forty of them had been fused together by their tails to create a single being. They were normal-sized mice, not the humanoid variety, all of them running together in a massive knot of pink feet and squeaking and gray fur.

"Mouse king." Gwen told him unnecessarily. "I call him Ted."

Midas closed his eyes and prayed for patience. It was astounding that anybody thought this woman was heartless. She'd created an un-petting zoo for freaks. As dangerous and illogical as this situation was, Midas couldn't help but be enchanted by her innocent do-Gooding. There was no one else in the world like his angelic wife.

"Finish looking for the wand, so we can get out of here." He told her, wondering why in the hell he'd been given such a Good-hearted True Love. Gwen truly did deserve someone better. "Then, I will hire a team of experts to care for your menagerie of unnatural beasts."

"Really?" She looked surprised. "You'd do that for me?"

"I would do anything for you." The words came before he could stop them. "Anything to make you happy."

Gwen gazed up at him silently. Once again, Midas had the feeling he was being examined from the inside out. He stared back at her, not looking away from her eyes.

Christ, she was beautiful.

"Thank you." She finally whispered and stepped closer to him.

"You don't have to thank me." Unable to help himself, Midas reached out to fiddle with her collar again, trying to smooth it down. "If you want something, I'll make sure you have it." He absently rubbed one of her curls between his thumb and forefinger, fascinated by the way it sprang back to its original shape when he released it.

She didn't tell him to stop, which was astonishing. Why didn't she tell him to stop? Big blue eyes stared up at him, unafraid. "Why?" She asked, instead.

"Huh?" Midas had lost the thread of the conversation. "Why what?"

It was hard to concentrate on anything but the desire coursing through him. All his life, he'd ignored the barriers meant to keep him from what he wanted and he wanted *nothing* as much as he wanted Gwen. Midas instinctively pulled her closer. His palms slipped down to the lapels of her coat, gripping them tight and tugging her forward.

Gwen gave a surprised gasp as he dragged her towards him. The quick, indrawn breath caused her chest to rise. Her breasts brushed against the back of his fingers and Midas' eyes nearly crossed. Fuck. A hiss of air escaped him, his body on fire for her.

Gwen blinked up at him, still not struggling to get free. "You're definitely touching something, now." She murmured and he almost thought her mouth curved.

"I know. I'm sorry. I'm..." Midas shook his head and began unfastening her jacket, trying to focus. "It's buttoned wrong." His voice was too rough. He cleared his throat and tried again. "That's why your collar isn't straight. Your coat is crooked."

She stood still, letting him adjust her clothes. "Fix it for me, then."

It was all he could do not to groan. Was this another test of some kind? Midas was too dazed to decide. His fingers slid over the buttons, feeling big and awkward. He should *not* be touching her. No one from Celliwig should ever touch such a classy woman. ...But he sure as hell didn't stop touching her.

He wasn't an idiot.

Gwen made a soft whisper of a sound, as his thumb inadvertently rasped over the tip of her breast. Even through the layers of fabric and the leather of his glove, Midas could sense her nipple bead. That response was all it took for him to become more aroused than he'd ever been. He got so hard, so fast it would be a wonder if he didn't permanently cripple himself.

His wife.

Midas' jaw clenched, trying to calm down. Shit. All he'd done was touch her coat and he was ready to come. He needed to stop this, before it went too far. He didn't have control. He *always* had control.

Gwen's pulse hammered in her neck. "Why do you want to make me happy?" She asked, obviously trying to get them back on track. "That isn't part of our Contract."

"Honoring and cherishing you *is* part of our Contract." Midas finished with his ministrations and reluctantly dropped his fingers. "I promised it in my vows."

Gwen frowned. "Well, I hadn't considered the actual ceremony part of our deal..."

Midas cut her off, sexual frustration making him harsher than usual. "*I* consider it part of the deal." The only part he cared about, as a matter of fact. "Is there something about our wedding ceremony that you feel wasn't contractually binding?"

"No, but from a practical sense, it could be hard to reconcile a..." she floundered for a beat, "a *traditional* person's view of a marriage contract with our very rational *business* Contract."

"I'm not having an issue with it."

"Well, I know we're fake-married, but..."

"We're *not* fake-married." Midas interjected unequivocally. "Our wedding was completely legitimate." It was the first time the law had ever worked in his favor, so he'd ensured every i was dotted and every t was crossed. "Our names are on a *real* scroll, witnessed by a *real* wizard, in a *real* wedding ceremony, where we said *real* vows."

"Yes, but..."

"It's all detailed in our very real and very valid and very *legal* marriage contract."

Gwen's eyebrows compressed like she wanted to argue her position, but wasn't exactly sure what her position *was*.

"I take all contracts seriously." Midas adopted a look of polite inquiry. "Don't you?"

"Of course I take contracts seriously! I'm just..." Gwen trailed off and took a deep breath. "I'm just going to go look for the wand. This is getting us nowhere." She turned back to Merlyn's room with a stubborn set to her jaw. "Stay there and don't touch anything else."

The only thing he wanted to touch was walking away from him, so that wouldn't be a problem. Midas leaned a shoulder against the wall, his lower body still throbbing. His eyes fixed on the shapely curve of Gwen's posterior, which did nothing to help the situation. Goddamn. However much he'd paid for those unadorned jeans she was wearing, they had been a fucking brilliant investment. He was going to order her about fifty more pair and...

The gunshot caught him by surprise.

Midas automatically ducked to the side and had the vague thought that it was astonishing anyone could miss him at close range. As a target, he was massive. Camelot's anti-gun laws were really not such a terrible thing. It meant that most people in the kingdom had rotten aim. The bullet sailed past his forehead, imbedding in the wall beside him. Instantly, Merlyn's self-cleaning, self-repairing house absorbed the bullet-hole, not leaving even a trace of it on the tasteful yellow wall.

Midas barely noticed, his gaze siting on the lone figure at the end of the hall. Apparently, there had been *five* of the King's Men lurking around. Son of a bitch. He did a quick scan for Gwen, who'd ducked back into Merlyn's room.

Percival gave a cackle of malicious delight. "I warned you, Kingpin. I *warned* you what would happen if you crossed me. You and that *gryphon* you hang around with." He sneered out the name of Trystan's people in disgust, hatred evident on his puckered face. "I fought in the Looking Glass Campaigns. I saw their barbarism, firsthand. It's *repulsive* that you would allow one of those winged devils into your home."

"The gryphon weren't the devils in that war."

"You're a fucking traitor, if you think that!" Percival shouted. "I'm not surprised. You're nothing but a mongrel, crawled out of a mud hole." He smirked. "You thought you got the best of me last night, but it will never happen! I'm *Good*. I'm *right*."

"You're an idiot. You always have been."

Percival didn't appreciate Midas quoting Gwen's entirely correct assessment. "Shut up!" He jabbed the gun in a blind fury. "I'm going to kill you, as *all* Bad folk should be killed! Then, the Scarecrow will have the woman and we'll control Camelot. It's ours, because we're *better* than you and your dirty, savage, flying friends. Now, hand her over!"

"My wife is going nowhere with you." Midas started forward, intent on killing the man or dying in the attempt. "Fucking shoot me and don't miss, this time. It's the only way you'll *ever* take her from me."

Percival's eyes narrowed in panic at such a direct attack. Raising the gun, he tried to fire. Maybe the second time would have been the charm or maybe he would have missed, again. Neither of them got a chance to find out.

Guinevere came up behind Percival and slammed something into the back of his skull. There was a sickening crunch and the sound of shattering glass. Then Percival was tipping forward, unconscious. The gun tumbled to the carpet, Percival falling only a heartbeat behind it. They both lay on the floor, subdued.

Midas moved to check his pulse. Well shit. The jackass wasn't dead, sadly, but still it was pretty fine work for a Good folk. He glanced at Gwen, his mouth curving with pride.

His wife.

"Hi, kitten." He said mildly. "Great timing."

"Thanks." Gwen smiled at him. "So, I didn't find Merlyn's magic wand." She shrugged and held up a clear orb with a newly created, gigantic crack running straight through its center. "But, I knew right where he kept his crystal ball."

Chapter Seven

Midas
Twenty Years Ago

Nothing grew in the village of Celliwig.

A century before, forest groves had covered the rolling hills, as lush and verdant as anyone could imagine. The trees there had a magic all their own. They soared as high as buildings and grew together in thickets as thick as weeds. Green and sprawling, the branches waved hundreds of feet in the air, cooling the shaded land below. Meanwhile, the trees' roots sunk deep into the marshy ground, anchoring the land so a town could be built.

The woods of Celliwig *were* Celliwig.

The lumber they provided made it one of the wealthiest villages in Camelot. Hundreds of people worked in the forest, chopping and sawing, and everyone got rich. Money seemed to rain from the sky like leaves in autumn. Buying timberland was a surefire, no miss, chance-of-a-lifetime investment and everyone wanted in on it. Soon thousands of people were cutting. Mansions sprouted up as the trees came down. Bigger and bigger, richer and richer, there seemed no end to Celliwig's prosperity.

Until, inevitably, all the trees were gone.

Within two generations, the thick forest had been seriously depleted. People realized the danger, of course. Talked about it. Wrote concerned essays and discussed it in serious tones. But solving the problem wasn't so easy when there was so much *money* to be made by simply ignoring it. Somehow the villagers convinced themselves that deforestation was just a temporary setback. That their lifestyle was sustainable. That millennia of growth could be replaced with a few rows of newly planted pines and a newspaper recycling program.

Another forty years of denial and logging left the woods decimated beyond repair and the ground as soft as a sponge. By that point, there was no turning back. Everyone who could leave Celliwig abandoned it, never to return. Those who couldn't leave were forced to live in mud and squalor and rotting stumps. Blackened acres of them covered the hills, like gravestones in a cemetery. A decade after the last tree fell, only the poorest, most hopeless villagers remained in Celliwig.

And, once upon a time, Midas had been the poorest and most hopeless of all.

Technically, he wasn't an orphan. He had parents. Somewhere. After a while, he couldn't recall their faces, but he remembered what mattered most about them. Remembered the bitterness and resentment that never left their beige house. Remembered sleeping in the attic, terrified of the dark. Remembered their constant fights about money and their countless schemes to acquire more. Remembered the scorn they'd showed him and the beatings and the tears.

Most of all, he remembered that fucking bologna sandwich.

His parents hated him. Midas accepted that. On some level, he even understood it. Their dreams had been drowned in oppressive poverty and, somehow, they channeled all their disappointment into despising their only child. They were Good, with grand and unfulfilled ambitions that ate at them every day. They'd prepared to pass down a spectacular legacy, except their timberland was nothing but a mud puddle, their once grand house was being repossessed, and Midas, their heir, was Bad. That kind of failure was enough to make anyone want to run away.

And so, one winter day, when Midas was nine, his parents did what everyone in Celliwig dreamed of doing: They packed up their meager belongings and left town forever.

They just neglected to tell Midas about their plans.

He came home from the ramshackle shed that served as the village school and found his parents gone. The door was locked, the windows boarded up, and a single bologna sandwich was left on the porch for his dinner. There wasn't even a note.

That was the part that angered him the most. They didn't have the balls to write a brief good-bye, or a half-hearted apology, or a simple explanation. They just made him the sandwich, piled his single change of clothes on the steps, and vanished without a word. They hadn't even left Midas his one "toy," the sock full of sawdust, so he could hold it while he cried himself to sleep.

For a few nights, he deluded himself with the idea that his parents might return and stayed right there on the porch, waiting for them. Then the bankers came to chase him away and sold the house to new owners. With nowhere else to go, Midas began living in alleyways. Unprotected and small, he would have died quickly, except an old woman had come along before any of Celliwig's desperate, immoral men found him.

Corrah Skycast was as forsaken as Midas, dying and broken in a foreign land. Quite possibly, she was the last female gryphon still free in the world and she intended to stay that way. She'd once been a warrior and she could still kill a man as easily as she flew. Remote and proud, she clung to the old ways like those customs were the only thing left for her.

They *were* the only thing left. Midas' people had stolen everything else.

Like all gryphons, protecting the young was a sacred responsibility for Corrah. ...Even the young of a race she despised. The innocent belonged to all who would care for them. There were no gryphon left to judge her actions or inactions, but that didn't matter to her sense of duty. She still lived by the code of her vanished people and she shielded Midas from the horrors of the streets.

Midas adored her, even though she couldn't feel the emotion back. She didn't have to. Her actions were enough. Corrah gave him most of the food-scraps she found, and taught him her language, and traded for books so he could read, and let him sleep wrapped safely in her wings when it snowed.

When he cajoled for long enough, she even grudgingly told him the stories of her people. Tales of rocking-horseflies so big that they carried children to the stars and mighty queens who swept down to save their clans from destruction.

But no one came to save Corrah.

She died in an abandoned building, less than three years after he'd found her. Midas wasn't sure if it was her age, or her ancient battle wounds, or her broken spirit that finally took her. But he cried when she left him, like he'd never cried over his parents' departure. Missed her far more than he missed them.

After she was gone, he was alone.

Nobody else in Celliwig was going to take in a Bad folk, even if he was just a child. Why would they? They didn't possess the gryphons' sense of communal responsibility for the young. There was no hope for Midas' future, so why invest in his food and lodging? He was a waste of resources.

Later, Midas would wonder why he hadn't turned to crime far sooner than he did, but, as a boy, it hadn't occurred to him to break the law. Instead, he'd gotten work in the stable, two doors from his old house. He received no money for the backbreaking labor, but he was allowed to sleep in the straw at night. Midas was big for his age and very smart. He read everything he could find and worked hard, every day, for two years... and got exactly nowhere.

Slowly, it dawned on Midas he would never get away from the servitude and loneliness of his dismal life. There was no escape hatch for Bad folks. No pot of gold waiting for them. No warm home and happy family, if he just tried his best and kept believing. Mucking stalls and staying hungry and wading through mud was all he could ever have. All he would ever be.

There was no hope for him, at all.

The day he had that realization was the bleakest of his existence. He sat down in an empty horse stall and wept as darkness settled over him. He had nothing. He would always have... nothing.

Through his misery, he cast around for someone to blame. For some reason he was so alone and forgotten. It didn't take long to find a cause. It was simple, in fact. In the end, he didn't blame his parents for abandoning him. Didn't blame the Good folk for their uncaring ways or even destiny for making him Bad.

No. He blamed himself.

More precisely, he blamed his own poverty.

Money was the root of all his problems. Or rather the lack of it. If he'd had money, his parents wouldn't have left. If he'd had money, he could have gotten a doctor to tend to Corrah and she wouldn't have died. If he had money, it wouldn't matter that he was Bad, because no one would look down on him. He could just *buy* anything he wanted: Friends, food, a house, respectability.

Class.

In that stable, at the lowest point of his life, Midas made a decision: He would be rich. He would be so rich that no one would ever be able to keep him from what he wanted, ever again. Hard work and prayers wouldn't do a damn thing to grow his pocketbook, though. He was going to need to steal and cheat... and use some magic.

And so Midas did what no one else in Celliwig would ever, *ever* do.

He went to see Vivien, Lady of the Lake.

Once Midas set his mind to something, nothing stood in his way. Certainly, not the fact that no one who'd visited Vivien's domain survived the journey. He had nothing to lose and everything to gain.

The Lady of the Lake had lived in peace with the townspeople, until they'd destroyed the dense forest where she lived. Now, she sought to ruin them for their disrespect. All of Celliwig knew that and so they stayed away.

All except Midas.

He was the first one to reach the shores of her lake in generations. The first Vivien didn't strike down with her magic. He wasn't sure why she let him come to her private sanctum. Maybe she was simply curious.

Vivien was ageless and beautiful, like most of her kind. Red hair fell to her waist and her green eyes missed nothing, even though she was older than the land itself. She watched him arrive, safe on her island in the middle of the lake. It was said that she would live forever, so long as she never left it. The island was the last place in Celliwig where trees still grew and no one else could reach the rocky shore, no matter how hard they swam.

Midas tried to think of something intelligent to say, but his mind was blank. Truthfully, he hadn't imagined getting this far. "I'm Midas." He got out, trying not to stare at the trees she protected. He'd never seen real ones before. Only pictures in books.

"Just Midas?"

"Just Midas." His parents had never wanted him to use their name, which was just as well, since Midas refused to carry it.

Vivien nodded. "I've seen you, Just Midas." She told him, calmly. "In the past and your deeds yet to come. The Great Queen will one day choose you over all other men. You are most welcome here."

Midas had no clue what she was talking about. No one had ever chosen him and no one ever would. Certainly not a queen. Ignoring that weirdness, he went with his original plan and dropped a single coin into the water.

A *gold* coin.

"That's everything I have." He told her, proudly.

He'd stolen odds and ends for over a year, and now he had gold. Crime paid, just fine. Anyone who said different was doing it wrong.

Vivien's head tilted. "You surprise me." She stepped to the edge of the water on her side of the lake, looking him over with deep interest. "And it takes much to surprise me. Come closer."

Midas edged into the lake, so it washed over his bare feet. For a second, he was overcome with its beauty. He hadn't known water could *be* that clean and clear. The deep, startling blue instantly became his favorite color. It was like peering into peace and magic.

"You owe me a wish." He persisted, refusing to be distracted from his quest.

"A sorceress *chooses*, boy. We choose our partners, and our families, and our paths. ...And we *especially* choose who we help. I do not choose to help anyone from Celliwig. I wish none of you to prosper."

Midas had been expecting her refusal. It didn't matter, though. Life had taught Midas one lesson well: If you waited for someone to *give* you what you wanted, you'd never have anything, at all. *Taking* was the only way to succeed. "It doesn't matter if you want to or not. You made a deal and you're honoring it."

His total assurance seemed to catch her off guard. "A deal?"

"You made a promise to the people of this town, long ago. You said that you would dispense magic to us, so long as we gave you all we have in exchange. Well, I come from this town. And *that*," he pointed to the gold glittering beneath the surface of the water, "is all that I have. I've upheld my end of the deal."

She looked amused. "This isn't a wishing well, child. You can't just toss in a coin and expect me to give you happiness and…"

Midas cut her off. "I want to be the richest person in the world. The richest person who's ever existed. Then, I'll *buy* myself happiness."

Vivien studied him for a long beat, taking in his dirty skin and tattered clothes. "Where's your family?"

"I haven't bought one, yet."

She shook her head. "Gold can't buy you that, I'm afraid."

"Then I'll get *more* gold." He retorted. "I want to keep getting more and more and *more* gold, so nothing can ever touch me. Until I have… everything."

Vivien arched a brow. "Everything?"

"*Everything.*"

"That is a very big word, Just Midas. A powerful word. It's why I used it in my vow to Celliwig. *Everything* can be a lot more than you think."

He glowered at her, prepared to play hardball. "I *think* that even you are bound by the rules of magic. You struck a deal with the people of this town and I come from this town. I want you to uphold your end of the bargain."

"I foresee many bargains for you, child. Only two will matter, though, and this isn't one of them." She gave him a strange smile. "But I'll give you what you seek."

He hadn't expected such a quick victory and it made him suspicious. "You will? You'll really help me?"

"No, it will not help." Her head tilted to the other side now, like a bird. "Not in the way you believe, anyway. But if you ever understand what it is you truly desire, you'll have a path to reach it. Choose wisely."

"What do you...?"

Vivien cut him off. Her hand waved out, power gleaming in the air and the coin disappeared from the bottom of the lake. "You will have more money than you can ever spend, Just Midas. You will grow richer and richer, but nothing will touch you. And the magic will go on and on and on, until you realize the truth. ...Until you finally have *everything*."

Before he could finish asking her what the hell that meant, she vanished right before his eyes.

Midas stood there, blinking and feeling exactly the same. Still, exhilaration filled him, because she'd said she'd granted his wish. He would be rich! He would finally have everything! He would never again have to be unhappy or afraid or hungry.

He'd done it.

A rocking-horsefly flittered by. He'd never seen one before. How could he? They lived in gardens, not mud holes like Celliwig. The mysterious, iridescent creature was the most delicate thing he'd ever beheld. It was probably the only one for a hundred miles and it was right in front of him.

For a moment, Midas thought of Corrah. She would be proud that he had fought for this prize and won. She wouldn't be able to feel the emotion, but she would still be proud. He reached out to touch the fragile insect in wonder, feeling exalted. If she were here she would...

Instantly, his excited mood turned to horror.

The rocking-horsefly froze in midair, its perfect, translucent wings becoming thick with gold. The tiny miracle fell to the ground with a thump. What had once been a magical part of nature was now a lump of cold metal lying in the mud.

Dead.

He'd killed it.

It was his wish. It had to be. Without meaning to, he'd taken something beautiful from the world. Something that could never come back. Midas looked down at his large, scarred hands. Confusion and dread and disgust filled him, as he tried to make sense of what had happened. He'd just wanted to touch something special and instead he'd destroyed it because he'd been thoughtless and greedy.

This was his fault.

And it was then that Midas understood his wish wasn't a wish, at all.

It was a curse.

Chapter Eight

Midas (no last name given) will furnish Guinevere Pendragon and her daughter with shelter, food, reasonable support in the face of their enemies, and the supplies necessary to enact her campaign, on the condition that she pay him back for all expenses once Camelot has been returned to her control.

He may offer input on the campaign, as he deems necessary, with the understanding that Guinevere Pendragon is in command of the offensive and in charge of *all* strategic planning. (Please note emphasis on the word "all.")

Clause 9- Partnership Responsibilities of Midas (no last name given)

"I think I should help with the planning of this war." Midas sat behind his hideously extravagant desk, looking exactly like a real businessman. Unbending, professional, intimidating... It was no wonder so many people missed the fact he was a marshmallow. "Things will be a lot quicker."

Gwen frowned. She'd just walked into the room and already she was lost. "Is *this* why you called me in here?"

She'd been hoping for a more "I'm the King of Camelot now and I want to learn about my new responsibilities" kind of topic. It worried her how little Midas cared about being king. Why had he agreed to marry her, if he didn't care about being king? It didn't make any sense and Gwen liked it when everything made sense.

"Yes." Midas clicked his pen, like he was poised to jot down some notes. "Ever since Percival attacked you yesterday, I've been thinking I need to take a more active role in your war. It's become imperative that we end this as swiftly as possible."

"Technically, he attacked *you*." Thank God she'd been there to save him.

"Well, now he's locked up in my dungeon and I want to help you win this war."

Gwen considered that. "Clause 9- 'Partnership Responsibilities of Midas' says..."

Midas cut her off. "I've read Clause 9 and it clearly states that I can offer input on strategies."

"Well, that's true, but..."

"So, I'm offering." He interjected and held his pen at the ready. "Now, what is the precise number of dead you'd find acceptable?"

"Um..." Gwen gave into the inevitable, trying to match his detached tone. His voice was always so damn calm and reasonable. "I don't know. A small number, I guess. *Very* small. I told you, I want to win with as little bloodshed as possible. That's why I need the wand. It can destroy Dark Science. My father promised it would cleanse the whole kingdom."

"But you have no idea where the wand is, correct?"

"Right. Merlyn just said, 'It's the very last place he'd want to look.' And I guess I haven't looked there, yet." She tilted her head. "Do you think Merlyn meant the last place the *Scarecrow* would look?" She mused. "I've been thinking he meant Arthur. Maybe *that's* why I can't find it."

"Regardless, searching for it will take far longer than open warfare. Are you *sure* you're only willing to accept a small number of casualties?" From the way Midas watched her, it seemed like he expected her to green-light the mass slaughter of half the kingdom.

"I don't care how long it takes. *We're* not the villains here, Midas. We can't act like it."

His brutally unhandsome face didn't so much as flicker. "Of course, I'm the villain. Bad folk are always the villains."

"No, you're not." Gwen sat down across from him, surprised he would say such a thing. She'd seen evil and this man wasn't it. "I wouldn't have married a villain."

Not again.

"Except you already have." He insisted. "*I'm* your husband. And I'm the Baddest man you'll ever meet, Guinevere. Everyone in this kingdom is scared of me."

He was right about that part. Which was why he was the best choice to protect Avalon. Gwen might not understand his motives for doing it, but she believed Midas would keep her daughter safe. He'd given her his word. Besides, she'd seen the corner of his mouth flick upward as Avi talked to him. All through dinner the night before, Avalon had chattered at him about the rocking-horseflies in the vast garden and Midas had patiently listened. In Gwen's book, that was far better than any arbitrary designation of "Good" on his birth certificate.

"We need to try every other option, before we resort to violence." She decided. "You know it's the right thing to do."

"I'm physiologically incapable of knowing right from wrong,

according to the prison psychiatrists." His tone stayed calm as he related the news, watching her for a reaction to that nonsense.

"That's ridiculous. You're a kind and gentle man. It's why I came to you."

She could read a glimmer of frustration in his eyes. "Someone *actually* told you that? Told you to come to me, because I was kind and gentle?"

"Of course."

"Who?"

"Why does it matter who they are?"

"Because, there is nobody in this land or any other who would advise you to trust me. Not unless they had some other agenda. Have you considered that?" He sounded irritated, like he didn't understand why she didn't understand. "I'm an *extremely* Bad person. Perhaps they're trying to set you up."

"They're not."

"How do you know?"

"Because I *know*, okay? And, I swear, they had nothing but positive things to say about you."

"Then they're a liar."

"I don't think so." The man was an impossible mix of contradictions. Suspicious and trusting. Unbending and generous. Cold and hot. ...God, he was really, really hot. More importantly, he was also honorable straight down to his soul. She looked into his eyes and knew that he'd do everything in his power to help her.

Gloved fingers drummed on his armrest, his restless energy seeking an outlet. "For a woman who's usually so blunt you seem to be very dodgy on the subject of who sent you to me."

"I just don't see that it matters."

"Was it your father? He could remember the future. Did he see... me?"

Gwen shifted uncomfortably. "Can we go back to planning how we'll save the kingdom?"

Midas wasn't satisfied, but he let it drop. "I can't depose the Scarecrow as efficiently, if we're going to be squeamish about the methods. *That's* what I'm trying to say. But, if you untie my hands, I could have this over within the week."

"A *week?*"

He held up his gloved palms. "I have extremely persuasive hands."

She studied his leather-clad fingers, wondering if he ever missed the sensation of touching things with his skin. He must. It made her sad to even consider it. Midas had done a lot for her. Maybe she could figure out a way to help him.

"Are you *sure* you can't cure your curse?"

"I'm sure."

"Because maybe I can figure out something you haven't thought of yet. I'm a very logical thinker."

He arched a brow. "The curse lasts until I get everything."

"Like... *everything*? Everywhere?"

"Like everything everywhere."

"Well, how are you supposed to get everything everywhere?"

"I'm not." He shrugged, like it was no big deal. "I've tried, of course. But, so far, I haven't been able to buy the entire world. I doubt I ever will. Hence, the permanence of my curse."

"Oh." She frowned, thinking that over. "Well, there must be a way."

"Can we go back to planning how we'll save the kingdom?" He asked, repeating her words, because he was a kind and gentle wiseass. "That's all that matters. Let me clear the path, so we can win this war *now*."

That was *waaaay* more tempting than it should have been. To have the fighting finally over... To allow Avalon to play outside without worry... To be able to sleep through the night... But what would the cost be?

Gwen took a deep breath. "If we did it your way, how many of Camelot's citizens would die?"

"Most of them?" It was a broad guess. "Perhaps more. But the majority will be Bad. The Scarecrow will send them into battle first."

"You think that makes me feel better?"

"It would make most Good folk feel *great*."

"I don't believe that." She shook her head. "We can defeat the Scarecrow without destroying our kingdom. Good or Bad, most of the people in Camelot are innocent. We can't become worse than the man we're fighting to stop."

"My God." Midas' eyes rolled towards the hideous fresco on the ceiling. Unicorns and centaurs frolicked against a garish sunset. Some poor soul must have developed permanent neck damage painting the acres of space and the result was an affront to art critics everywhere. "How in the hell do you have a reputation for being heartless? You're so damn *nice* it's a wonder you've survived at all. You've lived inside a palace your whole life, so you have no idea of the monsters that lurk in the dark."

"Oh, I have a pretty good idea. Things get pitch fucking black down in a dungeon."

That remark caught him off guard. Midas glanced at her sharply and a smile curled his mouth, softening the harsh angles of his unhandsome face. "It amazes me that you can make cursing sound so classy. How do you do that?"

"I went to a really progressive school."

"No, you didn't. You didn't go to *any* school, in fact. You had tutors training you from the cradle, preparing you to be Arthur's queen. Your father saw your marriage in a prophesy, on the day you were born, and no one seemed to question it, after that. That's all you've ever known."

He was trying to knock her off balance, but she wasn't surprised he knew about her past. Midas probably had his goons compiling research on her, trying to discover every hidden piece of her life. Real power came from information, after all, and he was a very powerful man.

In this case, though, it wouldn't do him a damn bit of good.

"It's pointless to bother searching for my nefarious secrets." She told him and it was true. The ones she had were too well-hidden, even for him. "I'm really not very interesting."

He scoffed at that.

Avalon came dashing through the door, blonde curls bouncing in a messy disarray. Leaves and twigs were all tangled into the bright strands, the ribbon that had been tied around her head long gone. No matter how hard Gwen worked at it, it was simply impossible to keep the girl's hair under control.

"Hi, Mommy." She sang out and then turned to Midas without waiting for a response. "I need a sword for Lyrssa." She told him, out of breath. "It's real important." To prove her point she held up one of her new fashion dolls. "She keeps losing all the fights!"

"Um…" Midas glanced over at Gwen for guidance.

She settled back to watch him squirm, in no mood to assist.

Midas' eyes narrowed, seeing that she was leaving him to his own devices. "Alright." He focused on Avalon and seemed to square his shoulders. "I don't own a sword for your doll. Give me an hour and I'll buy one. I don't know from *where*, but somebody must sell miniature weapons."

"I doubt it." Gwen chimed in unhelpfully.

"Lyrssa can't wait a whole hour!" Avalon sounded scandalized by the very idea. "She needs her sword *now*. She's losing and it's not fair!"

At this point, any experienced parent would tell the child that they would have to be patient or, more likely, explain that there was no such thing as a doll sword. Instead, the Kingpin of Camelot nodded like Avalon was making perfect sense. "I understand. We'll just have to make her one ourselves, then."

Avi perked up. "Good idea." She hurried over to Midas' side. "How we's gonna do that?"

Midas took the doll in one massive hand, looking her up and down. "Well, she's not very big."

"Trystan says size isn't important in battle, just you's willingness to kill and die for glory."

Gwen rolled her eyes skyward and looked over her shoulder to where Trystan was standing in the doorway. "*Really?*" She demanded.

"What? It's the fucking truth."

"Cursing is a no-no." Avi informed him.

Midas handed the doll back to Avalon. "Hold on, I have an idea." He began searching through drawers in his desk. "I have it here somewhere... Ah!" He pulled out a letter opener, which appeared to be made of platinum and studded with sapphires the size of raisins. "Here, this is the right size and not sharp enough to hurt little girls. Let's see if it suits Lyrssa."

Avalon wedged the priceless artifact into her dolly's hand and beamed at Midas. "Thank you!" Delighted that her toy was properly armed, she ran from the room, again. "Bye-bye, Mommy." She called as she went.

"Bye, baby."

Trystan sighed and trailed behind her.

Midas stared after them, a smile tugging at the corners of his lips.

"You're going to spoil her." Gwen warned, trying not to be insanely charmed by the big marshmallow. "Giving Avi presents is not a great way to ignore her."

He shrugged, pretending he had no idea what she meant. "The letter opener is a small thing."

"A small thing worth a big fortune, I'm guessing. What if she loses it?"

"Then, I'll buy her another." He didn't look worried.

"Clause 3- 'Care and Protection of Avalon' says..."

Midas cut her off. "It was just a letter opener, Gwen. Not a private island." He muttered defensively. "The child asked for my help and I gave it. I believe that fits within Clause 3's parameters. What would you have had me do differently?"

She sighed, because he was right. "Nothing. It's not that. I just don't want Avalon to be disappointed if our fake marriage…"

"It's a *real* marriage. There's a *real* marriage scroll to certify its authenticity, as I've reminded you before."

"…If our *business arrangement* doesn't work out."

Midas glanced at her through his lashes. "I think it's working out fine. Don't you?"

"So far, yes!" It was working out better than she'd even imagined. "But what if something goes wrong? Avalon is very sensitive and she likes you. …A lot."

Midas blinked, surprised and pleased. "I like her, too."

He didn't get it. Gwen picked her words carefully. "Avalon has had very little positive male attention in her life. Arthur never bonded with her and my father died before she was born. Mainly, it's just been Galahad. That's one of the main reasons I wrote Clause 3. If you're not careful, Avi could get... attached to you."

Midas arched a skeptical brow, like he couldn't imagine that happening. "So she's attached to Galahad?" He asked, because he always seemed to focus on the wrong part of her lectures.

"She loves Galahad. We both do. It hurt Avi terribly when he was banished." She would never forgive Arthur for that. …Or for so many other things. "I tell her that he'll come back soon and I can just hope it's true."

Midas' jaw ticked. "Who is the child's real father?" He asked abruptly. Maybe he was hoping to catch her off guard.

It worked. Gwen flinched a bit. "'The child' has a name." Which he never used, as if he was afraid it might taint her by association. "You can call her 'Avalon,' Midas. Lightning won't strike you dead."

"Who is *Avalon's* father?" He corrected, his face expressionless.

"Arthur is Avalon's father."

"She says otherwise." He paused. "*Arthur* said otherwise."

"Never publically. He always acknowledged Avi as his heir in public." Gwen met his eyes dead on. "This is going to be *her* kingdom, one day." That was another reason they needed to win the war without a slaughter. If Avalon came to her throne on a sea of Bad folk blood, half the kingdom would hate her forever. "You said you'd help me win it for her."

"And I will." He leaned closer to Gwen over the width of the desk, his gaze flicking down to her wedding band and then back to her face. "But, if something else is going on here, you should tell me about it *now*, before it fucks us both. If there is another man with a claim on you and Avalon, I need to prepare..."

Gwen cut him off. "*Arthur is her father, Midas.*" She stressed every word.

He wasn't convinced. "Avalon disagrees." He reiterated flatly.

Gwen weighed her possible responses to that remark and went with silence.

"We need to be partners in this." Midas pressed. "I don't think less of you for not feeling bound by your wedding vows to Arthur. I'm sure he gave you plenty of reasons to find someone else. He wasn't faithful, either. But, I told your daughter and I'll tell you: *I'm not Arthur.* You don't need to lie to me."

"I *know* you're not Arthur."

For one thing, Arthur would never ask to be her partner. He certainly wouldn't have wanted her "input" on anything of importance. He would've wiped out most of Camelot's peasants in his quest for glory, without a second thought to Gwen's wishes.

For another thing, when she was with Arthur, she'd never felt this... unsettled. Being close to Midas left her skin flushed and tight. It was exciting. That interlude when he'd fixed her coat had been extremely pleasant. So had their wedding kiss.

She wanted Midas. Why shouldn't she have him?

Sex was a completely natural part of life, after all. Especially when you were fake-married. It was very rational for a fake-wife to sleep with her fake-husband. In fact, the more Gwen considered it, the more natural and rational the idea became.

Except Clause 7- "Separate Lives and Other Relationships" allowed Midas his freedom.

Damn it, why had she included that part? Why had Midas *agreed* to it? He might project a cool exterior, but his eyes were molten as they watched her. Hungry. Logically, that *had* to mean he wanted her back. His golden gaze followed every move she made, burning a trail of primal heat and masculine focus. Gwen was a pragmatic, feet-on-the-ground kind of girl. She wasn't imagining this connection between them. He could feel it, too.

Probably.

"Did Galahad tell you to come to me?" Midas asked abruptly, switching suspects.

"Gal is banished. How could he tell me anything?"

Midas frowned at that non-answer. "*Why* was Galahad banished?" He tried. "There must've been a *big* reason for the Captain of the King's Men to get permanently expelled from Camelot."

"Galahad betrayed Arthur."

The pen snapped in Midas' hand and he didn't seem to notice. "Betrayed him with you?"

"Yes." He used one word answers all the time, why couldn't she?

Midas stared at her. "Oh." He said, clearly inferring all kinds of terrible conclusions from that single syllable.

Gwen should just leave it at that and let him think the worst. It would be much safer. Better to have him believe she was a cheating wife than let him continue poking around. He was way too clever. God only knew what he might piece together.

...Except, Gwen didn't *want* Midas to think the worst.

"Galahad helped me destroy the Dark Science laboratory." She blurted out. "The night I broke the animals out, he was with me."

Golden eyes sparked with hope. "*That's* how he betrayed Arthur?"

"Yes. I don't like to say he was there, because it wasn't his fault. It was all my doing and he's the one who paid for it." That was still hard to bear. "We burned the White Rabbit's first lab to the ground. That evil bunny rebuilt it, but we set the program back for a year. It was the right thing to do, regardless of what anyone says."

Midas set the pieces of the broken pen down and leaned back in his chair, looking relieved. "Tell me." He said simply.

And so she did.

Gwen had had no one to talk to in so long. The words just spilled out of her. "The Scarecrow had two perfectly innocent trolls kill each other right in front of us. It was *horrible*. Then, I found out about the animal experiments. Found out all the evil plots the Rabbit had been dreaming up. I couldn't allow anyone else to suffer. I tried to reason with Arthur, but," she shrugged in defeat, "he wasn't going to stop the madness. I needed to close down the lab myself. Galahad agreed and volunteered to help me come up with a plan."

"And the best plan you two could come up with was arson?"

"What else could we do?" She rubbed her temples, hating to remember it. "It seemed very logical at the time. It was all my idea, but Gal was the one who took the blame. Percival saw him that night. I'm not sure *how*, because Galahad is so skilled and Percival's an idiot. But, somehow he was caught and Arthur found out everything."

"Did Arthur know about your involvement?"

"Of course. I told him."

"You *told* Arthur you'd burned down his lab?"

"I was trying to save Galahad. He's my best friend. I thought Arthur would turn his attention to me, but Gal denied I was even there. He wanted to shield me, the way he always does. Arthur was happy to have his full confession and wouldn't listen to me. I think he just wanted us separated. Gal was convicted of High Treason and shipped off to who-knows-where."

"Galahad must have been very determined to protect you."

"Oh, Gal will always do what's right, no matter the cost. Always defend people who need help. It's the primary vow he took as a knight and a huge part of who he is as a man. Basically, Galahad is..." Gwen hunted for the right adjective, "perfect."

Midas' expression darkened, again. "Perfect." The word had a snarled edge to it that seemed out of character for such a soft-spoken man. "You *actually* just called Galahad perfect. Fucking hell. I can only imagine how *close* you are to your 'best friend' to have such a rosy view of him."

Gwen arched a brow, not appreciating his attitude and insinuations, even though she'd done nothing to help him understand. "Galahad *is* perfect. Ask anyone."

"Un-fucking-believable..." There was a laptop open on Midas' desk and it made a sudden chirping sound, signaling an incoming message. He glanced at the screen and arched a brow. "Well, it certainly took him long enough." He muttered. His eyes went from the computer, to Gwen, and then back again. A frown tugged at his mouth. "Would you excuse me for a moment?"

Gwen wasn't surprised. Arthur had always wanted to exclude her, too. There was no reason to expect more from Midas.

...Somehow she did, though.

Hiding her disappointment, she nodded and got to her feet. "Certainly." She murmured and headed for the door. "I'll just wait out in the hall."

Of course, she didn't say anything about closing the door behind her.

Leaving the gilded entry ajar, meant she could still see and hear everything that happened in the office. Since Gwen already had a sneaking suspicion it had to do with her, she had no problem eavesdropping on his mysterious call.

Midas waited until she left and then reached over to click the mouse. "Hello, Scarecrow. Calling to ask about wedding gifts?"

Chapter Nine

Each day, the parties will meet to frankly discuss new/developing issues that could impact their partnership.

Honesty is expected.

Clause 10- Communication Between Partners

Gwen couldn't quite stifle her gasp. Whatever she'd expected to discover with her eavesdropping, this wasn't it. The Scarecrow was calling Midas? Why? It took everything in her to stay out of sight and not storm back into the room.

"What the fuck do you think you're doing, Midas?" The Scarecrow demanded. "You think you can fuck with me and get away with it, you illiterate fucking hoodlum?!"

Gwen's eyebrows shot up at his wrathful tone and florid cursing. Holy cow! His language was even worse than Midas'. Usually, the Scarecrow tried to project an image of scholarly sophistication. Typically, that meant a lot more syllables and a lot fewer f-bombs. Maybe he only bothered to polish up his erudite manners and flawless taste for people he wanted to impress. Gwen's new husband clearly didn't make the list.

Just as clearly, Midas didn't give a damn.

"I think I'm becoming the supreme ruler of Camelot." Midas said easily. "Granted, I don't have a fancy degree, like you, but I *can* read. And it turns out our constitution is quite egalitarian, when it comes to women's rights. Queens continue to hold power, even when their spouse died. It's very progressive."

"That's only one interpretation…"

Midas cut him off. "It's the *only* interpretation. It's all spelled out in amendment six, article nine, paragraph seven: 'Rules for Succession in Event of Royal Death" enacted by the Second Congress of Wizards."

Gwen nearly smiled at how quickly he rattled it off. It was like the man could remember everything he read with photographic detail.

"So, don't try to bullshit me." Midas went on with total

confidence. "Guinevere's still the queen. I'm her husband, now. Ergo..." He shrugged. "I'm your new king. Couldn't be plainer, under our glorious governmental system."

"*The fuck you are!*" From his enraged shriek it seemed a good guess that the Scarecrow wasn't about to start bowing anytime soon. It was shrill enough to nearly shatter Midas' collection of priceless, ageless, incredibly gaudy magic mirrors. "That bitch might think she's won, but as long as she's intent on passing that illegitimate brat off as Arthur's heir, the Good folks of the kingdom will *never* support her. Not even you and your kneecapping henchmen can change that."

Gwen's eyes narrowed at the back of the laptop, hating the man.

"I find Avalon to be quite delightful." As usual, Midas' voice stayed utterly calm. "Given time, I think the rest of Camelot will come to agree. You'd be surprised at how persuasive I can be when I put my mind to it."

"Why are you doing this?" The Scarecrow sounded furious and frustrated and not at all like a smooth-talking politician. He was used to being three steps ahead of everyone else, analyzing patterns and calculating odds. Like Gwen, he must've suspected Midas was playing some bigger game and, also like her, he couldn't figure out what it might be. "You don't even *want* Camelot, Midas. Being king has never been your endgame."

"Career goals change."

"You don't have a career. You just have victims."

"And subjects." Midas' golden eyes gleamed like ancient coins. "It's good to be king."

"Is it Guinevere?" The Scarecrow demanded, like he'd just figured it all out. "You know she killed Arthur, right? She's probably planning the same fate for you, you fool. She wants your money."

Gwen scowled.

"I doubt that. She's drafting me a will, which leaves my fortune to my bodyguard, Trystan Airbourne. She was very insistent on it. There was a slideshow." Midas still sounded amused by that perfectly logical presentation. At least he sat still to listen to her estate planning lecture, though. Trystan had rolled his eyes and walked out. "Personally, I'm not worried about leaving this mortal coil." Midas continued nonchalantly. "I'm pretty hard to kill. Ask anyone."

"So was Arthur, but he's still dead." The Scarecrow retorted. "I mean, do you *really* believe his fall was an accident?"

Midas gave an unconcerned shrug. "Perhaps he jumped."

"Perhaps you're thinking with your dick." The Scarecrow sneered. "I'm not surprised. You've never been so close to an actual lady before, have you? All that shiny, blonde class must be hypnotizing to a mud-dweller like you. Of *course* you'd develop a hard-on for some expensive pussy."

"You *really* don't want to be insulting Guinevere." Midas warned, even though most of that had been insults directed towards *him*. "We're having such a pleasant conversation, but you're about to get on my Bad side."

The Scarecrow snorted, as if Midas' stupidity was all but confirmed. "Oh, don't even bother trying to play the white knight. It doesn't suit Bad folk. You aren't some defender of the innocent, Midas. You're just a big, ugly primate who got suckered in by a woman *way* out of your league. She is using you! Using *you* to win *her* war! And you're letting her do it!"

Gwen winced a bit, because there *was* some truth mixed in with the Scarecrow's lies and vile words. She *had* strong-armed Midas into this fight. He'd just been too much of a gentleman to stop her. Now she was getting him into a war with the most horrible monster in Camelot.

Maybe she should rush in there and save him.

"Guinevere wasn't just married to King Arthur, she was also fucking *Galahad*, for fuck's sake." The Scarecrow sounded incredulous, angry, and cruelly amused. "Have you s*een* Galahad? Read his resume? Watched his fucking adventures on his fucking TV show? He's perfect! I'm fucking straight and *I* would fuck Galahad. *That's* how fucking perfect he is."

Midas looked irritated for the first time. "Galahad had his own television show?"

"Two of them." The Scarecrow informed him nastily. "*That's* the kind of men Gwen's used to having between her legs. Kings and heroes. If she's letting *you* touch her, it's only because you're serving a purpose. You're usually smarter than this, Midas."

"People keep telling me that."

"You're a means to an end for her. You have to see it. A big, dirty, expendable animal she can keep on a leash. Once you aren't useful anymore, Gwen will be gone. You don't belong with her and you know it."

Something flickered behind Midas' eyes. Something like pain or resignation or loneliness. If she hadn't been watching him closely, Gwen would have missed it.

Then, Midas arched a brow, as if the moment had never

happened, at all. "Maybe I'm *not* her ideal husband." He agreed. "But, didn't she turn down *your* proposal entirely?"

The Scarecrow didn't appreciate that reminder. "At least I'm from her class and not some no-necked orangutan!" He snapped. "Look, you might have the woman *for now*, but I'll *never* let you have this kingdom. Whatever your goal is here, you don't have the men or brains to take Camelot by force, so we're at a standstill unless we reach a compromise."

"A compromise?"

"A deal." The Scarecrow translated, as if Midas was having trouble understanding long words. He took a deep breath, trying to get himself under control. "Guinevere for Camelot."

"I get the woman, you get the kingdom?"

"Precisely!" His vocabulary got fancier, again. "You and I are professional men, Kingpin. We can strike a mutually beneficial accord. Simply *make* Guinevere surrender the throne and her father's wand. In exchange, I'll give you the Queen of Camelot and you can do with her as you will. She's what you truly covet, correct?"

"Except I already *have* the Queen of Camelot." Midas remarked impassively. "You can't give me what I already possess. Also --and I *would* have thought you'd notice this yourself, because the woman isn't all that subtle-- Gwen hates you. She will *never* willingly hand you the keys to her castle." He tilted his head, like he was trying to recall the details. "Something about you locking her in a dungeon and threatening her child and stealing her throne...?"

The Scarecrow's temper sparked again, his vocabulary disintegrating once more. "You're a fucking hoodlum and she's a goddamn soccer mom! Stop pretending this is complicated. Just do whatever it fucking takes!"

Midas very slowly blinked. "And Avalon?" He asked. "What do you propose we do with the princess?"

The Scarecrow's veneer of civility slipped back into place. "The child's dangerous. You've probably witnessed it already." He heaved a regretful sigh, as if he'd done everything he possibly could to be reasonable. "I've tried to rationalize with the tyke," his voice got harder, "but she's as stupid and stubborn as her mother. If you take care of that brat, we'll call it even."

Gwen's knees nearly gave out. That son of a bitch wanted her baby dead. What was she going to do? She could barely breathe as panic set it. Oh God...

The Scarecrow continued pressing in his most persuasive tone. "You and I have never been at odds before, Midas. No need to start now. Once I have total control of Camelot, you'll be one of the Baddies I spare. *Someone* will have to supply the kingdom with its vices, after all. I'll give you free reign to run your business as you see fit. It's a fair deal for us both."

Midas sat forward in his chair. "It's a compelling offer." He admitted.

Gwen shot him an appalled look, wanting to scream.

"Of course, there is one small problem with the arrangement." Midas went on, before she could charge into the room. "I already have a competing deal in place with Guinevere. We have a Contract and everything. I've read the whole thing. Even the footnotes. ...And there were *a lot* of footnotes. It's all very official looking."

Gwen hesitated, her hand on the doorknob.

"Whatever she's offering, I can top it." The Scarecrow promised him smugly.

"No." Midas said with total assurance. "You *can't* top Guinevere's deal. There isn't another person in the world who can offer me what she does."

Relief flooded through Gwen, leaving her dizzy.

"Come on, now..." The Scarecrow drawled out with phony camaraderie. "Siding with me is win-win! You can expand your business with the blessing of the crown *and* keep the woman. What could be simpler?"

Midas' eyes glinted like he knew a secret. "Oh, I've never been one to do things the simple way. What would be the fun in that?"

Gwen's heartbeat sped up, seeing what the Scarecrow didn't. He believed he had the upper-hand simply because Midas hadn't been born in a palace or educated in some high-priced academy.

That was a mistake. A big one.

The Scarecrow's IQ tests might be the stuff of legend, but he had no idea who his opponent really was. Unless you were watching Midas closely --If you didn't spot the ruthless intelligence, because you were blinded by his unpolished accent and street-brawler profile and gentle nature-- it was so easy to underestimate him. To miss the brilliant mind lurking beneath the tacky suit.

The Kingpin might suck at contract negotiations, but he was in complete control of *this* meeting.

The Scarecrow kept chuckling, not noticing that he was about to fail in a spectacular fashion. "Now, don't tell me it wouldn't be a pleasant experience to have Guinevere naked and chained to your bed. Be able to play out whatever sick, villainous fantasies your kind can dream up. Arthur's wife helpless in your evil clutches."

"But she *isn't* Arthur's wife." Midas corrected as if the Scarecrow was a drooling moron. That alone was worth the price of admission. "Guinevere is *my* wife."

The air caught in Gwen's chest as she studied Midas' unhandsome face. Whatever happened next would change her whole life. There wasn't a doubt in her mind.

"Yes, but she..."

Midas just kept talking like the Scarecrow's words weren't even worth listening to. "*Mine.* You're stealing from... and insulting... and threatening... *my* wife."

"If you would just..."

Midas interrupted him again, his voice hard. "So, the only deal I will *ever* make with you is the one where I take *everything* and you fucking hide, you piece of shit. If I was you, I'd accept that deal, too. Because if you think I'm an animal now... You just *try* getting between me and what's mine."

"So you said some empty vows to that woman! What does that have to do with business...?"

Midas cut off the Scarecrow's desperate jabbering, again. "When I give my word, it's *never* empty. *Especially* not when I give it to Gwen. My wife wants Camelot back, so I'm going to get it for her. You're just the dead man I have to go through, before I win the war."

Gwen gazed at Midas, the whole world realigning itself. It had *always* been Gwen and Avalon on their side of the battle, with everyone else on the other. But apparently not anymore. Now Midas was with them.

"You stupid fucking fuck!" The Scarecrow completely lost his jocular façade, screaming in wrath and humiliation. "Gwen is my ticket to the throne and she *will* give it to me. I don't care what it takes. If you stand with that bitch, I will unleash hell on you."

Midas smirked and it was a thing of beauty. "Well, you *could* send more King's Men after me, I suppose. ...Have you heard back from the last bunch, yet?"

Gwen blinked.

The Scarecrow made a sound of incoherent fury. Not over his missing knights, but because he'd lost the negotiation and they both knew it. He'd never lost *anything* before, but Midas had just crushed him without even raising his voice.

It was one of the greatest moments of Gwen's life.

"You're nothing but a sewer rat, trying to claw his way up in the world!" The Scarecrow screeched. "You come from nothing! Your family was nothing! You *are* nothing! There's no way you can beat me! You have no idea the kind of power I have on my side! You don't know what I can unleash on you!"

"I know that I'm keeping my bride, right here in my evil clutches. *And* Avalon. *And* their kingdom." Midas retorted calmly. "And I know I'm going to kill you, very soon. That's a fucking *promise*." He arched a brow. "And, like I said before, I'm famous for keeping my word." He slammed the computer lid closed, cutting off the Scarecrow's bellow of protest. "What an idiot."

In that second, Kingpin Midas --notorious gangster, terrible dresser, and overall enigma-- became the greatest hero in the kingdom. Braver than any knight in shining armor. Stronger than any handsome prince. More honorable than any righteous king. The absolute epitome of manhood and chivalry. Midas had just put himself between Gwen and the Scarecrow. Between *Avalon* and the Scarecrow, which was so much more important.

It was amazing.

Gwen pushed the door open, not bothering to hide the fact she'd been listening to every word of the exchange, and stared at him in wonder.

Surprised, Midas glanced up at her and arched a brow. "Eavesdropping? Really?" He rolled his eyes. "I have no idea why I didn't expect that." He gestured for her to resume her seat. "Well, no matter. I'm just sorry you had to hear him threaten you and Avalon. I knew that was coming and I'd hoped to spare you."

Gwen sat back down and took a deep breath. "Thank you." She said simply.

Midas gave an awkward shrug. He always looked uncomfortable with her gratitude, like he didn't think he deserved it. "It was easy enough to deny the man. The Scarecrow is remarkably unlikable."

"It would've been a lot eas*ier* to just do what he wanted."

"In addition to lacking a sense of right and wrong, my prison psychiatrist informs me that I'm pathologically incapable of doing what Good folk want." Midas explained, like that nonsense was somehow true. "I'm also prone to disproportionally violent responses when people cross me. I'm selfish, greedy, narcissistic, and --in short-- irredeemably Bad."

"I don't believe any of that."

"You should. It's a matter of public record."

Gwen waved all that bullshit aside. "What you are... is an *amazingly* gallant man." She told him and it was true.

What Midas had was so much rarer than blueblood. So much more important. You could train legions of soldiers to fight monsters, but true nobility had to be born into someone's heart and soul. Had to be part of their very bones. There was no other way to get it.

Golden eyes flicked back to her face. "I'm not gallant." His voice was serious and sad. "You have no idea how much I'd pay to fix that. How much I would love to be a Good man for you, Gwen. But... I'm not."

"Good and Bad are just labels. They have nothing to do with who people are inside. Only our actions define us."

Midas shook his head, dismissing the very idea. "Arthur once called me a tawdry, feral animal." He shrugged. "He was probably right. But, I don't rape women or hurt little girls. *That's* what I need you to understand. Nothing could *ever* make me harm you."

"I know. I'm probably the only person in the world who's not frightened of you, *at all*. Nothing the Scarecrow said changed that. Nothing *anyone* said could ever change that."

Midas hesitated. "I killed the King's Men." He admitted quietly. Of course this man would have trouble with lies of omission. It was just in his nature to always be honest. "If you heard that part of the conversation, it's true."

"Were they going to kill you?"

"Yes."

"Then you didn't have a choice."

His brows compressed, as if her confidence in him was confusing.

"Why would you even be worried about this, Midas? Do you think I'd bring my daughter into your house if I thought you were a tawdry, feral animal? I *know* you'll protect us. I knew before I came."

What would Arthur have done in Midas' place? Would he have given aid to a desperate woman and her baby? Antagonized a powerful man? Aligned himself with the underdogs? No way in hell. So who was the real Bad guy in the story?

Gwen couldn't exactly tell what was happening inside Midas' complicated head, but she saw into his heart. This man was lonely and misunderstood and compassionate and kind. He fought for the innocent and let himself be strong-armed by someone half his size, just because he knew she was right. No one else in all of Camelot had been willing to help Gwen. None of the knights. None of the wizards. None of the Good folk.

Just the kingdom's greatest criminal.

This man wasn't a villain.

He was a hero.

Midas' gaze stayed steady, still trying to convince her of what she was already so sure of. "I'll keep you and Avalon safe, no matter what. You have my word."

"I know." Just like she knew that everything she'd secretly hoped before she met him was true. All of it. "Can I tell you something and you not ask me any questions about it?"

"Yes." The answer was immediate.

"Promise?"

"You can tell me anything."

Gwen nervously brushed back her hair. "If Galahad came back, right now, and offered to take care of me and Avi," she glanced at Midas and then quickly away, "I would still want to stay right here."

Midas blinked in astonishment. "With me?"

"Technically, that's a question, but yes. With you." Her eyes flicked to his again, unable to stop herself. "I like being here with you, Midas. Not just because I feel safest when you're around, but because..." She shrugged. "I like you. Very much."

Those incredible eyes glowed hotter than molten gold.

Gwen blushed, but she didn't look away, again. "What the Scarecrow said is *not* true. When I kiss you, it's just because I *want* to kiss you. And I know you're so honorable that you'd help me even if I *didn't* kiss you, so pretending to be attracted to you would be pointless, anyway. Also, I'm terrible at lying, so you'd probably guess, if I was faking. I know I'd make a mess of it. I really am a little bit brash around the edges. So," she finished nervously, "I just want you to know that I find you incredibly appealing."

Midas took a deep breath, like he'd forgotten to breathe while she was talking.

"Are you okay?"

"Yes. Um..." He cleared his throat. "Which part am I not supposed to ask questions about?"

Gwen expelled a self-conscious breath. "All of it."

"Alright." He studied her for a long moment. "Then, can I tell *you* something and *you* won't ask questions about it?"

"Sure." She nodded, still a little winded from rushing through that whole rambling speech. "That's fair."

Midas stared into her eyes, the lines of his face harsh and somehow beautiful. "If Galahad *ever* comes back... I will fight with everything I have to convince you and Avalon to stay here with me." It was a promise. "I like you, Gwen. Very much. And I find you *incredibly* appealing."

She smiled. "Really? You're getting used to having me around? Even with the brashness?"

"That's technically *several* questions, but yes. Brashness and all. My life would be very, very dull without it." He paused. "He really had *two* television shows?"

"And a mini-series of his life. Gal starred in it. It won --like-- fifty awards. He gave all the profits to charity."

"Fucking hell..." Midas sighed in disgust. "Anyway, I don't suppose any of this has changed your mind about waging total war, has it?" He asked, clearly hoping to change the subject.

"Nope." Gwen rallied herself, trying to focus. "I still don't want to murder thousands of people."

"I knew you would say that."

Which is why he'd asked. Because he knew it was wrong and that she'd stop him. He had such a gentle soul. "You'd rather me *not* tell you what I really think?" She challenged, already sure of the answer.

"No." He said quietly. "I'd always prefer the truth, even when it's not what I want to hear."

"Me, too." She took a deep breath of her own. "Equal partners, Midas."

That was more than she'd ever offered another soul, because she'd never met anybody who could reciprocate before. Gwen liked to strike bargains, but it was usually difficult to find someone who could uphold their end. With Midas, though, nothing ever went quite as it normally did.

Gwen held out her palm to him. "Deal?"

He glanced at it, his eyes lingering on her wedding band from Arthur. "It's not safe for us to touch, even with the gloves. My curse..."

"Deal?" She repeated, cutting him off.

He studied her face, as if measuring her resolve. "You know, someone once told me about this moment." He said abruptly.

"Huh?" Gwen's eyebrows compressed. "Who?"

"Vivien. The same woman who cursed me."

"Probably not a great person to listen to, then."

"She knew the future."

Gwen's heart skipped a beat. "Someone predicted you and I would be standing here?" It had to be an enchantress. Crap. What else had she seen?

"She told me I'd only make two bargains in my whole life that really mattered." Midas' glowing eyes fixed on hers, burning with something immeasurable and warm. "This is one of them."

Gwen's throat went dry under his intent stare, forgetting to be worried about the enchantress. "Are you sure?" She whispered.

"Yes." He said simply and took hold of her hand. "We have a deal. Equal partners." Huge, leather-clad fingers enveloped hers. For a second, it seemed like his thumb brushed her skin in a gentle caress.

Gwen felt her insides liquefy.

"And we'll win your war the hard way, if you want." He assured her, releasing her hand and settling back in his chair. "The Scarecrow will still die, so it's an acceptable choice. Just *far* less interesting."

Gwen exhaled in relief. "Thank you." She started smiling again, thrilled with their progress. "Want to help me look for the wand again today?"

"No. We're busy all afternoon."

"Busy?" Gwen echoed in disappointment, her mood nosediving. Not that she was expecting him to take her on a honeymoon cruise to Neverland or anything, but he could at least wait a whole weekend before...

Shit.

Gwen sighed at the bizarre sensation of hurt filling her. She was being an idiot. No matter what she was suddenly feeling, they were allowed to live separate lives. It was outlined in Clause 7.

"Of course." She said, trying to cover her dismay. Her imagination went wild with all the horrible places he had to rush off to. Maybe he had some beautiful girlfriend he still needed to inform about his fake marriage and that would take a while. The crying alone would no doubt be time consuming. "I'm sure you must need to explain a few things to..."

"I never explain."

Guinevere's eyes narrowed at that blasé interruption. It was both true and annoying. "Well, I'm sure there are a few ladies who will be wanting some kind of..." She stopped short, finally processing his words. "Wait, did you say *we're* busy today? As in you and me?"

"Obviously. Haven't we been discussing the necessity of working together?" He straightened his aggressively flashy suit, not bothering to wait for an answer. "Since you want to do this the hard way, this year's Round Table is a good place to start. If you're going to eavesdrop, you might as well just participate. Saves us both time and effort."

"The... Round Table?" She repeated, not sure she'd actually heard what she'd heard.

"Yes."

Holy shit, she *had* heard it. Excitement warred with trepidation. "That annual conference thingy where all the worst villains in the world gather together in one spot?"

"*Some* of the worst villains."

"And these horrible people make horrible deals and have horrible arguments and make lists of people to horribly kill?"

"Mostly it's just whining and lies and sometimes a couple deaths."

"And you want us to just... *go* to this meeting from hell?"

"I never *want* to go to a meeting, but you're not giving me much of a choice. Not if you wish to reclaim Camelot with minimal bloodshed. Don't worry. Some of them were witnesses at our wedding."

"And they were... horrible."

"I know." He arched a brow at her appalled expression. "Are you sure you wouldn't rather me just kill everyone?"

Chapter Ten

Galahad
Eighteen Months Ago

It was a disgusting scene.

Sir Galahad, Captain of the King's Men, stood in the door of the lab, repulsed by what he saw. Knowing that he had to do something to stop it. Knowing that when he did, it would mean he'd be caught and probably banished. Knowing he had no choice.

He was a knight.

The job, and responsibility that came with it, meant *everything* to Galahad. He'd forgotten his primary duty once and it still haunted him. The first and most sacred part of his oath now underscored every decision he made:

A knight protects those weaker than himself.

Guinevere would not be happy, though. When she discovered that he'd done this, she would blame herself. Hurting Gwen was the last thing Galahad would ever want to do, but she would understand. The queen was Good in the truest sense of the word. Honest and righteous and just.

Together they were in the process of destroying the Dark Science lab. Gwen was releasing the poor animals from their cages, while Galahad made sure it was free of people. It should have been perfectly safe. Galahad had stationed his men elsewhere, so there were no guards to interfere. It was night, so all the White Rabbits' lab techs were gone. No one would be hurt.

He'd already radioed Gwen, telling her it was okay to begin burning the whole building down. Incendiary devices were going off at that very moment, at strategic points around the building. Galahad had been so *sure* he'd thought of everything.

He'd never expected to find any Bad folk in the building.

King Arthur had promised no more testing on people, after the horrible deaths of the two trolls that the Scarecrow had pitted against one another. Galahad had believed him. He shouldn't have. He knew that now. He'd been naive to retain any faith in the king, just as Gwen had claimed. Galahad should never have trusted him.

Or Percival.

Galahad's second-in-command was torturing a gryphon.

Feathers covered the floor, shaved off the woman's wings. Now the magical appendages were just thin bones and bruised skin. Without the added fullness of the feathers, she looked fragile. Small. Whoever she was, though, she still fought. Her naked body was cut and bloody, but she was not willing to submit. When gryphons were in the midst of battle, a veil fell over their faces. A misty facade that obscured their human features, making them resemble fearsome eagles. The woman wore that shifting mask now.

She would not bow to her captors.

For some reason, that reminded Galahad of Gwen. Like his queen, this woman had the heart of a warrior.

"I've been waiting for this." Percival was telling the woman. There was an empty hypodermic needle in his hand, so he must have just given her a shot of the formula. "Dreaming of having you at my mercy, bitch." His voice shook with hatred and lust.

"I dream only of your death."

Percival scoffed at her words. "Insolent even now. I could make this easier for you, by just *telling* you to give in. Make you think you loved me, even, so it wouldn't be so hard on you. But you've done nothing to deserve any leniency. I want you aware of every single thing I'm doing and helpless to stop me."

"Because you're weak." The woman said contemptuously. "It's why your people will ultimately lose."

"Whose race is nearly extinct?" Percival shot back. "We've *already* won."

Maybe that part was true. The gryphon were nearly gone now and few mourned them. For his part, Galahad had been taught to despise the gryphon. Every day at the Academy, he'd heard tales of their monstrous natures, until he didn't even question the truth of the stories, now. He'd killed many of them in battle beside King Uther. Too many to even remember.

Except Galahad *did* remember. He remembered all of them.

His honor had been lost in those mountains. He doubted he'd ever reclaim it, but he would dedicate the rest of his life to the attempt. It was why Galahad was burning down the lab and why he would protect this injured woman who hated his kind, no matter the cost. He didn't care what race she came from. She was weak and needed his help. He would live by the code of the knights or die trying.

Galahad would never again allow the innocent to suffer, because the strong ordered it.

"As long as even one gryphon remains, you have won *nothing*." The woman sneered. "Do what you will to me. My kind will still see you dead, in the end."

Percival didn't appreciate her defiance. He grabbed a handful of her hair, yanking her head back. "Get on your knees, you fucking evil barbarian."

The woman tried to resist the compulsion. The strain of her internal struggle had blood trickling from her nose, but it was no use. She sank to the ground as if someone was pushing her down. The formula gave her no choice.

Percival's breathing was ragged and excited, disgustingly aroused as she knelt before him. "That's more like it, whore."

Galahad's jaw tightened, pulling his sword free. No. This wasn't going to happen. If it meant standing against his second-in-command to defend a gryphon… so be it.

The woman spotted him as he stalked into the room. Even thorough the gryphon's vapory mask, he saw her surprise. Galahad put a finger to his lips, wanting her to be silent as he moved behind Percival. To his shock, she actually gave a slight nod. It was possibly the first time ever that a gryphon had ever worked with a knight. On anything. Ever. For any reason. *Ever*.

"*Your* people are the weak ones." Percival spat out, his hands at his belt buckle. "It's why you're losing this war. God wants your heathen culture erased. Once you're all dead, the Good folk will… *Fuck!*" He gave a panicked shout as Galahad dragged him backwards, the sword at his throat.

"Go." Galahad told the woman. "Leave this place and don't return."

"What are you doing?" Percival shouted in outrage. "She's a prisoner. An enemy of Camelot! You can't just set her free!"

"Shut up." Galahad snapped. "You're a disgrace to your armor."

The woman slowly got to her feet. "You are releasing me?" She demanded, suspiciously. "Why? This savage is one of your kind."

"*I'm* not the savage here, slut!" Percival raged.

The woman went for him, intent on ripping him apart with her bare hands.

"No." Galahad dragged Percival back, not letting the woman near him. "The building is on fire." He told her. "You need to get out of here. Go straight down this hall and turn left. It will lead you outside."

"Fire?" Percival yelped. "What fire? What have you done, you traitor?"

Galahad pressed the sword deeper into his flesh, keeping

him still. "Shut. Up." He repeated quietly. "Before I let her have you."

"This winged-demon is right about one thing, Galahad: I *am* one of your kind and you're betraying me." Percival wheezed out. "Betraying the King's Men. I'll make sure you pay for this."

The woman's eyes flicked to Galahad. "This vermin is pathetic." She waved a repulsed hand at Percival. "He will tell your commander of this."

"Damn right I will!"

"You must slay this man." She warned Galahad. "Allow me to do it or do it yourself, but make sure he's dead before you leave this place. Otherwise, he will see you punished for your actions here."

Galahad shook his head. He wasn't going to kill Percival in cold-blood. That would do nothing to reclaim his lost honor. "I'm not ashamed of my actions. I will accept the consequences of them."

Her head tilted, like that answer intrigued her.

"*Go.*" He urged. "Get out of Camelot, while you can."

She headed for the door, pausing to look back at him. "Thank you for saving my life." She said simply. "When the rest of your vile kind dies in the fires of our vengeance, I will see that you are spared."

Galahad gave her a half-smile. "Thanks."

Chapter Eleven

Cooperation is the goal of this partnership. Parties will treat each other with respect and consideration. If need be, they will also provide a sounding board for ideas or offer appropriate support. If an issue is of importance to one party, they can request the second party's assistance, collaboration, or focus on said issue.
The second party will do his/her best to accommodate them without whining.

Clause 12- Respect and Cooperation Between Partners

She continued to wear Arthur's ring.

Each time he looked at the hunk of metal weighing down her finger, Midas seethed.

Guinevere was married to *him*. Under every law of the kingdom she belonged to Midas. Not that he gave a damn about laws, but *Gwen* sure as hell did. She was supposed to be a coloring-inside-the-lines, home-by-midnight, always-playing-fair *Good* folk. She wasn't allowed to break their rules like this. Granted, Midas hadn't exactly read the Good folk's imaginary, beige-colored Code of Conduct. Still, he was fairly sure one of the chapter headings was: "Wear the Wedding Band of Your CURRENT Husband."

And it was an important chapter, too. Like chapter fucking *one*.

Brooding about Gwen was a great deal more interesting than the stupid meeting he was sitting through. All around Midas, Baddies engaged in the Round Table. Once a year, the worst of the worst gathered for a few days in Camelot to map out territories, draft treaties, and negotiate prices. ...And to bitch a lot. It gave Midas a headache.

"Are you listening to this craziness?" Gwen whispered at him.

He didn't look up from his tablet. "I'm trying not to."

She was listening, though. His wife sat next to him, actually *listening* to that blubbering idiot Walrus gripe about his staffing issues. Everyone else was without sympathy for the flippered moron. Of the twenty-two other members of the Round Table, half of them were dozing as the Walrus jabbered. By and large, the group had difficulty in focusing on anything that didn't directly benefit *them*, so other people's problems were always dull. But Guinevere was taking the Walrus' complaints seriously, concentrating as he whined about his unreliable oyster brigade henchman.

Midas' mouth curved. Despite his annoyance over the wedding ring, he was incurably smitten by his Good little bride. Actually his smitten-ness was the reason the ring annoyed him so deeply. It was easy to *tell* himself to keep a practical distance from Gwen, but the decision was hard to follow through with when she insisted on being so fucking adorable.

He sent her a sideways glance, his gaze drawn to her like a magnet.

He couldn't sleep with his wife, but lust still throbbed whenever he looked at her. Or heard her voice. Or thought about her. The blue of her eyes and the golden shine of her hair and the delicate curves of her breasts... It all clouded his mind. The multitude of logical reasons why he couldn't touch her became a fog and there was just the overwhelming desire to feel her body beneath his.

"The Walrus isn't being reasonable about his employee practices." Gwen whispered, oblivious to Midas' dark, wet, hot thoughts. She leaned closer to him and he nearly groaned at the erotic scent of her hair. "You should tell him so."

Midas managed to hide his hopeless lust. Instead, he theatrically lowered his voice so it matched hers. "I would, but I'm extremely busy not caring about that asshole."

She flashed him a quick frown. "You really should pay more attention, Midas. Granted your business is illegal, but it's still a *business*. You need to know exactly what's happening with your competitors, if you're going to stay successful at crime. It's not just spreadsheets and math. Every detail could be important."

Midas couldn't help but be touched. Gwen was focused on the Round Table because she was trying to protect him. The woman really did want to be equal partners. She wanted to *help* him.

Was it any wonder he was so smitten?

"Nothing the Walrus says is important, Gwen." He assured her softly. He knew that, because he'd been mentally processing all of it. Sorting through the moaning and lies, just in case something vaguely interesting was said. Very little escaped Midas' attention... Even the unimportant shit.

"How would you know if it's important or not? You're ignoring everything he says."

"It's usually the best way to deal with an idiot."

She gave him a compassionate look. "These kind of negotiation aren't your forte, are they?"

He arched a brow. "Well, I do my best."

"Of course you do!" She said swiftly, clearly worried she'd hurt his feelings. "I mean, you're very talented at *many* things. I think you probably remember every single thing you've ever read, right?"

"Yes." He was surprised she knew that, though. No one else had ever noticed. Not even his teachers, back before his parents left and he'd attended Celliwig's decrepit school.

Gwen just nodded, like it was obvious. "You're very smart, Midas. *Incredibly* smart. I know that. But you're a bit too innocent to really understand that unscrupulous people try to weasel weasly things into contracts."

"Too... innocent?" Even as a child, he'd been old.

"There's no shame in it." She picked up a pen. "You're a naturally kind and trusting person. It's everyone *else* who should change, but they won't." She sighed. "Instead, they'll just take advantage of your gallant nature. The world is a hard place for honorable people like you."

Midas had no idea what he could say to that lunacy.

"Luckily, I'm here and I'm heartless." She continued. "Everyone knows that."

"I don't think that..."

She kept talking. "Why, I can already tell the Walrus is a cheat and a liar. It's lucky that I'm here, so you don't have to worry about jerks like him. I won't let anyone hurt you."

Midas weighed his options and couldn't think of a single reason to tell her he was actually a mean son of a bitch, who ruled the underworld with an iron fist. Why disillusion her about his "gallant" nature? What could possibly be gained?

"That's... very thoughtful." He murmured instead.

Gwen patted his arm, pleased at his acquiescence. "Here, I'll take some notes on ways we can outmaneuver him."

Midas bit back a smile. She thought he was lousy at running his empire. He wasn't sure why he found it so charming, but he was in no hurry to correct her misapprehension. He liked that she saw him as too "kind and trusting" for the seedy side of Camelot. He liked that she was trying to look out for him. It made him feel... special.

Even though he wasn't.

Until Gwen arrived, he'd had nothing special in his life, at all. He needed her more than he'd ever needed anything and it scared him. Gwen would one day leave and take all the light with her. Midas couldn't let that happen. He somehow needed to convince her to stay with him, no matter what.

To that end, he had men compiling reams of information on Gwen and everyone she knew, all of it forwarded to his email.

Midas angled the screen of his tablet to hide the fact he was prying into her life, scrolling past articles on formal balls, and her legendary father, and her happily-ever-after with Arthur. All of them featured perfectly staged photos and unobjectionable quotes. ...And *none* of them had a damn thing to do with the real woman. What the hell was he paying these imbeciles for? Could they uncover nothing of value? How could someone so famous be so hard to investigate?

"I don't understand why they just can't be grateful that I'm still hiring in this economy." The Walrus' huge tusks caused him to lisp every word. His voice was annoying and he talked a lot, which was a bad combination. "Oysters are fucking useless! We need to establish some kind of henchman temp service, so I can get some reliable help."

"Have you t-t-t-tried w-w-w-working with r-r-r-rats?" K-k-k-Katy the K-k-k-Kruel stuttered out. Her hair was in two pigtails and she carried a switchblade in her gingham pocket.

She was also the one who'd selected the meeting spot for the Round Table this year, which was basically just a deserted warehouse and some folding chairs around a long table. The damn table wasn't even round! It was totally unacceptable. Next year, Midas would have to take over the planning process. In this dump, he was afraid his delicate wife would get impaled by an exposed nail or contract malaria from the stagnant puddles on the floor. The roof leaked, its huge windows not closing properly. Given the constant drizzle outside, that ensured that everyone stayed damp and uncomfortable.

Midas flashed a disgusted look towards the dripping ceiling. God, he missed the sun. When was Camelot going to get over its damn "mourning for Arthur" and let summer come back?

"Yeah, rats are the way to go, Walrus." Dower, the jackass wolf, put in. "There are a bunch of those hairy bastards freelancing as henchmen, ever since Cinderella got her ass locked up."

The Walrus looked outraged. "I'm a *sea mammal!* What am I going to do with *rats* for henchmen? Can they even swim?"

"They swim off sinking ships, don't they?" Dower sounded bored. Who could blame him? "It's like their one and only skill. And you fail so often, they'll be backstroking around in no time."

"Rats are the only henchmen worth having." Hamelin, the Pied Piper, agreed seriously. He favored green tights and a jaunty hat with a feather in it. "They're smart and loyal and don't carry nearly as many diseases as people say."

The Walrus rolled his eyes. "Blah, blah, blah, blah, blah."

Well, the Walrus didn't *actually* say "blah, blah, blah, blah, blah," but it was all Midas heard. The words themselves weren't important enough to even register. His mind helpfully filtered them out, resuming its subconscious scan for someone to say something interesting. And really what were the odds of *that* happening?

God, this meeting was just going to drag on forever.

Information from the official palace sites was of no help whatsoever. Midas only learned the recipe for Gwen's famous pecan pie, a *looooong* list of charities she supported, and that her favorite color was red. Actually, that did intrigue him. It was such a bold shade for a queen. He would have guessed buttercup yellow or mint green or some other serene shade of pastel cutesy-ness. Still, he was frustrated by his lack of progress. Where was all the information that *mattered*?

He clicked on a link to a tabloid site, which looked more promising. It featured a picture of Arthur and Guinevere taken through a telephoto lens. They were in the middle of an argument inside the Queen's Parlor. The caption read, "Art Reacts to Rumors of Gwen's Secret Love." The king was caught mid-bellow, his handsome face red and angry. Guinevere was holding a much smaller Avalon to her shoulder, her hand protectively covering the back of her daughter's head. It looked as though Avalon's eyes were filled with tears and she was cringing away from her father's tirade.

Midas' jaw tightened. What the hell had Arthur been thinking, making his daughter cry? The man truly had been the biggest asshole in the land.

He scrolled down and saw another article, this one accompanied by a picture of Gwen and Galahad walking in a garden. She'd claimed they were friends, but they were *really* fucking good friends. Avalon rode on Galahad's wide shoulders, holding onto his clean, unscarred, uncursed hands for balance. They all looked happy and classy and... perfect.

They looked like they belonged together.

Midas got a sick feeling in the pit of his stomach.

Galahad was handsome and smiling and goddamn *perfect*. Gwen claimed she would stay with Midas, even if Galahad returned, but what if she was just kidding herself? Who could possibly want Midas over Camelot's most decorated hero? Especially if he was the father of her child? The son of a bitch even *looked* like Avalon. Blond hair and blue eyes. The author of the story must have agreed, because the headline was all in capitals: SOURCE CONFIRMS- GALAHAD IS PRINCESS' BIO DADDY!

Mother *fuck*.

Midas' fingers tightened on the edge of the tablet so hard it was a wonder the screen didn't crack.

"What about starting some kind of henchman school?" The Cat chimed in, absently strumming her fiddle, which was lying flat on the (not-round) table. It was a nervous tick. "They need training in the minion-ing arts. Those dishes and spoons I work with are fucking nymphos, constantly running off together. It's cutting into my bottom line, especially since the Cow jumped off to who-the-hell-knows-where." She looked over at Little Dog. "Am I right?"

Little Dog laughed, because Little Dog *always* laughed, because Little Dog was *always* high. Midas had no idea how the jackass got any villainy done when he was forever stoned out of his spotted skull.

Dower rolled his eyes. So did everyone else.

Except Gwen, who glanced at Midas. "Hey, what are you doing?" She asked, craning her neck to see the screen of his tablet.

"Nothing." Midas automatically pulled it back from her, even though she'd seen too much to believe that.

"Are you looking at pictures of Galahad and me?"

Midas didn't want to lie and he sure as hell wasn't going to admit the truth, so he said nothing.

Lake-blue eyes narrowed. "I can't believe you're still snooping around. I let the part where you looked into my schooling go, but you have no business reading tabloid articles about my past. It violates the Contract, Midas."

"No, it doesn't." He argued and it was technically true. He could recite her the exact language of the relevant Clauses if she'd like. "At most, it's a gray area..."

The door to the warehouse opened and Jill Hill came stalking in, interrupting his (kind of lame) explanation. Midas had never been so happy to see the woman in his life. All of Gwen's angry attention instantly went to Arthur's mistress.

Thank God.

"I knew you'd be here, Midas." Jill spat out. There was a huge bruise on her jaw, thanks to Gwen's fist. "You think I don't know what you're doing, you son of a bitch!?"

"Well, I wasn't really trying to *hide* it, so..."

"You shut down all the ports!" She interrupted at a shriek.

"You closed down *everything!*"

"Yes." Midas agreed.

He controlled Camelot's black market, so he could determine exactly what came in and out of the kingdom. That was a powerful weapon in war. His first idea had been to stop shipments of all illegal goods into Camelot, just to create some hardships for all the hypocritical Good folk who used his products. But then it occurred to him that he'd been thinking too small. Why not cut off *everything?* He had the power to shut every checkpoint and transit line in every direction.

And so he did.

Nothing was moving in the whole kingdom and it *wouldn't* as long as the Scarecrow was in power. Let's see how popular the bastard remained when the Good folk realized they could no longer get their cellphones, cigarettes, and coffee.

Jill threw a stack of reports at him. "You're going to lose hundreds of millions, you fool! And all for *her?*" She jabbed a finger at Gwen. "Because you want to own a queen? Are you out of your mind!?"

"Oh for God's sake, Jill." Gwen bounded to her feet, batting the falling papers away as they drifted to the floor. "Wasn't it enough to try and ruin my wedding? Now you have to show up here and yell at my husband?"

Midas heart flipped, his breath stilling.

"I totally get why the Kingpin's so damn pussy-whipped by the girl." Dower told the room at large. "She's fucking hot for a Goodie, right? Usually, I don't got a thing for 'em, but she's got some fire. You can tell."

Midas didn't even bother to hit the man. All his focus was on Gwen, still trying to process what she'd just said. She'd called him her husband. Out loud and in public.

Nothing had ever sounded so *right*.

"This is all your doing!" Jill ranted, stabbing a finger at Gwen. "My business will suffer, now. Men don't pay for escorts, when they're broke. You won't be happy until you've ruined my entire life, will you? Until you've robbed me of everything that's rightfully mine."

"Midas isn't yours." Gwen snapped. "He's *my* partner." She sent him a quick glance. "Aren't you mine?"

"Yes." He belonged to Gwen. He had from the moment he saw her.

"See?" She looked back to Jill. "Midas and I are business partners in this. Everything he's doing is to help our plan. A plan which *will* happen, no matter who stands in our way. So you need to back the hell off or I will knock your ass down, again." She paused and glanced at Midas. "And shutting down the ports is a really good idea, by the way." She tacked on a little belatedly.

"Thank you." He murmured, soaking in her words like sunshine.

"All you are is a trophy to him." Jill hissed. "Something of Arthur's he can show off."

Gwen frowned.

Midas' jaw ticked, seeing she'd been hurt. *No one* hurt his wife. "You should go now, Jill." There was no mistaking the warning in his tone. "You have a busy afternoon of trying to liquidate assets ahead of you."

She tossed her hair back. "What the hell is that supposed to mean?"

"It means I own every marker you owe and they're all being called in. *Now*. Every outstanding mortgage and debt will be due at start of business tomorrow." He arched a brow. "You think shutting down the ports impacted your bottom line? I'll make sure you don't even have an umbrella to sit under when it rains. And Jill?" He lifted a negligent hand towards the overcast sky. "It *always* rains in Camelot."

Jill paled.

Gwen glanced at him in surprise. "Midas..."

"That's me being my kindest self." He interrupted, anticipating her complaint. "Believe me. I could do much worse and Jill knows that I *will* if she bothers you, again."

Jill's lips thinned at the threat. "You bastard. You'll pay for this."

"I can afford it." He said calmly.

"We'll just see who comes out on top, asshole." She glanced back at Gwen. "Have fun pulling his strings, for a while. Arthur always said you were trying to steal his kingdom and now you can try to steal the underworld from Midas. ...For as long as he finds it amusing, anyway. Midas doesn't have a long attention span for his new toys. There's always something better to buy." Turning on her tall heels, she marched from the room.

"What a bitch." Miss Muffet muttered.

Gwen glanced down at Midas, like Jill's words actually worried her. "I'm not trying to steal your business from you." She said in a stricken voice.

Fucking hell. No doubt Arthur *had* complained about Gwen trying to save Camelot from his bungling. The woman cared deeply about this shithole kingdom. Of course she'd try to save it from an incompetent moron. And of course Arthur had resisted her efforts. The man's ego had no doubt been bruised that Gwen was a thousand times smarter than him.

"You're not stealing from me." Midas assured her firmly. Just the idea was ridiculous. Gwen couldn't steal from him, even if she wanted to. Everything he had was hers.

"I just want to help. Really." She still looked unsure. It broke his heart. "Midas, if I'm bothering you by being here…"

"I need you." He interrupted, not caring if anyone else heard him, just wanting her usual confidence back. "I like that you're helping me. I like that you let *me* help *you*. That's why we both signed the Contract, isn't it?"

She hesitated, chewing on her lower lip.

"Don't break our deal." Midas urged. "Don't leave me. Without you, I would be… alone."

She studied him for a long moment, like she was trying to read his mind.

Midas stared back. Every word he'd said was true, so this was one test he'd knew he'd pass. Sure enough, those big, blue eyes weighed him and, once again, they liked what they saw.

"Okay." Gwen let out a relieved breath. "Equal partners."

"Equal partners." God, it really was the best bargain he'd ever made.

Gwen sat down again and deliberately shifted her chair closer to his. She may have intended it to be a discreet movement, but the legs squeaked across the floor. The woman simply wasn't programmed to be subtle. After about half a second, she scooted her chair over again, so now the cushions actually touched. Then, she glanced up at him, as if checking to see if Midas noticed the noise or closer proximity.

His only response was to stretch out a proprietary arm, so it was resting along the back of her seat. Gwen didn't seem to mind the unmistakable show of possessiveness. She smiled and settled back with a cheerful sigh. Satisfaction filled Midas, his gloved fingers absently toying with the ends of her soft, shiny hair.

His wife.

"I like that you're trying to be more assertive." Gwen whispered. "I know it's hard for you to be as heartless as me, but it will really help you in business. And you're a doing a great job."

"It's coming very easily to me." He assured her.

"But maybe you could show a little bit of mercy to Jill."

Gwen went on. "Not a lot. But... don't ruin her. She's having such a hard time. She loved Arthur, you know. That's where all her anger is coming from."

The woman would be the death of him. Midas rolled his eyes and picked up his tablet again. "You and I have very different definitions of 'heartless, Guinevere.'" He muttered.

"Please?"

Midas' resolve faded into dust. He would have leveled continents for her, so showing mercy to Jill meant nothing. Until she'd gone bat-shit crazy, he'd liked the other woman. "Fine." He flashed her a look through his lashes. "For *you*, not her."

Gwen leaned over to give his cheek a smacking kiss and it was magical. "Thank you."

Midas' mouth curved, adoring her. Everyone in the room had to see how smitten he was, but so what? Any Bad folk in the world would kill to possess what he'd found. Truthfully, Jill was kind of right. His deepest instinct *was* to show Gwen off to everyone. Not because she'd been Arthur's, but because she was *his*. Midas wanted to make sure everyone in Camelot knew she'd married him. Bragging, arrogance, territorialism, pride... whatever you called it, he had no desire to hide his triumph.

Hell, he might just take out a billboard.

"Um... Ma-ma-ma-maybe we should go ba-ba-ba-back to the he-he-he-henchmen problem." K-k-k-Katy suggested, giving him an annoyed look. "S-s-s-some of us w-w-w-want to get this m-m-m-meeting back underway."

Midas nodded. "By all means."

And so they resumed whining at each other and Midas went back to ignoring them.

"Do you think anyone would mind if I made some suggestions about running their crime syndicates?" Gwen asked after a while.

Midas couldn't care less about their opinions. He was the most powerful man in this room and the others would do what Gwen wanted or face the consequences. "I give you full authority to speak for us." He told her, supremely content. "See if you can bring order to this god-awful mess."

Gwen beamed.

Pleased that his True Love was happy in his evil clutches, Midas stopped researching her past. He didn't want to upset her, again. Instead, he switched his attention to Galahad.

Was the knight Avalon's daddy? If not, then who was?

Questions plagued him. Was Galahad the one who'd sent Gwen to Midas? Why would he do such a thing? Did he think he could use Midas to fight this war and then reclaim Gwen later? That Midas would just give her up? Whatever delusions the man had, Midas had a morbid desire to know them all. He wanted to learn *everything* he possibly could about their relationship. Understand *everything* Gwen saw in Galahad and *everything* he'd ever done with her.

Then he wanted the bastard to die.

Horribly.

Midas scowled, reading reviews on Galahad's stupid television shows. Damn it, they were all glowing with praise. He needed to buy the TV stations and make sure even the reruns were canceled.

"Exactly!" The Walrus bellowed, about God only knew what. "I second the idea of a henchman school! If any of *you* have a better idea, I'd love to hear it, because..."

"Maybe if you didn't devour your oyster brigade by the dozen, it would be easier to hire replacements." Gwen interrupted, jolting Midas from his thoughts. "Who would want to work for someone who might eat them at any moment?"

Midas' head snapped up at the sound of her voice. He'd thought Gwen would be too intimidated by the wicked crowd surrounding her to risk interacting with them quite so forcefully. He should have known better. Nothing could scare this woman. She seemed ready to take charge of the meeting with her usual outspoken bluntness.

He didn't know whether to be proud or scared.

"Who wants to work for *any* of you?" Guinevere continued, heedless of how dangerous it was to be at the center of so much Bad attention. "Really, I think your only hope is an industry-wide commitment to less cannibalism and a higher quality of life for your employees." She arched a brow, glancing around the table. "For instance, do you guys offer them any health care options?"

Silence.

The other Baddies squinted as if she'd grown two heads. Actually, with *more* incredulity than if she'd grown two heads. After all, Hansel and Gretel, the serial-killing conjoined twins, were sitting at the table and nobody was gaping at *them* with appalled fascination.

Midas' breakable little bride didn't appear to notice their dangerously curious expressions, but he sure as hell did. He set the tablet down on the (annoyingly square) table, his body shifting even closer to Gwen. It was probably an animalistic response, but he didn't care. Anyone who upset his wife was going to see just what a tawdry, feral animal he could be.

"In fact, if you're going to be competitive in the market, you're really going to need to improve benefits." Gwen tapped her pen against the notes she'd made on her legal pad. "We should begin offering henchman pension plans. Vacation time. Assurances they won't be killed in some fit of villainous rage. That will improve employee retention."

Twenty-two sets of Bad eyeballs blinked at her.

Guinevere looked over at Midas. "Don't you think?" She asked guilelessly.

Twenty-two sets of Bad eyeballs switched to Midas.

Shit. It looked like he was going to have to pay attention to the Round Table, after all.

Chapter Twelve

Upon reclaiming the kingdom, Guinevere Pendragon promises to make Midas (no last name given) King of Camelot, with the understanding that Avalon Pendragon is to remain, now and forevermore, heir to the throne. He may rule by Guinevere Pendragon's side for as long as he wishes, provided that he does not wantonly oppress, torture, or enslave their subjects.

Clause 5- Oversight of the Kingdom

Midas sighed and grudgingly began participating in the meeting. "If you compensate your employees more than anyone else, you're most likely going to get better employees than anyone else." He agreed, because Gwen was one-hundred percent correct. "If you want the best, you have to pay for it."

Hell, that could've been his family motto. ...If he'd *had* a family, anyway.

Gwen smiled, pleased that Midas had sided with her, and then turned back to the others. "See? It's really very logical, when you think about it."

The Walrus scowled as best he could, given the cumbersome size of his gigantic tusks. "Maybe it's time we stop ignoring the elephant in the room." He snapped.

Guinevere looked over at a certain flying pachyderm, who was presently chained in the corner. "That's a fair point. Since you brought it up, I don't think it's right to ransom that poor elephant. I mean, aside from big ears, he seems pretty much..." She trailed off in apparent surprise, finally noticing that everyone was staring at her. "Oh, you mean *me?*"

"They mean you." Midas assured her, his golden gaze fixed on the Walrus. The jackass now had his full attention. "Tell me... What would you like to discuss regarding *my* wife?"

His quiet tone had half the table cringing.

The Walrus glanced around for support, but no one else was willing to risk Midas' wrath. Gwen might think he was "gentle and kind," but everybody else knew better. They were all suddenly fascinated with the ceiling, walls, and floor.

The Walrus scowled at the others and pressed on himself. "Well, this is supposed to be a gathering of Bad folks and she isn't Bad."

Gwen gasped as if she'd been maligned. "I may have been born Good, but I'm an outlaw now." She insisted hotly. "*Actions* are what matters, not biology. I'm almost-Bad!"

The *actual* Bad folk couldn't contain their skepticism.

Gwen glowered at them, irritated by their lack of enthusiasm for her villainy.

"Regardless of whether she was born Good or Bad, the queen wants to be here." Midas' voice stayed mild, but his fingers drummed on the tabletop in clear warning. "Of course, I'm a reasonable man, Walrus. Would you like to step outside and discuss the situation privately? I'm sure I can convince you to see things her way."

"No!" The Walrus's beady eyes went to Midas' gloved hand, correctly interpreting it as a threat. "No, Kingpin. She should stay. Of course your woman..."

"My *wife*."

"Your wife should stay! I'm already convinced."

"So stop talking."

The Walrus shut his mouth so fast, it was a wonder his tusks didn't stab right through his lip.

Gwen shot Midas a censuring look. "Intimidating your coworkers is not going to help your future business ventures." She whispered.

"They're *not* my coworkers. They're imbeciles I meet with once a year, because it's easier than killing them outright. Right now, I'm weighing the convenience factor against how damn annoying they are."

"Really, you can't blame them for questioning my presence."

"Yes, I can."

She disregarded that and smiled around the table. "Obviously, most of you recognize me and you're wondering what I can contribute to your evil consortium. I *was* born Good. I'm not denying that. Until last year, my life was spearheading social reforms and taking my little girl to ballet class." She paused. "And I was married to King Arthur. That must be hard to forget. We had one of those celebrity couple names and everything. 'Arthevere.'"

Midas made a face at the ridiculous moniker.

"I wouldn't blame you for distrusting me, a bit." Gwen continued. "But, I *am* a criminal, just like you. In fact, I'm the one the

Scarecrow hates the most. I have a bigger price on my head than anyone in this room. So it seems to me that," she shrugged, "I'm actually the biggest Badass here."

Midas smiled at that outrageous claim. He couldn't help it. God, she just enchanted him with her crazy ideas and gingerbread scent and Good-girly-ness.

"Now the Good folk have kept you down for years, even though you outnumber them." Gwen went on, oblivious to his helpless adoration.

"Because they have all the power." The Walrus whined.

"You *give* them the power." Gwen retorted. "But now we're going to take it back. This is my kingdom. If you help me defeat the Scarecrow, I will help you have an equal place in Camelot."

"Why should we trust you?" Dower demanded. "The wizards hate Bad folk and you need their approval to be queen. They'll *never* support you, if you support us."

That was a fair point.

"I'll deal with the wizards. In the meantime, I need the Bad folk to do everything they can to cause chaos for the Scarecrow and his regime. Show people what Camelot will be like with him in charge." Gwen nodded intently. "And we also need to stop him from going to other lands for support. Especially the Four Kingdoms. We need to cut him off, so it's just us and him. Then we beat him."

Midas had to admit it was a pretty good plan.

"You have the numbers to cause chaos. I have the crown to get us legitimacy with the Wizards Congress. Midas has the gold to finance everything." Gwen held up three fingers, ticking off her points as she spoke. "Soldiers, power, money. *That's* what wins a war and we already possess it."

At least half the villains present looked intrigued.

Hamelin was not among them. "No matter what you do, the Good folk aren't going to let *Midas* be king, though."

"Midas already *is* the king. I am the rightful ruler of Camelot and Midas is my husband. The Good folk can't change that."

No one would fucking change that. Not while Midas was still breathing. He didn't give a damn about any crown, but he would live and die as Guinevere's husband.

"Now, we're going to save the kingdom from that bird-filled bastard and you're going to help us." Gwen glanced at Midas. "Right?"

"Right."

Miss Muffet made a frustrated sound. Spiders crept along

her skin in a never-ending blanket of spindly legs. "You're really going to wage war on the Scarecrow for this girl, Midas?"

"Yes."

Her lips tightened at the simple reply. "You're usually smarter than this, you know."

People kept telling him that. In reality, the bargain he'd made with Gwen was the most brilliant deal any man had ever struck in the history of the world. What other stable boy from Celliwig had married a beautiful queen who called him gallant? What other tawdry feral animal knew the absolute contentment of listening to a little girl talk about rocking-horseflies at dinner? Midas now owned the most beautiful, valuable things in the kingdom. His success should be plain for everyone to see.

He gave Miss Muffet a smirk. "I'm just suddenly passionate about politics."

Miss Muffet looked pissed at his nonchalant attitude. "Use your head. The one with the actual *brain* in it. Jill had a point earlier. How is this plan going to be good for business?"

Midas shrugged. "Weapon sales will be up." He wasn't particularly concerned over lost revenue. Overthrowing a kingdom was a small price to have Guinevere beside him. You had to pay to have the best.

"You're turning into an idiot."

"Midas is brilliant!" Gwen interjected, apparently furious that Miss Muffet had just insulted him. "Yes, he needs to focus more on details. And granted, he threatens violence a bit too much in order to cover his gentle heart. And okay, he can be a little trusting..."

"'Trusting and gentle?'" Dower interjected incredulously. "*Midas?*" He looked at Midas. "*You?*"

Midas endeavored to look trusting and gentle.

"...But he's built a successful empire, all on his own." Gwen continued, ignoring the interruption. "*None* of us could do what he has." She jabbed a fingertip against the table to emphasize her words. "The man is a genius and you all know it."

Shockingly, no one argued that part.

Except Midas... "I'm not a genius." He argued, pitching his voice so only she could hear. He didn't mind her thinking he was "kind and gentle," but "genius" was too much even for him. It made him feel guilty to trick her. "I stopped going to school in the fourth grade and it really wasn't much of a school before that."

"That just makes your accomplishments even more impressive."

Midas blinked at her convoluted reasoning. "But..."

Gwen talked right over his protest, getting back to her speech. "Now, Midas and I are equal partners in this. And you guys need to help us make this plan happen. Otherwise, I will kill all of you and we can start over with some other, *smarter* Round Table."

Midas gave up his half-hearted effort to make her see his true nature. It had been a stupid, self-defeating impulse. He didn't know right from wrong anyway, so why even bother to try and figure it out? Why not just count his lucky stars that such a bright woman was so very, very blind about him? Feeling smug about his good fortune, he leaned back in his chair and just *basked* in his wife.

Miss Muffet crossed her arms over her chest and scowled at Midas' smitten expression. "Look, Kingpin, it can be disconcerting to find your True Love. I get it. It's bound to make anyone a little nutty. But, day-to-day, True Loves are more trouble than they're worth, especially when they're Good. Trust me. I keep mine all safe and sound, cocooned on a spider web, because of his bitching." She shook her head in exasperation. "Marriage is really pretty... lackluster."

Midas was getting damn tired of hearing that opinion.

"We're not True Loves." Gwen put in quickly. "We're business partners. In fact this whole arrangement was *my* idea."

Twenty-two villains scoffed in unison. Midas couldn't blame them. Gwen might not believe in True Love, but any Baddie could see why Midas was so sanguine about this plan and it had nothing to do with "business." Still, the very last thing he wanted was for Gwen to understand the depth of their connection. As soon as she knew the power she held, she'd be gone.

His eyes narrowed at the others and no one dared to press the issue.

"It's true!" Gwen insisted. "Midas, isn't it true that I'm the one who proposed?"

"Yes. You drove quite a hard bargain, too."

Dower somehow kept his mouth shut, but he rolled his eyes so hard he probably popped a blood vessel.

"Whatever you two have planned, I don't get why we should be a part of it." Hamelin interjected with unexpected insight. "What's in it for us? Why the hell would we help Midas takeover Camelot? He'll probably execute us all by the end of the fiscal year."

Midas lifted a shoulder. If not sooner.

"Because, the Scarecrow is coming for you." Gwen looked around. "That's why you all need to listen to us. He has plans for the Bad folk of this kingdom. Plans that include brainwashing and servitude and death. If we don't stand together, we'll swing alone. I promise you that. He'll pick us off, one at a time."

"Brainwashing?" The Walrus repeated. "How does he plan to do that?"

"Dark Science. He has a formula that will target Bad folk." She paused. "He wants to turn you Good."

The Round Table attendees exchanged sideways glances, murmuring amongst themselves.

Midas' eyebrows soared. For one timeless moment hope surged through him, blocking out rational thought. Dark Science could turn him Good? Guinevere would never accept a villain for a True Love. He knew that. The woman wanted someone kind and trusting, for fuck's sake. But, if there was a way to undo Badness --If he could somehow become Good-- then maybe she would stay with him. If there was even a *chance* of success, he'd take it regardless of the cost.

He would pay anything to have her.

"W-w-w-will the formula w-w-w-work?" K-k-k-Katy demanded and Midas had a feeling she was thinking the same impossible thoughts.

"No." Gwen shook her head and Midas' heart sank. "Neither magic nor science can alter that. Not really. It can just cover up who we are, and twist it, and pollute it."

"There are people who will tell you Bad folk are already polluted." Midas said, struggling with his disappointment. "People who will tell you this formula is a blessing. That it's right to change us."

"Good and Bad mean *nothing*." Gwen snapped. "I told you, it's our actions and choices that determine who we are, not some blood test. My daughter is Bad and she is *perfect,* just the way she is. I would *never* want her changed. No mother would."

She was very wrong about that. Midas' mother would have fed him a goddamn *death* formula, if she thought it would change him into someone socially acceptable. Only Gwen would battle to keep her Bad child Bad. Only Gwen had that pure of a heart.

Midas had no idea how he'd survived so long without this woman.

"This formula will make you slaves." She continued passionately. "It will erase who you *are* and fill you up with who the Scarecrow *wants* you to be. And --trust me-- you do *not* want to be who he wants you to be. He is going to scoop out your freewill and personalities until you mindlessly serve him."

"Damn." Dower muttered. "That's going to really suck."

"Eighteen months ago, Galahad and I saw what they were doing and we destroyed the lab." She sighed, clearly ready to canonize her "best friend." "He was somehow caught and then banished for it. It broke my heart, but he was so brave."

Midas' teeth ground with such force they were nearly pulverized into dust.

Miss Muffet shot him an arch look, also noticing Gwen's enamored tone. "See? She can't feel what you do. It's not in Good folk's programming."

The glare he sent her probably scorched a few spiders dead.

Gwen seemed oblivious to the byplay. "I thought we'd gotten rid of all of the formula, but some survived and the Scarecrow is obsessed with it. He rebuilt the lab. So far, he can only administer the formula in shots, but soon he'll be able to make it airborne. It will infect all of Camelot."

"Which is why you need your father's wand?" Midas guessed.

"Yes! The wand is the one thing that can destroy Dark Science, once and for all. The magic in it is unsurpassed. Without it, you and Avalon and everyone at this table could be *gone*."

No one argued with her. In fact, Midas had never seen the Round Table so focused. Five minutes of talking and his wife was now firmly in charge of the most ruthless criminals in the land.

The woman truly was a queen.

The door opened and waiters marched in all carrying lunch trays.

"Finally!" The Walrus clapped his flippers together as a silver cloche was placed in front of everybody. Maybe he was the one who'd hired the caterers. "What are we having?"

"Pie." One of the waiters told him with a professional smile. He was some kind of elf, dressed in a crisp white uniform. "It's our specialty." In unison, all the waiters raised the lids from the trays to reveal the neatly baked shells.

Gwen's eyebrows compressed as she looked down at hers.

"Pie?" The Walrus repeated, skeptically. "For lunch?"

"It's a pot pie." The waiter called, heading for the door with his co-workers. They all seemed Good, which was odd. Servants were usually Bad. "Enjoy!"

Gwen went pale.

Midas picked up his fork. He hated to admit it, but the pie did look delicious. Before he could break through the top of the crust, though, the silver cloche was slammed back over his tray like a guillotine. Midas nearly lost three of his gloved fingers. He sat back in surprise, his eyes cutting over to Gwen, who'd just stopped him from eating. In fact, she had her palm flattened on the lid, just in case he tried to open it back up again.

"You don't like pot pie?" He hazarded calmly. Given the woman's unpredictability, it was as good a guess as any.

"I love pie. I bake pie. I *know* pie. And this is *not* a pot pie."

"The waiter was mistaken?"

"The waiter was lying." Her voice was absolutely sure.

Well, shit. Midas put his fork down. He wasn't sure what was happening, but he completely believed her warning. "Everybody *stop*." He ordered. "Don't eat anything. Something's wrong." He looked around the table. "Who ordered this food? Where did it come from?"

"The waiters brought it, dumbass." Dower cut into the golden-brown crust with a derisive sniff, refusing to stop his meal, because wolves *always* refused to listen to reason. "What, did you go blind or something? They were just…? The wolf didn't get a chance to finish his snarking.

As soon as the blade of his knife cut into the pie, the blackbirds attacked.

Chapter Thirteen

The parties agree to lead separate lives. They will do their best to not infringe upon the private business of the other party. Midas (no last name given) is free to pursue outside affairs, so long as he does not bring strangers around Avalon Pendragon (a minor).

Guinevere Pendragon will not pursue outside affairs while married to Midas. She will be given her own bedroom, with a lock.

Clause 7- Separate Lives and Other Relationships

Gwen let out a panicked cry as four-and-twenty blackbirds shot out of the pies and began dive-bombing the room.

The Scarecrow's minions!

His feathered assassins were at least three times the size of normal birds and trained to kill. He enjoyed sending them out after enemies of the state, laughing as his pets returned with the pecked-off noses of their victims. The grisly hunks of flesh hung like trophies in his office, with little brass nameplates beneath them, announcing whose face they'd been ripped from.

The Pied Piper screamed as a half-dozen razor-sharp beaks stabbed at him, trying to gouge his nose free of his cheeks. He flailed backwards in his chair. Blood spurted from his torn flesh. Miss Muffet crawled under the table, desperately trying to protect her precious spiders. Little Dog stopped laughing and ran for the door, his tail tucked between his legs. In the process, he knocked over the table, sending food and silverware and laptop computers in every direction.

Midas pushed Gwen out of her seat, as she sat there frozen, trying to process the scene around her. She fell to the floor, Midas's body shielding hers. "Stay down!" He ordered. Huge arms came over her head, forming a protective barrier.

Chaos reigned.

Dower grabbed a fork from the table setting and succeeded in jabbing a blackbird in the chest. Four more swooped in to attack him and he bellowed in rage. The Walrus waddled around in a helpless circle, ineffectually waving his flippers at the blackbirds as they pierced his blubbery skin. Hansel and Gretel tried to push each other into the line of fire to protect their own ass. ...Which made no sense, given the fact they were *attached*, but no one was thinking clearly.

Except Midas.

Gwen switched her attention to her husband's very appealing, unhandsome face and saw that he was already figuring out a plan. The man might not be much of a contract negotiator, but heroics were right up his alley. Midas was lying on top of her, so she had an up-close view of the determination glinting in his eyes. ...Also she couldn't help but notice that his lips were perfectly shaped and he smelled incredible.

Midas swore with incredible fluidity and quickly settled on a course of action. She *so* admired decisiveness.

"Gwen, wait here." He jerked off his silver pinstriped jacket and draped it over her head. "Protect your eyes. And whatever you do, *don't touch me*." Then he was moving away from her, stripping off his gloves.

Gwen turned to watch as he got to his feet. "What are you going to...?" The answer to her question came before she even finished asking it.

Several of the massive blackbirds launched themselves at Midas. Instead of ducking, he held out a hand and the first winged assassin flew right into it. When its feathers touched Midas's bare fingers it became abundantly clear what his plan was. His curse acted so fast that Gwen didn't actually see the blackbird transform. One second it was zooming towards Midas. The next, it was falling from the sky, its wings forever frozen in mid-flap. Two more quickly followed.

Their metal bodies fell beside her with sickening clangs.

Midas glanced down at his hands and then back at Gwen, like he was trying to gauge her reaction.

Did he think she was going to be revolted? She couldn't imagine why she would be, considering he was about to save her life. "I don't think your curse is a curse today." She told him over the screaming of the others.

"It's always a curse." He said, but he went back to work.

He might have spent the entire meeting complaining about the Round Table, but his first instinct was still to help them. Nobility was just a part of him. Midas reached Dower, his hands swatting the gigantic birds away from the wolf's bleeding neck. They met the same fate as their flockmates, their shiny black feathers becoming glinting gold.

"Be-fucking-careful!" Dower bellowed, ducking out of range, just in case Midas accidently touched him. "I don't feel like becoming a gilded lawn ornament today!"

"Nobody would put your ugly ass on their lawn." Midas retorted, the idea offending his keen decorating sense.

Three more birds hit the floor. Every time one got within striking distance, it became an expensive paperweight. Gwen watched wide-eyed as he flicked another blackbird away from Miss Muffet, instantly turning it to gold.

They tried to attack him, again and again, but Midas was invincible. He even stopped to unlock the baby elephant's chains, so the poor thing could fly to safety. It soared out of the warehouse, flapping his ears fast enough to send some of the birds scattering and squawking.

"Hey, that elephant's ransom was going to pay for my mom's Christmas present this year, dickwad!" Dower objected hotly.

Midas ignored that complaint.

K-k-k-Katy ducked behind Midas' massive body, trying to hide. "H-h-h-help!" She cried, grabbing at his vibrantly-patterned shirt. "Do s-s-s-something!"

Midas glanced back at her and then grabbed the tablecloth from the mess on the floor. He tossed it over K-k-k-Katy, so her nose would stay attached to her face.

Gwen frowned in annoyance, suddenly noticing that the other woman wasn't so terribly hideous for a villain. It was nice of Midas to help her, but did he have to be *so* nice to women who weren't hideous?

Meanwhile, the birds were beginning to regroup. The largest member of the flock had red eyes and an ear-splitting shriek. It called to its companions, as if reminding them of their real target. The rest of the flock stopped trying to maul the Round Table attendees.

Instead, they turned on Guinevere.

In unison they descended on her, with flapping wings and grasping claws.

Gwen gave a shout of alarm as she was surrounded. The huge birds latched onto her, their talons digging into her clothing and flesh. They were so strong and all working together. Gwen felt her body begin to leave the ground as they lifted her upward.

Oh God, they were going to take her back to the Scarecrow!

"*Midas!*" Screaming for him was pure instinct. She frantically grasped hold of the nearest chair back as the birds tried to take off with her. They were too big for her to stop on her own. "Help!"

His head snapped around, taking in the situation. "God*damn* it!" He leapt across the scattered furniture to reach her. For a man of his size, he was surprisingly agile. Under other circumstances, it would have been impressive to see him cross the distance so quickly and with such grace. It was like watching a predator move through the jungle, sited on its prey.

Gwen tried to tear herself free of the blackbirds' grip and only succeeded in losing hold of the chair. Within a heartbeat of time, she was eight feet off the ground. "No!" She automatically grabbed for Midas as he appeared below her.

He began to reach for her. His hand was the size of a catcher's mitt and nothing had ever looked more reassuring to Gwen.

"Shit!" Midas suddenly jerked his palm down again, remembering that he wasn't wearing his gloves.

Gwen's fingers closed onto thin air as Midas pulled back. "*Midas!*"

"*Shit!*" He bellowed again, looking tortured. "Hold on!" He backed up, his eyes on her, gauging the distance between them. "Stay still, Gwen!"

Stay still? Was he crazy?

The birds were trying to get her to one of the broken windows. Gwen fought them with everything she had. She managed to wrench her hands free and cracked one of the bird's wings like she was snapping a tree branch. She felt the bone fracture with a sickening wet crunch. The bird let out a screech of pain and loosened its grip enough that the whole flock sagged in the air, like a balloon losing altitude.

"I'm going to get you down, but you have to *stay still*. If you're moving, you might accidently touch me!"

She tried to process what Midas was saying, but panic was telling her to do everything possible to stop the birds from leaving the building with her. If they reached open sky, they would soar too high for her to escape. They'd return her to the Scarecrow and he'd toss her in the dungeon and this time she'd never get out. She'd never see Avalon again. She'd never see Midas or...

"*Gwen!*" Midas roared, cutting through her frantic thoughts. "Fucking listen to me!"

The command was such a departure from his usual calm tone that it got her attention. She looked down at him, pausing in her efforts to free herself.

"Trust me." He said simply, golden eyes locked on hers. "Equal partners."

Trust him.

She'd never trusted any man, except her father. It was why her Right Man list always seemed so unattainable. Nobody had *ever* measured up to one of her criteria. ...But in that moment she looked at Midas and she knew he wouldn't let her down. It was mind-blowing and exhilarating and terrifying, but she trusted him to save her.

Oh God.

Gwen stopped fighting the birds and forced herself to stay still.

Oh God, oh God, oh God...

Midas leapt up on the edge of the sideways table, using it as a springboard. Gwen had no idea how he kept his balance, but he didn't so much as wobble as he hurtled towards her and snagged hold of her coat hem.

With his massive weight anchoring her, Gwen was yanked back down towards the ground. It was like the sudden downhill drop of a rollercoaster.

The birds let out squawks of anger and surprise as Midas tore the whole flock from the air. Their talons dug into Gwen's skin hard enough to draw blood, trying to hold on. They fought to stay airborne, while not releasing their grip. Gwen was now in a tug-of-war and it was no secret which side she wanted to win.

Unable to stay *totally* still, she kicked out with her foot, sending one bird careening into the wall.

Midas pulled against the power of the prehistoric-sized blackbirds. They were strong, but Midas was stronger. No one was as strong as her husband, certainly not the Scarecrow's minions. Once he had her low enough, Midas slammed his free hand into the flock of vicious birds, catching the largest one by the throat.

Golden eyes glowed with rage as he squeezed. "Let go of my wife. *Now*."

It was hard to say what killed the bird first: Midas crushing it in his fist or Midas turning it to gold. Either way the effect was the same. The bird was gone before Midas even finished issuing the order. The blackbird transformed into a misshapen golden statue, its beak open in a soundless wail.

With their leader dead, the other birds dropped Gwen in panic, flying for the nearest exits. Suddenly released, she tumbled downward. Midas didn't try to catch her, still afraid of accidently brushing her skin. But he did move so he was directly beneath her, breaking her fall, while keeping his hands out of range. That *so* wasn't good enough. Gwen grabbed hold of him. Her arms wrapped around his neck and her legs wrapped around his waist. She clung tight to his massive body.

Safe.

She was safe.

Her eyes closed tight as she embraced him. "Thank you." She whispered.

Just for a second, she thought Midas was going to hug her back. She felt a shudder of relief pass through his humongous form. His head dipped down so it rested against hers, his breath rushing out in a long sigh. His arms moved like he wanted to cradle her against him and just melt into her body.

...Then he thought better of it.

Shit.

"Are you alright?" He demanded, looking her over for injuries, instead.

"Yeah." She nodded her head, too winded to say more.

"Good." He stared down at her, all his wild emotions looking for a new outlet and apparently seizing on "anger." "Then explain what the hell you were thinking?!"

"Me?"

"Yes, *you*. You could have been killed! Do not ever, *ever* touch me. No matter what is happening, you need to stay far away from my hands."

"I wasn't thinking about your curse. I just knew you'd save me." He'd inadvertently ticked the first box on her Right Man list. A list which was pretty much unachievable for everyone else on the planet.

It was amazing. *He* was amazing. Midas really could do anything.

His expression grew darker, not nearly so amazed. "You *always* need to be thinking about it." He held up his fingers, so she could see the damaged skin. His palms had once bled from manual labor, scars and callouses crisscrossing his skin. "Look at them, Gwen! Do these hands look honorable to you? Are they the hands of a king? Hands you would want touching your body or caring for your child?"

Actually... yes.

He kept shouting, without waiting for her to answer. "You saw what I can do with them and you *still* fell right into my arms. Just *fell*. What if something had gone wrong?"

"It didn't. You said to trust you and you were right."

That just seemed to make him angrier, his accent getting thicker as he raged. "If you understood *anything*, you'd see why you're not *supposed* to trust me. I'm not anything like you think I am.

You don't *see* me."

"You're *all* I see, Midas." From the minute she'd spotted him on the stairs, he'd occupied her every thought. Long before that, if she was being honest.

"I'm not kind and gentle." He pressed on, caught up in his frustration. "Not naïve. Not fucking honorable. You want some perfect knight and that's not who I am. I'm *cursed* and big and coarse and Bad and I don't have any class! Everybody sees it! How do you not see it, too?"

Gwen scoffed at that nonsense. "Of course you have class." In her whole life, she'd never met anyone so gallant. "You've been a gentleman to me from the moment we met."

"A gentleman?!" He echoed incredulously. "Are you fucking kidding me? You have no *idea* where I came from."

"That doesn't…"

He cut her off. "Do you know what it takes to crawl out of Celliwig?"

Her eyes widened in horror. He was from Celliwig? That place gave hellholes a bad name. Technically, it was part of Camelot, but no king had dared to visit it in three generations. The pollution and poverty kept everyone but the destitute and desperate away. TV news images of grime and death and crying children were as close as any respectable person got to the town. Anyone who escaped had to do it all on their own.

It explained so much about Midas.

If Arthur hadn't been born a king, he never could have risen up in the world. He simply hadn't been capable of it. Take the money and power away from Midas, though, and he'd figure out a way to regain everything he'd lost. He'd fight back, no matter the odds. Resilience and self-confidence were simply a part of him. He hadn't been handed his position the way Arthur and the Scarecrow had. Everything he'd ever done, he'd accomplished through his own nerve and brains and determination.

"Midas…"

He kept going, almost talking to himself now. "To escape that place, you have to be willing to do the things that *no one* else is willing to do." He shook his head. "You have to be meaner and stronger and go farther than *all* of the other assholes willing to do anything. You have to do *more*. You have to cross lines that shouldn't be crossed and you have to *keep going,* because, if you don't, you will die." He gave a shudder, like he was seeing it all again. "There is a trail of blood and dirt behind me that will never wash away."

"Midas, please don't..."

"I will *never* be a gentleman, Gwen. *Never* be gallant or Good. I will never be anything but a tawdry, feral animal, trying to steal what isn't his. Everyone in Camelot knows that... except you."

"No." She put her hands on either side of his face, forcing him to meet her eyes. "You're *not* a tawdry feral animal. Why in the world would you allow Arthur's words to define you, Midas? He wasn't half the man you are. Why would you ever believe something so ridiculous and *wrong?*"

Midas shook his head, not even hearing her. "It would be better for you, if you left me now, before I do something to crush the purity you and Avalon have brought..."

This time, *Gwen* interrupted *him*. It was actually pretty easy to do.

She just kissed him.

Midas drew in a shocked breath, automatically jerking his gigantic, glove-less hands up and out of the way of her skin as she leaned into him. Under other circumstances, Gwen would've laughed. For once, her "tad bit of brazenness" was landing her right where she wanted to be. Midas was at her mercy. He couldn't exactly push her away, even if he wanted to. He was helpless.

...And it was *amazing*.

Gwen's mouth parted against his, her arms winding around his neck, again. Yesyesyesyes. The magnetic pull of the man dragged her under. Logic and reason were lost. Vaguely, she recalled being an idiot teenager, resenting the fact that she had to settle for Arthur and his soulless pecks instead of the sweeping romance of real passion. Of course, what she knew about "real passion" she saw on movie screens, but still *this* was how she'd pictured kissing the Right Man would feel. Alive and free and out of control.

Midas gave a low groan and she could feel his arousal pressed against her. Huge and hot and already desperately throbbing to be inside of her. The wildness of her husband spurred her own desire even higher. Her body rocked against his. Accepting him.

"Gwen." He got out, kissing her back like he just couldn't help himself. Like he was drowning and she was all that kept his head above water. "Oh *fuck*." The defeated curse was music to her ears. He linked his hands behind his back to keep from touching her, letting her do whatever she wanted to him.

Victory had never been so sweet.

Midas' mouth slanted over hers, taking everything she had and giving her more. He might be inscrutably secretive about most things, but there was no doubt he wanted her naked. She'd *known* she was right about that! Without even thinking, she began yanking his garish tie off and he didn't utter a word of protest.

"Midas," she got out, "please. I need…" She couldn't focus long enough to finish that request. "Please, Midas."

"Anything." His eyes met hers for a beat, glowing like ancient coins. "Anything you want. It's yours."

Not want. Need. She *desperately* needed him. Just him. She needed to do all kinds of amazing things with his amazing body. It was the only way she'd ever be satisfied. Her lips found his again, her entire system on fire. She was so tight and overheated that she actually whimpered on the edge of pain. The primitive growl Midas gave in response did spectacular things to her insides. This man was *hers*. She was going to have him and then everything would be perfect. He'd said she could have anything she wanted and she wanted *him*, naked and begging. Once she got the rest of his clothes off, she could…

"What the hell was *that* about?" Dower's angry voice boomed from right beside them, cutting through Gwen's passionate haze. "Hey, would you two cut that out and pay attention?"

Huh…?

She blinked, trying to reorient herself to the world outside of her own desire. Oh shit, it had happened again! She'd totally forgotten that they weren't alone. Kissing Midas was like downing a memory potion. All her former thoughts got washed clean in the tidal wave of desire.

Gwen scrambled backward, her eyes on his. This time she didn't apologize for kissing him, because she wasn't at all sorry. Besides that would have taken a lot more oxygen than she had to spare. She just stared up at him, her chest heaving as she tried to catch her breath.

Midas made a snarling sound of frustration when she pulled away, his head snapping over to glower at Dower. "You stupid fucking son of a *bitch*." That golden gaze glinted like death. For a split second, Gwen saw why so many people feared her husband. He looked fully capable of wolf-icide. "That is *twice* you've done this to me."

Dower took a wary step back, but he still didn't shut up. "When you two start kissing, you forget everything else." He snapped, which --admittedly-- was kind of a little bit true. "We got real shit to talk about here. Why did a goddamn army of birds just attack us, huh? It must be something *you* did."

Midas moved forward, like he was already imagining how

much a twenty-four karet Dower statue would be worth.

Gwen quickly jumped between them before Midas did something he'd regret. "The blackbirds work for the Scarecrow." She told Dower, holding up a palm so Midas didn't just stalk around her and kill the moron. "He sent them after us."

"Hell." The Walrus grumbled dabbing at his various bloody wounds. "Seems like everyone can get worthwhile henchmen but me."

Chapter Fourteen

In case of the death of Guinevere Pendragon, Sir Galahad is granted guardianship of Avalon Pendragon (a minor) and full control of her estates. If he cannot be found, Midas (no last name given) will assume responsibility.

He will try not to screw it up.

Clause 17- Instance of Guinevere Pendragon's Death

"So, the *actual* queen of an *actual* kingdom married *actual* you?" Marrok Wolf's voice was amused. "Damn. The poor girl must be *massively* desperate, huh?"

Midas's fingers tightened on the phone with enough strength to crack its plastic casing. "Let me talk to your wife." He ordered, refusing to rise to the bait. He'd barely restrained himself from killing Dower earlier and he wasn't sure he could be so controlled if another one of their asshole kind pissed him off today.

Wolves were so damn annoying.

After the blackbirds' attack, the other Round Table attendees had run back to their homes to hide. By and large, villains always panicked when Good folk struck back at them. They were used to losing, so they were usually quick to admit defeat. Midas wasn't so sure they would help to rally the Bad folk to Guinevere's cause, like she wanted. Oh, they'd promised to spread the word to their followers about causing chaos, but who knew if they really would.

It didn't matter. Midas would win the war by himself, if he had to. Regardless of Gwen's misconceptions about his gentle nature, when it came to bloodshed and plotting, no one could beat Midas.

For the "smartest man in the kingdom," the Scarecrow was clearly an idiot. That son of a bitch had *attacked* Guinevere, forcing Midas to show her his curse up close and in person. That had been the *last* thing he'd ever wanted to do. So now Midas would take his frustration out on every inch of the Scarecrow's bird-filled body.

And he was going to hire a shitload of lunatic killers to help him.

"Letty's busy crying, because *you* could be in charge of

Camelot." Marrok reported. "You know her grandfather was born there, right? This is a huge blow to the whole family."

"Give me that." Marrok's wife, Scarlett, grabbed the receiver away from him. She sure didn't sound like she was weeping. Midas could hear the exasperation in her tone. "Why do I even let you out in public?"

"Actually, Red, I'd be a lot happier if we could just stay all alone in private." Marrok teased and there was no mistaking Letty's answering snicker of laughter.

Midas looked up at the very expensive fresco on the ceiling of his office, praying for patience.

Letty's voice finally came on the line, breathless from what was undoubtedly Marrok's kiss. "Midas?"

"Hello, Scarlett. It's been a while."

"Yeah, I'm pretty sure the last time I saw you, you were making macaroni necklaces in prison. Craft time was the pits, wasn't it?"

Midas was in no mood to reminisce about their time in the WUB Club. "I need an army." He told her, cutting to the chase.

"Uh-huh..." She drawled out with the humoring cadence of a customer service rep. "And who are we murdering today?"

"The Scarecrow. He's seized control of Guinevere's kingdom and I've promised to stop him."

"Because Guinevere Pendragon is your.... wife." Scarlett sounded like she was still trying to wrap her head around that news. Who could blame her? Midas could barely believe it himself.

"Yes, she's my wife." Possessive satisfaction filled him at the words.

"*Why* is she your wife?" Scarlett persisted. "I mean why are you doing this? It can't be about wanting Arthur's bland, tasteful palace. Because, that place is *totally* not your style, Midas. I've seen it and it's –like-- all bland and tasteful and beige."

Midas suppressed a shudder of revulsion. "Trust me, that asshole's ugly castle is hardly my dream home. I can't fucking stand beige." It reminded him of his parents' home and Celliwig was the very last place in the world he ever wanted to think about.

"So what the hell are you doing, then?" Scarlett repeated. "I've never known you to care much about politics, so is there *another* reason you're picking a war with a megalomaniac?"

"Gwen asked me to."

Letty made a "huh" sound. "That's very *altruistic* of you." She drawled.

"I've recently been told I'm extremely kind." Midas didn't like the direction this conversation was headed. "Are my motives really vital to our discussion?"

"No, but we're discussing your True Love, I'm guessing." Letty surmised in a knowing voice. "So you can't blame me for being a *little* curious."

Midas hesitated and that was all the response she needed. Scarlett had always been perceptive.

"Well, alright then." She said in a far cheerier tone. "*Now,* it's all making sense. Congrats! I can see why you would want to get Camelot back for her. Sure to be a lovely wedding gift."

Midas' gloved fingers drummed on the desktop. "Can you help or not? I'm willing to pay a lot of money for anyone willing to fight for me."

"The Enchanted Forest isn't just a bunch of disposable mercenaries, Midas. I'm not going to risk my people, so you can impress your new bride and…"

"The Scarecrow has a formula that will turn Bad folk into mindless zombies." Midas interrupted.

Scarlett gave a gasp. "What?"

"He's using Dark Science --which is just as terrible as it sounds-- to brainwash Bad folk. He's going to sell this idea as making us 'Good,' but it's really just erasing who we are. Forcing us to be pliable slaves."

"He can't do that! It's impossible!"

"According to Guinevere, it's *real* fucking possible." Midas didn't see the point in sugarcoating it. "If we don't fight him now, he'll come after *all* of us. He'll start with Camelot and then move onto other kingdoms. My wife is the only thing stopping him."

Scarlett was silent for a long moment. "What do you want from me?"

"I told you, I need an army to keep the asshole busy, while Gwen works to stop the formula. Surely some of your followers would like a steady job slaughtering people and causing disorder. It's what they do for fun, anyway."

Letty took a deep breath. "I suppose I can ask around the Enchanted Forest. See if anyone is interested in hiring onto your little insurrection. …*If* you were to do something for me."

"Aside from stopping a madman, you mean?"

"You could be lying about that."

"I could be, but I'm not." It wasn't worth arguing over, though. "How much gold do you want for the men?"

"I don't want *gold*, idiot. I want Ez."

What the hell was she talking about? "Esmeralda?"

"Yes. She's still missing. I want her back."

"Well, *I* certainly don't have the witch." Midas hadn't seen Esmeralda since the prison break. The memory was quite vivid. He'd been frantically wondering how to escape the poisoned gas filling the WUB Club, while she strolled by nonchalantly fiddling with her fingernails. Even in an asylum filled with crazy people, it was easy to recall someone so crazy.

"I know *you* don't have her." Scarlett retorted. "But *somebody* does. No one has seen Ez in months." Clearly, this was worrisome to Letty. God only knew why. Most people would've been *happy* not to have a wicked witch hanging around.

Midas rubbed his forehead and wondered why everyone he knew was so irritating. "Do you have any evidence that she's been abducted or that she's in some kind of trouble?" He asked, very much doubting it.

"Not exactly, but..."

"Well, why not just wait for her to contact you, then? Esmeralda *is* an adult." Technically, anyway. Her maturity-level was another story. "For all you know, she could have just moved and not bothered to send you a forwarding address."

Scarlett ignored that. "You have connections and money in every land. Can you find her? If you can, we have a deal."

Midas would rather eat mud than get involved in this mess. Still, Scarlett was a master at getting smart people to do dumb things. "Why is this witch so important to you?"

"I love Ez. Tuesday share circle sticks together. We want her found and returned to us.

By "we" Letty meant her sister Drusilla, Marrok, Prince Avenant of the Northlands, that annoying blue bridge ogre Benji, and herself. The Tuesday share circle really did stick together. The six of them had an unbreakable bond. Midas had the brief thought that it must be nice to have a family like that.

Somewhere to belong.

The Monday share circle he'd shared with Dower hadn't been nearly so chummy or intelligent. Midas blamed Arthur. If Camelot was a more important kingdom, Midas' crimes would've gotten more international notoriety. Then, he would have been in with a more prestigious group of villains.

Midas sighed in aggravation. In any case, he needed that damn army. How difficult could it really be to find one green-skinned girl with a fancy manicure? Esmeralda always stood out in a crowd. "I can find her." He agreed. "Send the men and you have my word, my people will track her down, no matter how long it takes."

"Great! I'll gather the information we have on Ez's disappearance and be in touch." Letty hung up the phone without waiting for an answer, no doubt to start faxing him pointless maps of forgotten lands.

Damn Tuesday share circle. Why couldn't they just ask for gold?

Midas made a face and set the receiver back on its cradle. Still, making Gwen happy was worth doing all kinds of exasperating things, even rescuing witches who probably didn't need to be rescued. For Gwen he would do… anything. His new bride consumed every single thought in his head.

And all of them were confused.

She'd kissed him. Again. He still didn't understand it, but it had really happened. The woman was delicate and soft and tasted like magic. And she'd kissed him. Again. It was a miracle. He wanted her more than he'd ever wanted anything and she'd kissed him like she might just want him back.

Why?

Just because he couldn't help himself, Midas looked down at his hands. Covered in gloves and far too large, he'd always hated them, even before the curse made it impossible for him to touch anything living. He flexed his fingers, sighing at the massive size of his fist. They were the hands of someone who came from the poorest village in Camelot, and who fought other boys for food, and who worked in a stable until he was too exhausted to even sleep.

Hands like that weren't meant to touch a queen.

Sighing, Midas opened the palace budget report lying on his desk. If he was going to be morose, he might as well be morose over Arthur's substandard bookkeeping. Gwen had put him in charge of bringing Camelot back to fiscal solvency, but it was like trying to patch a hole in a boat, after it had already sunk to the bottom of the sea. Dear God… Arthur might as well have just passed out his ATM pin number to any maniac walking by on the street. It would have resulted in the same depressingly red numbers that Midas was seeing, now. Hell, he might have even *saved* money. The moron had spent so much that…

The door to his office creaked open, interrupting his mental ranting. Midas' head snapped up. Avalon was standing there with her thumb in her mouth and dressed in a frilly pink nightgown. Hadn't

Gwen already put her to bed?

"The child reports that she can't sleep until she says good night to you." Trystan announced from behind her, answering Midas' unspoken question.

Midas felt a genuine flash of panic. The only times he'd interacted with Avalon, Gwen had been there to mediate. What the hell did he know about kids? What if she started crying or somehow broke? For reasons that were beyond his understanding, the little girl seemed to like him, so far, and he lived in fear of screwing it up.

"Okay." Midas cleared his throat and focused on Avalon, hoping for the best. "Good night." He intoned and was pleased with himself. He'd done it! Thank God.

He waited for her to leave.

Instead, she kept staring at him expectantly.

Midas stared back. A full minute ticked by and she still didn't move. Clearly, he was missing a step of this procedure. "Ummmm..." He hunted for something else to say. "Would you care to sit down, for a bit?" He tried and motioned for Avalon to come inside the office.

That seemed to do the trick. "Okay." Avalon beamed and hurried over to crawl into the massive chair across from him. "Wanna tell me a bedtime story?" She asked and it wasn't really a question. She clearly anticipated that he'd do her bidding, just like Trystan did. The gryphon was aggravatingly comfortable with children, something that Midas couldn't help but envy.

"A story?" Midas echoed, hoping he'd misunderstood the words.

"Uh-huh." She arranged herself on the thick upholstery, her face excited. "A nice one. I like stories!"

"Um..." Nothing in Midas' life had prepared him for such a terrifying moment. He looked at Trystan for some hint on how to proceed. "Do you know any nice stories?"

"We should tell her about the time I saved you from prison."

"*You* saved *me?* Are we going for a fictional tale, then?"

"We can take her down to the dungeon to see Percival. He woke up, you know, and had quite a few opinions to share about my people. It was an enlightening discussion."

Midas mentally winced. "Did he survive it?"

"I broke both of his arms." Trystan looked as amused as a gryphon could look, considering their lack of emotions. "It's quite funny to see them bend in all the wrong directions. The child will be most entertained."

Midas narrowed his eyes at the idiot. "You'll scare my

daughter with that kind of talk." He snapped in the gryphons' language.

Gryphons had never been ones for shades of meaning, so they didn't have a word for 'stepdaughter.' A child was theirs, simply because they claimed it. Still, saying "daughter" in any language threw Midas off-balance for a beat. He'd never thought there would be a time in his life when a child was *"his"* anything. Especially not one who only wore clothing that was the color of bubblegum and covered in shiny bits of shiny stuff.

He actually blinked, his brain trying to catch up with the idea.

"The girl *should* be scared." Trystan retorted in the gryphons' dialect, not noticing Midas' distraction. "When Guinevere got rid of that rat-bastard king, she should have killed the Scarecrow and Percival, too. It was sloppy to leave enemies free in the world. It's why I plan to slay all of mine, at the earliest opportunity."

Midas gave his head a clearing shake. "There is no proof Gwen killed Arthur."

Trystan made a considering face, conceding that point. "Yes, she did well at covering up the crime." He admitted. "I give your woman credit for doing *part* of the job correctly."

Midas nearly rolled his eyes at that very Trystan-ish response.

Trystan crossed his arms over his chest, deep in thought. "But the Scarecrow is still a threat. He seeks to steal your woman and make her his own. And you said that he plans to kill the child." He paused. "Do we know *why* he is so determined to do that, by the way? Because it seems important to know."

"Not exactly, but I'm sure it has to do with her magic." He could feel Avalon's power and so could Trystan. It was impossible to miss. "She must be a danger to him somehow."

"Then he'll just keep coming until she's gone."

Midas nodded, his insides sinking. Who could possibly want to hurt this girl? She was innocently watching them speak back and forth in a language she couldn't possibly understand, with no idea of how much trouble she was in. She smiled up at him, looking totally at ease, her bare feet dangling ten inches off the floor.

Son of a bitch.

Midas took a deep breath and turned back to Trystan. "Hire more guards." He ordered. "Hire everyone with a heartbeat and a sword in a hundred mile radius. I don't care what it costs, have my daughter watched twenty-four hours a day."

This time he didn't jolt at the word.

"I can kill thousands, but more men will come for her, until we deal with the underlying issue." Trystan predicted.

"What do you suggest, then?" Midas snapped. "We just wait for the asshole to harm her?"

"We need information, not more guards." Trystan arched a brow. "I can talk to Percival again. Your woman wants to know about possible places that wand could be hidden, yes? Places the Scarecrow would not want to look? Perhaps Percival has some suggestions."

Actually, it *did* seem like a good plan.

"*I'll* talk to him." Midas said quickly, forgetting to use the gryphons' language. "You stay here and tell Avalon a story." The gryphons had countless tales. Surely Trystan could remember one.

"I want *you* to tell me a story." Avalon reminded Midas in a definite tone. "A nice one."

"Yes, *you* do it, Midas." Trystan headed for the exit, before she could change her mind. "I will be out here, relishing the quiet and lack of glitter." He paused with his hand on the knob. "Lyrssa bless you, my friend." He intoned as if Midas was off to battle a hydra and closed the door behind him.

Midas barely noticed his quick and cowardly exit. His gaze stayed on Avalon, watching her like she was a cobra about to strike. Were bedtime stories even allowed under Clause 3 of the Contract? He was supposed to be ignoring the child, after all. Retreat seemed like the best option.

He all but jumped to his feet. "Why don't I go hire someone more qualified to...?"

"My daddy *loves* to tell me bedtime stories." Avalon announced happily not letting him finish the offer. "He's really good at it."

Midas' eyes narrowed a bit at that news... and he sat back down. "He is, huh?"

"Yep." Blonde curls went flying every-which-way as she bobbed her head. "He's the best storyteller in the whole kingdom. He's really good at *everything*."

Of course he was. Midas' lip nearly curled back in a snarl. In his mind, Avalon's "daddy" was handsome, noble, and talented at all kinds of ridiculous shit that little girls and their beautiful mothers appreciated. It set his teeth on edge just thinking about the asshole. "You spend a lot of time with your father?" He asked, because he just couldn't help himself.

"I will soon!" She bounced up and down in her seat excitedly. "We's be a family!"

A... family?

No. A crazed buzzing sound filled Midas' ears. *No*. Anguish and rage blocked all rational thought. Another man planned to steal away *Midas'* True Love and *Midas'* new step-daughter? Give them his name? Claim them as his own, while Midas went back to that cold front porch alone?

Oh *fuck* no.

"Your father is arriving soon?" Somehow he kept his voice level. "Does your mother know?"

He doubted it. Not after kissing him like that. Gwen was the most endearingly, crazily, horrifyingly direct person he'd ever met. If she was waiting for a knight in shining armor to show up and save her from her villainous husband, she'd probably just say so.

"Oh, Mommy doesn't like it when I talk about my daddy." Avalon rolled her eyes like she was the only sensible person in town. "But it's okay if I tell you, I guess. We're best friends."

Midas certainly wasn't going to argue. "Is Galahad your daddy?"

"Nope."

Relief flooded him at the simple answer. "Are you sure?"

"'Course I's sure." She scoffed. "I know my own daddy when I see him. He's all the time in my head."

Midas felt a surge of hope. "This man is just in your imagination?"

"No!" She made a face, as if that was crazy talk. "But I..." She stopped and looked over her shoulder, making sure no one was listening in. Satisfied they were alone, she turned back to Midas and leaned in closer to the desk. "I see things before they happen." She announced in a stage-whisper and pointed to her forehead. "Everything but the blackbirds. I don't like them, because I can't see them. They's scary."

Midas blinked at her.

Avalon smiled guilelessly. "Mommy says I's not supposed to tell you 'bout the stuff I see, because you might be upset, so *shhh!*" She held a finger to her lips. "It's a secret."

The child could predict the future?

Midas hesitated, trying to process that bombshell. This wasn't just Merlyn's ability to remember backwards. This was prophesy. Shit. He'd sensed that Avalon was powerful, but that was pushing the bounds of known magic. Very few beings had abilities like hers. *This* was why the Scarecrow wanted her dead.

Because Avalon was a superweapon with heart-shaped

barrettes in her hair.

"I'm not upset." Midas lied, his mind trying to process this new twist. Why could nothing with these two ever be easy? "So you're a sorceress, then?" He surmised.

Just like the Lady of the Lake had been. Sorceresses were some of the most powerful beings in all of creation. Which was why it was fortunate for all the righteous people out there that they were universally born Good. ...Up until Avalon Pendragon, anyway.

She was the first Bad folk in history with the potential to be unstoppable.

"I'm just Avalon." Avalon corrected. Blue eyes, the same shade as her mother's watched him closely. "Are you's mad at me? Arthur always got real mad when I said stuff he didn't want to hear." Her lips compressed into a disapproving pout. "I's didn't like him. He frowned a lot and he smelled funny."

If she kept saying things like that, Avalon really *would* become Midas' best friend. "No, I'm not mad at you."

But Arthur had apparently feared the child because of her gifts. What a fucking moron. No wonder she refused to acknowledge him as a parent. Still, he hated the idea of Avalon feeling abandoned by her dickhead of a father. That seemed like something that would damage a kid. Midas' father had left him and look at how *he'd* turned out, for God sake.

"Maybe Arthur wasn't really mad, either. Maybe he was worried about what you'd foresee." He offered that lame-ass excuse, wanting to make her feel better. It was the closest he could come to defending the dickhead.

"No," Avalon shook her head, like it was all quite obvious, "he just didn't love me."

Midas wasn't sure what he should say to that. Disagreeing would no doubt be a lie and agreeing seemed cruel. If Arthur wasn't already dead, Midas would've definitely found a way to kill him. Somehow that didn't seem like the best thing to share with a kindergartener, though.

Avalon didn't mind his silence. "I made him scared. I's tried not to, but," she shrugged and sighed at the same time, "I can't lie about what I's see. It would be wrong."

Midas studied her for a long moment. "My father didn't love me, either." He finally murmured.

"I know." She agreed with an earnest nod. "I's seen it."

"I'm sure you did." For a girl who could foretell the future, seeing the past must be no trouble, at all. He found himself trying to explain some of the God-awful pictures that were probably in her head. "My family were Good. I wasn't. There were… issues."

"My daddy says: Sometimes the first family you get isn't the right one."

"Yes."

And sometimes you just never got a family, at all. Especially if you were Bad. He wasn't about to tell Avalon that, though. As much as Midas despised him, Avalon's daddy was right to shield her from the harsh realities of the world. She'd know them for herself, all too soon.

The idea burned at Midas. No one should ostracize this girl. No one should *ever* think her less. "There are people in this world who will never be as we hoped." He said, wishing he had better words to offer. "That doesn't mean we shouldn't be as we *are*. It doesn't mean that *we* are the ones who failed. You and I were born this way. It was our *fathers* who failed in not accepting us." Until he said it, he hadn't known how true it was.

Avalon looked at him in surprise. "But Arthur *wasn't* my daddy." She reminded him.

"Your mother thinks he was. Seems as if she would know."

Avalon tilted her head. "My favorite color is pink." She told him apropos of nothing.

…Except he'd learned Gwen's favorite color earlier, so perhaps the child was picking up on his memories.

"I've noticed you like it." He agreed. "It's why I had the painters redo your bedroom." Before it had been purple. Pleasing Avalon was surprisingly important to him, so everything in the room was getting pink-ified. And bedazzled.

"Is *your* favorite color pink?" She persisted.

"My favorite color is gold."

"No," Avalon's head tilted to the other side, considering him closely, "I don't think it is."

Midas refused to be distracted by her rapid-fire subject changes. "How long have you been able to predict the future?" He asked, wanting to stay focused. Smalltalk with this child still made him nervous. She seemed very smart, but what if he accidently frightened her? Maybe he should use a softer tone or shorter words or rhyme something.

"Forever." She swung her tiny feet, back and forth, and he noted that all of her toenails were painted in glittery peppermint polish. He could only imagine that was Gwen's handiwork. "And my visions are never wrong." She preened at bit. "I'm 'mazing. Mommy said so."

Midas's mouth curved. "I've come to realize that your mother is usually right."

Guinevere had also grown up with Merlyn, the greatest wizard in all of Camelot. Her devotion to the man and her trust in his powers was unquestioned. Why wouldn't that faith carry over to her daughter's magic?

It explained so much.

His gaze stayed on Avalon. "Did you tell your mother to come to me, when she escaped the Scarecrow? That I would help her save Camelot?"

There was no one else who could have done it. He realized that now. No one else Gwen would have trusted. And no one but his new "best friend" would ever have positive things to say about him.

"'Course." Avalon said easily.

Midas stared at the girl. Of course. It was so obvious. "You told her I was an honorable man?" He asked, just to be sure.

"Yep." Avalon beamed at him with unearned trust. "You take care of Mommy and me. You protect us from the Mean Thing. I's seen it. You was waiting for us. You met Mommy and you was happy."

Midas' pulse sped up, understanding what she meant by that merry little remark. The child knew Guinevere was his True Love.

Damn it, what was he going to do, now? Avalon must not have told her mother the whole truth, yet. Maybe she was too young to even realize it. But if she ever explained the bond to Gwen, it would be the end. Guinevere would know she didn't need to uphold her end of the Contract to persuade him to help her. She'd leave. He'd have nothing.

"It's okay." Avalon said, interrupting his frantic thoughts. She leaned closer again, like she sensed his internal distress and wanted to comfort him. Her voice dropped to another loud whisper. "We take care of you's, too."

Midas blinked at that reassurance and, amazingly, his panic... faded.

Avalon was wise beyond her years and she was going to keep his secrets. He could see it in her small face. For whatever reason, their interests aligned. She grinned at him like they were on the same team, her tiny nose wrinkling in delight, and a frozen spot melted inside Midas' chest. A place for this girl that could never ice over again. Avalon Pendragon was one of a kind.

And Midas was somebody who valued rare things.

He took a deep breath. "I appreciate your faith in me." He

told her in a very formal tone. The child had entrusted him with her mother, after all. Gwen was undoubtedly her most valuable possession and Avalon was counting on him to guard her. That called for a solemn vow.

She nodded easily. "Okay."

"I will protect both of you." Midas assured her, just as he had her mother.

"I know." Avalon didn't seem worried about his commitment. "I seen it."

She said that a lot, but he wasn't sure what it meant. "*When* did you see me...?"

Avalon cut him off, grinning happily. "Your favorite color is blue!" She exclaimed, as if she'd just puzzled out a difficult riddle. "Like the magical lake. Like me and Mommy's eyes."

Midas' mouth curved. "Yes." He allowed, blown away by her abilities. One day this little girl was going to rule the world. "That color blue is my favorite. You're right."

"I's always right." She switched topics again, faster than he could keep up. "I like the way you talk!"

His eyebrows soared. The girl liked his rough Celliwig accent? That was a first. Midas hunted for a response. "Thank you."

"I think you should talk some more. ...Like maybe if you were telling me a bedtime story!" She clapped her hands together, obviously thinking she'd been quite crafty with that segue. "You should tell me about rocking-horseflies. They's my favorite!"

Midas couldn't quite contain another smile. "You certainly have your mother's talent for subtlety."

And, like Guinevere, the child seemed to think she could strong-arm him into doing her bidding. No one else in the world thought he was such a pushover, because he *wasn't*. Usually. There was just something about Gwen and Avalon that made him want to give them whatever they wanted. To keep them happy, and by his side, and thinking he was a kind man, he was willing to pay any price.

Even write some kind of (God help him) bedtime story.

Midas took a deep breath. "I can tell you a story." He could recall some of Corrah's old fables. Or perhaps Avalon would like to hear tales of some of his more profitable business deals. "May I ask you something first?"

"Sure."

"Are you *certain* your daddy isn't just in your head?" Maybe Avalon rejected Arthur as her family, because he rejected her. Maybe she'd invented a new father to fill the void. He'd once read that small children sometimes invented make-believe friends.

Avalon laughed as if that was a hilarious joke. "Oh no, my daddy is a *real* person." She sounded positive. "I's told Arthur about him and he got super mad."

It sickened Midas to have anything in common with Arthur, but he fully understood the dead king's feelings on the subject. He hated Avalon's daddy, too.

"Well, is there anything I can do to dissuade your father from claiming you and your mother, then?" Preferably, a way that didn't end up with the jerkoff dead in a ditch. No matter how much he detested the bastard, Midas didn't want to murder Avalon's beloved daddy. It would no doubt upset the child.

Avalon shook her head, admiration in her tone and shining from her eyes. "*Nothing* can stop my daddy." She gushed. "He's too strong. A *hero!* The most strongest man in the kingdom."

God, Midas really wished he could just slaughter that fucker. "Why don't you tell me his name and I'll ask him myself."

She giggled like he'd told another joke, understanding his plans as soon as he concocted them. "You's can't *buy* Mommy and me, silly!"

"Oh, I know that." Midas assured her in a sincere tone.

Although, he was *completely* willing to buy them. Logically, it was the most efficient and practical idea. He didn't have a family of his own, so he would just buy one. The only one he wanted. The *best* one. It made perfect sense. There was nothing you couldn't buy, if you offered enough money.

"You think you can buy *everything*." Avalon told him, her eyes burning right through to his deepest thoughts. "I seen it. But you's can't."

Midas arched a brow at her naivety. Avalon might be the most idealistic Bad folk in the kingdom, but that didn't mean her "daddy" was. The man would surely be open to a deal. Midas was willing to pay *anything*, so they wouldn't even need negotiations. The bastard could have the goddamn moon, just so he relinquished his claim on Gwen and Avalon. Midas would write a check for whatever it took and then everyone would be happy.

Especially Midas. No price was too high to have the best.

"My daddy won't *ever* sell us." Avalon continued with total and complete faith in the son of a bitch's integrity.

Midas had several counting houses to bet on the fact she was wrong. If her daddy left forever, he'd be richer than he'd ever dreamed. Very few people would turn down an opportunity like that.

"We'll see." He murmured, not wanting to disillusion the girl.

"My daddy loves me and Mommy *way* more than gold." Avalon smiled like she saw every Bad idea in Midas' head and already knew they were doomed for failure. "He's the smartest man in the kingdom."

Chapter Fifteen

Trystan
One Year Ago

There was no light in Trystan's cell.

They'd taken the single light bulb out of the flickering ceiling fixture after his first week in prison, because he'd shattered the glass and blinded two guards with it. There were no windows, either. They knew better than to give him any access to the outside world. There wasn't even a soft glow seeping under the bottom of his cell door, because there was no cell door. His cage was a square of stone and metal, sealed tight on all four walls. No one else entered it. They were all too afraid of the creature they had trapped down in the pit.

What did you do with a monster, after you'd captured it?

His food was dropped through a metal shaft, which was electrified, into his iron cage, which was also electrified. It had been three years since he'd spoken to another person. So long that he'd mostly forgotten what voices even sounded like. He was locked in the deepest part of the prison, safely chained away from everyone else in the world.

Trystan knew too many secrets to ever be free and too many secrets to ever kill.

The only thing they could do with him now was lock him up in the deepest hole they could find and wait for him to break. And so, for thirty-seven months and eleven days, he'd stayed in the darkness.

...Until the Tuesday share circle staged their prison break. Scarlett Riding was no dummy. Before she and her friends escaped, she cut the power to the whole building. By accident or design, that ensured that every villain trapped within the thick walls of the Wicked, Ugly and Bad Mental Health Treatment Center and Maximum Security Prison suddenly had a chance at freedom.

They just had to grab for it.

In his darkened cell, Trystan wasn't sure what was happening upstairs. Hell, he'd never even *met* the Tuesday share circle or any other captives of the WUB Club. He was isolated from everyone. Legally, he wasn't even supposed to be there, but laws meant nothing to those who wrote them. They created them to oppress *others*, not to follow them themselves. Trystan would not give them what they wanted and so they punished him with something far worse than death.

He was forgotten.

But he was alive. Not crazy. Not gone. He endured and he waited. When he felt the electricity die, he knew his patience had finally paid off.

The high-pitched hum of energy that sang through the bars day and night, night and day ceased so suddenly that he nearly missed it at first. He'd become so used to the never-ending sound that it barely even registered anymore. Just a continuing, droning noise that vibrated his mind and added another element of torture to his confinement. When it was gone, it took him a minute to realize that, for the first time in forever, he was hearing… nothing.

Just silence.

Trystan's eyes slowly opened. He was sitting cross-legged in the middle of his cell, as he spent most of his time. Thinking was the main way he passed the endless days in solitary confinement. His gaze drifted upward towards the ceiling. Towards the metal chute that they used to drop him his rancid sandwich and single bottle of water each day.

When he spent his days thinking, he dwelled on three main topics:

1) Ideas on how he should have killed his enemies in the past.
2) Ideas on how he could kill his enemies in the present.
3) Ideas on how he would kill his enemies in the future.

He could do nothing about the past, but the other two options were suddenly possible, because that metal chute was suddenly undefended. The high-voltage wires protecting it were suddenly dead and suddenly his wait was over.

If you could call thirty-seven months and eleven days "sudden."

Trystan got to his feet in one smooth movement. Exercise was difficult here, but he still did it every day so his body would be ready for just this moment. There was an enspelled chain cinching his wrists together and then attaching him to the floor in Y-configuration. It was unbreakable. Or so they'd told him when they'd snapped the locks in place and nothing since had proven them wrong. His captors wanted him to stay on the ground and, for three years, he had.

But, he'd spent all three of those years thinking.

The bolt holding the bottom of the chain was sunk into an

ordinary stone. A *huge* ordinary stone, granted, but still just a stone. It had been cemented into place and surrounded with many other huge, ordinary stones to make up the floor of his cell. Luckily, when you had over a thousand days to kill, sitting on a stone floor and contemplating three things in an endless loop, it was surprisingly easy to dig the mortar out from around a big rock.

His eyes fixed on the metal chute, Trystan wrapped the chain around his hands to improve his grip and began pulling the stone upward. He couldn't break the links holding him *to* the floor, so he'd break the floor itself. There was always a way, if you waited long enough and pushed far enough and thought deep enough.

Teeth grinding with effort, Trystan managed to heft the rock free. It weighed hundreds of pounds, which meant nothing to him. Besides thinking and digging at mortar until his fingers bled, his only other pastime was keeping his body strong. When you had a list of people to kill as long as Trystan's list, you needed to stay prepared for the slaughter. He lifted the stone into his arms, muscles straining.

That was the easy part.

His massive wings unfurled, stiff from lack of use. Flying had been impossible when he was chained to the floor, so it had been three years since he even attempted it. Being in the air was still an intrinsic part of who he was, though, and his body knew exactly what to do. His wings adjusted quickly to the unfamiliar movement. It took him a moment to gain altitude with the extra weight of the stone, but determination drove him on.

Drove him *up*.

Three giant flaps and he was at the opening of the chute. It was small. *So* small. Too small for someone of Trystan's size. And then there were the spikes. As one final, low-tech, sadistic plot to keep him contained, they had added nails to the inside of the shaft. Jagged barbs, guaranteed to rend and puncture. If he tried to squeeze through, he would be sliced to ribbons.

But he had no choice. This was the only escape route and he *would* escape.

Or die trying.

The edges of the chute tore at his body, as he forced his way into the tiny opening, the rock still weighing him down. For once, he was glad for the darkness. He didn't want to see the damage he was inflicting on himself. Bad enough he could feel it. The spikes had been coated with some kind of poison that burned through him with every scratch. With his wrists shackled, it took twice as long as it should have to climb the long shaft and each inch was agony. Blood and sweat and feathers rained down like tears.

His wings took the brunt of the damage, the sharp metal shredding the delicate appendages to the bone. They would never be the same. He knew that. The wounds were going too deep, scraping off his flesh in jagged sheets with their poisoned edges. He would be lucky to ever fly again.

But still he climbed. Like an animal chewing off its own foot to escape a trap, freedom was his only focus. Until, finally, he clawed his way to the top of the shaft.

Pulling himself out of the chute, he stood for a second, trying to function through the sensory overload. Even with the electricity off, the increased light aboveground hurt his eyes, making it hard for him to see. There was a fire raging somewhere nearby, affecting his sense of smell. Screaming and crashing and the maniacal laughter of rioting prisoners left his ears ringing and head swimming. His body was one huge open wound. Pain was crashing through him like an avalanche, threatening to drive him to his knees.

Trystan's hand came up to steady himself on the slimy wall, leaving a long smear of blood from his lacerated palm. The rock slipped from his grasp, slamming into the ground, and Trystan mentally swore.

P'don.

He took a deep breath and looked around. Where the hell was he? His straining eyes cut around the deserted room and piles of trash. A garbage area? That explained the rats that were always making their way into this cell. Trystan took a step forward, forgetting that the rock anchored him to the filthy floor. He tripped when it brought him up short and staggered against the wall, his legs barely supporting his weight.

He gave his head a clearing shake.

After three years in a dark cell, he was weakened and overwhelmed. The poison and the tremendous amount of blood he'd lost in the chute drained what was left of his reserves. This wasn't good. Trystan struggled to stay conscious and focus.

He wasn't strong enough to fight. And there *would be* a fight. There was *always* a fight. But, for the first time in his entire life, Trystan knew he would lose.

So be it.

He'd fight anyway and keep fighting, until he could fight no more.

Centering himself for the task ahead, he looked around for a weapon. A bloody cleaver was jutting from a butcher-block cutting board, a small and scraggly animal partially eviscerated on the wooden surface. One of the rats perhaps? He'd never been exactly sure what the undercooked meat was in the sandwiches they dropped down to him, but he knew it was some kind of rodent. Whatever the creature had been, it appeared someone had been half-heartedly preparing its maggot-filled carcass for his meal tomorrow, when they'd been interrupted by the riot.

While he squinted down at it, the door behind him slammed open and Trystan reacted. He grabbed the cleaver, turning to face the intruders. A dozen prison guards came dashing into the room. Perhaps more. Perhaps less. He still wasn't seeing properly. They had high-powered flashlights that burned his eyes, so he shut them.

He would kill the men using his other senses.

Trystan sank back into the shadows of trash, waiting.

"He came this way." One of the men shouted to the others. "I saw him head down one of the garbage chutes. We'll cut him off, before he gets outside."

"Make sure he's dead this time." Someone else ordered. "King Arthur is only paying us, if we can show him a body. This riot is a fucking gift for us. No one will question why the Kingpin is dead. Just don't get too close to his hands."

They were almost on him, now. Trystan took a deep breath and mentally recited the gryphons' death prayer. Generally, it was only said once in a warrior's life, as he entered his final battle. It asked for the strength to kill many of his enemies, before he stood among his ancestors.

And then it was time.

The misty veil of battle fell over his face, transforming his features into an eagle's and heightening all his senses. Wrapping his hand around the chain for leverage, Trystan swung the rock like a mace. That took out the first two as they came around a pile of trash. The slab of stone connected with their skulls, crushing bone like eggshells. He heard their brains splatter to the ground along with their blood.

The other man screamed in panic, having not anticipated the attack.

For a final battle, this one was pathetic. Even partially blinded and chained to a rock, he could tell these enemies were beneath him. Trystan's training took over where his faltering eyesight left off. He slashed out with the cleaver and another man lost his arm at the elbow. The guard scrambled backwards, bellowing in panic, while others pressed forward. Guns and clubs and fists.

"*Who the fuck is this guy?*" Someone shrieked.

Trystan acted without conscious thought, his instincts driving him onward. More men came at him and he killed them, too. He lost count of how many rushed into the room, drawn by the sound of the fight. He lost track of the time that past. Nothing mattered besides slaughtering his enemies. When he entered the halls of the afterlife, he needed to prove himself worthy to join his ancestors.

A metal *clang* vaguely registered in his brain, but he was too caught up in the choreography of death to figure out what it meant.

At the zoo, the gryphons had been called "the savages of the civilized world" and Trystan did his best to prove the epithet correct. It took ten of the poorly-trained men to finally drag him to the ground. Trystan felt the stone floor beneath him and he knew it was the end.

One of the prison guards wrapped his hands around Trystan's throat, trying to strangle him, while others held down his arms. "You stupid fucking animal!" The man was out of breath. "We're not even here for you!"

Trystan lifted his head and used his teeth to rip out the guard's throat. Blood spurted out, warm and wet, coating him. The man screamed as best he could, considering several inches of his windpipe were missing. He toppled sideways, hopelessly clutching his gushing neck.

Trystan spat the hunk of flesh from his mouth, grimly satisfied with his final kill. He would die free and covered in his enemies' blood. No gryphon could ask for more.

And then, oddly, the men holding his arms were gone.

No. Not gone. They were still there, but there grips went cold. *Hard.*

The flesh that had been touching his own, biting into his arms and legs, became... metallic? *P'don.* That didn't seem right. He was used to death and killing, but this was strange. Whatever was happening, it concerned Trystan more than the dozens of men who had tried to murder him. He struggled free of his captors' frozen grips. His straining eyes focused long enough to note that they had been turned into golden statues.

What the hell was *this* about?

Another strangled cry sounded from the left of Trystan. Then another and another and another. He staggered to his feet, swiveling his head around, trying to make sense of it. A shadow moved and the last guard in the room became still. Even his malfunctioning vision could pick up the expressions of horror left frozen on the men's golden faces.

"Hey," a new voice said, "are you alright?"

Trystan responded by grabbing the cleaver and doing his damnedest to decapitate the man.

"Jesus *Christ!*" The guy jumped back in the nick of time, barely keeping his head attached. "Are you fucking trying to kill me?!"

Of course he was. Trystan growled low in his throat and swung at him again.

The guy somehow avoided another blow. "I just saved your life, you deranged lunatic!"

Trystan hesitated, his brain telling him that was true. *Why* had this man helped him, though? No one would help a gryphon without a deeper purpose. It must be a trap. He backed into the shadows, waiting for another opening.

"Look, I got no fight with you, so don't start one." The guy held up his palms. He was large for his kind, with dark hair. His eyes glowed gold in the dim light, trying to get a good look at Trystan. "Enough people want to kill me. I don't need to add you to the list, whoever the hell you are."

Trystan's head tilted, trying to make sense of the words. He'd learned to speak the common tongue as a child, but he always *thought* in the gryphons' language. Since he hadn't spoken aloud for years, his skills were rusty. Plus, this man had an accent which added to Trystan's difficulty in understanding.

"They were after me." The stranger said, nodding to the bodies on the ground.

Trystan watched him narrowly, translating that as best he could.

"I'm only down here to avoid the gas." The stranger jerked a thumb towards another metal tube, this one leading from upstairs. "I came through the garbage chute and found you slaughtering all the men sent to murder me. So... thanks."

Gas?

That word registered easily. Trystan glanced upward. Men he could simply disembowel, but how did one fight a gas?

"It's the sleeping kind." The guy informed him. Apparently guessing that Trystan was struggling with a language barrier, he pantomimed sleep by resting his cheek on his clasped palms. "You know...? It knocks you out."

Trystan grunted, piecing his meaning together.

Since no attack seemed forthcoming, he edged back into the dim light to try and find a key for his manacles. The stranger was dressed in a red sweat suit, which was the WUB Club's standard uniform for its worst offenders. Trystan had no idea why the other inmates consented to wear them. He refused to don clothes provided by his enemies. It was a matter of honor.

"My God." The guy's eyes widened. It was hard to say if he was more surprised by Trystan's nakedness, injuries, or wings. "You're a gryphon."

Trystan disregarded that inanity, stripping the dead guards of anything useful in his fruitless search for a key.

"I have not seen one of your kind for many years. I thought you were all gone."

Trystan's head snapped up to gape at the man. It wasn't the words that mattered. It was the fact he'd used the gryphons' language to communicate them. The informal dialect, which no outsiders spoke. This man had been claimed by someone. Part of a clan.

For the first time, he regarded the stranger with real interest.

"I knew a gryphon, long ago." The man continued. "She lived in Celliwig, when I was a boy. She must have been a refugee from the Looking Glass Campaigns, but she never spoke of it." Unlike many, he didn't smirk when he used the sanitized name his kind used to describe the wholesale slaughter of Trystan's people. "I was alone and she shielded me from danger. Kept me alive. I still think of her, every day, with love and respect."

Trystan believed nothing told to him by these people, but he believed that story. Gryphons were typically born without emotion, but they always cared for children. It was their way.

"Her name was Corrah Skycast."

Corrah.

Trystan's head tilted. Yes... She would have protected an orphaned child from an enemy race. The Skycast Clan's honor had been unsurpassed. They had ruled the Principal Mountains with ruthless justice and unquestioned authority. Corrah had been their last queen, before they fell forever. Trystan had beheld her once, with black wings that seemed to blot out the sun and eyes that beheld far too much. Such a woman would have done her duty to the very end.

"You knew her, too." The stranger guessed, seeing Trystan's face. "She was old, when she was with me, but she taught me to survive. She was a great and selfless woman. The *best*."

Trystan grunted. Corrah had been a warrior. And she'd apparently died on the ground, among her enemies, which was a degradation she'd done nothing to deserve.

"Look," the stranger pressed on, "we need to get out of here. If we get hit with that gas upstairs, only a kiss from our True Loves can wake us up." He did his damnedest to look everywhere but at Trystan's nudity. They were such a puritanical people. "I don't know about you, but I don't currently *have* a True Love, so that's not going to work for me. I have someone I need to kill, back in Camelot."

Trystan watched him carefully, the cleaver still in his hand. "Who...?" His voice was hoarse and rusty from lack of use. Just saying one word led to a coughing fit.

"Who do I plan to kill?" The guy guessed with a snort. "King Arthur. He's the dipshit who put me here and who sent all these fuckers to kill me." He nudged a golden body with his toe.

Trystan shook his head, waving that aside. ...Although Arthur, son of Uther, *was* a worthy choice of victim. "Who... are... *you?*" Even speaking in his own language hurt his atrophied vocal chords.

"Midas. Who are you?"

"Trystan Airbourne, last of my Clan." He raised the cleaver higher as Midas took a step forward.

"Relax." Midas picked something up off the floor, which looked to be a glove. "All I'm focused on is escaping this shithole." He put the glove on and he headed for the door that the guards had rushed through. "I have nobody, either, so you're welcome to tag along, if you like."

Trystan's eyes sharpened as the man went past him, still waiting for some kind of trap to spring. "As if I would ever accompany one of *your* kind, anywhere." He rasped.

"You might want to take stock of your injuries before you start refusing help, regardless of who offers it. I've never met you before, but I'm betting that you've looked better." Midas glanced at the battered appendages hanging limply from Trystan's back. "Especially your wings."

Trystan refused to consider the damage, even as blood seeped from a hundred different places on his skin. Warriors did not tend their wounds in the midst of battle and he was still fighting. This man could be nothing but a clever foe. "How did you turn the guards to...?" Another hacking fit made it impossible for him to finish the question.

P'don.

With the adrenalin fading, his body was beginning to fail. The poison and the blood loss and the pain from dozens of injuries was too much. He tried to push past it all and concentrate. Tried to keep going. To do anything else would be admitting defeat and Trystan would never be defeated. He was a *gryphon*. Stronger than a thousand of his enemies. He could block out the pain and...

The floor was suddenly rising up to meet him. By that point, he was too far gone to even put out his hands to brace himself. He just hit the ground with a reverberating crash and lay there barely conscious.

"Well shit." Midas said very distinctly in his own tongue. His feet came into Trystan's line of sight and then he was crouching down to meet Trystan's eyes. "Alright," he sighed, switching back to Trystan's language, "it looks like you're going to have to accompany me, whether you like it or not." He grabbed Trystan by the shoulder, hefting him up.

With his last bit of strength, Trystan swung the cleaver at him again.

"*Really?*" Midas knocked it away, with an exasperated oath. "You almost cut off my nose! God, you're a fucking maniac, you know that? Why the hell am I wasting my time rescuing you?"

"I don't know." Trystan got out, but he stopped struggling and let himself be half-carried to the door. "Perhaps you have plans of your own. Perhaps you are designing to lock me in another cage."

Midas scoffed at that suggestion. "*Perhaps*, I'm just repaying a debt. Corrah helped me. I will help you. My only 'design' is to get the shackles off you, dump you someplace to heal, and then go back to Camelot. The *last* thing I would want to do is keep you around, believe me."

This man had no intention of killing him.

Trystan shook his head in disgust, as he accepted the truth. Midas was not a clever foe. Midas was an idiot. He tried to break that news to the idiot gently. "You are an idiot."

"And you're an asshole, so we're even."

"Only an idiot would offer assistance to a man such as me, in a place such as this. Especially, when others seek your death." Trystan clarified in a slower voice, but it was like explaining the mechanics of flight to a kangaroo. Midas did not understand.

Like Corrah, he was a being of honor. Like her, it would no doubt be his end.

"I guess I'd just hate for the best fighter I've ever seen to die in a trash heap. I've always respected the best." Midas shrugged. "The way you were cutting through those guards...? It was art."

Gryphons detested art, so that was hardly a compliment.

Still, no one else in the universe would have helped Trystan. That said much for the man's integrity, no matter his race. It would be a shame to just let Midas perish from his own stupidity. This soft, trusting fool was saving his life. His own honor dictated that Trystan do all he could to return the favor.

"I will come with you to Camelot." He decided with an aggravated sigh.

"Who the fuck invited you?"

"I will ensure that you are safe from your enemies." Trystan continued, ignoring the protest. The man clearly was not intelligent enough to form any worthwhile opinions, so it would be a waste of time to even consider his words. "Then I will continue on my quest to kill all who have opposed my people."

"Yeah," Midas muttered in a humoring tone, "that all sounds very epic, but you might want to focus on getting unchained from that giant rock first."

Chapter Sixteen

At any time, any portion of this Contract may be renegotiated by the parties, to reflect their current and/or changing circumstances. Both parties must agree to the changes, without duress, or the Contract cannot be altered.
Once altered, the changes will be binding. Unless they want to alter it again.

Clause 14- Renegotiation of the Contract

Gwen checked on Avalon at least three times a night, so it didn't take her long to realize her daughter was missing. When she saw that Avi's ridiculously pink bedroom was empty, panic seized Gwen's heart.

"Avalon?" She yanked open the jam-packed closet, looked under the overwrought canopy bed, peered behind the gigantic dollhouse in the corner, and searched beneath the ever-growing mountains of toys that Midas wasn't supposed to be buying, but the little girl was nowhere to be seen.

What if the Scarecrow had her?

Gwen turned and dashed from the room, heading for the massive staircase. "Avalon!" She raced downstairs, her eyes scanning for the familiar mop of messy curls. "*Avalon!*" Her gaze fell on Trystan who was leaning against the wall, whittling on a piece of blackened wood with a machete-sized knife.

That son of a bitch was supposed to be watching her daughter!

Furious and frightened beyond imagining, she advanced on the gryphon. "*Where is my baby!?*" She would rip his wings off with her bare hands if...

The sound of Avalon's laughter cut through Gwen's terror like a bucket of cold water. She nearly sobbed with relief, dashing for Midas' office. The door was partially open so she could see that Avalon was safe and sound, sitting on one of Midas' gaudy chairs.

"Oh thank God." She braced one hand against the door jam, trying to calm down. She didn't want to let Avalon see her so upset. She covered her eyes with her other palm, barely holding back tears. Avi was safe. That was all that mattered.

"The child wanted Midas to tell her a bedtime story." Trystan reported from behind her.

"A bedtime story?" Gwen repeated incredulously, her heart still hammering in her chest.

"A 'nice' one." He sneered out the word. "Apparently, suffering prisoners are not suitable, no matter how amusing their broken limbs are to witness."

Gwen had no idea what that meant. "Midas is supposed to be ignoring Avi. It's all outlined in Clause 3 of the Contract- 'Care and Protection of Avalon Pendragon.'"

"That child is impossible to ignore. Believe me." He refocused on his whittling. "I finally realized it's easier just to choose a damn doll, rather than listen to her nag."

That muttered complaint actually diverted Gwen's attention for a beat. "You played dolls with Avalon?" The gryphon was -- without question-- the scariest man she'd ever met. The scarred wings were like something out of a nightmare and his arms were the size of tattooed tree trunks. It was hard to picture him sitting on the floor of that frilly pink room and accessorizing tiny fashion outfits.

Trystan sent Gwen a glower. "It was not 'playing.' It is *training*. We reenacted epic battles of old."

"Oh." What else was she supposed to say to that?

He kept talking, not convinced that she *fully* understood. "The child must learn the strategies from great wars, if she is ever to wage her own. I fashioned her doll to represent Lyrssa Highstorm, vanished empress of my people and tyrant of the skies, seeking glorious vengeance upon all who wronged her."

"This is the doll that Midas armed with a letter opener, I take it." It wasn't really a question. "Avalon likes to draw pictures of Lyrssa, too." She'd been doing them for months. Imagining the lost queen of the gryphon seemed to comfort her.

Trystan grunted. "Once Lyrssa was properly outfitted, her foes were slain by the score. Their entrails rained from above, for hours upon end." He paused. "The child now needs more toys. Many died in the slaughter."

Gwen squinted at him, wondering if Midas knew his most trusted guard was a lunatic. "Do you drink a lot?" She asked bluntly.

"Only the blood of my enemies."

Gwen's eyebrows climbed. Maybe he was joking. He *had* to be joking. "How many people have you killed?" She asked, before she could stop herself.

"Not enough." Trystan intoned darkly, glancing her way

again. "And, unlike *some*, I've never killed a king."

She frowned. "When are you going to stop accusing me of killing Arthur?"

"When I'm satisfied you have no plans for a repeat performance."

Gwen sighed in frustration. This just wasn't going to work, unless one of them bent a little. She took a deep breath and went out on a limb, trusting her daughter. Avi had spent hours listing all the reasons why the gryphon was her second best friend in the whole world. Surely that meant he had some redeeming qualities buried deep.

Really, really deep.

"Avalon has powers." She told him grudgingly. "I'm sure you've noticed." It wasn't like Avi tried to hide her gifts. God only knew what she'd told Midas already. Clause 3 was completely out the window, at this point.

Trystan studied her. "You say she draws pictures of Lyrssa Highstorm?"

"Yes."

"She also sketches my people's ancient temples." He admitted cautiously. "Accurate maps of places that were burned before she was even born. I do not know all her gifts, but I recognize they are vast. I suspect that's why the Scarecrow wishes her dead."

"It is."

"I will not let *anyone* harm that child."

"I know." Gwen wouldn't be here if she doubted it. "Avalon loves you. And Avi is *never* wrong about people." Hopefully, that would mean something, even to a man born without emotions. "She says you're special, and important, and part of our family. It's why I trust you with her."

Trystan's head tilted. If Gwen hadn't known better, she would have sworn he was affected by the words. His eyes got brighter and more focused.

"We need to come to an agreement. We're on the same side, fighting for the same two people." She gestured towards Midas' office. "The four of us are connected, whether you like it or not. It makes no sense for you and me to be enemies."

Trystan considered that for a long moment. "Gryphon are hunted by the 'civilized' kingdoms. Massacred. Our lands stolen. Our customs ridiculed. I was taken from my home when I was young and shipped off to live in a cage."

She frowned, wondering why he was telling her this. "They

sent a little boy to prison?"

"No. To a zoo. The prison came later."

"A... zoo?"

"An exhibit of primitive peoples. Your kind worried we'd become extinct before they learned all our secrets. They'd hoped those of us left might breed --In controlled conditions-- and help them rape more of our culture." His voice was matter of fact. "In the meantime, we were put on display behind bars. Many came to stare and laugh and throw things."

Gwen simply didn't know what to say to that.

"So, I learned very young that I have *many* enemies." Trystan's gaze stayed locked on hers. "Midas is not among them. He is the only clan I have left." He paused. "Did he tell you that he was raised by a gryphon?"

"No." But it didn't surprise her.

"Corrah. One of our greatest queens. Had my people still been alive, she would have brought him to us as her son. I know that. She told him things a gryphon would only tell a member of her clan." Trystan tapped his chest, just above his heart. "She *claimed* him, which is sacred. When a gryphon claims someone, they put that person above all else. They fight for them. They die for them. They protect them. *Above all else*."

"And now you claim Midas, too." Again, it wasn't a question. "Look, I'm not a threat to him. That's what I'm trying to tell you."

"A reassurance which would mean more if you weren't a husband-murderer."

"Arthur's death was an *accident*."

Trystan scoffed at that claim.

Gwen scowled at his rude sound of skepticism. "You don't have to believe *me*. There was an investigation that *said* it was an accident."

Trystan wasn't impressed by the official findings. "Why can't you just admit you are a remorseless killer?"

Her jaw dropped in outrage. "Because I'm *not* a remorseless killer!"

"Understand that Arthur's life meant nothing to me." Trystan waved a dismissive hand. "I do not care that you killed him. I only care *why* you killed him. At first, I assumed that you were just a deranged, soulless maniac, like so many of your kind. Seeking power in blood."

"I wouldn't assassinate my way onto a throne, Trystan."

"No. I see this, now. You would likely have your kingdom

already, had you agreed to disavow the child. Instead, you shield her. You are not blinded by greed or ambition. You fight for love. For your young. I would do the same."

"There is nothing I won't do for my daughter."

Trystan nodded. "Like all great queens, you protect your people and crush your foes without remorse." He shrugged, philosophically. "So long as you do not harm Midas, I will leave you to it. I see no profit in warring with you. I suspect both of us would die."

"Well, you can relax then, because I'm not going to remorselessly kill Midas. Queens protect their people. You just said so yourself."

Trystan mulled that over. "You claim Midas as part of your clan?"

"Yes." Gwen didn't even hesitate.

"It is a sacred thing." He reminded her. "Far more than your hollow mating ceremony. You cannot take it back."

Gwen had no intention of ever taking it back. "Midas is my people."

Trystan squinted, like he was thinking something over. "I claim the child as part of my clan." He finally decided in a very formal tone. "She is my people."

"Yeah, someone told me you'd say that."

Trystan grunted, not bothering to ask who. They both knew it was Avalon. "Midas insists that I protect you over him, you know. No matter what."

Of course he did. Her new husband's size and reputation blinded people to his marshmallow-soft center. "Midas will always put his own safety last. At the Round Table, he fought to protect *everyone*. Even the really sucky people."

"I've no doubt. When we met, I tried to behead Midas at least twice. And he still saved my life." Trystan muttered with a sigh. "It's long troubled me that he is so... gallant. It's bound to lead him into trouble."

"Exactly!" Gwen was glad he was making sense. "The Scarecrow is *evil*. He will cheat and kill, if he has to."

"He will cheat and kill even if he *doesn't* have to. It's in his nature."

That was true. "You and I are alike. We're heartless enough to do whatever it takes to survive, but Midas isn't. He has a much gentler soul."

More silence. "The innocent belong to all who would care for them."

"Yes." Gwen agreed quietly. "So you and I will care for them. Midas and Avalon are *our* people. I don't care what he's told you about protecting me first, we keep *them* safe, before anything and anyone. Is it a deal?"

Trystan shrugged. "I'm still not sure that I like you.... and I'm *positive* that I hate everyone else." He arched a brow. "So, yes. It is a deal. I will protect Midas and the child first. Keeping them safe is all that matters."

"Thank you." Gwen nodded pleased with how well that conversation had gone. She grinned up at Trystan. "You know, you're not nearly so terrifying as I first thought."

"Four hundred and sixteen."

Her smile faded. "What?"

"That's how many men I've killed. Not counting all the leprechauns."

Her lips parted, staggered by the triple-digit number. "Why in the world would you kill any leprechauns?" She blurted out. "They're harmless."

"And delicious."

"...Oh." Gwen sure wasn't about to pursue that line of questioning. Instead, she turned back to the office door and struggled to focus on something else --*Anything* else-- even as her mind raced with images of leprechaun-burgers. Ew. The graphic, shamrock-and-blood colored imagery danced in her brain, which was why it took her a moment to realize that Midas was indeed telling Avalon a bedtime story.

Kind of.

"But, of course, I had already negotiated that all the spinning wheels had to be *magical*." He snorted as if the whole situation had been absurd. "Why would I spend a fortune importing *regular* spinning wheels? I don't think anyone even knows *how* to use them for actual cloth production, anymore. These days, it's all casting spells and spinning gold. Mal was trying to fuck me over. Obviously, I wasn't going to let that stand, so we went to court."

Gwen winced a bit at his casual swearing, trying not to laugh.

For once, Avalon didn't chide someone for the bad language. Gwen wasn't surprised. Midas cursed more than anyone she'd ever met, but he was also *Midas*. The man could say anything he wanted and Avi would be fine with it. ...Up to and including telling her a "bedtime story" that was really a contract dispute.

Avalon leaned forward, fascinated with the spinning wheel debacle. "How come she'd do that?"

"She's a wicked witch. They think they're smarter than everyone else. But, in the end she got stuck with six hundred and seven useless spinning wheels, because she tried to violate the contract." Midas nodded, as if making a profound point. "A contract is the one thing in this world that a Bad folk can rely on."

"I'm Bad." Avalon announced.

Midas hesitated. "Yes." He allowed. "But that's not always such a terrible thing. Bad folk can do many things Good folk can't."

Gwen felt her heart warming in all kinds of soft and sappy ways as she watched them. Midas could love Avi. It was obvious. She'd been so right about his gentle nature. So right to hand her baby into his arms. So right to *trust*. He was already putty in Avalon's tiny hands.

Just that quickly, another of her Right Man requirements got ticked off the list.

"Bad folk can do *lots*." Avalon nodded, disheveled blonde curls swinging. "We know our True Loves as soon as we find them."

"We do." His mouth curved. "And that skill is worth quite a bit." Midas studied her for a moment, like he was trying to find the right words to explain something important. "As you grow, Good folk will want you to settle for second-rate things. They will tell you that it's easier and smarter and even right. But don't *ever* accept less than your True Love, Avalon. You hold out for the *best*."

"Like you always do?"

"Always."

Gwen stomach knotted, her soft, sappy emotions taking a veering turn into panic. So Midas *did* want his True Love. She'd *known* it. She'd even agreed to that fucking proviso in Clause 11- 'Reasons for Nullification and/or Termination of Marriage,' giving him an out if the bitch ever showed up. *Shit*. Why in the world had she made it easier for him to leave her? How could she have been so stupid?

"Only settle for the *best* and then take excellent care of it." Midas continued. "That's an important rule to follow. Nothing else you will ever own is half so valuable as your True Love."

"Can't own people." Avalon told him importantly.

"Of course you can. They just own you back."

"Avi?" Gwen stepped into the room, not wanting to hear any more about the fated homewrecker her husband was pining for. It was just pissing her off. "Sweetie, you should be asleep."

Midas glanced up, surprised to see her there. He really should be used to her eavesdropping by now.

Gwen flashed him an unrepentant glare. Maybe his oh-so-valuable True Love would politely knock at his office door, but this was *her* house for now and she'd do as she pleased. He was lucky she didn't drag the invisibility cloak out of her closet and follow him everywhere.

"'Kay, Mommy." Avi hopped off the huge chair and bounced over to hug Midas. "Night!"

He looked panicked at the contact, jerking his hands back so even the gloves wouldn't accidentally brush against her. "It's not safe for you to touch me, Avalon." He warned and looked at Gwen. "You didn't tell her that?"

"I told her, although I'm sure she already knew." They'd apparently been alone together for at least twenty minutes, so there wasn't a doubt in Gwen's mind that Avalon had given him a complete rundown of her abilities. Since Midas wasn't demanding answers from her, though, Gwen could only assume that Avalon hadn't told him *too* much. That was something, at least. "Did you even read Clause 3, by the way?"

Midas frowned. "Yes and it says *nothing* about bedtime stories, so I'm well within my rights."

"How are bedtime stories i-g-n-o-r-i-n-g her?"

"Have you ever tried i-g-n-o-r-i-n-g this child?" He scoffed in the exact same tone Trystan had used. "The girl is a tyrant in pink sequins."

"For a man with such a fearsome reputation, you really are a marshmallow."

"Only towards certain blondes." He looked back at Avalon and took a deep breath. "I'm cursed." He informed her, not accepting the fact that she already understood more than anyone else alive. "When I touch something living, it turns to gold."

"You should fix your curse, silly."

Midas squinted. "Fix it?"

"Make it go away. You'd be a lot happier." She stopped to get a kiss from Gwen and then skipped towards the door. Her tiny palm reached up to grab Trystan's gigantic hand, her fingers barely reaching around his thumb. "Wanna play dolls before bed?" She asked him in what she obviously hoped was a surreptitious tone.

Midas shook his head, as if he was trying to clear it. People did that a lot around Avalon. "You're playing dolls, Trystan?"

The gryphon flashed him a deadly look. "It was not 'playing.'" He intoned. "I was *instructing* the girl. She had much to learn if she plans to lead a kingdom."

"They're reenacting epic battles of old." Gwen put in. "It's part of the training. Trystan made her a doll to represent Lyrssa Highstorm, vanquished empress of his people and tyrant of the skies." She arched a brow at the assassin/nanny. "Who ritualistically m-u-r-d-e-r-e-d Arthur's father during the last Looking Glass Campaign, by the way."

"I know." Trystan smirked as if the image of King Uther's abject suffering was a constant source of emotionless delight. Who could blame him, really? "The girl can learn much from such a worthy example." He scooped Avi up and set her on his massive shoulder, his scarred wing curving a bit so she could hold onto it for balance. "Come, child. I will teach you how to gut a man with an axe. Every great ruler must know this."

"Please *don't*." Gwen called after him. "Stick with training with dolls. Or read her a *real* history story, if you want to teach her about the past. God knows, there are plenty of books up there." Midas had bought out the children's section of the local library.

Literally.

"Real history is never written down." Trystan snorted, as if that suggestion was ludicrous. "Those who would tell it truthfully all perished in its forging."

Gwen threw her hands up as the crazy person headed back upstairs with her innocent baby daughter. Why had she even briefly considered him reasonable? "Our babysitter is a lunatic. You know that right?" She shook her head in exasperation. "Maybe we should find him a girlfriend or something. I think he needs to get out more."

"His online relationship profile would be interesting." Midas got to his feet. "Do you think he'd list how many people he's killed or is that a third-date conversation?"

"Four hundred and sixteen. Not counting leprechauns."

Midas glanced at her. "Trystan said that?" He sounded surprised.

"Yes." Hope blossomed. "Why, do you think he's lying? Padding the total to look like more of a Badass?" That would be a huge relief.

"I think he's just very... *optimistic* about the recoveries of a thousand other men he's fought." Midas looked amused. "Perhaps, he only counts the enemies he beheaded on the field and not the ones who crawled off to die with two missing legs and arrows in their lungs."

Gwen winced. Wonderful.

"Don't worry about Trystan." Midas came out from behind his desk. "When he wants a mate, I'm sure he'll steal himself one. In the meantime, there isn't another man I trust with Avalon. No one who comes against her will survive. I promise you. Trystan adores her."

"He's not the only one." Gwen arched a brow. "Which reminds me: Why are the gardeners erecting hundreds of rocking-horsefly feeders out back? You and I have had numerous discussions about not buying Avi every crazy thing she wants."

"Well, I purchased those for myself. It's just a coincidence that she asked for them, too."

"You got them for *yourself*? They're decorated with baby unicorns and plastic pinwheels."

"I have excellent taste." He said straight-faced. "Everyone knows that."

Gwen rolled her eyes. "Just be sure you're adding all this crap to my bill."

"Your what?" He asked, like he genuinely had no idea what she was talking about.

"The *bill*, Midas. We agreed I'd pay you back for all the money you spend on us, remember?"

"Oh right. Yeah… I'm keeping a tally. Don't worry." He smiled, walking her towards the exit. "I got *a lot* of great discounts, though, so you owe a surprisingly low amount."

The man was impossible. "Midas, you have to put the *actual totals* on the bill or it's all meaningless. Let me see the receipts. You're supposed to be the math-y one here, but you're doing a terrible job. I think I need to audit you."

"No need. I'll add everything up tomorrow." He opened the door. "First thing."

Gwen frowned. "Are you trying to get rid of me?" She asked suspiciously.

That accusation surprised him. "No, of course not."

"Well, it seems like you're about to go somewhere that you don't want me to know about." Arthur had usually done that when he planned to visit Jill. Her stomach tightened at the idea of Midas hurrying off to see another woman. Maybe he was looking for his True Love. "You can just tell me, if you're meeting someone." She didn't really want to know, but it was far better than living with lies. "I mean, you're *allowed* to have your own life. It's right there in the Contract, so…" Her voice trailed off unhappily.

"I'm about to go down to the dungeon." Midas said after a moment. "Trystan says Percival woke up. I'd like to ask him some questions."

"Oh." That cheered her up. "Well, I'll go with you, then."

Midas hesitated. "The man is apparently... broken." He admitted. "Trystan took my earlier request to 'see if you can wake him up' as a creative challenge. It won't be pleasant to see."

"I don't care about his health and safety. He tried to murder you! All that matters is we figure out how to stop the Scarecrow. It's important that I be there. I know Percival, so I can help."

Midas didn't look convinced, but as usual he gave into her strong-arm tactics. "Very well." He swept a hand towards the door, indicating that she should go first. "If you feel... bothered, at any time, just tell me and we'll leave."

"Thank you." Gwen patted his arm. Midas really was the most reasonable man. "Don't worry. I'll be fine... and I'll make sure you are too."

"That's very kind."

She gave him a pointed look, sensing he was amused by her promise. "I'm the one who knocked him out in the first place, you know."

"I know. You can handle anyone, I have no doubt. You are..." His gloved palm moved like he wanted to touch her hair, only to stop without making contact. Instead, he cleared his throat. "But you've somehow missed the fact that I am a villain."

"I'm sure you think that's true." She assured him kindly. "But I see you a bit more clearly than you see yourself." It was a wonder his business rivals didn't have him dead and buried, given his gentle disposition. "Just because you were born Bad, doesn't make you a villain."

"I'm sure you think that's true." He murmured.

"It *is* true. *Actions* are what define us. And your actions are not villainous. I have never met anyone so generous and noble and unselfish." She shook her head. "And I'm going to make sure you aren't hurt because I strong-armed you into this deal. I *swear* it."

"No one strong-arms me into anything. I am doing this all for me. I promise." He guided her towards a random, mile-long hallway off the foyer. His whole house was a maze of gilding and corridors. "In other news, you'll be happy to know that I'm in the process of acquiring you an army from Scarlett Riding-Wolf. At this rate, I calculate we'll win this war in a few weeks, with minimal bloodshed, and then you'll have your kingdom back."

"Our kingdom back." Gwen corrected.

He concentrated on pushing back a hidden panel on the wall and opening the decorative gate of an antique elevator. ...Because of *course* he had an elevator in his house. "Yes, our kingdom." He murmured, politely holding the grate back for her.

Gwen frowned at his tone and followed him into the ornate car. It looked really familiar. In fact, she was pretty sure it had once belonged to the Swan Princess. ...Before she'd been imprisoned for bankrupting her land with callous overspending. The woman had flited around in feathered headdresses and tutus, consigning her subjects to squalid mines, so they could dig for pretty gemstones. Which explained the kaleidoscopic rainbow of jewels sparkling from the walls and the huge ballet-slipper-pink velvet bench built into the back of the elevator car.

Gwen rolled her eyes. Midas must have purchased the pointlessly extravagant thing and then installed it in his home, just because he could. Every bit of it was handmade, massive, shiny, and no one else could *possibly* afford it.

In short, it was exactly her husband's taste.

"It's *our* kingdom, Midas." She emphasized again, because she could tell he still wasn't keen on the whole "becoming king" aspect of her plan. That made no sense. Why had he even married Gwen, if he didn't want to rule Camelot? Maybe he was just helping her to be nice, with no intention of sticking around after they saved the kingdom.

Maybe he was thinking of his True Love.

Damn it, he *couldn't* just leave her. Not when everything was feeling so... right. Gwen wasn't going to be the only one feeling these soft and sappy feelings. He needed to feel them back. Midas had already completed most of her Right Man list and he wasn't even trying! If he just put a *tiny* bit of effort into wanting her as much as she wanted him, everything could be... amazing.

What could she do to convince him of that?

Gwen's brow furrowed. Seducing him seemed like the most obvious plan. Midas obviously liked it when she kissed him, so how hard could it really be to push him farther? Gwen was a problem-solver by nature and extremely almost-Bad, so using her feminine wiles would no doubt come naturally. Surely, she could figure out a way to trick him into bed. And a smart first step to the process would be keeping Midas away from his True Love.

"We should redraft Clause 7." Gwen blurted out, not caring that it was a non sequitur.

Midas glanced down at her, his eyebrows compressing in apparent bafflement. "What?"

"Clause 7- 'Separate Lives and Other Relationships?' We

need to X it all out."

"I know what Clause 7 deals with." He snapped, like he was getting ready for an argument. "It says *I* get a separate life. Not you." He stabbed the button for the bottom floor with his thumb, yanking the gilded gate closed. "We're not renegotiating *anything* that allows you to be with another man. I don't give a shit if he's your 'family' or not. I told you, I won't…"

"Not for *me*, doofus." She interrupted, a bit insulted that he was trying to turn this all around. *She* wasn't the one filling Avalon's head with fantasy stories of True Love. All Gwen wanted to do was seduce her idiot husband, like any loving wife. "I want to change it for *you*."

That caught him off guard. "What?" He said again.

"So long as we're equal partners, I don't want you to be with other women. I think it's a perfectly fair alteration to the Contract."

Midas' head tilted, like his mind was changing gears so fast it was hard for him to keep up. "I'm not interested in other women." His tone suggested that she wasn't making any sense.

"I heard you talking about your True Love." She crossed her arms over her chest. "I know that's who you're looking for. I don't even blame you." *Much.* "I know you think she's out there. But, until you find her and break the Contract," or *try* to break it, because she'd fight him, "I don't want you sleeping with anyone else. It… hurts me to think of it."

Midas' expression softened. "Kitten, you don't *ever* have to worry about me cheating on you."

The endearment warmed her insides. "Except I *do* worry." How could she not? Everything between them was so right --so *logical*-- but Midas refused to see it. "It wouldn't even be cheating, under the Contract."

Midas watched her with that penetrating gaze. "It would be cheating." He said quietly. "And I don't cheat. I'm not Arthur."

"I know that." Sex with Arthur was icky and painful. Gwen had been happy when he got a mistress and stayed away. She didn't feel that way about Midas. Not even close. "But, the two of us need to be… united." She tried to look business-like. "We're doing all this for the good of the kingdom. Adding other people into our deal will just complicate things. I know we're only fake-married, but it's still *married*." The last part came out like an accusation.

"We are *real*-married." His voice was unequivocal. "There is a scroll to prove it."

"Except you also have a Contract with Clause 7."

"You're the one who wrote that in there."

"You're the one who's looking for his True Love!"

Midas was quiet for a beat, studying her fuming face. "Some people would argue that finding your True Love is bigger than a marriage." He finally said in an unreadable voice.

"*I* wouldn't. One is a legally-binding contract and one is some harebrained fantasy."

He didn't seem to take offense at that opinion. "Would you have left Arthur, if you found your True Love?"

"I don't believe in True Love." She took a deep breath, trying to calm down. "And anyway, I'm focused on finding the Right Man. Not some make-believe soul mate."

Midas' eyebrows drew together again. "And who's the Right Man?"

"He's the person I've been searching for all my life. Merlyn said I would find him. I wrote a list of attributes he'll have. It's very organized and rational and real. ...Unlike *some people's* idiotic quest for cosmic perfection."

"I see." He said, even though he clearly didn't. "What exactly does the Right Man need?"

"I want someone I can trust." Gwen explained. "I want someone who loves Avalon. I want someone who wants to be with me, as much as I want to be with him. *That's* the Right Man. Nothing to do with destiny or True Love. It just matters who he is inside." She tapped her temple. "*He's* the one I've been looking for."

Midas didn't look thrilled with that news. "You're still searching for this guy?" He had the nerve to sound pissed about it.

"Just like you're still pining for your True Love." She retorted. "The woman who you think is 'the best.'" She added air quotes around the word.

"Is it Galahad?" Midas persisted, apparently as annoyed as she was, even though he had no right to be.

"Huh? What in the world does poor Galahad have to do with your intention of... of... just *giving* yourself to this True Love person the second she shows up?" Gwen demanded barely paying attention to his question. "No matter who she is, or what she's done, or why she's even here, you think she's *the best* and that's enough. Do you seriously think that's a solid basis for a real relationship?"

"I think True Love is the *only* basis for a real relationship." There wasn't even an ounce of doubt in his tone. "Everything else is settling."

Gwen looked away, the simple words hurt more than any of

Arthur's betrayals. Her first husband had had no loyalty to anyone. Her second had incredible amounts, all of which he directed at some skanky stranger. That was so much worse.

"Well I think having somebody you actually *know* is a better foundation for a marriage." She said stiffly, her mind whirling with possible schemes to change his mind. "That's not settling; it's *logic*. Something you've obviously left behind for children's stories."

He made a scoffing sound. "Only you would suggest I'm operating from romantic fancy. I'm the least whimsical man in this kingdom, Gwen. Everything I do is logical."

"Bullshit. *I'm* focused on business. *You're* planning your dream wedding to a figment of your imagination." She was seething at his irrational attitude. "So, fine. When our Contract ends, you can have your mythical 'True Love' and I'll stick with my practical, foolproof, *logical* checklist for the Right Man." She slanted him a glare. "And when I find him, he *will* get in line with the practical, foolproof, logical deal I propose."

She'd make sure of it.

Dickhead.

Midas' eyes fixed on the lighted numbers above the door. Weighed down with precious gems, the elevator was painfully slow. Anyone rich enough to own it didn't have to worry about getting places quickly. "Avalon says her daddy is coming soon."

Gwen glanced at him sharply from the corner of her eye. Midas' voice remained tranquil, but she still heard... something in his tone. Suddenly, it occurred to her why he'd been pressing her about Galahad.

"Avalon says a lot of baffling things." Gwen told him, carefully. "Sometimes, the visions in her head can be hard for a five year old to explain.

Midas wasn't convinced. "She says he's the smartest man in the kingdom."

"Did she?" Gwen snorted. "Well, even Avi can make a mistake." She kept her eyes on the elevator doors. "I never slept with the Scarecrow, if that's what you're asking." Just the idea made her shudder.

"I'm asking about Avalon's father. Is he the practical, foolproof, logical Right Man you're waiting for?"

"Avalon's father is dead." Gwen reiterated firmly. "Believe me. I saw Arthur fall off the balcony myself."

That golden gaze sharpened. "Did you?" Just like that, Midas' nimble brain swerved onto a new and dangerous path. "You

were there when Arthur died?"
　　...Well shit.

Chapter Seventeen

In the event that the Contract is terminated or nullified, each party will leave the marriage with the property they brought into it. Therefore, Guinevere Pendragon will retain all estates inherited from her father and/or former husband (provided she can retrieve them from her enemies), her wedding band from Arthur Pendragon, and sole custody of Avalon Pendragon (a minor).

She will not pay alimony to Midas (no last name given).

Clause 20- Disposition of Property of Guinevere Pendragon in Event of Contract's Termination

Gwen glowered over at Midas, pissed that he'd gotten her to say more than she'd intended. "Clause 8- 'Privacy and Disclosure' *specifically* says that I don't have to tell you about Arthur."

"It says you don't *need* to tell me… but it doesn't say I can't ask."

Shit. He was right about the contractual language. As usual. She should refuse to answer him, anyway, but he was looking at her with those hypnotic gold eyes and words just started flowing. "Our bedrooms shared the balcony. Of course I saw Arthur fall. How could I miss it?"

Midas watched her closely. "That must have been traumatic for you."

Gwen nodded, still not liking this topic. "*Very* traumatic."

"How did it happen?"

"It was late. He was drunk and leaning over too far. He lost his balance."

"Exactly what the official report said. A tragic accident."

"*Very* tragic."

"The report didn't say you saw him fall, though."

"I'm sure it did."

"No." Midas sounded one-hundred percent certain. His steel-trap of a memory no doubt recalled every word on every page. "It didn't. Your statement said you were sleeping. Which seems odd, because it *also* said that one of the panes of glass on your balcony door was broken. Seems like the noise of it shattering would have woken you up."

"Oh, that broke long before Arthur died."

"Not according to the maid who cleaned the room that day."

"Well, she's confused then." Gwen shot back. "The palace has a lot of windows, so it would be easy to get mixed up. And *I* was confused, if my statement said I was asleep when Arthur fell. I was understandably upset at the time, so I'm not surprised it got all muddled around in my mind. My husband had just fallen to his death."

"Yes, the whole kingdom mourned. Just check the daily weather reports."

"Pfft." Gwen rolled her eyes at that nonsense. "Camelot's climate was bad way before Arthur died. I don't care what the Scarecrow says, it's the *pollution* making it so gray, all the time. Once I have the crown back, we're instituting a much more comprehensive environmental program. That will fix the gloom and bring back the sun."

Midas' eyebrows soared at her very scientific take on the weather.

"Oh." Gwen mentally winced. Maybe it wasn't the best time to discuss her thoughts on Camelot's abysmal air quality. She should act more grief-stricken. "But obviously, everyone was *very* sad about Arthur." She hurriedly tacked on. "Very, very... sad."

Midas took a deep breath, like he was getting ready to jump into unknown waters. "I wasn't sad." He said distinctly. "I'm still not sad. I always thought Arthur was a colossal asshole. I'm glad he's gone."

Gwen's jaw dropped. No one *ever* criticized Arthur. Even Galahad had made excuses for him. Everybody thought Arthur was perfect. Camelot's shining ideal of manhood. It was astonishing to hear somebody else realize that he was a bastard.

Midas gauged her reaction. "Arthur locked me in the WUB Club, of course, so I'm bound to hold a biased opinion." He went on warily when she didn't respond. "Perhaps he was different in private. With you."

"No." Gwen took a deep breath and jumped into the pool, too. She was never afraid of drowning when Midas was around. "The more you knew him, the more of an asshole he became, actually."

Midas processed that unfiltered response for a beat. "Tell me." He finally said.

And so she did.

"Arthur terrified me. He was violent and malicious and he

hated both me and Avalon. If there had been a safe way to leave him, I would have done it."

Something savage gleamed in Midas' eyes.

"At the beginning, Arthur was just a terrible father, a philandering husband, and a disinterested king." Gwen went on. It was relief not to have to pretend. She sucked at subterfuge. "He was spoiled and arrogant. I could tolerate that. But things changed after Avi was born. He wanted to use Dark Science to 'cure' her and he was furious that I wouldn't go along with it. By the time he died, he was... unhinged."

"You weren't in love with him." It was a statement.

"God no! Not even for a day. I've never loved any man, because none of them have been the *Right* Man."

Her father had seen that Arthur was her destiny --that their child would be a gift to the world-- and so Gwen had done her duty and married him. It had been the logical choice. She'd trusted Merlyn and he'd been right. Avalon *was* a gift. Gwen had never regretted listening to him, because Arthur gave her Avi.

At first, Gwen had even entertained some childish fantasies of her own, imagining their life together. Even if he wasn't the Right Man, she'd hoped they could have a happy family. Those dreams had died quickly in the face of Arthur's cheating and drinking and cruelty. It was always pointless to try and hide from reality.

Before he died, though, Merlyn had left Gwen a recording, promising her that the Right Man was coming. He'd told her he'd seen it. Seen *him*. And, like Avalon, her father was always right. Gwen had been clinging to that hope for years. Sometimes it was all that got her through.

"You love Galahad." Midas persisted. "You told me so."

"But not romantically. Lord, I have no idea how this rumor of our supposed 'affair' keeps circulating."

"Possibly because you have nothing but glowing things to say about the man. Repeatedly and often, across all forms of media. I believe the term you used to describe him to me was 'perfect.'" He bit off the word as if it was coated in poison.

"Of course I said that! Galahad is a *wonderful* person. My best friend." She hesitated, looking at Midas. "One of them, anyway. But, I'm not *in* love with Gal. We're not attracted to each other. No chemistry." She'd always been drawn to rougher, darker, Badder men. Case in point, the rougher, darker, Badder man beside her. "I mean Gal's got *such* a great heart and he's *so* ethical and just *fabulously* gorgeous."

"Oh for God's sake…"

"Well it's true." Gwen defended. "However, he's also very, very, *very*… perfect."

Midas slanted her a quick sideways look, intrigued by her tone. "Wait. Perfect is a *negative* thing to you?"

"Perfect is… beige." Gwen explained. "There's nothing wrong with beige, but nobody is ever excited to see it show up on a date, ya know? It's just inoffensive and easy and… classy." She made a face. "But, classy can be so boring, don't you think?"

Midas' brows climbed up his forehead.

Gwen looked him up and down, taking in his outrageous clothing and wonderfully unhandsome face. "You are *never* beige." She told him happily.

That made him laugh. The unexpected sound caused her stomach to dip in all kinds of pleasurable ways. Gwen had never heard him laugh before. She doubted many people had. The chuckle burst out of him, as if the humor caught him completely off-guard, and it was beautiful.

"I hate beige." He admitted with a grin.

"Why, I never would have guessed." She waved a hand around the bejeweled elevator.

"I do like classy, though. I don't find it boring, at all." He smiled, like a weight had been lifted off of him. "Alright." He said in a lighter tone. "So to recap: you're not in love with beige Galahad."

"Nope."

"And you don't love asshole Arthur."

"*No*. How many times do I need to say it? When he died, I was mostly just relieved."

"Then why is his ring still on your finger?"

Gwen looked down at her wedding band. Truthfully, she'd forgotten it was even there. She'd never much liked the ugly hunk of metal, which was emblazoned with Arthur's crest. Certainly, whatever sentimental attachment she'd once had towards it was gone now. It was the one valuable object she had left, though.

"I wear it in case Avi ever needs food or a place to sleep, of course. It's all I have to sell. The Scarecrow took everything else."

Midas blinked. That pragmatic answer clearly wasn't what he'd been expecting to hear. "You see the ring as currency?"

"Of course. Gold is *money*. You, more than anyone, know that, Midas." Out of habit, she rubbed the smooth surface with her thumb. "It's like a safety net, I guess. No matter what happens, I have *this* and so I know Avalon will be okay."

Midas' brow knitted, staring down at the ring. "I'll buy it from you." He said abruptly, his amusement gone.

"Huh?"

"How much do you want for it? I can pay any amount." He shrugged dismissively. "Millions. Tens of millions. Name it and it's yours."

"I'm not going to take money from you Midas!"

"Why not?" He looked annoyed. "I have plenty. You can use *my* gold to care for Avalon, instead of that damn ring."

Gwen shook her head. "It's not the same."

Jesus, Midas really did think he could purchase anything, didn't he? The countless dolls, and handbags, and rocking-horsefly feeders that he bought for them were one thing. She was confused by the barrage of stuff, but she mostly found it quirky and cute. Gwen got exasperated by his inability to keep track of costs, of course. In her heart, though, she knew Midas was only trying to make her and Avi happy.

But *this* was just insulting. Why did he even want the ring? As a trophy?

Jill's words filtered through her head. *All you are is a trophy to him. Something of Arthur's he can show off.* Gwen trusted Midas, but it was hard to get past the fact that he liked to own things. They couldn't have a real relationship if he thought she had a price attached.

"How is my money not the same as Arthur's money?" Midas demanded, like he was one who should be offended. "Because I'm a criminal and he was the king?"

The man made her want to rip out her hair. "*You're* the king now!"

Midas snorted. "You are alone in that opinion, I assure you."

"It's not an opinion, it's a *fact*. Just like it's a fact that nobody can remove a wedding band from someone else's finger without permission. You know that. You can't even cut it off. They're enspelled." She held up her hand. "No one can *ever* take this from me. Even if you want to enact Clause 11 and end our marriage, I will still have enough money to ensure Avalon eats."

"I'm not going to steal my gold *back* once I pay you, Gwen." He looked really pissed now. "And I'm never going to end our marriage. *Ever.* And I sure as hell wouldn't vanish and leave Avalon out in the cold without any goddamn food. I'm not my fucking parents!"

Gwen's head snapped around. "What?" Only one part of

that really registered with her. "My God, Midas. Did your parents really vanish?"

Midas blinked, like he hadn't expected to tell her that. "I... I don't want to talk about it." He muttered, refusing to elaborate. "All I want to do is buy the damn ring."

She ignored that evasion, imagining him as a little boy, hungry and alone. No wonder money and buying things meant so much to him. He'd spent his childhood in that mud hole of Celliwig, without a family to rely on. How had he survived? Everything Midas had he'd fought for or paid for, all by himself.

"Midas, I think we *should* talk about your parents." She studied his face with stricken eyes. "What happened to you? Trystan said you were raised by a gryphon. Did she take you in after they disappeared? Did they die?"

His jaw ticked. "Clause 8 says I don't need to disclose my past."

Gwen's lips tightened at that stubborn answer. "Clause 8 was written in for me, not you! And you have a hell of a nerve bringing it up, *at all*, considering you've spent days researching my whole life."

"That was well within the parameters of the Contract." He retorted, but now he looked guilty. He liked to pretend he didn't know right from wrong, but his honorable nature wouldn't let him snoop around in shades of gray without his conscience bothering him. "You never had to tell me anything you didn't want to. I simply hired investigators and found it out myself. That's not against the rules."

"It violated the spirit of our agreement and you know it!"

"So, sell me the ring. Then, you'll have plenty of money to hire detectives and do the same thing to me. Quid pro quo."

Gwen crossed her arms over her chest, frustrated with him for a variety of reasons. "My ring is not for sale."

"Everything's for sale."

"*I'm* not."

He glanced at her sharply from beneath his lashes.

"Once you understand that you cannot just buy me," Gwen continued, in a tight voice, "I'll consider your offer."

The elevator bing-ed, finally reaching its destination. Midas muttered a curse and slid the iron gates open to reveal a long, antiseptic hallway lined with neatly numbered doors.

Gwen glanced around. "Your dungeon looks like a hospital." She informed him in a not so pleasant voice.

"I built this house." Midas stepped out of the elevator, gesturing for her to follow. "You think I would build something old and filthy?"

"Why in the world did you build a dungeon, at all?"

He was obviously still mad. "Arthur had a dungeon. Did you ever ask him why *he* had it?"

"No. I knew why he had it: Because he liked to have power over people. He liked to hurt them. It fed his ego."

Midas sent her another sideways look. "That's *not* why I have it."

Gwen sighed. It was so difficult to stay irritated at the man. Even when he was brooding and obstinate, he was just impossibly appealing. "I know."

Midas' first instinct was always to defend those weaker than himself. She wondered if he knew that was the primary duty of a knight. Part of their code. Probably not. Midas lived with honor, without ever being taught their oath. It was just his nature.

He wasn't satisfied by her instant agreement. "I built it, because I was designing a castle and castles have dungeons. It's why I have a moat and throne room, too. I wanted to create the best." He hesitated, looking around. "Until today, no one's ever been locked up down here."

Somehow that didn't surprise her. Midas was so gentle.

She wasn't.

"I never could see the profit in keeping your enemies confined in your home. Practically speaking, it makes more sense to just get rid of them." She paused, thinking it over. "While we're on the subject, I think *I* should be the one to talk to Percival."

"That's a disturbing idea."

"I'm serious. I'm sure I can make him talk."

Midas stalked down the hall. "The man has information we need. If he's going to talk, he must stay alive. With his head attached and his vocal cords functional." He flashed her a pointed look. "Understand?" He actually sounded like he expected Gwen to slaughter their captive right then and there.

"Well, I'm not planning to walk in and kill him!" She protested indignantly.

"With you, I find it's better to prepare for all kinds of possibilities." He stopped by one of the cells and tapped a code into the keypad on the wall. A light flashed green and the door unlocked. "Sometimes you shoot people. Or punch them. Or bash them in the skull."

"Hey, all that stuff just randomly *happened* to me. I'm extremely nonviolent."

Midas didn't look convinced. "Just don't execute the man, yet." He began to pull the door open, only to stop short with his palm on the handle. "I wasn't trying to buy you." He said abruptly, not meeting her eyes.

"It sure felt like it, what with the money being offered and all."

His jaw ticked. "I just want the ring. And when I want something, handing over a great deal of gold is usually the fastest way to get it."

"If you want something from me, the *only* way to get it is to ask. Nicely."

"Ask... *nicely?*" Midas mulled that over, like it was a riddle. "Fuck. Alright." He cleared his throat. "Will you *please* sell me Arthur's ring?"

For a brilliant man, he could be extremely slow at times. "Nope."

Midas glowered at her and yanked opened the door of the cell. "You make everything more complicated than it needs to..." His words halted mid-sentence.

The cell was empty.

Except for the bomb.

Chapter Eighteen

In the case of Midas' (no last name given) death, his estate and property will be dispersed according to his Last Will and Testament.

(Note: As he inexplicably *has* no Last Will and Testament as of the writing of this Contract, Guinevere Pendragon will help him draft one as soon as possible. Until then, his verbal instructions are that his entire estate pass to Mr. Trystan Airbourne, with the understanding that the man: "Give it all to who I'd want to give it to. He knows who I mean. And --f*ck-- tell him to buy himself a really fancy axe or something fun. Live a little.")

Clause 18- Instances of Midas' (no last name given) Death

"GO!" Midas grabbed Gwen by the arm, dragging her back from the cell.

He recognized the bomb on sight. The enchanted device was adhered to the stone wall, a counter ticking off the seconds until it detonated and magical energy blasted out in a shockwave of destruction.

"Oh my God!" Gwen's eyes were huge. "Avalon. Midas, I have to get Avalon!"

Midas was already reaching for his phone, stabbing in the security code for the house. Instantly, the alarm began to blare. "Trystan has her." He herded Gwen down the hall, dialing the gryphon's number. "He'll get her out."

"*I'll* get her out!" Gwen bellowed back. "You think I'll leave my baby...?" Midas passed her phone, cutting her off. "What is this?" She automatically put it to her ear, even though it was on speakerphone. "Hello?"

"I have her." Trystan said on the other end.

"There's a bomb." Gwen's voice broke on a sob, as close to hysteria as Midas had ever heard her. "Get her out of the house. Please."

"We're already out."

Her voice rose even higher. "How in the hell could you already be out? The alarm went off three seconds ago!"

"I can fly."

"Hi, Mommy!" Avalon's voice called. "We's in the sky!"

"Oh God." Gwen closed her eyes, swaying like she felt lightheaded. Her hand grabbed onto Midas' arm to steady herself. "Thank you." She looked up at Midas. "He got her out."

"Good. That just leaves us, then."

"Keep her safe." Gwen told Trystan frantically. "Just keep her safe. Please."

"I have the child. You focus on Midas. We have a deal, woman. We protect them first."

Midas scowled. "What the hell...?"

"I have him." Gwen interrupted. "Don't worry. I won't let anything happen to Midas."

Midas grabbed the phone back from her. "You told my wife to protect *me*, you son of a bitch? Are you out of your goddamn mind?"

"Get out now. Yell at me later." Trystan hung up.

"Crazy, fucking lunatic." Midas glowered at the phone and then at Gwen. "Do not *ever* protect me over yourself. Ever. The only thing that matters to me is keeping you alive." Instead of heading back towards the elevator, Midas headed the other way. "We don't have time to get back upstairs. We need to go through the tunnels."

"You built *tunnels* into your dungeon?"

"All the best castles have tunnels." Midas reached the end of the hall and pressed against a sequence of stone blocks. A hidden door swung open and he pushed her through it. "They had to go on the bottom floor, so my architect tried to tell me it was them or the dungeon. I opted for both, of course. And then hired a new architect."

"Who I'm sure you didn't listen to, either."

"It's my house." Midas said simply. He clicked on the flashlight app and gave her the phone again. "You have to hurry. If the bomb goes off, this tunnel could collapse." He'd paid a fortune to have it built with the finest materials, but he had no idea how strong the bomb might be. "I'm going to go see if I can defuse the damn thing."

"What?!" Gwen's fingers gripped his sleeve, when he tried to duck back into the hall. "No! You're not going back there!"

"I have to. It could take out half my house."

"So you'll build another one. You'll probably do that anyway, the minute you start getting bored." She reached around him to slam the door closed, sealing them into the tunnel. "Do you even know anything about magical explosives?"

"Well, I read a book once..."

"Now's not a great time to show off how smart you are." She interrupted. "You're worth more than a big house, Midas. Worth more than some expensive furniture."

"But, it's *my* big house." The only home he'd ever had. Midas was so angry that he wasn't thinking straight. He knew that, but it didn't help to calm him down. "*My* expensive furniture. I built and bought and designed every piece of..."

"And I'm your wife."

He stopped short, staring down at her.

"I'm your *wife*, Midas." She repeated firmly and then she frowned, like she recalled the circumstances of their wedding. "I mean, maybe it's just a fake marriage..."

"It's not a fake marriage."

She kept talking. "But I still care about you. Very much. And I won't leave you to die."

He felt himself hesitate. "I'll be right behind you."

"You'll be right *beside* me, even if it means we both stay here."

"You can't stay here. Are you crazy? There's a bomb about to go off, Gwen!"

"*Exactly.*"

Midas squeezed his eyes shut. Fuck. He had a lot of confidence in his ability to figure things out. There were six minutes left on that timer. He was pretty sure he could defuse the bomb in six minutes. ...But, what if he couldn't. Was the house or anything in it worth the risk?

No.

Not if it put Gwen in danger. She was more valuable than anything else in the world. Since she wouldn't leave without him, then Midas had to go. There was no other choice.

"Fine." He seized her arm and propelled her down the tunnel. "You owe me a hell of a lot of priceless antiques, though."

"You can add it to my bill."

The passageway was long and rounded, with steel-tiled walls that rose from a neatly paved floor. Midas had seen no reason to commission a substandard tunnel, so he'd even added electricity to it. It took him a second to locate the switch, but, once he hit it, recessed sconces blinked on in a seemingly never-ending row. The metal surface of the walls shone like chrome in the atmospheric light. They also illuminated some priceless statues of naked mermaids and a swimming pool he forgotten he'd built.

Gwen glanced up at him, unimpressed with the spectacle of

excess. "*Really?*"

Midas shrugged. "I was assured it's the best."

She rolled her eyes and headed down the corridor. "You really need to find a better outlet for your shopaholism. If you're going to compulsively spend gold, you could find more worthwhile ways to do it."

"In about five minutes, I'm going to be spending a fortune to put a roof back over our heads. That seems worthwhile."

"It depends on how gilded the roof is." Gwen still had his cellphone, the flashlight bouncing off the walls in the dim glow of the lamps. "Midas?"

"Yes?"

"How do you think a bomb got into that cell?"

"Someone put it there, of course. Someone I know is working with the Scarecrow, freed Percival, and wants us dead. Someone who knows my house well enough to slip in undetected and figure out the code to the cell. Hell, they probably used these tunnels to do it."

"Percival could have had the bomb hidden on him."

Midas shook his head. "Not only did Trystan and I both search the asshole, but he was locked in a room, with two broken arms. He *had* to have help. Someone betrayed me."

Gwen made a face. "I know it won't make much of a difference, since it's *your* house that's about to explode, but the person probably thought he was just betraying *me*. I don't have the best reputation when it comes to keeping husbands alive. He might think he's saving you from me."

"I don't want to be saved. I'm quite content in your Good little clutches."

Gwen sent him a smile.

"Don't be alone with *anybody* except me and Trystan." Midas continued. "Someone I know is working against us. And if that someone thinks they can get away with playing double-agent, they're sadly fucking mistaken." His accent was getting thicker, his anger boiling below the surface. "It's got to be one of those morons from the Round Table. They were here for the party, so they could have figured out a way back in." His eyes narrowed. "I'll bet it's Dower. I should have killed the wolf back in share circle."

"No." Gwen's voice was suddenly very sure. "It was Jill."

"Jill? I mean, I know she's pissed about Arthur's death, but..." He stopped mid-sentence, spotting the figure standing in the tunnel ahead of them.

Jill.

"She ruined my happily ever after with Arthur." There was a two-shot revolver in her hand and it shook with the force of her emotion. "Now you're trying to steal my business, because of her, Midas. I can't let her get away with it."

"Midas isn't going to foreclose on your mortgages." Gwen said, her gaze on the gun. "He's way too kind to ever do something like that."

"Bullshit!" Jill shouted. "He's a villain, just like me." Her eyes were wild as she looked at him. "I thought we were friends, but you took *everything* from me, just so you could fuck Arthur's wife."

"She's *my* wife." Midas shifted so he was in front of Gwen. "Just mine."

"She's brainwashed you. It's magic or something. Everything that's ever gone wrong in my life is because of *her*."

"It's hard to see you as the victim, considering you're trying to kill us." Gwen snapped.

Jill tried to level the gun at her around Midas' huge form, but he wasn't moving. "Jill, you're blaming the wrong person." He kept his tone very even, using her name to try and reach her. "*I'm* the one who threatened to call in all your debts."

"For her!" Jill spat out. "You did it for *her*. It's always about *her*. I was walking out of here, my job done, and I heard her horrible voice echoing, pulling me back. She can't even let me have *this*." She shook her head. "How do you not see it, Midas? Even now you're protecting her."

Midas certainly couldn't dispute that. He kept his body between Gwen and the shaking weapon. "Where did the bomb come from?" He asked instead.

"The Scarecrow. He has a price on your head. He's offering a free pass to any Baddie willing to stand against you." She shrugged. "So I thought... Why not? I remembered these tunnels from your housewarming party and the Scarecrow was only too happy to supply the explosives."

"He wants Gwen alive, though. I'm sure he told you that." The lunatic's whole plan involved marrying the Queen of Camelot and stealing the throne.

"Well, I got him Percival back, instead." Jill retorted. "A bit of a surprise, but it should be enough to smooth over his anger. And if it's not, I'll just deal with him, too. I'm done with men walking all over me." She arched a brow. "I have to look out for myself, now. It's not as if anyone else is going to do it. Not since *she* killed Arthur."

"Arthur's death was an accident." Gwen said quietly. Her hand came up to rest on Midas' back, tapping lightly with all five of her fingers.

He had to stop himself from looking back at her in confusion.

"You killed him and we all know it!" Jill raged, gesturing with the gun. You see?" She looked at Midas, like she expected him to be on her side. "Even now she's trying to spoil things! I was going to be *queen*! Arthur promised me! He would have left her and married me, but she killed him before he got the chance."

Gwen made an aggravated sound, as if this was an old argument. "I was married to Arthur for years before you even met him, Jill. If anything you were the one trying to take him away. And I never interfered, because I didn't really care if the two of you wanted to have an affair..."

"*He was my True Love!*" Jill screamed. "You were the other woman, not me!"

Shit.

Arthur had been Jill's True Love? That was really, *really* bad news.

Jill had loved the bastard and she believed Gwen had murdered him. What would Midas do if someone murdered his True Love? How fucking off-the-rails would he be? How far would he go to get revenge? Blowing up a house would be nothing.

He would burn the world to ash, hoping to die in the blaze.

His eyes met Jill's in a silent moment of understanding. Gwen thought the woman would eventually come out of her grief. She was wrong. No Good folk had any idea what Jill was feeling. The loss and the pain. For God only knew how long, she'd been all alone. Then, she'd found magic, only to have it snatched away. She would kill everybody she deemed responsible for sending her back into the abyss. Any villain would.

There was nothing he could say to stop her.

"True Love?" Gwen repeated in surprise.

"I loved him." Jill's voice cracked. "I loved him so much and now he's *gone*."

"I'm sorry, Jill." Midas actually meant that. "There can be nothing worse than losing your True Love. I can't imagine the darkness." He didn't want to, either.

Gwen tapped his back with four fingers.

"Arthur swore that he'd leave her." Jill continued, willing him to understand. "He promised me that we would be together. He would have made me his queen, if he'd just had more time."

No. Arthur never would've done that. Midas knew it and, deep down, so did Jill. No Good folk would put a villain on Camelot's throne. He was actually confused as to why Gwen hadn't given up on the notion of making him king, yet. He kept expecting her to realize it was a hopeless idea.

Behind him, Gwen tapped his back with three fingers and Midas realized she was counting down to something. He had no clue what she was planning, but he was willing to go with it. It was probably better than his current idea of just making Jill shoot him twice, so Gwen could get away. They were running out of time.

Midas resisted the urge to check his watch. "That bomb is going to go off soon, Jill." He warned.

"After he died, I thought," Jill swallowed, not even hearing him, "'at least Guinevere would be punished. At least everyone hates her. At least she's locked in a dungeon. At least the Scarecrow will take her crown.'" She shook her head. "But then *you* had to get involved. And I know you, Midas. You're going to make sure she has *everything.*"

"Yes." There was no sense in denying it. Gwen tapped his back with two fingers and Midas gave an almost imperceptible nod.

"I can't let it happen. I *can't.* Guinevere has to die." Jill wiped at her eyes. "But, I don't want to kill *you*, Midas. I've always liked you. You're ugly and cold and crass, but you never made me feel cheap. Not even once."

Gwen gave an outraged gasp, although Jill had meant her words as a compliment. "Midas is none of those things!"

"Shut up!" Jill shrieked. "You're about to kill him, just like you killed Arthur! *He* can walk out of here, right now. *You're* the only one I want dead. If he dies, it's *your* fault."

Gwen hesitated. "You'll let him go?"

"Of course I will. *You're* the one I hate. He can leave, but you stay."

Gwen actually started to move around Midas, willing to make that deal. "Fine. Yes. You and I will do this, Jill, and Midas can go. That's fair."

"No." Midas put his arm back, keeping her behind him.

"Yeah, but..."

"Stay right where you are." He flashed her a warning look. "I have never been more serious in my life."

She frowned, but stopped trying to get around him.

Jill snorted. "You used to be smarter than this, Midas. I swear to God, you did."

Midas glanced back at her. "I won't leave my wife." He told her softly. "I won't go back into my own darkness. I can't."

Jill's lips parted, understanding what he meant. Realizing for the first time that Gwen was his True Love. Knowing that he was going to fight and die to protect her. "No." She frantically shook her head. "*No!*"

Gwen gave up on her idea to be a martyr and tapped his shoulder with one finger.

Midas moved. He leapt at Jill, taking a chance that he could survive long enough to get the gun from her grasp. At the same time, Gwen shined the flashlight right in Jill's face.

"Shit!" Jill instinctively shut her eyes, turning away from the beam. The bullet she fired at Midas, went wide, slamming into his arm. The same damn arm that the King's Man had injured at Merlyn's house. Son of a bitch, the fucking thing had just started to heal.

"Midas!" Gwen screamed.

He wrapped his hand around Jill's wrist, forcing the muzzle towards the ceiling. The two of them spun around, locked in struggle. "God*damn* it, Jill. This is stupid." He could have broken her bones with little effort, but that wasn't what he wanted. "Just give it up, so we can get out of here."

She tried to shoot him in the head, but the bullet ricocheted off the ceiling, instead. The sound was deafening in the tunnel. The gun only had two shots, though, and she'd just spent them both. Midas wasn't taking a chance that she'd reload. He wrenched it out of her hand.

Gwen was already beside him, latching on to his wounded arm and surveying the damage in the dim light. "Oh my God, you're bleeding! He's bleeding!" She gave Jill an angry shove. "You psychotic *bitch!*"

"Don't touch me!" Jill staggered backwards, close to deranged. "I'm not going to spend my life in prison or as some golden statue for the two of you to laugh at!" She took off running, back in the direction of the dungeon. "I'll be with Arthur, somewhere where you'll never steal our happiness!"

"Fucking hell." Midas tossed the gun aside and started after her. "Come back! *Jill!*"

"No!" Gwen gripped his shirt sleeve, tugging him to a stop when he would have followed her. "You were right. We have to *go.*"

"She'll die back there."

"That doesn't mean you have to."

"I can't just..."

"It was her choice, not yours. You're not wasting your life for someone who just tried to shoot you and blow up my baby." Gwen pulled him towards the exit. "We can't have much more than a minute to get out of here, Midas. You *can't* go back for her." She shook him as best she could, considering their size difference. "*I'm* the heartless one. Listen to me and not your damn gallantry. There's no time! Avalon needs us. *Please*. You know I'm right."

She was right.

Shit.

He only had a matter of seconds to get his True Love to safety.

Midas' jaw tightened. "Go." He seized Gwen's arm, half carrying her so she could keep up. "Goddamn Arthur just killed her." It incensed him to even think about it. "He fucking killed her, just as much as the bomb will."

"I didn't know." Gwen insisted, running alongside him. "I knew she loved him, but I didn't know she thought Arthur was her True Love. I don't even believe in True Love." She sounded out of breath. "Arthur never said anything about it. Maybe he didn't know either."

"He knew." Arthur would have known the truth the moment he slept with Jill. No doubt he'd been simultaneously thrilled with his control over her and disgusted that she was Bad. He would have done everything he could to tear her down, all the while using her devotion for his own ends. It was no wonder she went crazy.

"He *also* never said he was leaving me. I swear, I would have let him. Happily."

"He was never going to leave you for Jill." Midas scoffed.

Give up Merlyn's classy, pedigreed daughter for a villain who ran a gentlemen's club? Not fucking likely. Arthur was a man who liked having his cake and eating it, too. Why wouldn't he keep his Good queen *and* his Bad mistress? It made total sense, if you were a sociopathic narcissist.

"But Arthur would want to be with his True Love, right? That's the way it's supposed to work."

"It works that way if you're Bad. Arthur was Good." Biologically, anyway. "He would never link himself to a Bad folk, no matter who she was. True Love doesn't mean as much to Good folk."

She looked incredulous. "Your explanation is that Good folk don't feel love?"

"Maybe they feel it, they just don't care."

Gwen didn't like that answer. He could tell from her

expression. But he didn't have a better one to give her.

They reached the end of the tunnel, bursting out into the moonlight. They were in the gardens, which was right where he wanted to be. Midas did a quick look around, orienting himself, and spotted a wall separating the manicured lawn from the woods beyond. It was nine feet high, two feet thick, and made of brick forged in dragon fire.

The very best wall money could buy.

"This way." He stomped right over the carefully tended flower beds, trying to put as much distance between the house and Gwen as he possibly could. Avalon's new rocking-horsefly feeders were knocked over. No matter. He'd buy her more. "I'm going to lift you up and you get over that wall, okay?"

She shook her head emphatically. "No, way. I'm too heavy and you're bleeding too badly..."

"I'm fine." He interrupted. Growing up in Celliwig, you learned to block out pain and survive. He'd cleaned stables with broken bones and gaping wounds, lifting far heavier loads than his petite wife. He didn't even wince as he grabbed her around the waist and hefted her above his head. "Up you go, kitten."

Gwen had no choice but to go along with the plan. Muttering curses, she clambered onto the top of the wall, looking back to make sure he was following her. "Midas?" She extended a hand down to help him up, which was simply adorable, considering he outweighed her by at least a hundred and forty pounds.

"I'm here. Just stay right where you are." Midas scaled the bricks by himself, pausing beside her to touch her hair. "It's going to be okay." He swung his body around so he could drop to the other side. The landing jolted his injured arm, sending agony coursing through him. He ignored it. "Alright." He held out his hands. "Jump and I'll catch you."

Even in the darkness, he could see her shaking her head, again. "I'll hurt you. Give me a second and I'll figure out how to get down on my own."

"We don't have a second. Just get down here, *now*."

"Are you crazy? You'll be injured even worse than..."

The explosion cut her off.

The entire left side of his house detonated, sending fire and wreckage into the sky. No way had Jill survived a blast of that size. The shockwave alone sent Gwen catapulting from the top of the wall.

"*Fuck!*" Midas threw himself at her, grabbing her as she fell. He twisted his body in midair, ensuring that she landed on top of him, both his arms cradling her against the impact. The two of them hit the ground hard enough to knock the wind from his body. Gwen lay across his chest, ominously still.

"Gwen?" He instantly flipped her around, so she was beneath him. The massive wall stopped the main force of the bomb, but fiery debris was raining down. Midas made sure his body was shielding her from it, even as he tried to revive her. "Gwen?"

She was unconscious.

Oh God...

Midas put his hands on either side of her face, terror filling him. "*Gwen!*" For one horrible second, he was nine years old again, huddled on a porch in the cold night. Without Gwen, there was no light. This tiny, fragile being was all that stood between Midas and the darkness. "Don't leave me. Gwen, don't leave me all alone!"

She came to with a gasp, her fingers grasping his wrists. "Midas." She got out.

"I'm here." Relief had his voice breaking. "I'm here. Oh God, thank you." He swallowed hard, trying to check her for injuries. "Are you hurt? Where are you hurt, kitten?"

"I'm okay." She tried to sit up, but he pushed her back down. "Midas, I'm okay. I promise. You're the one who was shot."

"It just grazed me." He spared his arm a disinterested look. "I'll heal. You're the only thing that matters to me."

She didn't respond to that, looking around and noticing all the flaming rubble surrounding them, for the first time. Noticing that Midas was sheltering her from it with his body. Lake-blue eyes cut back up to his and her head tilted. "You saved me. Again."

"I'll always protect you."

"Why?" She asked softly.

Feeling exposed, Midas eased back from her. "You know why." Everyone knew why. He might as well just take out that billboard and announce it to the world. In fact, sooner or later, he probably would.

Gwen followed him, sitting up. "Because I'm your wife?"

"Yes."

"What does that mean to you, though? Am I just a possession?"

One day he would figure out how her mind worked, but today wasn't it. "What?" He demanded, rescanning her for head injuries.

"Am I just something you collected, because I was Arthur's wife?"

Why the hell were they discussing this nonsense *now?* "No."

The one-word answer didn't satisfy her. As usual. "I'm not a trophy, Midas."

"I know that."

Her hand wrapped around his vividly patterned necktie. "What do you want from me? Be honest, because our connection feels real to me and if it's not for you..."

"It's real." He offered no resistance at all as she tugged on his tie, bringing his head down to hers. "Everything I've ever said to you is real." Her lips were millimeters from his and he nearly groaned. She was safe and beautiful and smelled like gingerbread. "Everything I feel for you is real, Gwen."

"Good folks can feel things, too." Her free palm came up to rest on his cheek. "I promise you." She lifted her mouth to his, giving him the gentlest kiss imaginable.

Midas' eyes drifted shut.

The wash of emotions he experienced around Gwen was far more than just satisfaction at finding his True Love, or arrogance at owning a queen, or happiness that he was no longer alone. It was so much *more* than any of the half-hearted excuses he'd come up with. So much simpler.

He was just head over heels in love with this crazy woman.

Fuck it. The billboards were going to be neon.

Chapter Nineteen

There is no expectation, implied or stated, that the parties' union will ever be consummated.

Clause 4- Physical Activity Between Parties

"The wizards finally called me back." Gwen said, three afternoons later. "They want to meet us."

Midas grunted, looking completely unenthusiastic about the prospect of traveling to the Emerald City. "Fine. I'll take you out there tomorrow."

He was working to repair his bejeweled elevator, standing on a ladder with the control panel open and lots of impressive tools lying around. The bomb had knocked it out of alignment and Midas didn't seem to trust anyone else to fix it properly.

Carefully vetted contractors were already working to rebuild the rest of the house. Midas' palace was huge, so the bomb hadn't impacted most of it. The bedrooms and kitchen were fine. He'd just sealed off the East Wing, so the repairs could be finished without impacting life for anyone living there. The most upsetting part of the whole ordeal had been digging out Jill's body and giving her a proper funeral. Otherwise, everyone had bounced back quickly. Midas' shoulder was healing, Gwen didn't even have a twinge of a headache, and Avalon couldn't stop talking about how Trystan had carried her up into the sky.

"The wizards want to meet *us*, Midas." Gwen reiterated, stressing the pronoun. "They want to talk to you, too."

He glanced at her and she could see his doubts. "About what?"

"You're going to be king." She stood in the gilded doorway, watching him work. "They just want to be sure you're not all the vile things Arthur said you were."

His jaw tightened. "And if I am?"

"You're *not*."

He didn't seem convinced.

"This will work, Midas." She assured him. "Besides the Scarecrow *hates* the Emerald City. If my father hid the wand with that jackass in mind, 'the last place he'd want to look,' will be somewhere inside those walls. This could be our best chance to find it."

Midas sighed and rotated his shoulder.

Gwen was instantly concerned by the uncomfortable motion. "Are you feeling okay?" A witch-practitioner had come to hasten the healing of his bullet wound with magical medicines, but you couldn't be too careful. "Do you need to sit down?"

"I'm fine."

"You're doing too much. You should be resting. Why don't you go lay down and I'll make you some soup? Wait. Shit, I have no idea how to cook soup. A pie!" She nodded enthusiastically. "I make an excellent pecan pie. Do you want a pie?"

His lips quirked up at the corners. "Maybe later." He climbed down the ladder to stand in front of her. "Let's backtrack to the wizards. They aren't going to support you for queen, if you're married to me. That's the bottom line here."

"Of course they will. They have to. It's the law."

"No Good folk will ever put a Bad folk on the throne, regardless of what the rules say. Trust me." He crooked a finger at her, beckoning her closer. "Stand out of the way, kitten. I'm going to test the door.

She stepped into the elevator car, her eyes staying on him. "If the wizards won't support our partnership, then we'll win Camelot without them."

Midas didn't respond to that. He hit the glittery "close" button and the door slid shut.

Gwen smiled. He'd done it. She'd never had a doubt. Midas could do anything. "Besides, the wizards will love you." She assured him. Nobody who met this man could fail to see how special he was. "Really. You don't need to worry. My father was friends with all these guys. That's why they're opening the gates for us. They're like my uncles."

"And I'm just the guy every man wants for a nephew-in-law." He muttered, climbing back up the ladder to secure the control panel.

She made an "umm" sound, barely listening. When he stretched his arms up to screw the door closed, the muscles in his biceps bulged and it was... awesome. She could've happily watched him all day.

Midas didn't seem to notice her mentally undressing him. "Gwen, we need to have a serious talk."

"I was thinking the same thing."

"Were you? Well... good. I expected that. By now, you're

seeing this whole idea is crazy, right? Trying to make me king is just not going to work. I'm glad we agree."

"Huh?" What was he talking about?

He looked frustrated, realizing that she wasn't paying attention. "It would be better if you tried to work out a deal where you would be queen, *without* me being king. They'll give you the crown a lot easier."

Gwen squinted. "That's ridiculous."

"It's not." He argued, warming to his topic. "We can stay married, but I don't have to be involved in ruling Camelot or..."

Gwen cut him off. "I can't do this without you, Midas. Equal partners."

He studied her determined face for a moment. "Fuck."

Gwen bit back a grin, hearing victory in the quiet oath. The man cursed *waaaay* too much, but he could infuse "fuck" with so much meaning that it was hard not to appreciate his talent. "Now that we've settled that, why don't we discuss what *I* wanted to talk about? It's really a lot more interesting."

"Fine." Midas dropped down from the ladder, looking annoyed at the world. "What's on your mind?"

"Us."

"Us?" He echoed warily and sent her a suspicious look. "You and me?"

"Yes, you and me! What other 'us' is there, dummy?"

"I'm not sure. I've never been part of an 'us' before, so..."

Gwen cut him off, focused on her new goal. "We need to think about taking the next step, Midas." She'd given him time and it was glaringly obvious *he* wasn't going to initiate anything, so she'd just do it herself. Unlike some huge mobsters, she wasn't particularly shy. "I know you're feeling hesitant, but there's really no sense in putting off the inevitable here."

He squinted, like he was waiting for the other shoe to drop. "Which is what?" He hit the button for the third floor, testing the mechanics, and the elevator slowly started moving.

"I'm glad you asked." She slammed her thumb down on the elevator's emergency stop button, ignoring the way Midas had to brace his hand on the wall to stay steady as the car lurched to a halt. She was on a mission, now. "You said that if I ever had needs, we could renegotiate the Contract, remember? The very first night we met. Well, I have needs."

Midas' head snapped around to gape at her. "What?"

He just wasn't getting it. Luckily, Gwen was a woman who

knew how to drop subtle clues. "We should have sex. Right now."

Midas slowly blinked, a mystified expression on his face.

Gwen pressed onward in the face of his silent astonishment. "I mean, we're married, and I want to, and you said we could."

"You want to have sex? With me?"

"Of course with you!" Why was he so confused? "You're my husband, aren't you?"

"Yes." The air left his lungs in a rush, like the word had knocked the breath out of him. "I'm your husband." He made no move to restart the elevator.

"So --I know it's a business deal-- but maybe we could also be *closer*. It's probably the most practical choice, all things considered. I mean, I'm very content with our arrangement, so far. I don't see me breaking the Contract soon." She braced herself. "Do you plan on breaking it soon?"

"I don't ever plan on breaking it." Total surety echoed in his tone.

Gwen sagged back in relief.

"But touching you isn't safe." He continued. "*I'm* not safe. I told you that."

"So we'll be careful. It will be okay if you keep your gloves on, right? Isn't that how you manage with other women?"

"You're not other women." Midas muttered, but she could see him mulling it all over in his lightning-fast brain. He was focused on this idea.

Gwen took that as a good sign.

"I want to reopen negotiations on Clause 7- 'Separate Lives and Other Relationships'." She said candidly. No matter what people said about "tact" and "diplomacy," she always found it was better to just put it all out there. "Then we can begin having sex and fulfilling my needs."

"Clause 7 never mentions sex between us."

"Well, *I* say we can't have sex unless we are both exclusive. So no more separate lives." She shook her head. "Now, you said you'd fulfill my needs, if I ever wanted it. That's verbally binding. We just need to do some negotiation on the fine print and we'll have a workable deal."

"Why are you doing this?" Midas seemed genuinely baffled. "Why do you want to have sex with *me*? You could have anybody. Knights with TV shows, for instance. There are far better candidates for kings and husbands than some…."

She cut him off, before he could call himself a tawdry, feral animal again. "I'm attracted to *you*, Midas. I want to be with *you*. You're in my head all the time."

Midas flinched at her words like he felt them as a physical blow and looked away, breathing hard. "*Fuck*." For once, he actually seemed rattled. "No. *No*. We can't... It would... complicate things if we had sex." His hand came up as if he desperately wanted to hit the proper button and get the elevator moving again.

Gwen stepped in front of him, preventing him from pressing it. "Do you not want me back?" It came out in a smaller voice than she'd intended. Maybe these new feelings were all one sided, after all.

That golden gaze jumped to hers, burning and hungry, and relief filled her.

"Don't be a fool, Gwen." He said softly. "I have wanted you from the second we met. You had to have seen that. Everyone else in Camelot has seen it. I just don't... Sex isn't..."

"You don't like sex?" She guessed excitedly, cutting him off. "That's okay. I've always found it lackluster in the past, but there are other things we could do." Her incredible attraction to Midas made her positively creative. She had all kinds of wonderfully shocking ideas. "We could try them instead."

She had his full attention, now. "...We could?" He asked in a strange voice and his hand dropped away from the start button.

"Absolutely." Gwen nodded, ready to hard-sell the details. She felt a little bad about strong-arming Midas into another deal, but she couldn't stop herself. She just *had* to convince him or she'd go out of her mind with lust. "I'm thinking we could agree to a safe, simple test of --like-- third base behavior. Once a day, we could engage in said behavior and see if we enjoy it."

Midas' brows rose. "See if we *enjoy* it?" He echoed incredulously.

"Exactly. We can alternate days of who's --um-- satisfied. If we don't enjoy it, we can stop and go back to the way we are now. If we *do* enjoy it, we can just... continue. It's a very practical and no-risk arrangement." She paused. "*If* you agree to void Clause Seven. No other women, Midas. Not even if you find your wonderful, perfect 'True Love.'" She added air quotes around the word, again.

It had rattled her deeply to hear him discussing Arthur and Jill's relationship in such black and white terms. Not only did Midas want his True Love, he wanted her to be Bad. He thought Good folk were cold and unfeeling. He clearly had a picture of this girl in his head and Gwen needed to change it for him. He could thank her later.

"Finding my True Love isn't going to be an issue." He assured her.

"*I* know that, but I don't think you do."

He arched a brow. "And what if you find your Right Man?"

Gwen shrugged, hoping he couldn't tell her heart was pounding in her chest. "Until one of us wants to end the Contract under Clause 11- 'Termination of Marriage,' we're monogamous." She stipulated. "Just you and me and no one else."

The edges of his mouth curved. "Just you and me and no one else." The words were dark and full of promise. "Always, Gwen."

That sounded reassuringly definite. Still... "If you cheat on me, I'll leave you." She warned, not even considering what that would mean for Camelot. "The very first time, will be the end of our marriage."

Midas' head tilted. He didn't look upset over the threat, just intrigued that she'd issue it. "Why didn't you leave Arthur, when *he* cheated on you?"

"I never trusted him, so it didn't matter who else he slept with." Her eyes met his. "But I *do* trust you, Midas. So it *would* matter. A lot. When you tell me we're equal partners, I believe you. ...Because I believe *in* you and in the fact that you're an honorable man."

Midas stared at her, not saying anything.

"So is it a deal?" She prompted after a long moment of silence.

He swallowed. "You think I'm an honorable man. I'm not." His voice was serious. "But, for you, I'm going to try one more time to talk you out of the plan. It *will* complicate things."

"Is it a deal?" She repeated, not worried about his dire predictions.

Midas sighed and gave up. "Of course, it's a deal. What the hell do you think? I'm a fucking villain, Gwen. Obviously, I'm going to say 'yes' to a plan that contractually guarantees my right to do Bad things to your Good little body."

"Excellent." She held out her hand, ready to shake on it, only to pull back as she remembered another important point. "But try not to call me by anyone else's name when we're together. I don't like that."

Midas's eyes went wide again. "Arthur...?" He trailed off, pinching the bridge of his nose as if he was in pain and muttering something like: "Be glad you're dead, you fucking son of a bitch."

Gwen frowned in confusion. "What?"

"Never mind." He took a deep breath, raising his voice to

normal volume. "That's fine. I want to add a caveat to the deal, too."

Gwen nearly pouted. "What kind of caveat?" Damn it, he was usually willing to agree to whatever deal she put in front of him.

"Clothes stay mostly on. If we're naked, I'm not going to be able to hold back and I don't want to risk losing control. If we have sex, it would be… problematic."

Maybe someone had mistreated him in the past and now he was scared. She couldn't imagine why else he'd be so reluctant to consummate their marriage. Celliwig was a terrible lawless place, so God only knew what had happened to him as a child. Gwen's heart broke, just thinking about some monster hurting him. Midas might be a huge gangster on the surface, but underneath he was so gentle. So kindhearted. It was a wonder he'd survived, at all.

"Of course." She agreed softly. "We don't have to do anything you're not comfortable with. I promise."

He glanced at her sharply, as if reading her mind, and his mouth curved. "You truly are a Good person, Gwen." He murmured. "Not because you were *born* Good. Because you *are* Good. You're right. It's actions which define us and yours are always pure."

What a sweet thing to say. He was totally wrong about her, but it was still sweet. "I'm not always Good, you know." For instance, sometimes she pressured her gallant husband into sexually compromising situations, before he was ready.

…And didn't even feel guilty about it.

He shook his head, not believing the truth. "You are the best person I've ever known." He reached over to touch her hair and she expected him to pull his hand back at the last second, like he usually did. Instead, his gloved fingers hesitantly brushed her blonde curls and he let out a long sigh. "The very best, Gwen."

Well, nobody could say she didn't warn him. "So we're doing this, then?" Gwen smiled and extended her hand before he could change his mind. "As usual, it's a pleasure doing business with you, partner."

"Likewise." His fingers left her hair to shake her outstretched palm. Instead of releasing her after the handshake, he tugged her closer to his huge body. "Shall we begin?"

Her insides dipped at his deep tone. "Right now?" She looked around the elevator. "Here?"

"Right now." He maneuvered backward, towards the pink velvet bench at the back of the car. "Here. You have needs, remember?"

"Well, the agreement is to alternate days, so you can go

first." She offered, nerves jangling inside of her. As usual, Midas was going along with her plan, but suddenly she wasn't so sure she could pull it off without looking like an idiot. What seemed easy in her head was a lot more daunting in reality. Midas was probably used to someone with way more... pizzazz. What if she was too beige for him?

"I can take my turn tomorrow." She nodded, wanting to do a good job of seducing him. "Would you rather me use my mouth on you tonight? Or my hands? I'm almost positive I'd be incredible at that."

Midas' eyes glazed over for a second, like he was picturing that idea in his head and liking everything he saw. "No." He shook his head, trying to clear it. "Don't distract me."

She blew out an anxious breath as the backs of her knees hit the bench. "Midas?" She whispered, suddenly uncertain. Self-assurance usually came easily to her, but this all felt so new and fragile.

One of his arms came up to brace against the ornate wall of the elevator behind her, caging her in. It was all she could do not to spontaneously combust. "Yes?"

"I've never been with anyone but Arthur."

He seemed startled. "No one?"

"Until you, I've never even kissed anybody else. I *would* have," she added, because she wanted to be totally honest, "but everyone stayed away. From the time I was a child, everyone said I was Arthur's."

"They were wrong."

"Well, nobody else seems to think so." She brightened. "You are a *much* better kisser than he was, though."

Midas' mouth curved. "You'd be surprised at how often I hear that."

"I just wanted you to know. About the not-having-a-lot-of sex part, I mean." She paused. "You believe me, right?"

"Yes." His voice was gentle and predatory at the same time. "Do you want to stop and think about this some more, kitten?"

"No, of course not. I'm just..." She hesitated, trying to marshal her thoughts. "Arthur was really bad in bed and it was *such* a disappointment."

Midas smirked, not looking very sympathetic.

"I'm telling you all this, because I really want to enjoy sex, so..." She trailed off and blew out a breath, wandering how to phrase her request in a not-brash-around-the-edges way. "So don't suck at this, okay?"

"I'll do my best." He assured her dryly.

"And I'll tell you if things start going lackluster."

"Oh, I'm sure you will." Golden eyes glinted with amusement.

Damn it. Her wording had probably been too blunt, but she wasn't sure how to soften the offer. "You can tell me if I'm lackluster, too." She tacked on, trying to make it better. "I don't mind feedback. I mean, I'm sort of new at this, if you don't count a few times with Arthur."

"Believe me, I never count Arthur."

She took a deep breath, confidence returning. "I think I'm going to be *awesome* at sex, now that my partner isn't a total asshole. Still, everyone can grow from constructive criticism." She waved a hand. "So feel free to offer advice and I'll do the same."

Midas shook his head, his expression filled with something more than just lust. "I have no idea what I did with my days before you came along, Gwen. Everything must have been so drab and predictable." He dipped his head so it was next to her ear. "Sit down on the bench for me."

She looked behind her and then back up at him. "Really?"

"Now."

Well, when he put it that way… Gwen sat on the bench, the pillow-y cushions nearly swallowing her. It felt decadent.

"You might want to lie back." He suggested, his gaze hot. "This could take a while."

"Really?" Gwen said again. With Arthur it had never taken long. Sitting on the bench and looking up at Midas felt kinda interesting, though. He was so big and strong as he loomed over her. It made her insides feel delightfully fizzy.

"*Now*." He knelt down in front of her, still a head taller than Gwen. His hands slipped under her skirt and slid up the inside of her legs. "Just lay back and try not to worry so much."

"I'm not worried. But I know I pushed you into this, so if you feel uncomfortable or your arm hurts or you want to take a break, we could…" His palms grazed the inside of her knees and Gwen lost her train of thought. She felt herself sinking backwards over the cushions.

"So Arthur cheated on you, but you didn't cheat on him." Midas mused quietly, still focused on her not-really-*that*-important confession. "Why bother to stay faithful to that jackass? Even if you didn't want Galahad, there must have been others."

"I was married. It would've been wrong." Of course, that staunch moral stance would have lasted about two seconds if Midas had shown up. The man was irresistible. His gloved hands were strong and gentle and not at all like Arthur's. Gwen found herself melting into them.

"Right and wrong are always so clear to you. I envy that."

"Not really." She hated to deceive him about herself. "I'm pretty heartless. I mean, strong-arming you into this is wrong, but I did it anyway. I know you would rather wait for your True Love."

"I'm sure she'll understand." His thumb brushed higher, skimming the inner flesh of her thigh, and she jolted. "Is it getting lackluster, yet?"

"No, I just…" She blinked rapidly. Something hot and wet was beginning to tighten inside of her. Something she'd never experienced before with anyone else in the room. Since the world had kept other men away from Gwen, she'd invented her own. Usually it was just her and a vibrator and some fantasies about strapping stable boys. "You're really not sucking at this so far."

"Thank you. I appreciate feedback, too. Especially when it's positive."

"Just… um… let me know if you want to stop. We can even come up with a safe-word or something, if it makes you feel more secure."

"That's very considerate."

Long minutes went by as he explored her flesh and it didn't seem like he wanted to stop. Neither did Gwen. She forgot about everything except Midas. He nudged her knees, wanting more access, and she parted them as willingly as water. Big hands reached the edge of her panties and then glided back down to her ankles.

The hot, wet tightness was getting tighter. And wetter. And hotter. Okkkayyyy. This was new. Gwen's breathing got faster. "I think… you can touch me higher, if you want." She finally decided, needing his fingers to go just a little bit farther. "That would be okay."

He made a low sound of approval. "You have beautiful legs, Guinevere." He leaned forward to kiss the curve of her calf, his teeth nipping her skin.

"You think so?" She asked in surprise.

"I *know* so."

"I always thought they were too short." Someone like Midas was probably used to tall, curvy showgirl types. "Maybe a little lackluster?"

"No. They're absolutely perfect." His tongue rasped across a freckle and she stopped arguing. Her eyes drifted shut in pleasure, as his hands traveled back up to her thighs and his mouth followed it.

"You are definitely not lackluster, either." Without even thinking about it, her palms caressed his thick hair, still urging him higher. "Whatever you're doing, you should just keep it up. I think you're really onto something here." There was a hitch to her voice now. "Please, just a little higher."

The small plea sent a rumbling growl through him. Teeth grazed her inner thigh and she could barely breathe.

"In fact, you should probably do *more*." She recommended. "Do more and don't stop. I know I said you could stop, but don't stop. Please, please, *please* don't stop."

"I'm not going to stop, kitten." He assured her in a husky tone. "Don't worry. Nothing in the world could make me stop."

His head was between her legs now and she barely noticed. It was hard to focus on anything except how hot and wet and *tight* she felt. "Midas." She needed more, but she wasn't sure how to ask for it. "Please." Her hips instinctively arched towards him.

He met her gaze over the length of her body and his hand finally slid under the edge of her panties. Unerringly, he touched the spot that was throbbing for his attention and Gwen sighed in relief. *Finally*. Even through the gloves, he could no doubt feel the moisture coating her hidden thatch of curls. That should probably embarrass her, but it didn't.

Gwen just wanted more.

"Oh *yes*." Her head went back as he played with her weeping flesh. Her knees fell all the way open, giving him total access. "Oh God." Her eyes were wide and sightless. "Oh please." She didn't even notice when the panties were tugged off completely, all her attention on the massive finger filling her. He tunneled it deeper, stretching her small channel, and Gwen gave a desperate cry.

"Jesus." He was sweating, now. "You're so *tight*." He watched his hand move with a rapturous expression. "So beautiful. Can you take another one, kitten?" He began squeezing a second finger into her, without giving her a chance to respond and Gwen whimpered in need. The sound had his breath sawing in and out. "That's it. That's my Good girl."

She wasn't feeling very Good at the moment. In fact, she felt wonderfully, gloriously Bad. Gwen bit down on her lower lip, trying to hang on. Not even her strapping stable boy fantasies were this amazing.

"So tight." His voice was thick as he pressed both fingers home. "And small. Fucking hell, you're small." He shook his head, as if he was trying to focus. "Goddamn it, I'm *so* much bigger than you,

Gwen."

"I *know*." It came out as a purr. The weight of his fingers felt incredible inside of her. Gwen's hips moved, riding them up and down, needing something just out of reach.

"*Goddamn it*." He said again and it was somewhere between a snarl and a groan. "This is wrong. You're too delicate for me to touch. I'm rough and coarse and you're like fucking silk and magic." He started to draw back. "What am I doing? My hands shouldn't be on you. I could *hurt* you. I can't..."

Her palm came up to cradle his face and he stopped talking, like he'd been hypnotized. Golden eyes locked on hers, his cheek unconsciously leaning into her touch. In that moment, the Kingpin of Camelot was totally at her mercy.

"You're not hurting me." She promised. "You would never hurt me, Midas."

"You want me to keep touching you?" He sounded like he needed to make sure.

"*Yes.*" She smiled up at him. "I'm not going to break. I promise. I'm just the right size for you. Do whatever you want to do, just keep doing it."

"Whatever I want?"

"Anything. Just don't stop. Please."

He slowly smiled at that and dipped his head. "Alright." He gently blew over her soaked flesh and Gwen saw stars.

"*Midas.*"

The sound of his name had him growling in lust. "My wife." His mouth settled on her wet, naked, aching core. "Mine."

Gwen screamed, her hands fisting in his dark hair. Wanting to push him away. Wanting to pull him even closer. His tongue and his lips and his teeth... It was all too much. It was happening too fast. She tried to twist beneath him, afraid of the sensation building inside of her. Those massive hands seized her hips, not letting her escape. Demanding all of her. Licking and sucking and it was actually going to happen! She was going to...

He stopped.

Gwen gave a choked cry, her horrified eyes finding his. "What are you doing?" She wailed. "Don't *stop*. I told you not to stop! You promised you wouldn't stop!"

"I'm renegotiating." He was out of breath. "Next time, you're naked. My clothes have to stay on, but you're fucking naked in my arms, Gwen."

She needed to climax so badly she was shivering. She'd

never come with another person before. She hadn't thought she *could* come with another person, but Midas was making it happen. "Your pants come off." She got out, because he'd never respect her if she took the first offer. "Now fucking *finish*."

He gave an un-Midas like grin at her negotiating and leaned over her. One hand braced by her head, while his other pressed open the swollen folds of her body. "I just *love* that it's impossible to know what you're going to say next." Those big fingers surged inside of her, as deep as they could go, and there was no way to hold back.

"*Oooohhhh*." Gwen's whole body came off the velvet bench, the force of her orgasm bowing her back. "MidasMidasMidas*Midas!*"

The hand beside her head fisted, his expression savage, as she chanted his name. Those magnificently Bad fingers kept up their relentless assault, triggering another explosion even stronger than the first.

"Oh *yessssss!*" She was shouting and she didn't even care.

Neither did Midas. He stared down at her in awe. "So, that's what it's like to finally have the best." He murmured hoarsely. "No wonder everything else felt like a cheap imitation."

Gwen barely heard him. Waves of pleasure beat at her senses, wiping her mind clean of everything except him. It was just liked she'd imagined sex would be before she'd actually experienced it. With Midas, it wasn't painful or icky. It was *perfect*. Like something out of a really dirty storybook. His perfectly imperfect face hovered above hers, drinking in her blissful expression as she finally went limp.

"That was *not* lackluster." She got out breathlessly. "My God. You're even better at this than you are at kissing. You are like a sexual genius."

A smug smile curved his lips. "It's a team sport, kitten."

She swallowed, still trying to rearrange all her thoughts. "Are you okay?" He looked okay, but she needed to be sure. This idea had worried him from the start and it had been *way* more intense than either of them could've expected. "Was it too much for you? We didn't come up with a safe-word for you."

"I'll brainstorm some for next time."

"I'm serious. I really did strong-arm you into this." Belated guilt flickered inside of her, despite her happiness. "I'm *always* strong-arming you into things."

"I told you, no one strong-arms me into anything."

She nearly snorted, because that just wasn't true. She'd been dragging Midas into messes since they met. "Are you --like-- regretting this deal or anything?"

Midas gently touched a knuckle to her face. "You are the best deal I ever made, Guinevere." He assured her and dipped his head to lap at the moisture coating her thighs, coaxing every last aftershock from her body. "God, I love the way you taste.

Gwen's fingers tangled in his hair, relief and pleasure filling her. Sex had been shockingly simple with Midas. Not at all degrading or awkward. He'd sent her whole body into meltdown in a matter of minutes. The man was as brilliant at sex as he was at everything else. His girlfriends probably lined up around the block, reveling in what he could do to their shapely, Bad bodies. What if one of them turned out to be his True Love?

Gwen winced. "I think Arthur must have been doing something wrong." She blurted out, not wanting to dwell on the image of Midas with anyone else and spoil the mood. "Arthur couldn't do anything even *close* to that. No way. I always knew it was his fault things were so lackluster."

"The man was an asshole." Midas reiterated gravely, his perfect tongue beginning to do perfectly Bad things again. "If he made sex unpleasant for you, then *he* screwed up. Not you. I promise, I can do a *far* better job."

She gave a contented sigh. "I know you can. You can do anything." He'd certainly proven that enough times. She should never have doubted that he'd make this perfect, too.

Midas was the Right Man.

He was already two-thirds of the way through the list. If he could just want her the way she wanted him, everything would be exactly as she'd always dreamed.

Unfortunately, her jackass husband seemed determined to screw up all her plans. They'd renegotiated the Contract, but Gwen still didn't feel secure. The second Midas found his "True Love," he'd want out of their deal. She knew it. He'd never want Gwen as much as she wanted him, as long as that (hopefully) imaginary woman was standing in the way.

Gwen's eyes narrowed. There was only one thing for a practical, logical almost-Bad girl to do, really.

She needed to make her fake-husband fall in love with her for real.

Chapter Twenty

If a situation occurs not foreseen by this Contract, but needing action, the parties will mutually agree on an appropriate solution. Guinevere Pendragon will lead the discussion.

Clause 16- Unexpected Situations

The Emerald City was filled with people who hated him.

It was an exclusive gated town at the center of Camelot, populated exclusively with wizards, who were exclusively Good. Midas was used to being surrounded by enemies, but usually they were enemies he could kill. There wasn't a damn thing he could do to the wizards, though. Not when his True Love considered them all her uncles.

He sat in the office of Suffrah Moghrabi, Chair of the Congress of Wizards, trying not to draw attention to himself. Which was hard, considering Midas was the only un-green thing in a five mile radius. All the buildings were green. The furniture inside of them was green. The citizens who lived in them favored green clothes and green hair-dye. Even Gwen was dressed in a striking green jacket and coordinating skirt, which did amazing things for her eyes.

Midas was wearing black.

Black suit, black shirt, black tie, and black shoes. It was the simplest outfit he owned. Putting together anything even halfway classy was completely beyond his skill set, but at least he matched. His entire goal for the day was to just... get through the day. He wanted to keep his mouth shut, let Gwen do whatever royal-ish stuff she needed to do to get the wizards' backing, and go home with her still safely married to him.

It was a great plan.

Except Suffrah was not in the mood to let it happen.

Like the other two men sitting behind the long table in front of him, Suffrah was a level five wizard, wearing long robes, a long beard, and a disapproving expression. Unlike the others, his green eyes stayed fixed on Midas while Gwen talked.

The bastard was thinking of ways to break up their marriage. Midas could tell. Wizards were the only beings alive who could void a marriage contract. Suffrah would need Gwen's permission to do it and access to their marriage scroll, of course. Neither of which seemed likely to happen, but it was still a risk. Midas didn't take risks with his wife. It was why he hadn't wanted to come to the Emerald City, in the first place.

"So you see," Gwen continued enthusiastically, like she didn't notice the man's glower, "if you and the rest of the wizards would back us, we could stop the Scarecrow from destroying the kingdom, Uncles. If we stand together with the Bad folk, he won't even have a chance."

Suffrah kept staring at Midas. "Was this your idea?" He demanded.

"No."

"It was my idea." Gwen put in. "Midas is not entirely thrilled about the whole 'becoming king' concept. But, he's going to be amazing at it." She smiled over at Midas, her eyes bright and happy.

She couldn't *possibly* think this meeting was going well, right?

One of the other wizards, named Nim, arched a gray brow at Midas. "Arthur was an unworthy king." He declared as if Midas had suggested otherwise. "The Scarecrow is even worse with his depraved use of Dark Science. The wizards want no part of that madness."

"Neither do we." Gwen assured him. "That's why we're here." She looked at Midas for support. "Right?"

"Yes."

Gwen frowned at his abbreviated answer, but Midas wasn't saying one word more than he had to. The meeting was doomed and had been from the start. He'd *told* Gwen that. He just wanted to get his wife out of there, before someone tried to take her and he had to kill them. It would really not win Gwen a lot of points with her uncles if Midas slaughtered them all.

Uncomfortable, he checked the distance to the door, again.

"We want no part of a war, either." Suffrah spared Gwen the briefest of glances, before refocusing his scowl on Midas. "Good folk are above such things."

Midas met his stare levelly, not saying a word.

"Not always, Uncle. The Looking Glass Campaigns were all started by the Good. Historically, I think we can all agree that most wars begin with Good folk trying to..."

"We must look at eons, not just today." The third wizard, named Chryson, interrupted. "Patience is a virtue. In the end, the world always rights itself. You do not need your crown *today*, my dear."

Gwen's face fell in disappointment.

Midas' jaw tightened, forcing himself to stay still. He wasn't going to get involved. If he got involved it would make things worse for her. The wizards were looking for a reason to deny Gwen her crown *forever* and Midas was one hell of a big, Bad, cursed reason.

"But the Scarecrow has the formula. I told you, he's going to put it in the air and brainwash all the Bad folk." Gwen shook her head. "I can't let that happen. I have to stop him *now*."

"Camelot will make its own choices, Guinevere." Nim tutted. "There is no reason to risk wizards' blood as they make their mistakes. Perhaps they will learn from them."

"What about other people's blood?" The words were out before Midas could stop them. "How many will die while you lock your gates and let innocent people learn from the Scarecrow's mistakes?"

Gwen looked over at him in surprised gratitude.

Suffrah's eyes narrowed. "What others do is no concern of ours. As Nim said, we all must make our own choices."

"Well, make them while you can." Midas crossed his arms over his chest. "The Scarecrow hates the wizards nearly as much as Bad folk. Didn't you guys turn him down for entrance into the Academy or something?" He glanced at Gwen. "Didn't you tell me they turned him down?"

"They turned him down." Gwen nodded. "Like four times."

"Well, no wonder he's holding a grudge." Midas arched a brow. "So, after he's done erasing all the Bad folk, it stands to reason the Scarecrow will be coming here." He gestured around the green office and to the green city beyond. "To steal freewill from *you*. To enslave *you* with Dark Science and get his revenge. ...And there will be no one left to stop him."

Suffrah's scowl deepened. "You think the wizards would do better under your illustrious rule, *Kingpin?*" The nickname was a taunt.

"Everyone will do better under his rule." Gwen interjected. "Midas is the best king we've had in generations. He was born with nothing and look what he's accomplished!" Her voice radiated sincerity, as if she truly believed what she was saying. "There isn't a man alive with a kinder heart or a nobler nature. And smart! Oh my God, he's *so* smart, no one else can even compare."

Midas blinked, moved and shaken by her enthusiastic praise.

"Smart?" Chryson pursed his lips, scanning Midas as if he was a horse who could perform tricks. "He doesn't *look* smart. Can he even play catur?"

"Of course he can." Gwen answered instantly.

Midas' eyes widened. No, he couldn't. He'd told her that. "Wait, let's not…"

Chryson talked right over him. "Monkeys can move pieces on a board, but they cannot *win*." He argued. Still, he looked a bit intrigued with the idea of Midas being more than a mindless goon. "Can your man win?" Even Suffrah and Nim were eyeing Midas speculatively, now. "Catur requires rare talent, after all. It is a game of gentlemen and scholars, not thugs."

"Midas is the most talented man I have ever met." Gwen sounded supremely confident. "He can beat anyone at anything."

Chryson's stroked his beard. "Are you willing to bet on him, then, my dear?"

Gwen smirked. "Absolutely."

Midas' saw the floor opening up beneath him. "Gwen, don't." He warned.

Everyone ignored him.

"If the boy wins, the wizards will help you in your quest for the crown." Chryson offered. "If he loses, we won't. We will seal our gates and leave Camelot to its fate. *Forever*."

"Deal." Gwen agreed with a victorious clap of her hands. "Get the board."

Midas squeezed his eyes shut.

Fucking hell.

Chryson bounded to his feet. "Well, we'll see how right you are about this man you married, Guinevere." He pointed at Midas. "I warn you though, boy, I've been grandmaster of the Emerald City Catur Club for thirty-three years."

Fucking *hell*.

Midas leaned closer to Gwen, lowering his voice to a hiss. "I've never played catur a day in my life. Blue-blooded, Good, *classy* people play catur. Not criminals from Celliwig. Are you out of your mind making this deal?"

"Didn't you say you read a book on catur?"

"Yes, but…"

She cut him off, lake-blue eyes full of unearned faith. "Then, you can beat him." She summed up with a nod. "I know it."

Midas' heart flipped and sank at the same time. "This is way outside my skillset, Gwen. Bad folk aren't even allowed to own a catur board."

"Really?" She glanced over at her uncles like she didn't

believe that. "*Really?*"

Saffrah was back to watching Midas like he was a bug skittering across the clean, green wall. "Of course Bad folk are forbidden to play this game. They lack the higher thinking abilities and strategic mindset to understand its subtleties."

Midas' eyes narrowed at him.

"Well, that's a stupid law and I'm changing it." Gwen shot back. Her hand came over to touch Midas' arm like she was shielding him from the wizard's antipathy. "Everyone should learn to play, if they want."

"Which will do the boy no good *today*, since he's apparently never played before."

"It's a game of higher thinking abilities and strategic mindsets, remember?" Gwen arched a brow. "Midas doesn't need a game board to practice those skills. He does it every day, just being himself."

Fucking.

Hell.

Midas ran a hand through his hair, trying to find a way out of this mess. "Why can't *you* play this game?" He asked her. "You've played before, right?"

"Because, I suck at catur. I'm too aggressive and… blunt. I need you. You're calmer and way better at seeing moves three steps ahead. It's why we're such a great team." She smiled at him. "We balance each other out."

Midas sighed in defeat. How could he possibly tell his True Love "no" after she said something like that?

"Okay." He gave in to her, because what choice did he have? Trying and failing was better than not trying at all. "I'll do this. I will. But," he lowered his voice, so only she could hear, "if I lose this game, are you going to use the Termination Clause of our Contract and leave me?"

She sent him a mystified look. "No, of course not."

He didn't completely believe her reassurance. Since they'd met, Gwen had been looking at him and deciding he measured up to whatever invisible scale she had in her head. This was a test he would fail, though. He knew it. And when he failed, she might very well enact Clause 11- "Reasons for Nullification and/or Termination of Marriage." If Midas couldn't give her what she wanted, why would she stay with him?

Gwen also looked worried, now. "I thought we agreed in the elevator… um…" she blushed a bit at the memory, "that… uh… we were *happy* with this deal." She whispered. "Are you not happy anymore?"

"Our deal is the happiest I've ever been." He said honestly.

And ever since she'd come up with the idea of him stroking her to orgasm every other day, it had been even better. The scent of her skin and the soft sounds she made and the taste of her... He needed nothing else to be happy. He was perfectly content just touching Gwen in every possible way she'd allow.

Midas hadn't even taken his turn, yet. He was afraid he'd lose control and have sex with her. It was fucking killing him to know she'd allow it and *he* was the one holding back. Of all the crazy things that had ever happened to him, that was the craziest. But he was afraid to reveal they were True Loves. Already the physical desire between them was growing hotter. Bigger.

That morning his need for her had made it impossible to sleep, so he'd knocked on Gwen's door at an ungodly hour with a new idea. She'd been surprisingly excited to see him. Especially, when he'd asked to amend the Contract, so he could trade his days in and pleasure her instead.

"You want to touch *me*, again?" She'd echoed, wide-eyed. "Are you sure?"

"Yes."

"Right now?"

"*Immediately.*"

"Damn, you really are the best partner ever." She'd yanked him into her bedroom, standing on tiptoe to meet his hungry kiss.

It had been one of the most magical moments of his life. The woman brought sunshine to his gloomy world. She gave him joy and warmth and laughter. A *family*. His existence before Gwen and Avalon arrived was nothing but a dark, cold porch.

And now he was about to lose *everything* because of a fucking board game.

Gwen's eyes searched his face. "Just do your best."

"What if it's not enough?"

"Then we'll think of something else." She shrugged. "But it *will* be enough. Believe me, you're going to be a natural at this."

Midas rubbed his temple so hard, it was amazing his fingers didn't drill right through his skull. She trusted him. Needed him. He couldn't let her down. "Fine." He muttered.

Fucking hell.

Midas watched in resignation as Chryson came bounding back in and set up the board. There were four painted quadrants and traditional chess pieces, mixed with elephants and chariots. That news did Midas very little good. He'd never played chess, either.

"I'll be white." The wizard announced, looking over Midas' solid black clothing.

Like it mattered.

Midas shrugged, studying his pieces, recalling the one and only book he'd ever read about this damn game. It had been in the WUB Club. The prison library had been a grim and desolate place, filled with ranting treatises against Badness and dull textbooks, so old they crumbled in your hands when you turned the pages. Midas had read them all, though, because even terrible books were better than no books, at all.

One of the forgotten, mildewed tomes had been entitled: *Catur's Classic Stratagems and Philosophies.*

Illustrations of the author's favorite moves and descriptions of his most cunning attacks had been chronicled in that ancient volume. Midas always remembered what he read, even the boring shit. Since this was the most important game he would ever play, he was going to use every advantage he had.

Midas' glanced at his opponent through his lashes. "White goes first, I believe."

Chryson slammed his chariot forward and gave Midas a challenging look.

Apparently, that was a bold opening. Hell if he knew why. Midas frowned, trying to recall how the elephant moved. The book said if your opponent led with a chariot, you needed to immediately bring out your elephant. Taking a chance, he slid the black pachyderm forward and arched a brow at Chryson.

Chryson's mouth curved in appreciation, settling back in his chair. "Ahhh... perhaps this won't be so dull a game, after all."

Gwen smiled knowingly.

It took four hours. Four unrelenting, tense hours, where Midas had to pay attention to every move Chryson made and then try to match it up to the information in the book. It took every ounce of his concentration to keep up. His infantry was gone in the first ninety minutes and his cavalry depleted soon after. The elephant, though... The elephant was amazing. Once Midas' got the hang of using the little bastard, he decimated the wizard's ranks. His opponent favored the chariot and it cost the man dearly.

Nim and Saffrah watched in amazement as Midas took Chryson's queen. Now there was only one queen left on the board.

Midas' queen.

He automatically looked over at Gwen, who was fiddling with her phone. He didn't know whether to be flattered or exasperated by how little attention she was paying to the game.

"Son of a toad." Chryson muttered, on the run now. "Who taught you to play like this, boy?" He tried shifting his king into a safer position, but it was no use.

Midas followed him, boxing him in. "You taught me." He answered calmly.

Chryson flashed him a baffled look. "I did? I don't recall that." He tried one more time to evade capture, but the elephant was relentless and the king fell. Chryson sat back with a frown, not looking too upset over the loss. "Although, that defense with the queen *was* familiar. Almost a…"

"A classic stratagem." Midas agreed, relief coursing through him. He'd done it. He'd passed another test and now his wife would stay with him. "Gwen?" He called and was pleased that his voice stayed steady. "It's over."

"Oh good." Gwen straightened in her chair, not even asking about the outcome. "Now we can go looking for the wand. I'm really hoping Merlyn hid it around here somewhere."

"I won." Midas informed her quietly. Maybe she didn't know that. Maybe she was afraid to ask.

She tilted her head. "Well, of course you did." She smiled like it was no big deal that an uneducated gangster had just defeated a wizard in the kingdom's most elite game. "You can do *anything*, Midas."

For the first time in his life, Midas felt pride.

His mouth curved, realizing the game hadn't been a test, after all. To Gwen, the outcome had simply never been in doubt. His wife completely believed in him. If he'd lost the game, she *still* would have believed in him. The value of that was beyond measure.

Chryson squinted at Midas. "A classic stratagem, eh?" He repeated, comprehension dawning.

"Yes." Midas cleared his throat. "Page eighty-one, I believe."

Chryson grinned. "What ho! The boy's read my book!"

"I read your book." Midas agreed. It had allowed him to predict Chryson's moves and understand his tactics. He might not fully understand catur, but he'd understood how *his opponent* understood catur and that was far more important.

"Told you no one could beat my husband." Gwen informed her uncles and Midas' breath caught at her casual use of the word.

"And FYI, when Arthur made the Scarecrow his chief advisor based on a catur match...? It took the Scarecrow *two days* to win, against a far less worthy adversary." She snorted. "Smartest man in the kingdom, my ass."

Chryson looked over to the other wizards. "You see what my teaching can do? Do you see why I've been Grandmaster of the Emerald City Catur Club for thirty-three years? Because no one can match my stratagems, not even me."

"No one can match *the King of Camelot*." Gwen corrected, standing up. "Midas could lose a thousand games and still be the best ruler this land ever had. You know he's even read the stupid budget reports? I'm telling you, you've backed the right man for the job."

"You could rule without him." Saffrah said, making one last ditch effort to ruin Midas' life. "We'll ensure you're queen, now. You can stay here and we'll support you, until you have the crown. You've no need for the Kingpin, anymore, Guinevere."

Midas started to rise out of his chair.

"Of course I have need for him." Gwen scoffed, not noticing the deadly look Midas was leveling at the bastard. "We're equal partners." She extended her palm. "A deal's a deal, uncles. Midas and I look forward to your support, as we win our war."

All three wizards shook her hand with varying degrees of reluctance, sealing the bargain.

And Midas realized he'd just become ruler of a kingdom.

Gwen had actually gotten the Congress of Wizards to put a Bad folk --a former stable boy from the worst town in Camelot-- on the throne. Holy shit! Of everything Midas expected to happen at the meeting, being named king was the very *last*. Gwen had maneuvered everyone perfectly and come out with everything she'd wanted.

His wife really was one hell of a negotiator.

Chapter Twenty-One

**The Scarecrow
Yesterday**

"The fucking wizards are on her side now!" The Scarecrow paced around the throne room, the blackbirds in his coat restlessly flapping. "Scarlett Riding-Wolf's army is causing havoc twenty-four hours a day, Midas is blocking every-fucking-thing at the ports, the Round Table is supporting her, and *now* she's gotten the fucking Congress of Wizards kissing her ass, too!"

Percival watched him, both of his arms in casts. "You swear a lot more now than you did before." He observed with puritanical disapproval. "It's unseemly for a king."

Like the Scarecrow gave a fuck.

It *did* bother him that the little turd thought it was acceptable to speak to him that way, though. Percival had never treated Arthur with anything but respect. It was further proof that the Scarecrow was losing his grip on Camelot. Nearly all the King's Men had abandoned him, now. Either killed by Midas, prisoners of Scarlett's forces, or unwilling to cross the wizards. The Bad folk were all laughing at him, betting that Gwen would win. Even foreign leaders were staying away.

He was a king without a kingdom.

The Scarecrow closed his eyes and took a deep breath, trying to think. Guinevere was boxing him in at every turn. The woman was smarter than he'd given her credit for. She was meeting him, move for move. And she'd recruited a pet goon who'd pay any amount of money to fulfil her whims. Midas *had* to be her True Love. There was no other explanation for the cash he was putting into her war. He could outspend the Scarecrow, hiring more men and buying more supplies.

Not to mention the goddamn media blitz.

Every fucking channel was all Gwen all the time. Commercials ran around the clock, all of them explaining how the Scarecrow's policies were ruining life in Camelot. All of them espousing the glories and wonders of Queen Guinevere. Then there were the op-ed articles, the radio spots, the countless blogs... One day, the Scarecrow would wake up and there would be fucking billboards. He was sure of it.

There was already an endless marathon of Galahad's damn television show airing on Midas' new TV network. Kids were sending the palace sad letters, wondering why the Scarecrow was keeping their favorite knight away. *Arthur* had banished that prick, but Midas' PR firm had flipped it all around, so the Scarecrow was responsible for season four's cliffhanger not being resolved!

Frustrated and furious, he collapsed onto the throne.

He couldn't win this war.

Gwen was building too much support in the kingdom and Midas was too powerful. If the Scarecrow was going to gain his throne, he needed that meddling whore as his wife and he needed Midas out of the picture.

The only way to achieve either of those things was Dark Science.

His gaze cut over to the White Rabbit, who was fiddling with his bowtie. "How much longer until you can get the formula airborne?" He demanded.

"Ummm... not long, sire. I've been working quite hard on it, just as you requested."

"What's the hold up?"

"Well," the scientist nervously smoothed down his ears, "I can't make the effects permanent, yet. The formula will only last a day or two on most Baddies. Even less if they are particularly strong-willed." He brightened. "But, I *have* figured out a way to trigger them into following our orders from a distance, so..."

"Gwen will find the wand imminently, I suspect." The Scarecrow interrupted, calming down enough to use the erudite vocabulary he preferred. There was no sense in being a genius if people didn't know it. "If she does, all our experiments will collapse into ruins. Time is of the essence."

"Well, that's true, sire." The Rabbit admitted. "Merlyn was a level six wizard. Those are quite rare. He put a great deal of power into his wand, so it could be an issue for us."

Even dead that asshole was causing problems.

"Dark Science can defeat most magic, but not at that strength. Not yet anyway." The Rabbit gulped, seeing the Scarecrow's *extreme* unhappiness with that news. "But I've set up a magic detecting sensor. As soon as the wand is located by Guinevere, we'll know. Its energy is too..."

The Scarecrow cut him off again. "As soon as she has it, we'll have to act immediately, no matter our level of preparedness." He pursed his burlap lips. "What about the Camlann Project?" He demanded. "How is that progressing?"

If he couldn't win, he'd make sure Gwen didn't either. That was the bottom line. For the last week or so, he'd been hounding the Rabbit to complete the Camlann Project. That little bitch Avalon had actually given him the idea. If the worst happened and he lost this fight, the Scarecrow would make sure that Midas and Gwen didn't get their happily ever after.

It was the least he could do.

The Rabbit gulped. "It's not even *close* to being ready, sire. I've told you that. If I even try to... to... do what you're asking, it would take months to perfect the proper serum. Years of tests, before it was right."

The Scarecrow snorted at that nonsense. "Just get close enough to fuck up their lives."

"Horrible, *horrible* things could happen though, sire! What you want is impossible and immoral and..."

The Scarecrow was beginning to lose his patience. "Allow *me* to do the planning. You just stick to the science."

"But... The Camlann Project plan is a *terrible* plan you're planning, sire."

"So you've repeatedly conveyed." His twig-fingers drummed on the arm rest. "I don't put much credence in your opinion, however. *I just want to know if it will fucking work!*" The last part came out at a bellow.

Inside his coat, the blackbirds shifted in agitation, their red eyes fixing on the Rabbit. If the bunny wasn't the only creature in the kingdom capable of mastering Dark Science, the Scarecrow would have had them peck the little bastard to death.

His babies were hungry.

"It will work." The Rabbit backed towards the door, gazing at the blackbirds in dread fascination. "I swear, I will have it working by this time tomorrow. At least for a trial run. In fact, I'll just go work on it right now..." He scampered from the room so fast, his cottontail nearly got caught in the door.

Twitchy little coward.

"We don't have time for him to fuck around much longer." He muttered. "Gwen is too clever. She'll find that wand soon. I know it."

"None of this will matter, so long as that winged demon is

still alive." Percival argued, bigotry always uppermost in his feeble mind. "When we get rid of Midas, Trystan will come for us. He's brainlessly loyal to his master. I battled those half-naked barbarians during the Looking Glass Campaigns. They're too stupid to quit, even when they're doomed to lose. We should kill Trystan *first*."

The Scarecrow rolled his eyes, sick of Percival's whining. Ever since he'd escaped Midas' dungeon, all he'd done was brood about Trystan snapping his arms like they were sticks from that stupid little pig's house. Percival's hatred for the gryphon blinded him.

"Gryphons are nothing." The Scarecrow scoffed dismissively. "Anachronisms who dwell in caves and eat raw meat."

"They're cave-dwelling anachronisms who are trained to fight to the death."

"Then we'll make sure Trystan fights *to the death* as quickly as possible. If we have the formula, we can compel him to fly into the ocean and drown himself. Or maybe a bug-zapper." Restless, the Scarecrow got to his feet and prowled over to look out the window. "And he can take all the fucking wizards with him."

He hated those smug bastards.

Hated them.

First they denied him admission to the academy and now they aided his enemies. Once he had control of Camelot, he would burn the Emerald City to the ground and...

No.

The Scarecrow winced a bit, rejecting that idea. Not fire. A bomb perhaps. He had a morbid fear of flames that only someone made of straw could ever understand. He wouldn't use that. Not even to kill the wizards.

Percival arched a brow. "They say Midas beat Chryson at catur, you know. Won the game in less than four hours. No one's ever done that. ...Not even you."

The Scarecrow's teeth ground together in fury.

For as long as he could remember, he'd been the smartest man in the kingdom. Everyone knew it and respected it. Now, for the very first time, he was afraid he... wasn't. That ill-bred ape was outmaneuvering him. Even with Gwen's help, that shouldn't be possible. Midas had been spawned in a mud hole on the ass-crack of Camelot. He'd lived in a goddamn stable for four years, sleeping with farm animals. He was tacky and common and uneducated and Bad.

How in the hell could he *possibly* be winning this war?

"Did you send men to that other wizard's house?" He demanded, gazing out at the lawn. A maid was doing laundry, vainly hoping that the linens would dry in the damp weather. "That drunken, stuttering fool who married Gwen and Midas?"

"Yes, but it was no use. The scroll wasn't there."

"What do you mean it *wasn't there?* It has to be there. Wizards always keep the marriage scrolls of the couples they wed."

"My men searched the house from top to bottom and couldn't find it, sire. It's not there."

The Scarecrow's painted-on eyes narrowed. *Midas.* That shrewd fucker had stolen it first!

The Scarecrow couldn't marry Gwen, if she was already married to Midas. Unless that scroll was destroyed, it was basically impossible to dissolve their marriage. The Scarecrow had been hoping to get his hands on it, but of course that dirty mongrel *had* to ruin his plans.

Dissatisfaction ate at him. Self-doubt. Rage. Needing a handy target for his roiling emotions, the Scarecrow's painted-on eyes fixed on the maid in the garden. She was hanging out the clothes. Like most people, she was probably supporting Gwen.

And his babies were hungry.

The Scarecrow made a clucking sound with his tongue. Instantly, the blackbirds swarmed out of his body, swooping down into the courtyard. It was a black cloud of feathers and wings and ravenous squawking.

The maid looked up at the sound, her mouth parting in horror. The fool actually tried to run. She took a few panicked steps, but his babies were already upon her. Talons tore into her body, knocking her to the ground. She helplessly screamed, desperate to escape, but it was no use. It was impossible to stop his blackbirds once they tasted blood.

...Unless you had a golden touch, like that murdering dickhead. The Scarecrow would never forgive Midas for that. He detested the man for so many reasons, but he'd *never forgive* that monster for turning a dozen of his precious babies to gold at the Round Table. He would have vengeance for the massacre.

He would take away something Midas loved.

Down in the courtyard, the blackbirds feasted on the woman, as she wailed and uselessly tried to protect her face. Beaks stabbed into her eyes, straight through to her brain, and then she was quiet. Blood pooled on the cobblestones, seeping out around her still form. It seemed they were going to need another laundress.

The Scarecrow smiled as one of his babies pecked off her nose.

...And he imagined it was Gwen.

Chapter Twenty-Two

In the event that the Contract is terminated or nullified, each party will leave the marriage with the property they brought into it. Therefore, Midas (no last name given) will retain his gold, his house, his horses, his business, and all material belongings related to any of the above.

He agrees to pay Guinevere Pendragon any alimony she wishes, even though she has repeatedly tried to talk him out of it.

Clause 19- Disposition of Property of Midas (no last name given) in Event of Contract's Termination

The next week was the happiest that Midas had ever been.

Every morning, he'd knock on Gwen's door, before the sun was even up, desperate to watch her come apart in his hands. ...And she always let him in. His wife would drag him inside her room, like she'd been waiting for him, eager for his touch. Even better, she then spent the rest of the day with him, saying delightfully unpredictable things and smiling. For the first time in his life, Midas truly belonged with someone.

With *two* someones, actually.

Avalon owned him. The little girl followed him around, asking non-stop questions, and proclaiming them best friends, and Midas was helpless to resist her. He didn't even *want* to resist her. He was perfectly content. He could go down to breakfast and Avalon would beam at him and Gwen would look at him like he was special. And Midas would know that he'd somehow acquired the impossible.

His very own family.

It cost him stacks and stacks of gold to hold onto such a valuable commodity, but it was all worth it. He would have gladly paid in blood, if that's what it took to keep them. The dozens of armed men he'd hired, and the weapons he was stockpiling, and the massive losses to his business were all the wisest money he'd ever spend.

Midas finally had the best.

So long as Avalon's "daddy" stayed away and Gwen never found the Right Man, Midas could keep his newfound riches. ...But he wasn't sure how much longer his luck would hold. He was fairly sure

Avi's father and Gwen's dream man were the same person. Someone Gwen hadn't even met yet, but who Avalon saw coming. Some handsome hero who would love them and give them his name.

Someone who would rip Midas' world apart, given half a chance.

And that son of a bitch wasn't the only dark cloud in his precariously happy existence. Gwen remained determined to track down Merlyn's wand. They'd scoured the Emerald City from top to bottom and come up empty. Midas was beginning to think it would never turn up and he was tired of waiting. It suited Gwen not to have bloodshed in the streets, but Midas preferred a more hands-on approach. He wanted the Scarecrow dead, as soon as possible.

He had so much to lose.

At least he had an army, now. The Round Table had actually come through, plus Letty had sent a mass of Bad folk to Camelot. Together, they were doing their damnedest to ruin the Scarecrow's day *every* day. Their mayhem wasn't exactly carried out with military precision, but it would do. Midas did worry that Scarlett would order her people back again if he didn't soon find her the witch, though.

Wherever Esmeralda was hiding, it wasn't in the Four Kingdoms, Camelot, Neverland, or Oz. Midas had had all of them searched from pole to pole and come up with nothing. All witches loved Oz! Why couldn't Esmeralda just be normal? It was beginning to annoy him that the woman was so well-concealed. Maybe Ez and Merlyn's wand were together someplace, which would explain why neither could be found.

"Your colonel is ridiculously attired and unfit for battle." Trystan informed him with a scoff. "It's no wonder your puny people starve."

"We're not fuc…-*p'don* starving." Clause 3- "Protection and Care of Avalon Pendragon" said Midas had to try to watch his language around the child, so he'd begun swearing in the gryphons' dialect, whenever possible. That way Avalon couldn't understand him and couldn't be shocked. Not that she ever corrected his missteps, anyway. She lectured everyone else about cursing, but she allowed Midas to say whatever he liked. For some reason, that made him feel smug. Special.

They were best friends.

Trystan was *also* his friend, even when he was an annoying jackass. Midas felt closer to the man since Avalon and Gwen arrived. Caring about *them* made it easier to care about others. The gryphon was the only other person on the planet Midas felt a bond with. The only man he completely trusted with his family.

Trystan definitely sensed the shift in their relationship, too. He seemed capable of feeling more than Corrah had been able to feel, but Midas couldn't be sure how *much* more. He'd never actually discussed it with the gryphon, because --well-- he was Trystan. Still, there was no doubt that Trystan could get pissed off pretty fast for a man without emotions.

When Midas had offered him a huge raise to compensate for his expanded duties as Avalon's bodyguard, Trystan had just about lost his damn mind.

"I will take no money to protect a child. Especially *that* child." Trystan had been speaking in the gryphons' language, without even noticing. His jaw was set defiantly, his tone furious. "I take *no money* to perform a sacred duty of my clan."

He'd dropped the heavy bag of gold right back on Midas' desk like it was tainted.

Instantly, Midas knew he'd fucked up. In this case, he'd known right from wrong... and he knew he'd been wrong. "I'm sorry." He'd quickly taken the gold back, haphazardly tossing it aside. "That was an insult to you. Forgive me, *j'ah*."

The word was hard to translate into the common tongue, but its meaning was profound. "Comrade in arms." "Most loyal friend." "Brother." Gryphons only used it with the men they fought beside and trusted the most.

With their clan.

Trystan's eyes had jumped to his.

Midas hadn't looked away, still using the gryphons' dialect. It was easier to say what he really meant in that language. "Guinevere claims I try to buy things that aren't for sale. She is teaching me better ways, but it's a difficult lesson."

Some of Trystan's tension had eased. "You *are* slow, but you'll eventually learn." He'd muttered. "One *hopes*."

Midas had inclined his head. "I rely on you. The gold was wrong, but the sentiment is real. You guard the things I value most. I thank you."

Trystan had grunted, still not completely appeased. "I need no thanks for guarding your woman and child. I do it for myself. They have come to us and now I awake each day, without..." Trystan paused like he wasn't sure how to articulate it in any language, "darkness."

Midas had known *exactly* what he meant. "Yes." He'd agreed.

"So, they are yours, but they belong to me as well." Trystan went on stubbornly. "The innocent belong to all who would care for them. You know that, *j'ha*. Your mother taught you. The Skycast Clan always honored our ways and so must you, as the last of the line."

Midas had blinked. Trystan had just declared him the final member of the Skycast Clan. The heir to Corrah's people. In a ceremonial sense, he'd just made him a gryphon. There was no higher compliment and Midas took the honor seriously.

"I will do my best to follow the old customs." The words had been formal and sincere. "My family is your family. My clan is your clan. Always."

Finally satisfied, Trystan had nodded sharply and stalked out of the room.

That was how Midas realized he had mother he'd loved and a lineage he was proud of. ...And an incredibly devoted, winged brother, who aggravated the hell out of him, most of the time.

"The citizens of Midasburg are doing just fine." Midas insisted in what he thought was a dignified tone. "We're recovering from the last battle faster than we'd dreamed."

Of course, the statement wasn't entirely true. His army had been significantly depleted after the last assault by the Trystantonia hordes and everyone knew it. Damn it. This game was far more challenging and enjoyable than catur. He really wanted to win. Maybe it *would* be better if his colonel tried a different outfit.

He scanned the available options and settled on an orange hat, studded with tiny rhinestones. Wedging it on the doll's head, he assessed the effect and gave a grunt of satisfaction. There! He slammed Lady Kimberly down and fixed Trystan with a "Now what, asshole?" kind of look.

Trystan gave a contemptuous snort and adjusted his own commander's dark hair back into a lopsided ponytail. He'd already used nail polish to decorate her face with vicious tribal markings. The Trystonians weren't a subtle people. "The hat is a desperate bid for attention. Lady Kimberly tries too hard to impress, but all it reveals is her mental weakness. Captain Kill-botica will bury your pathetic colonel in her pointless finery."

Trystan's doll wore a trench-coat and miniature boots, which, Midas had to admit, looked much more intimidating than Lady Kimberly's tangerine rhinestones. ...And why did he get stuck with "Lady Kimberly," while Trystan got to be "Captain Kill-botica?" It seemed unfair.

Avalon finished arranging Queen Lyrssa's forces and flopped down between the two men. "I think this will be the best battle yet!"

She informed them happily.

The floor of her bedroom had been divided off with different colors of markers to represent the various terrains of the dolls' world. Midas imagined that the permanent ink had ruined the hardwood, but so what? There was no time for such a paltry concern in the midst of war.

Avalon's dolls all had construction paper wings. "That one is Corrah Skycast." She told Midas, indicating a white-haired warrior. "I named her the same as your mommy. I seen her." She tapped her forehead. "She told you stories about rocking-horseflies. They's my favorite."

Midas' throat tightened with unexpected emotion. "They're my favorite, too." His mouth curved as he looked down at the doll. "My mother was a great warrior. She would have liked you very much."

"Everyone likes me." Avalon gave Corrah a place of honor in her regiment.

Trystan ignored the byplay, scowling down at a different member of Avalon's flying army. "Something is gravely wrong here, for Suzanna Sun-Catcher perished yesterday."

"Nuh-uh."

"Yes, she *did*." He insisted. Gryphons took all warfare seriously, even if it was waged with fashion dolls. "My people slayed her in the Cupcake Village Massacre and you know it."

Avalon shrugged. "She's a zombie. She came back."

Trystan gasped in outrage.

"Wait, we can have zombies?" Midas perked up at that news, because it would bolster his flagging forces if he could reanimate some of his numerous dead. He glanced over to the doll graveyard, where all the plastic victims were arranged in shoeboxes. "Lady Stephanie and Lady Heather are both zombies, too, then." He decided.

"Fuck that!" Trystan roared. "You two only want zombies, because I'm winning!"

"Cursing is a no-no." Avalon told him piously.

"Yeah, Trystan, watch your *p'don* language." Midas grabbed his sparkly soldiers back. "You're being a sore loser."

Avalon smiled up at him.

Midas smiled back, because it was impossible to do anything else. Love filled him. Every day, the feeling grew stronger. Deeper. The child was a part of his soul, now. Losing Avi would be as horrible as losing Gwen. He'd die before he gave up either of them.

Unfortunately, Midas already knew that Avalon's daddy was

not going to give them up, either. Not without a fight. It had been ridiculous to think he could buy the man's family. Midas could offer that heroic fucking hero all the gold in the world and it *still* wouldn't be enough. Nothing would *ever* be enough to part with Gwen and Avi. They were priceless. Anybody could see that. You might as well offer to buy someone's beating heart, right out of their chest.

For the first time, the Kingpin of Camelot had found something that simply wasn't for sale. ...So, Midas would just have to steal what he wanted.

No matter who Avi's son of a bitch father was, the man wouldn't stand in his way. *No one* could keep Midas from the family he'd claimed. His True Love and her baby daughter were secure in his evil clutches and he'd *never* let them go. He'd start a *second* goddamn war first.

Avalon glanced up at him again, seeing every thieving thought in his head and not looking particularly concerned. "Can I have a ballet room with singing wallpaper in the new wing you's building?" She randomly asked him.

Midas shrugged. "Yes."

"Can it be pink wallpaper, with kitty cats and dragons?"

"Of course." Just so it wasn't her daddy, she could have anything she wanted. "You can pick some out with the decorator tomorrow." That pattern sounded like a special order, though.

"And I get my swing set soon?"

"It's installed on Monday. Just like I promised."

"It gotta be big." She warned. "You and Trystan's gotta fit, so we's can play."

"It'll be exactly what you want or the builder will start all over again." Gwen would no doubt accuse him of spoiling the girl, but Midas couldn't help it. If it was up to him, Avalon would have Christmas every day.

Avalon nodded in satisfaction. She never seemed surprised by how tightly Midas was wrapped around her finger. "Thank you." She chirped happily. "Mommy and me will get you a present, too."

"You don't have to get me anything, baby." Just having them there was enough.

"I'm not losing this game." Trystan growled, not caring about singing wallpaper samples or jungle gyms the size of small cities. "*You* are losing, Midas. And now you wish to cheat in an effort to prevent your inevitable failure, as do all of your treacherous kind."

"Hey, my Midasburgians are an honorable people, not like your crazed barbarians." He flung a hand towards the sharply-dressed thugs who populated Trystantonia. It was a wonder they could sleep at night, with all the depravities they'd committed on the battlefield.

"And Clarissa of the Clouds is a vampire!" Avalon proclaimed holding another fallen warrior aloft. "She was only *pretending* to get her head chopped off." It was a cunning deception, since her rubber skull was missing. The doll was decapitated at the neck.

Trystan threw his palms up in exasperation. "It is chaos to train you." He declared. "This is no game, child. You need to treat each strategy in a grave and thoughtful manner, because, one day, you will need to defend your kingdom and protect your people." He paused. "Also, Clarissa of the Clouds cannot just reattach her head. It was burned in the pyres of Demonica Rex." He pointed to another one of his dolls, who looked customarily smug about her countless victories and flawless wardrobe.

Midas hated Demonica Rex. She was such a stuck up bitch.

Avalon frowned over at Demonica Rex, too, obviously thinking the same thing. Not even she could think of a way that Clarissa of the Clouds could have escaped the general's flames, though. Demonica Rex was ruthlessly efficient. She reluctantly surrendered Clarissa of the Clouds back to Trystan.

"*Thank* you." He tossed poor, headless Clarissa aside. "She returns to the grave, eternally unmourned."

"Most zombies do." Avalon allowed philosophically, moving onto other matters. "Lyrssa gets to have the sword again." She informed them, balancing the platinum letter opener in the queen's hand.

"She *always* gets the sword." Trystan whined and he wasn't wrong.

"Because she's the queen of Avalon City," Avalon sniffed, "and it's their ultimate weapon."

Trystan wasn't appeased. "Using the same weapon again and again can become predictable to your enemies. Why doesn't Captain Kill-botica take the sword, for a while?" He held out a hand and nodded persuasively. "Then, your people can develop new and better techniques."

Avalon eyed him like he was crazy. "You must think I'm an idiot."

A muffled laugh sounded from the doorway.

Midas glanced up to see Gwen standing there, watching them play.

"Hi, Mommy." Avalon cried cheerily. "Wanna go to war?"

"I don't know, baby. It seems unfair. Midas and Trystan are

always so helpless against us." Her eyes met Midas' and she smiled at him like he was everything she'd ever wanted in a husband.

Midas' heart swelled. So did other parts of him.

"Stop being smug and come defend Gwenville from the heathens." He tossed Gwen a doll from her stack of soldiers. "Just because you win every single time, doesn't mean you'll win, again."

"Maybe not, but I like the odds." She caught it and headed into the room, not even mentioning Clause 3. She hadn't reminded Midas to ignore Avalon for days, now. It was like she'd forgotten their agreement entirely and he certainly wasn't going to remind her. "You realize, of course, that bedtime was twenty minutes ago."

"Children should sleep when they are tired. Eat when they are hungry." Trystan opined. "You people make everything more complicated than it needs to be, with your reliance on clocks."

"What can I say? Gwenville's success is based on discipline." But she didn't press it.

Instead, she made her way across the battlefield and settled on Midas' lap like it was the most natural thing in the world. Midas' breath caught in his throat. For a second he was afraid to move, for fear that she'd leave. Gwen's body curled into his, comfortably fitting herself against his chest. Not afraid of the vast differences in their sizes or worried about showing affection in front of Trystan and Avalon.

It was… magical.

Midas' eyes met Trystan's and he knew the other man could sense his awe.

"*Ha'na*." Trystan said softly.

Gwen glanced over at him. "I've heard you say that before, but I don't know what it means. How come you never tell me what any of your words mean, Trystan?"

"If you spoke my language, Midas and I could not secretly talk about you."

Gwen threw her fashion doll at him and Trystan came as close to smiling as a gryphon could possibly come. The two of them spend most of their time bickering with each other about nonsense and listing reasons why Midas was hopelessly trusting. It seemed to work for them.

Trystan met Gwen's eyes. "Fine. To my people, *ha'na* is… 'light.'"

That wasn't the translation. Midas arched a brow at Trystan, who glanced away.

Gwen accepted the explanation, moving onto the doll battle.

"Hey, what happened to Clarissa of the Clouds?"

Trystan seemed eager not to discuss the gryphons' language. "She is now a dead decapitated zombie." He delivered the news with a pitiless smirk. "Demonica Rex will soon eat her bones."

"Bitch." Gwen muttered, flashing Demonica Rex a glower.

Midas carefully wrapped his arms around Gwen's waist, reveling in the fact that she didn't pull away. "We should team up to destroy her." He offered, running a hand over her hair. Frustration flickered, even through his happiness. Midas never hated his curse so much as when he touched his wife and wasn't able to feel her warmth. "We can divide Trystantonia between us. Equal partners."

She tilted her head back to grin at him. "We do make an excellent team."

Midas could no more have stopped himself from kissing her than he could have stopped the moon from shining in the night. His lips dipped down to brush hers, love suffusing every part of him.

"Ewww." Avalon wrinkled her nose at Trystan. "They're kissing again. Queen Lyrssa never kisses nobody. It's gross."

"Married people get to kiss whenever they want." Gwen told her good naturedly, cuddling into Midas' embrace. "It's one of the perks."

Midas' grip instinctively tightened on her. She hadn't said "*fake* married." She'd just said "married." The word was beautiful.

"This is why no queen should ever take a mate." Trystan instructed Avalon. "It makes you soft. Remember that as you ascend your throne. Queens need only slaves and consorts."

Gwen arched a brow and looked up at Midas, again. "Are you my slave or my consort?"

"Both." His check rested on the top of her head and realized everything he cared about was sitting in this room. He could lose every piece of gold in his counting houses and it wouldn't matter, just so he still had these three people around him.

"I'm going to have a firebird on our team." Gwen decided, adding a stuffed parrot to Midas' troops. "Her name is Harriet."

"Good Lord... She'll burn down Midasburg." The veterinarians he'd sent to oversee Gwen's Dark Science-y pets were quick to report Harriet's feathers were still aflame.

"Oh, she will not. Harriet and I have been working with a dog whistle, I told you. She's getting *much* better at controlling the fire." Gwen gave the toy parrot a pat on the head and then looked up at Midas again. "Hey, what were you doing locked in your office all evening? I missed talking to you."

Midas' heart melted. "You should have come in and talked to me, then. I would have been *thrilled* to see you, believe me. I was working on financial reports, trying to drag Camelot out of imminent bankruptcy."

"Really?" She seemed surprised.

"You told me to fix the kingdom's finances." He reminded her, not sure why she would be startled. "That's what I'm attempting to do, but it's a Gordian knot of make-believe math and poor decisions. If you want me to stop, I would be..."

"No, I don't want you to stop! I'm just really excited you're doing something to help Camelot run better. I know that being king isn't your dream job."

Midas shrugged. *She* was his dream. Saving Camelot was a simple enough way to make her happy. In a way, Midas was enjoying the challenge of the convoluted spreadsheets.

"I think it's awesome that you..." Gwen broke off mid-word. "Why is there ice cream melting all over the brand new area rug?"

"That's Celliwig." Avalon told her distractedly, busy cutting through her enemies with the letter opener. "It has mud." She gestured to the puddle of chocolate-chip fudge seeping into the pink carpet. "That's the mud."

Gwen sighed, her gaze flicking between Midas and Trystan. "You two will just let her do anything, won't you?"

"The child is a creative thinker." Trystan defended. "My people honor such gifts. You would prefer we stifle her genius?"

"No, of course not. That's the very *last* thing I would want you to do. But, there are ways to encourage a child without damaging all the furnishings..." Gwen stopped talking again, her attention jumping back to fake-Celliwig. "The very last." She whispered. "The very last place he'd want to look. Midas!" She grabbed his arm, excitedly. "He meant *you*."

"What?"

"My father remembered backwards! When he told me where he hid the wand, he said, 'It's the very last place he'd want to look.' Only Merlyn didn't mean Arthur or the Scarecrow. He meant *you*." Her voice rose in exhilaration, her sentences coming out in a rush. "He *knew* you were coming into my life. That I'd eventually figure out what his words meant, but no one else would understand! Because they don't know you, like I do."

Midas frowned. "You think the wand is...?"

Gwen cut him off. "Yes!" She pointed at the brown stain on the rug that represented his hometown. "It's in Celliwig! The very last place you'd ever want to go."

Midas' eyebrows compressed, thinking that over. "...shit." He finally muttered.

"Cursing is a no-no." Trystan taunted.

"We have to go there first thing in the morning." Gwen bounded to her feet. "Avi, sweetie, it's time for bed. Mommy has a very busy day tomorrow."

Midas stayed still while she tucked the little girl under the covers and while Trystan scooped the dolls back into Avalon's backpack. All except Lyrssa, anyway, who stayed hugged tight in Avalon's arms.

Celliwig.

A cold sense of dread crawled through Midas. Whenever he thought of that hellhole, he was nine years old again and all alone on a cold porch. It really was the last place he'd ever want to go. Especially with Gwen. Having her see where he came from --the dirt and misery and harshness of the village-- would be a nightmare. For reasons known only to God and Good-hearted blondes, she believed Midas was honorable. Once she saw where he'd been born, though, all her pretty fantasies about his gallantry would be over.

No one kind and gentle had ever come out of Celliwig. It was impossible. Gwen was too smart not to realize that. After tomorrow, she would never see him the same way, again.

Son of a *bitch*.

"A trip to Celliwig will take supplies." Trystan announced. "I will see to them."

He paused by the bed to touch Avalon's forehead, his thumb sliding from her hairline to the bridge of her nose. It was a pledge of devotion. Midas had never seen Trystan use the gesture with anyone except this little girl, but he recognized it. Corrah had done it to him, just before she died. That small ritual was the highest form of affection gryphons could show each other.

Gwen might not understand the full meaning behind it, but she knew the gentle action was important. She glanced at Trystan and gave him a sad smile.

No gryphon offspring had been born in decades. It was a hard blow for a race who had always seen the young as their future. Now their future was dead, but their instincts remained. All of Trystan's energy and loyalty had swung behind Avalon, like she was the last daughter of his vanishing kind. In a way, she *was*. The Princess of Camelot, granddaughter of the genocidal madman who'd slaughtered Trystan's people, was quite possibly the final child a gryphon would ever help to raise.

Trystan was training Avalon to be a warrior, the same way Corrah had trained Midas. To survive. More strikingly, though, Trystan was telling Avalon about his culture. The heroes and villains and rituals and wars. Stories that Midas had never even heard from Corrah. Legends and myths, straight from their gods. Tales of creation and ancient spells and forgotten magic that spanned farther back than any other people could possibly recall.

Trystan taught Avalon *everything* about the gryphons. As if he wanted her to understand who'd they'd been and what they'd believed. As if he expected that, one day soon, she would be the only one left to remember that they'd existed, at all.

"I will see you on the morrow, child." He said quietly, pretending not to see Gwen's sympathetic look. "You are safe this night."

"I know." She smiled and yawned at the same time. "Good night, Trystan. I love you."

He grunted, scanned around once more to ensure nothing was lurking in the shadows to threaten her, and then strode out of the room.

Gwen sighed and clicked on Avalon's nightlight. "Damn it, I think I adore that maniac."

"Gryphon are the best." Midas said quietly. "I wish I had been born one. I wish I had come from their villages, high in the mountains, instead of..." He waved a defeated hand at the melting ice cream that signified Celliwig. "You would like me so much more."

Gwen crouched down in front of him. "It's kind of impossible for me to like you more, Midas." Lake-colored eyes met his, sensing his distress. "I know you're scared to go back to Celliwig and you don't have to *ever* see that place again. I can find the wand by myself." She caught hold of his hand and gave it a reassuring squeeze. "I would *never* ask you to re-live something so painful..."

"No." He interrupted, her words cutting through the fog. "Fuck, no." He shook his head, incredulous that she would even suggest such a thing. "You're not going there alone." Was she out of her mind? He'd sooner send her, unarmed and blindfolded, into battle with a minotaur. No Good folk could survive ten minutes in Celliwig. The people who lived there would scent her innocence like hungry sharks scenting blood in the water.

"It'll be fine. I can take Trystan with me and you watch Avalon."

"No. *I'll* go with you." There was no other option. He was

the only one who knew that shitty town. Midas rubbed a hand over his face. "I'll go. Celliwig is..." He tried to find the right words to convey the abject vileness of the muddy cesspit, but there were none. "It's just a very Bad place. So, be ready. You might look at me differently, afterwards."

She *would* look at him differently and it would fucking kill him.

Her palm came up to rest on his cheek. "I could never look at you differently, Midas." She whispered. "You're my husband."

His heart turned over in his chest, as it always did when she called him that. "Just be ready." He repeated and got to his feet.

Gwen shook her head and backtracked to pet Avalon's hair. "Sleep tight, baby."

"Night, Mommy." Her eyes had drifted shut. "I love you."

"I love you, too." Gwen glided out of the room, shutting off the overhead light.

Midas followed her, stopping by the bed to kiss Avalon on the top of her head. "Good night, princess." He whispered.

"Night." She murmured, half-asleep now. Midas was already to the doorway when he heard the rest of her reply. "I love you, Daddy."

Chapter Twenty-Three

Guinevere Pendragon agrees to limit surprises to three (3) a day.

Clause 13- Limitation of Surprises

Midas' whole body went still.

For one endless moment, he stood frozen in the doorway, his hand on the knob. It seemed to Gwen like she could actually see his mind switching gears at high speed, trying to process what he'd heard. By the time his head had swung around to look back at Avalon, she was fast asleep, cuddled up with Queen Lyrssa. He blinked rapidly, staring at her in the soft glow of her rocking-horsefly shaped nightlight.

Gwen nearly laughed at his astonishment. "Really, Midas, I would have thought you'd have figured this out by now." She chided.

"She just called me 'Daddy.'" He sounded blindsided. "Did you hear that?"

"Of course I heard it." Gwen touched his arm. "Who else would her daddy be?"

Midas still wasn't getting it. "That's impossible. You and I have never…"

"She's not *biologically* your daughter, obviously. But, that doesn't matter to Avalon. She… claims you. She always has."

His attention was still riveted on Avalon. "That is my child?"

"Yes." Gwen shrugged. "I don't exactly know why she selected you to be her father. In her mind, there isn't a question about it, though. Sorceresses see more than we do. They pick their own path. They can choose. … And she chose you."

Midas didn't move.

"It's why I put in Clause 3- 'Care and Protection of Avalon Pendragon.'" Gwen added, a little worried by his silence. "I was afraid of what might happen if you didn't choose her back. If she got used to having you around and something went wrong. I worried how you would react, if a little girl just showed up and called you 'Daddy.' I thought it would be better if you ignored Avi, until I could be sure…"

He cut her off. "That is *my* child." This time it wasn't a question. Golden eyes swung around to impale her. "You wanted to keep her from me?" He looked almost betrayed.

"I *brought* her to you." Gwen retorted firmly. "Despite my fears and when it made no goddamn sense, at all, I walked into this house and handed my baby to *you*."

"You did." Midas seemed to be having a hard time focusing, like he wasn't sure whether to be angry or hurt or happy or confused or ten other things. "You *literally* did." He shut the bedroom door and leaned against it, staring at nothing. "I never understood why, but you just... put her in my arms."

"And you took care of her." Gwen agreed. "In my heart, I knew you would. It's why I came here. Why I trusted her with you *and* with Trystan. A gangster and a gryphon and I trusted you two with my little girl. Because Avalon is *always* right and she said you were both hers."

"We are hers." He whispered.

Gwen smiled at the surety in his tone. "For two years, all Avalon's talked about is you, Midas. I had nowhere to go and no one to help me, when I escaped that dungeon. Then, Avalon said, 'I want my daddy' and I didn't even think about Arthur. I knew she meant you."

"She meant me." He ran both hands through his hair, still looking dazed. "She chose me. A sorceress chooses her path." He gave a slightly crazed laugh. "She told me that, when I was fifteen years old and so fucking alone I wanted to die."

"What?"

"*Vivien* said it. She said there would be a great queen who chose me over all other men. I didn't believe her, but she was talking about Avalon. She saw Avalon coming to me when I was only fifteen. Our paths have *always* been the same."

Gwen's eyebrows compressed. "Is this the same Vivien who cursed you?"

Midas didn't even hear her, lost in his own head. "Avalon's mine. She's *always* been mine." His expression shifted to reflect a fierce, primitive satisfaction. "I *knew* she was mine. I fucking *felt* it. That is *my* daughter."

"I know." Gwen agreed simply.

"Two years." Midas repeated, his brain snapping pieces into place. "For two years, she's said I was her father?"

"Yes."

"That's why Arthur sent me to prison." Again it wasn't a question.

Gwen winced. "It wasn't Avi's fault you..."

"No, it was *his* fucking fault! That son of a bitch tried to keep me from my daughter!" He sounded ready to drag Arthur's body from his tomb and kill him all over again.

"To be fair, she was Arthur's daughter, genetically."

"What the fuck does that have to do with anything? She didn't want him. She wanted *me*. She chose *me*."

"Arthur hated to lose. He didn't care about Avalon, but he *hated* that she saw someone else as her father. She talked about you and your wonderfulness, all the time. It hurt his ego."

"I don't give a shit about his feelings! Avalon claims *me* as her father. I claim her as my child. She's *mine*." Midas sliced a furious hand through the air as if everything was clear, undisputable, and legally binding. "That girl was mine fifteen years before she was born."

He and Avalon were clearly on the same page about the paternity issue. Which happened to be the gryphons' page, come to think of it: You claim what you want and fight for it. But how else should something so important be decided? Trystan's people weren't so primitive, as the "civilized" kingdoms thought. They kind of had the only logical system.

"You should have come to me sooner." Midas continued. "That fucking asshole should never have been near *my* baby for even one day..."

"He would have killed us both, before he let that happen." Gwen interrupted baldly. "Believe me. He was unhinged, when it came to you."

Midas stopped talking so fast his teeth clinked together. There was a long pause and she could see the final puzzle getting solved inside of his razor-sharp brain. His head tilted to one side. "How did Arthur die, Gwen?"

She hesitated. He'd never asked her that before.

Midas watched her. Waiting.

"Everything happened because you kept getting yourself on television." Gwen finally told him. She moved to sit on a green-and-black checked bench that was arranged in the hallway. "That new PR firm of yours would not have approved of all the negative coverage."

Midas watched her, not saying anything.

"The first time I ever saw you was in a mugshot on the news. You were being investigated for something. I honestly don't remember the specifics. I just remember... Avalon." She sighed, picturing it all as it played out. "She was toddling around the Queen's Parlor, as I watched TV. And Arthur came in, for some reason. It was rare that I saw him, at all, so it was just bad luck that he was there."

"He stayed away from you, even back then?"

"Always." Gwen shrugged. "I was happy with that, though. We both were. Still, it might've all gone differently for him, if he'd been any kind of father. If Avalon hadn't been forced to go looking for a better daddy." She glanced up at him. "For you."

"No." Midas sounded very sure. "It always would have happened this way. You two were always meant to be mine."

"Arthur wanted me to get rid of her when she was born, you know. He said she was deformed, because she was Bad." It was mindboggling how blind he'd been. How unwilling to see past his bigotry. "I hated him, after that. If there had been a way to leave him…"

"How did he die, Gwen?"

"Arthur always had such dreadful timing." She rubbed her forehead, lost in the past. "Just as he walked into the Queen's Parlor, the newscast showed that close-up of your mugshot. Avalon saw it. ...And her expression lit up." Gwen recalled it all so clearly. "My God, you would've thought she'd just seen Santa Claus. She screamed -- screamed, mind you-- 'Daddy, Daddy, Daddy! Mama, it's my daddy' and she put her teeny little hand right up on the screen like she could touch you."

Midas' mouth curved, looking smug. "*My* daughter." He said quietly.

"Arthur, as you can imagine, was not as pleased as you appear to be." She informed him archly. "Avalon had never called *him* anything but 'Arthur.' I doubt it occurred to him to care about that before, but now he was furious. Afraid that someone else would hear her say *you* were her father. He said it would humiliate him if that rumor got around."

"He knew I'd show up on his doorstep, if I heard about it." Midas corrected. "I would have been there to see the child, even knowing it was impossible that she came from me."

"Either way, it was a side of him I'd never seen." She would never forget it. "Usually he was just spoiled and callous, but suddenly he was on a rampage. I tried to calm him down, but he was shouting curses at you, and accusing me of cheating on him, and threatening to disinherit Avalon." She glanced at him. "There were already so *many* rumors of my infidelity, you see."

"I'm sorry I ever, *ever* doubted you about that, Gwen."

"Well, you were kind of right. Avalon *wasn't* Arthur's daughter, in any way that mattered. I just wasn't sure how to explain that to you." She rolled her eyes. "'Hi, I'm Gwen and I know we've never met, but my baby thinks you're her dad.' I mean, it's not exactly a great conversation starter with a man."

"It would have worked *great* on me. I promise you."

"Well, how could I know that, then? How could I be sure you wouldn't refuse her or even kick us out? That first night you told me you didn't even like children."

"I never said that."

"Close enough. You said you wouldn't bond with her and that you'd make a terrible father and that you wanted to just ignore Avi. I was very worried that she'd somehow gotten you all wrong, Midas."

"That's why you almost left." He blinked, remembering their initial meeting. "You asked me about rocking-horseflies and I told you I loved them. That was the only thing that made you stay. I couldn't figure out why."

"They're Avi's favorite. She said they were your favorite, too. I thought if she was right about that, she was right about everything."

"*That's* what saved me? Liking those sparkly bugs?" He paled like a man who'd come within a single step of a thousand foot cliff. "Holy *fuck*. One call to an exterminator and I would've lost my wife and daughter."

"No." Gwen shook her head. "Right after that, you insisted on buying Avi a doll. I would have stayed with you then, regardless, because I thought that was very cute and promising."

"Buying things is always a great first step." He agreed. "How did Arthur die?"

Gwen made a face at him. "Anyway," she went back to her story, "after Avalon called you 'Daddy,' Arthur was so upset he wouldn't listen to me. He kicked the TV screen in. He was shouting at Avi, and she was crying, and I was so afraid of what he might..." She trailed off. "There are tabloid pictures of it. You've probably seen them."

"Yes."

"That's why I got the gun. After that, I knew I might need it. Galahad bought it for me."

Midas scrubbed a hand over his face. "I guess I can't hate the Beige Adonis anymore, if he protected you. Which is a shame, because I really fucking hate him. I even hate rerunning his stupid show on my new network, although it's working against the Scarecrow." He paused. "...And it makes *great* ratings. I hate that."

"Galahad always stood up for me. Always shielded Avalon. Aside from you, he's my best friend. I just wish I knew where Gal is, so *I* could help *him*, now."

"I'll find him for you."

That surprised her. "You will? Why? You just said you hated him."

"So what? You want him back."

Gwen smiled at that profound answer. "Thank you."

He grunted. "Just remember when he gets here: You're not attracted to boring heroes."

"That's true. I'm only attracted to one hero and he's certainly not boring."

Midas' mouth kicked up at the corner, but his eyes were grave. "How did Arthur die, Gwen?"

"After that day, Arthur had you arrested for whatever random crimes he could think of, probably for things you didn't even do."

"No, I did all of them." Midas admitted without even blinking.

She flashed him an exasperated look. "Regardless, I blamed myself. All I could think of was how you were unfairly targeted because of me."

"I would be sent back to prison a thousand times over for you."

"Well, I got it into my head to free you. I offered Arthur a DNA test on Avalon. I'd never really cared enough to bother, before. Let him think what he wanted, the ass. At least he was staying away from us. But I wanted to help you."

He smiled at that. "You're so fucking Good, it breaks my heart."

"Well, it didn't work. I'd hoped that the results would calm him down. Any paternity test would show him where Avi came from. I *never* cheated on Arthur, so I thought I'd solved everything. That he would stop with his obsession and let you go free. Instead, when he got the envelope back from the lab, it just seemed to make him more... unhinged."

Midas' gaze sharpened. "Whose blood did he test?"

"All our blood. Once he arrested you, he said it was legal for him to get your DNA. So he sent off his blood, my blood, your blood, and Avalon's blood. It was a waste of resources, because all he needed was his and Avalon's to show a match. I told him that."

"But he tested your blood and my blood, too? Together?"

She frowned at the intensity of the question. "Yes. Why?"

Midas didn't respond to that, staring off at nothing, again. "That son of a bitch knew." He murmured. "He knew I'd take them both. That's why he wanted me dead."

Gwen blinked. "Arthur tried to kill you?"

"Yes." Midas moved to sit next to her on the bench, his arm resting along the back rail behind her. "Did he try to kill you? Is that what happened the night he died?"

"No. He tried to kill Avalon."

Midas' fist clenched along the back of the seat, but he kept his voice low. "Tell me." He said.

And so she did.

Chapter Twenty-Four

Guinevere
One Year Ago

"Daddy's coming home!" Avalon bounced up and down on Gwen's bed, overcome with enthusiasm. "The mean place is burning up! Mommy, Daddy's coming home, now!"

Gwen stared at the television set on the wall, her own heart pounding. The Wicked, Ugly and Bad Mental Health Treatment Center and Maximum Security Prison was on fire. Half the walls had already fallen. Guards couldn't hold back the tidal wave of inmates. Chaos reigned, hundreds of people escaping into the night. Most would never be recaptured.

The Kingpin was free.

Hope swelled inside of Gwen. Crazy and illogical, but there just the same. If Midas was out, then he'd come back to Camelot. From all reports, the man was too arrogant to do anything else. He'd return to confront Arthur and reclaim his business. And if he came back to Camelot, everything would change.

She knew it.

Arthur swore Midas was nothing but a "tawdry feral animal." All the court documents would seem to back him up. Midas ran the biggest criminal organization in Camelot. There seemed little doubt of that, even if Gwen didn't fully believe that he'd committed *all* the crimes he'd been convicted of. To hear the prosecutors tell it, Midas was simply a flashy-dressed street thug. A violent, uneducated commoner, who'd bullied himself into a position of power. Any sane person would agree he belonged in prison. A jury of his (entirely Good) peers had rubber-stamped his guilty verdict in record time.

Except Avalon steadfastly believed that Midas was a hero. Kind, honorable, and gentle. She called this Bad man, with an even worse reputation, her daddy.

...And Avalon was always right.

Avi might be a small child, but she was also the granddaughter of Merlyn. A sorceress with powers beyond anything the world had ever seen. If Avi said Midas was special, Gwen believed her. In fact, the more Arthur and the rest of the Good folk railed against Midas, the more convinced Gwen grew that this "tawdry feral animal" was something far more important than anyone was letting on.

Her eyes scanned the hectic scene at the prison. "Is Midas hurt?" She heard herself ask, trying to spot him. In pictures, the man towered over everyone else. She knew that because she'd spent a lot of time looking at photos of Midas. An embarrassing amount of time, actually. You'd think his giant form would be easy to see on the TV screen, even in the darkness of night.

"Daddy's okay." Avalon kept bouncing. "He's with Trystan. Trystan's nice. He belongs with me and you and daddy. He's my second best friend. He has big wings."

Gwen nodded vaguely, not able to look away from the blaze on screen. Avalon's visions were accurate one hundred percent of the time. Why wouldn't she be right about this? Midas was safe and he was coming home.

"Daddy will be with us soon, Mommy! I'm happy, happy, happy!"

A smile curved the edges of Gwen's mouth. "So am I." She whispered.

The door leading from the veranda slammed open before she could say anything else, one of the glass panels shattering. Arthur stood there, breathing hard and violently drunk. "You whore!" He screamed. "You think I don't know you're involved in this?!"

Gwen's heart dropped, shocked that Arthur was in her room. He hadn't crossed the threshold since Avalon was born. Whatever was about to happen it would be horrible. She knew that without question.

"Avalon, run." She looked over at her daughter. "Run, now."

Avi didn't run, she stood on the mattress watching Arthur with grave eyes. "He smells funny." She whispered.

It was the liquor. *Shit*. Gwen tried to think through her panic.

"You probably helped him escape!" Arthur didn't even look like himself, his handsome face twisted and reddened in rage. "You and that fucking little brat that you pretend is mine, have been working against me." He waved a hand at Avi, hating her simply for being born.

"Stay away from my child." Gwen automatically moved, so she was standing between Arthur and Avi. Damn it, the gun was in the nightstand on the other side of the bed. How was she going to get it?

"Avalon, go back to your own room."

Avi ignored her, her attention on Arthur. "You's making a bad choice." She told him quietly, quoting the warning that Gwen always used on her when she was being naughty. "One last chance to fix your behavior and then you're going to be in *big* trouble."

"It's your mother's fault this happened. She'd rather fuck a gangster than a king." He whirled back to Gwen. "I thought you'd moved onto Galahad, but it's always been that tawdry, feral animal, hasn't it?"

"I've never even met Midas. You know that. I had nothing to do with his escape." Aside from silently cheering it on, anyway. Gwen edged towards the nightstand. "Please leave my room."

"You're a lying bitch." Arthur advanced on her, seething. "You and that ape probably sat around *laughing* at me, while you plotted and schemed. Is that what you do? Laugh at me, when you welcome that dirty primate into your bed!"

"You're out of your mind." Fear coursed through her, as he stalked closer. She tried to hide it, refusing to retreat. "Get out of here. *Now*."

"Or what? You'll call your brainless oaf of a boyfriend to protect you?"

"My daddy will always protect us." Avi glared at Arthur. "He's the bravest man in the whole kingdom. And the smartest. And the handsomest. And the..."

"*Shut up!*"

"Avalon, leave this room!" Gwen shouted, but her daughter wasn't listening.

"My daddy," she told Arthur, her voice ringing with the absolute certainty of an all-seeing sorceress, "will save me and Mommy from mean things like you... and there's nothing you can do to stop him."

"*I will never let that fucking villain win!*" Arthur lunged at Avalon,

"No!" Gwen tried to block him and he punched her.
Hard.

His fist slammed into her stomach, knocking the air from her lungs. No one had ever hit Gwen before. Despite everything, it shocked her. She fell, her head smacking against the bedpost and leaving her stunned for a moment. She lay on the ground, dazed and struggling for air.

Arthur grabbed Avalon right off the mattress. Avi struggled to get free, kicking, but Arthur was five times her size. He dragged her towards the balcony.

"*No!*" Gwen staggered to her feet, charging after them. "Arthur, stop!"

"Mommy!" Avalon caught hold of the doorway, trying to reach Gwen. Arthur roughly pulled her away, picking her up, so she couldn't escape.

Oh God.

"*I'm* the King of Camelot." The rain was pouring down, soaking all three of them. "No one else." Arthur backed towards the railing. "*Me!*"

Gwen followed him, her heart pounding out of her chest. The gun was still in her nightstand, but she couldn't go back for it. She was afraid to take her eyes off Avalon, for fear of what Arthur might do.

"No one's saying you're not the king." She flashed Avalon a warning look, before Avi could say that very thing. "You're becoming upset over nothing. Midas isn't a threat to you." Gwen had never been much of a liar, but she did her best to sound convincing and to calm him down. "You're much too powerful for anyone to challenge."

"That son of a bitch is coming back here! He'll find out the truth! No one will follow me. I'll be ruined. *Humiliated!*"

Gwen had no idea what he was talking about. She didn't even care. All she wanted was Avalon. "Arthur," she kept her voice as steady as possible, "put Avi down. You've been drinking. It's making you confused. You don't want to hurt your own daughter."

"She's *his* daughter." Arthur spat. "She belongs to *him*, not me." DNA test or not he would never accept Avalon as his child. "No Bad folk could *ever* be a true Princess of Camelot."

Avalon wouldn't accept him, either. She vainly tried to squirm free of his grasp, still expounding on Midas' virtues. "My daddy is the *real* King of Camelot. He will be the best king ever. Way better than you. I seen it."

"I knew it!" Arthur was half sobbing, half screaming, and totally beyond reason. "He's going to take *everything*."

"How in the world could he *possibly* become king, Arthur?" Gwen threw up her hands. "It doesn't even make any sense." Avalon was always right, but that seemed like a bizarre prediction even for her. "He'd either have to inherit the throne or marry someone who has it and Midas can't do either. You aren't thinking straight!"

He reached the banister, his eyes wild. "My fucking father must be enjoying this, watching and chortling from Hell. Do you think I'll let him be right about me being weak?"

"Uther is dead and gone. You don't need to worry about him. Just put Avi down and..."

"I'll kill you both, before I lose you to a Bad folk!" Arthur held Avalon out over the railing, so she dangled four stories above the hard ground. "I'll see you dead, before you beat me!"

Gwen gave up on reason and launched herself at the bastard.

Galahad had taught her some basic self-defense moves, but she wasn't sure if she used them. She was too desperate to get her baby back to think straight. She was hitting Arthur as hard as she could, flailing her arms out, trying to grab Avalon back from him. He was probably hitting her, too, but she didn't feel it. All that mattered was Avi.

"Midas can scrape his daughter from the pavement!" Arthur released his hold on Avalon.

"*Mommy!*"

Gwen threw herself forward, snagging her daughter's nightgown. Avalon hung by the cheerful cartoon-patterned garment, suspended over the unforgiving cobblestones. Focused only on saving her child, Gwen stopped fighting Arthur and concentrated on dragging Avi back up. Straining with everything she had, she lifted Avalon high enough so the little girl could latch onto her hand.

"Mommy, help!"

Gwen held tight. "I got you, baby." They would both go over or they would both survive. There was no way in the world she'd let go. She instinctively wrapped her ankles around the decorative balusters to anchor herself.

Seeing an opening, Arthur moved in for the kill. Screaming obscenities, he tried to shove Gwen over the edge, while she was distracted. His manicured hands pushed her, wanting her to go over and drag Avalon with her.

Too bad for him, her feet were still locked around the railing's spindles. Gwen wasn't going anywhere. Instead, she slugged him with her free hand, putting every ounce of power she had into the blow.

Maybe it was luck, or maybe it was fate, or maybe it was being a mother. But somehow her blow impacted him in the perfect spot. Arthur reared backwards, arms spinning. Off balance and caught by surprise, he didn't have time to brace himself. He hit the wet railing, slipped, and toppled backwards.

Arthur's face would be frozen in her memory forever. The shock and horror he felt when he realized there was no more ground beneath him.

"Gwen!" He clawed desperately for her, trying to save himself. "*Help me!*"

She didn't help him.

Reaching for Arthur would mean letting go of Avalon and no force in Heaven or Hell could make Gwen release her daughter. Instead, her free hand locked around Avalon's other wrist, dragging her up. "Don't watch, baby."

"*Jilllllllll....*" Arthur screamed the woman's name as he spiraled downward, impacting the pavement like a pumpkin exploding.

Blood pooled around him, mixing with the rain and staining all the puddles a ghastly crimson. There was no mistaking the fact that Arthur was dead. Gwen gazed at the grisly spectacle, reconciling herself to what she'd done and all the problems it would cause.

She'd just killed the King of Camelot.

Shit.

Jill was going to be pissed.

Chapter Twenty-Five

Parties agree that their partnership is exclusive and monogamous. Additionally, each day, they will alternate mutually agreed on physical contact (ie: third-base behaviors). The purpose of said activity is the satisfaction of needs.

Clothes will stay mostly on.

Clause 21- Amended Physical Contact Agreement (Containing Nullification of Clause 7-Separate Lives and Other Relationships)

"I couldn't save them both." Gwen said faintly, finishing her story. "I wasn't strong enough. I could only pull one to safety."

Midas nodded. "So you chose Avalon." It wasn't even a question.

"So, I chose Avalon." Gwen concurred. "I held her tight and I let him fall." She was quiet for a moment. "He really wasn't so terrible in the beginning. I never loved him, but he wasn't evil. Just self-indulgent and egotistical. Something dark took root in him."

"Or maybe he was always evil and you were too Good to see it."

"I'm not so Good. I punched him. That's why he died."

"He died because he was an abusive maniac."

She barely even heard that assurance. "It all happened so *fast*. I was frantic to get her back and then... he was just *screaming* all the way down. Screaming for Jill." At the end, maybe he'd realized what a terrible mistake he'd made in not treating her better. "That scream went on forever and then it stopped, but it was even louder, somehow." She sniffed back more tears. "Do you think it's true that I murdered him?"

"It was an accident." Midas insisted firmly. "An accident *he* caused."

She wanted to believe that, but it was so hard to be sure. "I'm not a violent person. I wouldn't have *deliberately* killed him. Not unless there was no other option to save her."

"I know." His hand smoothed down her hair. "I'm so sorry, kitten. This is my fault."

"Yours? That's ridiculous. You weren't even there."

"Once I escaped the WUB Club, I planned to kill Arthur." Midas brushed a tear from her cheek. "I would have, *should* have, except he died before I got back to Camelot. So, you have *nothing* to feel guilty about. If he hadn't died with you, he would have died with me. The bastard would be dead right now, regardless of how things happened that night. I just wish I had been the one to do it."

"He died the same day you escaped. There was nothing you could have done."

"If I had known you then, I would have come for you sooner, no matter what it took." It was a vow. "I would *never* have left you and Avalon with that man. Not even for a day. Arthur was right. I would have stolen you both away."

"You wouldn't have had to steal us." Gwen met his eyes. "I would have come with you willingly and I would have given you my daughter."

Midas liked that answer. "Yeah?"

"Yeah." Gwen gave him a watery smile, shifting closer to him on the bench. "I was swept up in you before we even met." She confessed. "Avi would tell me things about you. About how kind you are. And honorable. And gentle. And I swear I could feel you. It was like we were already... connected."

"We *are* connected." He shook his head. "Except I'm *not* kind and honorable and gentle. You don't believe that, I know. And I don't try hard enough to make you see the truth, because I'm afraid that you'll stop looking at me like I'm important to you."

"You and Avalon are the *most* important things to me, Midas. For two years, I've thought about you. Do you really believe I don't know who you are inside?"

"You have no idea who I am inside and I hope you never find out." He lifted her body so she was on his lap. "You are in my head every second of every day. Until you and Avalon came home to me, I was empty." He held her tight. "I had *nothing*. And now there is nothing I won't do to keep you both beside me."

Gwen cuddled closer, comforted by his warmth. "Do you think Arthur sensed that I was thinking about you so much? I worry *that's* why he tried to hurt you and Avi." She blinked up at him, confessing her deepest fear. "Do you think it was because of me that he targeted you two and...?"

"*No*." Midas interjected emphatically. "No, Gwen. You did nothing wrong." He kissed the top of her head. "You and Avalon are the victims in this mess. Everything that happened was because Arthur wanted what was mine. That son of a bitch is lucky he's dead." Midas brooded for a beat. "He'd better be fucking dead." He muttered. "I wake up at night, afraid he's somehow alive and you'll be his wife again."

"I would *never* be his wife, again." Gwen vowed with a shudder. "Ever. But, he *is* dead, Midas. I saw his body. He's gone." She laid a hand on his shirtfront. "And we're here. That's all that matters."

His cheek rested against her hair for a long time. "Thank you for saving Avalon." He finally whispered. "Thank you for coming here and trusting me with her."

"Thank you for protecting our daughter, when I had nowhere else to go." She tilted her head back. "You're the one who gave us a place to hide... *Oh!*"

The "our daughter" part of that comment had made Midas *extremely* happy. His mouth claimed Gwen's, his lips slanting over hers. Good *Lord*, but the man could kiss.

Emotions running high, it only took a moment for passion to take over. Clause 21-"Amended Physical Contact Agreement" said that they would alternate days when they pleasured each other, but, so far, Midas had spent all his days touching her. She'd tried to get his pants off on numerous occasions, but he'd always talked her out of it. The man could be so damn persuasive when his fingers were doing naughty things. This time, Gwen wasn't going to give him a chance to distract her. She shifted, so her knees were on either side of his hips, her hands reaching for his belt buckle.

"Gwen." He tugged her blouse open, nuzzling the valley between her breasts. His teeth grazed her delicate skin, marking her, and she whimpered. The small sound enflamed him. "I need to touch you, kitten. Come back to my bedroom and let me... Holy *shit*."

Gwen grinned in triumph. "It's your turn." She managed to get his pants open and then he was at her mercy. "We need to follow the rules of our Contract to the letter."

He caught hold of her wrist, keeping her still. "If you do this, I won't be able to go back." He warned. "I'll need you even more than I need you now... and that seems fucking *impossible*. You need to be sure."

"I have been sure about you from the minute I saw your mugshot, Midas." She gently tugged against his hold and he released her. Her fingers wrapped around him and he gave a harsh groan of bliss. "Are you sure about *me?* Do you still want me, even after everything I just told you?"

"Of everything in this world, you are the thing I am most sure about, Guinevere Pendragon."

She leaned forward to kiss him, loving that answer. "We really should find you a last name, so Avalon and I can change ours. I have a feeling you don't want to be a 'Pendragon' with us."

He kept his eyes open as their lips touched, like he was afraid to look away. "You'd share a name with me?" No one had ever linked their name to his before. He looked amazed.

"Well, only if it's really cool." She grinned, her palm massaging the massive evidence of his desire. "Nothing beige."

"Pick anything you want. Just so everyone knows that I belong with you and Avalon."

"We belong *together*." She corrected. "I guess we'll have to amend Clause 2- 'Change of Names' and update the marriage scroll, too. But, we can get that from that drunken wizard who performed the ceremony."

Midas dragged his attention from watching her fist caress him. "I have our marriage scroll." He admitted warily.

"*You* have it? How did you get it?"

"Trystan stole it for me." Midas' focus drifted to her breasts, again. "I asked him to. Our marriage can't be officially dissolved unless the scroll is destroyed, so I thought it would be better if I just held onto it. For… safekeeping."

"Oh." Gwen wasn't sure what to make of that. "Well, I guess that will make the name change easier."

Midas nodded. "Very logical." He couldn't work the bra's small closure through his gloves, so he just ripped it off of her. Gwen was used to that. In the last week, he'd shredded at least eight others in the same way. "God you're beautiful."

"I'm not going to keep buying lingerie, if you keep destroying it."

"Good. I'd be happier if you didn't wear a fucking thing." His mouth dipped to suckle her taunt nipple, making a hungry sound.

"No. I mean, *you're* going to be the one paying for…" Gwen gasped. "*Midas*." She arched against him and his hands smoothed over her body, memorizing the curves.

"I want to feel you, without the damn gloves in the way." He snarled in frustration. "I would give anything to be able to touch you for real."

"You *are* touching me for real." She tightened her grip on his shaft. "And I'm touching you."

"*Fuck*." He gave a hiss of pleasure. "You keep that up and

this will be over fast, kitten."

"Then, we'll just have the opportunity to start it all, again." She teased breathlessly. "Unless you have something better to do with your evening."

His smile was filled with something deeper than lust. Something huge and warm and real. "There is *nothing* better than you." He said quietly. "You are the very best, Gwen. I knew it from the minute I saw you."

She blinked back a new rush of tears at the soft words, the final requirement of her Right Man list checked off. Midas definitely wanted her as much as she wanted him. She could see it all in his eyes. Gwen's forehead dipped forward to rest against his. In that moment she'd never felt closer to anyone.

Midas' expression turned more solemn, like he sensed it, too. Their breath mingling, as her hair fell around them like a curtain. He lifted a palm to cradle her cheek. "I wish I could touch you for real," he whispered again, "half as deeply as you touch me."

Her lips brushed against his, her fingers moving faster. Her free hand came up to thread through his fingers, holding it against her face.

Midas' head tipped back in ecstasy. "God, kitten. I want it to last, but I can't. I need you too much." He shifted her open palm, so he could kiss it, only to stop suddenly. His gaze locked on the place where her wedding band rested. "Gwen?" He gave his head a clearing shake, like he was trying to concentrate. "Would you take his ring off?"

That surprised her. "Right now? Why?"

"Because I'm asking you. Nicely. I'm asking you nicely to give it to me and not to wear it anymore." He paused. "Please." He added, like that might help with the "nicely" part.

Gwen had to admit, it was fairly convincing. "Are you going to try and buy it, again?" She asked suspiciously. "Because that was really tacky and not in your usual cute way."

He shook his head, his breathing ragged. "I won't offer to buy it." He got out. "I just don't want to come in your hand, when you're wearing Arthur's ring. I want it to be you and me and no one else."

Gwen blinked. The wedding band was just money to her. It had nothing to do with Arthur. Obviously, it symbolized something else to Midas, though. It wasn't just a trophy for him to acquire, like she'd thought. It was a sign that she was still connected to another man. *That's* why he wanted it. She should have realized it sooner.

Midas could be sentimental, at times.

"Once I remove it, it won't be enspelled, anymore. I won't know for sure that no one can *ever* take it." It was a risk for her to give up her safety net of guaranteed funds. "It would lose the magical connection to my body."

"I know." It was a snarl of satisfaction.

"What will protect Avalon, if something goes wrong?"

"I will."

Gwen considered his intent face for a beat and then nodded. "Alright." She murmured, agreeing to give him far more than a hunk of gold. "Since you asked me nicely, you can have it."

The tendons in Midas' neck went taunt, his body swelling, but still he tried to focus. "You'll give it to me? Right now?"

"Well, I have my other hand full, right now." She nipped his ear. "If you want the ring gone, you'll have to do it yourself."

His gaze leapt to hers. "You'd let me remove it?"

"I would let you do just about anything, Midas." Since no wedding band could be removed without permission of the owner, though, Gwen figured she'd better be more explicit. "Please take my ring off." She held up her left palm for him.

Midas pulled it free so fast it was a wonder he didn't dislocate her joint. "About fucking time." He survey the naked finger, like he'd just singlehandedly felled a rampaging dragon. Triumph glittered in his gaze. "Mine." He tossed the wedding band aside and pushed her newly liberated palm towards his lap. "Use this hand. I want all those pretty, bare fingers wrapped around me."

Gwen arched a brow and did what he wanted. It was strangely arousing that he was so fixated on a simple circle of gold. "It *really* bothered you that I was wearing Arthur's ring, didn't it?" She surmised, feeling him grow impossibly harder in her grip.

That incredible golden gaze flashed up to hers again, burning hot. "Yes." He intoned and she heard all his suppressed frustration in the word. "It really bothered me."

Why was his possessiveness such a turn on? With Arthur, jealousy had been suffocating and scary. With Midas, she just wanted to sooth his frown away. The difference was all in the man and how deeply she trusted him. Her nails lightly scratched over Midas' velvety tip and his whole body jolted.

"*Gwen*." His teeth ground together like he was barely holding on.

She kissed the side of his jaw, pleased with that response. "It's just a ring, you know."

"I've bought you safes full of jewelry since you've been here." Midas panted. "Every ring for sale in the whole goddamn kingdom."

"*That's* why you've been doing that?" Lord, he was so impractical. It was part of his romantic, gallant nature, she supposed. "Do you have any idea how much all those rings must've cost? It's going to add a fortune to my bill and..."

"I don't care." He interrupted. "I care that you didn't wear them. You still wear *that* ring. Day after day. The one that marks you as Arthur's wife. The one that says you still belong to him."

"I don't see it that way. Really. I just saw the wedding band as my safety net."

"I see it as *his*."

"I'm sorry." She said honestly. "I truly didn't know it was such a big issue."

"How could it not be a big issue?" He'd clearly been storing up a huge list of grievances about one tiny ring. "You put that ugly chunk of metal right in *our* Contract. You said you wanted to keep it, just in case something went wrong with *our* marriage. Use *his* gold to buy food for *our* daughter, instead of any of the gold *I* gave you."

She made a *tsk* sound. "I should have remembered how sensitive you are. Let me make it up to you."

"I'm not sensitive. I just don't..." He trailed off with a moan as her body slid off his lap, so she was kneeling on the floor. "Oh *Christ*, yes. Make it up to me just like that. Just like that." His legs shifted, giving her room. "I need your mouth on me." His fingers tangled in her hair, urging her towards his throbbing shaft. "I need it, kitten. I need it so bad."

She dipped her head, but she didn't give him what he wanted. Instead, she nipped the inside of his thigh, enjoying his frustrated oath. "Do you know *why* I let you take the wedding band off?"

"Please." He got out, his jaw like granite. "Now, Gwen. Please." He was about to lose control.

"Because, I don't need it to be my safety net anymore." She continued. "I have you."

"You have me. God, you have all of me. You are my goddamn life and soul." He shuddered as her tongue flicked out to measure the length of him. "That's the reason I stole the scroll. So our marriage can't be broken. I can't ever give you up. I can't go back to the darkness."

She glanced up at him, through her lashes. "Why Midas,

stealing from a wizard sounds like something a *Bad* man would do and you're always such a gentleman." It was also pretty hot. She rewarded him by taking one deep, tantalizing taste of his pulsing flesh.

"*Fuck!*" Midas' whole body arched and she knew he was at the end of the game. "I'm not a gentleman. I'm Bad and you're mine and I'm taking you. Open. Now." He nudged her lips, wanting entrance. "And *never* put his ring on again." He added, like he still wasn't over the whole wedding band issue. "No one else *ever* marks you as theirs."

"Alright." She agreed, completely turned on by his wildness.

"I mean it, Gwen. Never again. I can't fucking stand it."

"Never again." She stopped teasing and gave him what he wanted. "I swear it, husband." Her lips sealed over him, but it was calling him her husband that sent him over the edge.

Midas erupted with a hoarse shout. His hand fisted in her hair, like he was afraid she would pull away and leave him bereft. "Gwen! Oh God. *Gwen*." His hips jerked, sinking deeper into her mouth and she suckled every drop from him. "Oh fuck yes."

Damn, but she rocked at seduction.

"My wife." Midas whispered when she was done. He said the words every time they finished, like he just couldn't believe she was really married to him. It always made Gwen smile.

"Yours." She told him, because he needed the reassurance. "I'm yours, Midas."

He pulled her into his lap, his face buried in her hair. His lips pressed against her temple in something like reverence. For a man who fought and paid for everything he possessed, he always seemed shocked at how easily she allowed him to hold her.

"But you're mine, too." Gwen continued, pretty damn smug with how well that had gone. "Equal partners."

"Equal partners." He kissed her full on the mouth, looking arrogant, now. "Do *not* wear another man's ring." He commanded, like maybe his feelings on the subject still weren't clear enough. "Not unless I'm dead in the ground. It drives me insane."

"I noticed."

"I want the Contract to say you can't get jewelry from any other men."

"Now you're just reacting emotionally, again. It's not your fault." She patted his cheek. "You're a very passionate man. It clouds your logic sometimes."

"Clause 14- 'Renegotiation of Contract' says I can renegotiate at any time." He insisted, still panting for oxygen. "That's *very* logical.

I want the contractual right to slaughter any bastard who gives my wife so much as a paperclip."

"We'll discuss it later, when you're not overcome by your delicate sensibilities." She pushed back her hair and ignored his skeptical snort. "Would you do something for me, right now?"

"I would do *anything* for you."

"Good. Make love to me." She ordered, feeling exhilarated. "Let's change the Contract and be together without any restrictions."

Midas hesitated and she saw a flash of longing on his face. He wanted her. His eyes dipped down to her breasts, to the small marks his teeth had left on the soft globes. She could actually feel him hardening again, recharging at a furious pace at the idea of being inside her the next time he came.

"...No." He said anyway.

"No?" Gwen hadn't expected that. "You just said you'd do anything."

"Anything but that."

"Why?" She demanded, stung by his refusal to do what they both wanted. She scrambled off of his lap, ready to argue her side.

Midas didn't try to hold her, which wasn't like him. "You'd just be unhappy afterwards." He said dully.

"I *seriously* doubt that."

"It's true. You wouldn't stay with me." He shook his head. "And if I lose you and Avalon, I would die." The words were stark and certain.

Her heart flipped over. "Avalon and I aren't leaving you, Midas. Why would you even think such a thing?" It had to come from his childhood. He said he'd lost his parents when he was nine. That had to create abandonment issues. "My love," she tilted her head to meet his gaze, "we will *never* leave you." This man was the only place in the world she wanted to be.

It was like he didn't even hear her reassurance. He lowered his face to his hands, not wanting to maintain eye contact, and rubbed his forehead. "My life is *perfect*." He was talking to himself, now. "I can't risk that. Not for anything."

"Perfect? We're at war with a madman and people are trying to kill us."

"That's a temporary situation." He assured her distractedly. "The Scarecrow will be dead soon and I'll have everything I ever wanted. You and Avalon will be happy, and safe, and looking at me like I belong with you."

"You *do* belong with us."

"For so long, I searched for what you've given me, Gwen. I didn't even have a *name* for it. I think I thought it was fucking class," he snorted, "I was an idiot."

He was still being an idiot. "Midas..."

He cut her off. "But now I wake up to it every single day. I'm not going to take a chance on losing that, no matter how much I want you." He swallowed. "God, how I want you. You have no idea. Sex with you would be... magic. You don't think I know it would be goddamn magic? You think I don't want you so bad that I can't sleep?" He plowed a hand through his hair. "But I come downstairs in the morning and you're *here*, Gwen. In this house. Smiling at me. Calling me your husband. And *that's* what I want more than anything."

It was difficult to be angry when he said things like that.

"Bad enough I have to take you to Celliwig tomorrow," he continued, in increasing agitation, "I'm not going to do *anything else* to jeopardize our marriage. I don't care if I have to live in cold showers for the rest of my life. I'm not going back out onto that godforsaken porch!"

Porch? What in the hell was he talking about? "How would sleeping with me jeopardize our marriage, Midas? Married people have sex all the time. It's really very common."

"You'll leave." He said again and his tone was utterly sure. "You won't need me with you anymore and you'll leave."

Whatever was happening in his mind, he'd somehow connected sleeping with her to the end of their marriage. Midas wasn't thinking rationally. She'd accidently hit on an issue that went straight down into his deepest and most instinctive fears.

And that triggered hers....

"Is this about your True Love?" Gwen blurted out.

Midas hesitated for a beat too long.

"It is!" She cried, not giving him a chance to answer. Her own insecurities took over, driving her on. "You're waiting for *her* and so you don't want to sleep with me. Is that it?"

"What?" His head snapped around. "No." He gaped at her like she was speaking in tongues. "God, no. I don't want anyone else." He sounded incredulous and kind of a little bit insulted. "How can you even *think* that?" He paused. "I mean, I *know* why you're thinking it. Because Arthur was a cheating bastard." Golden eyes narrowed. "That asshole is *still* trying to take you from me."

"This isn't about Arthur." Gwen retorted. "I was perfectly happy with him dating Jill and staying away from me." She waved them both aside. "I am *not* happy with you dating other people, though, because *you* are my husband. Arthur was just some guy I was married to."

Midas' eyes gleamed with that hungry light they always got when she called him her husband. "I waited my whole life for you, Gwen. Every minute of every day. You don't *ever* have to worry about my True Love coming between us."

"Of course, I'm worried about her!" The woman weighed on Gwen's mind so much that she'd started stalking the internet for information on True Love, hoping to find a way to cure it. So far, she'd found nothing and it made her eyes fill with tears. "You said only Bad folk could feel things, but that's *not* true."

He cringed, realizing that he'd hurt her. "I know it's not true. Gwen, you have so many beautiful, pure feelings. I see them in everything you do. I *love* how Good you are. And I would never want anyone but you. It kills me that you'd be upset over this woman, when..." He tilted his head back, like he was trying to find a way out of a maze. "Fuck."

She sniffed, only slightly appeased. "Even if you don't want this other girl yet, you *could*. What if some beautiful stranger shows up and you instantly fall head-over-heels in love? Huh? You'd probably do any crazy thing she wanted, no matter how illogical and dangerous and bad for business."

Midas' gaze flicked to hers. "You think?" His mouth curved, although it wasn't the least bit funny.

"It's not just some romantic fantasy!" She declared, thinking he was scoffing at the idea. "It's actual science. They can do blood tests and know when two people will match-up. It's --like-- biology."

"So you believe in True Love now?"

"I believe *something's* happening. Something that could be life and death, Midas. People will do *insane* things to be with their True Love. Like really insane. That could be you. I've read studies online that claim Bad folk just know their True Loves, as soon as they see them. I heard you and Avi talking about it, too. They say it's instant."

"I've heard that rumor."

"So, we should have a plan in place, just in case this woman arrives. I mean, are you going to leave me? If you just look up and she's there, will you break our Contract?"

"No."

That characteristically simple answer made her feel better, but it wasn't enough. "Would you *want* to leave me?"

"No."

"So you're going to just stop desiring your True Love?" She challenged. "I don't even think that's possible." And it sure didn't seem like him. The man was uncompromising when it came to having everything he considered "his."

Midas stood up, focusing hard on fixing his clothes. "This whole conversation is pointless. Cross the True Love part out of the Contract if it makes you feel better. As a matter of fact, I'll willingly sign away the entire Termination Clause. I have no intention of *ever* ending our marriage. You're the one who insisted on adding it. I thought it was a waste of paper and ink, if you recall."

Gwen wasn't fooled by his exasperated tone. "Are you going to stop looking for her?"

"I've *already* stopped looking for her."

"Impossible." Gwen jerked her top back into place, not even bothering to try and salvage the bra. "You said every woman but your True Love was settling." That remark still stung. "You've never settled for anything in your life, Midas. You really expect me to believe that you'll just give up on this girl?"

"I'm not settling. You and Avalon are exactly what I want."

"That's not an answer. Are you going to give up on your True Love? Tell me the truth."

Another long pause. "Give up on her?" He repeated carefully.

"Yes or no."

Midas began to look hunted. "*You* are my wife." He spoke slowly, like she was the one being unreasonable. "For me, there is no one else. I give you my word."

"Still not an answer." And if he wasn't answering, it was because he wasn't giving up on the bitch.

Midas scrubbed a hand over his face. "Why are we arguing about this? I won't *ever* leave you for another woman. *Ever*. I'm not stupid, Gwen. I'm not going *anywhere* until you kick me out. Even then, I'd probably try to find my way back in. I just don't get what else you need to hear."

She wanted to hear that he loved her, dammit! Was she being fucking subtle about it?

Why wasn't he just saying the words? She was madly in love with this idiot. The least he could do was return the sentiment. Forget his bimbo of a True Love, he *had* to love Gwen back. There was no way she was the only person feeling the connection between them. He said he felt it, too! No one looked at a woman the way he looked at her unless he was completely smitten.

Right?

Annoyed at herself, and especially at *him*, Gwen got to her feet. "I'm going to bed. *Alone*."

"It's not fair of you to be mad at me about not sleeping together." He called after her, sounding pissed off. "*You're* the one who wrote Clause 21- 'Amended Physical Contact Agreement.' I'm well within my rights of our partnership and you know it."

"Sweet dreams." She called, ignoring that logical, truthful, and one-hundred-percent-certified dumbass argument. "I'll just go give *myself* an orgasm." Unfortunately, she wasn't going to be able to use her standard strapping stable boy fantasy to accomplish it, because Midas was the only man who seemed to turn her on, anymore.

Damn it.

He groaned like he was in pain. "Really? You're going to tell me something like that and just walk away? Please, don't..."

She slammed the door to her room, cutting him off.

The man was the biggest moron in the kingdom. Totally unfeeling and without the slightest idea of how to make a girl happy. It was a wonder she'd retained even a shred of sanity having to deal with the gigantic dickhead all day long. She'd be better off married to a toadstool. At least it might show some potential for emotional growth. Midas was totally, *totally* hopeless. Why had he even married her if he was going to be such a jackass?

She hesitated in the middle of her mental rant.

Actually, why *had* he married her? That was at the heart of everything. Why had he agreed to this deal, in the first place? She'd never been able to figure it out.

Despite the wizards' backing, he still showed no real interest in ruling a kingdom, so that couldn't possibly be his motivation for their partnership. Even Gwen could admit that she'd done a pretty crappy job of initially selling him on the wonders of a "lackluster" marriage. He'd never even *heard* of Dark Science before she came along, so that wasn't the reason for helping her, either.

In short, there were zero incentives for Midas to sign their Contract.

No.

Gwen's head tilted, fragments of conversations and bits of information coming together in her mind. No... Actually there could be *one* incentive, if you were lucky and Bad and very careful. If you were really talented at not saying too much and really clever about seeing the catur board from an entirely different angle.

If you were the smartest man in Camelot.

And, just like that, Gwen suddenly beheld the single blinding answer to *all* her questions. Why Arthur had never shown her the results of that mystio-physiological screening done on Gwen and Midas' blood. Why Avalon had always been so sure that Midas was her daddy. Why Gwen knew in her heart, nearly from the first moment, that Midas would be the Right Man. Why Midas was so evasive about his True Love and so reluctant to sleep with Gwen.

It was all so clear she was amazed that she hadn't understood it before.

All this time, Midas had been working a deal of his own!

He'd let her do the hard work to make everything happen, while he sat back and got what he wanted. Their negotiations played right into his hand, because Gwen had been focused on everything *except* what Midas actually cared about. No wonder those golden eyes had gleamed with satisfaction as she'd presented him with the final Contract. A Contract that gave him *exactly* what he'd been seeking, without Midas having to write a single clause, give up anything that mattered to him, or reveal his actual motivations.

That tricky bastard.

He'd married her because he *wanted* to marry her.

Gwen had believed she'd strong-armed him into their agreement. In reality, Midas would have done *anything* to finalize it. Given her anything. *That* was what he was scared of her discovering, if they had sex. To his mind, Midas was in an impossibly weak bargaining position and he'd done everything he could think of to hide it from her.

And it had worked.

To hell with catur, the man should be a poker player. He'd bluffed and obfuscated and maneuvered his way into total victory, before she'd even understood the game. He hadn't boasted about his strategy. He just masterfully and discreetly shifted cards around, all the while letting Gwen think *she* was the one dealing. Until he held the winning hand. Until he had the one and only thing he was truly after.

His True Love.

Their entire Contract was simply about Midas marrying his True Love, because he never, ever settled for less than the best.

Gwen slowly smiled as she finally realized the truth:

The Kingpin of Camelot wasn't such a terrible businessman, after all.

Chapter Twenty-Six

Parties agree that Guinevere, Avalon (a minor), and Midas will share a single, new and permanent last name, just as soon as they find one they like.

Clause 23- Sharing a Name
(Containing Nullification of Clause 2- Change of Names)

Celliwig looked exactly the same.

Unfortunately.

Everywhere Midas looked there were still dead stumps and acres of mud. The rundown buildings still listed on the uneven ground. Gray clouds in the sky still blocked out the sunlight, just as the clouds of dirt on the ground still blocked out all hope. The people were still ragged and malevolent specters, peering out with silent contempt as the rest of the world past them by.

Seeing it all again, Midas was transported back in time twenty years. He half expected to look down at himself and see a half-starved teenager, dressed in filthy rags.

He shook his head and glanced over at Gwen, taking in her shocked expression. He'd tried to warn her, but he'd known it was impossible. How could she possibly have prepared herself for this kind of place? The woman had no frame of reference for Celliwig and the people who dwelled there.

That wasn't a complaint. Truly, Midas would have spent his entire life in this dismal town before he had Gwen experience it for even an hour. She belonged in magical palaces.

He didn't.

She was never going to see him the same, now that she knew when he really come from.

Sighing in resignation, Midas reigned in his horse and hopped to the ground. Instantly, his boots sank into brown sludge. He'd worn his tallest, thickest pair, but it was like trying to hold back a typhoon with a bucket.

"We're here." He told Gwen emotionlessly.

Her eyes darted over to the decaying building on their left. Unlike Merlyn's hidden castle, this structure wasn't disguised to *look* like a ruin. It *was* a ruin. Once, it had been one of the largest homes in town. Now it was just a barely erect pile of unpainted wood and broken windows. The wide, muddy yard was filled with trash.

"Here?" She asked, taking it all in with a slight frown. "This is your house?"

"No. This was my parents' house. I just own it."

It was one of the first things he'd bought, after he was cursed. He wasn't sure why. Maybe he'd thought they would somehow come back. They hadn't, of course, and Midas had quickly left Celliwig. For twenty years, the building had rotted away. Abandoned by everyone and everything. He'd *never* returned to this spot to check on the property.

It was the last place he would want to go.

Midas lifted Gwen off her horse, his hands on her waist. Every time he touched her, it reminded him how damn small she was. Her personality was so forceful and big, it was easy to forget that any mid-sized villain could've snapped her bones between his fingers. What the hell was someone so delicate doing with a man like him?

"Midas?" She prompted, when he didn't immediately set her down. She braced her palms on his shoulders. "Everything okay?"

No, it wasn't okay. Nothing was okay about this place.

He awkwardly held her off the ground. Looking around, he wasn't sure where to put her. He didn't want to drop her in the mud. The thick muck was nearly to his knees. His tiny wife would no doubt sink waist-deep into the mire. There was nowhere clean and safe and *clean* she could walk.

Christ, he hated this town.

Midas shifted his grip, swinging Gwen up into his arms. Fuck it. He'd just carry her. It was the best solution. She was so light he could have kept her aloft with one hand.

Gwen gave a squeak of surprise, instinctively gripping him tight as he swept her towards the house. "I can walk." She assured him breathlessly, cradled against his chest. "I don't mind getting a little dirty."

"I mind."

He didn't want anything in this God-awful place to touch her. He just wanted to find the wand as quickly as possible and get Gwen back home, where she'd be shielded from all the grime and sadness that festered in this hellhole. After that, he would take a damn scrub-brush to his skin and pray that his wife would somehow still think he was a kind, gentle man. Then, he might just drink until he passed out. All in all, he thought it was one of his better plans.

Lake-blue eyes darted up to his set face. "It'll be okay." Gwen told him softly. "I'm right here with you."

"I'm fine." He wasn't, but hopefully he could fake it. Humiliating himself in front of her was the one surefire way to make this horrible day even worse.

Gwen smiled, like she sensed how tense he was and wanted to make him feel better. He'd been concerned that she'd still be mad, after their fight the night before. She'd been in remarkably high spirits, though. This morning she'd let him bring her to orgasm, as usual. He'd knocked on her door and, five minutes later, they were on her bed, with his head between her legs and her voice sobbing his name. Being with her as the sun came up was his favorite part of the day. It was like Gwen's pleasure brought the light and chased away the darkness.

She hadn't asked more questions about his True Love, either. Given the woman's pushiness, Midas couldn't explain her reticence, but he wasn't about to question his good luck.

"If you put a little extra effort in, this part of our trip could actually be sort of romantic, you know."

He snorted at that.

"It's true." Her arms wound around the back of his neck and she leaned up so she could whisper into his ear. "For instance, brides like it when our big, strong husbands pick us up like we're teeny tiny."

Jesus. He was just going to spontaneously combust one day. All they would find would be some sexually frustrated ashes. "You *are* teeny tiny." He retorted, giving her a light toss in his arms.

And he was a tawdry, feral animal.

"Well, you're about to carry your teeny tiny new bride across the threshold of your childhood home. See? Romance." She kissed his jaw. "There's a country song in there, somewhere."

"I never had a childhood home." He corrected, because even seeing this desolate town, she *still* wasn't getting it. "I never had a childhood."

"Well, you're presently giving Avi the most expensive one ever experienced, so you're making up for lost time. I saw the plans for that jungle-gym you ordered. It'll be visible from space. And for once, I actually believe that it *is* something you'd buy for yourself, even without her prompting."

Despite himself, Midas felt his mouth curve. Gwen had a point. The toys and treehouses and go-carts he bought were as much for him as for Avalon.

That morning, before they'd left for Celliwig, a whole cadre of plastic dolls had come downstairs to say good-bye with Avi. She'd taken to carrying the entire Avalon City army around in a pink backpack, nearly as big as she was. It was the most adorable thing he'd ever seen. Midas would have given years off his life to be able to stay home and play games with her.

Instead, he'd crouched down so they were at eyelevel. "I finally figured out who your daddy is." He'd told her, quietly.

She'd popped her thumb in her mouth, like she was suddenly nervous. "You." She'd whispered.

"Me." Midas had agreed.

Avalon had given him a shy, hopeful smile.

"*I* am your daddy." He'd continued, his heart swelling with pride. "Forever. That's the contract I'm offering." He'd held out a palm. "Deal?"

Vivien had foreseen the moment, back at the lake. In his whole life, she'd promised, just two deals would really matter. She'd been right. These bargains he'd struck with Avalon and Gwen were the only ones that gave him what he longed for.

They gave him his family.

"Deal!" Avalon had exclaimed in relief. "I *told* everybody so! I *told* them who you were!" She'd grasped his palm and shook it with customary enthusiasm. "I was right! I's always right!" Exuberant, she'd thrown her arms around him.

Tears had burned the back of Midas' eyes. "I love you." He'd never said the words to anyone before, but there was simply no way to stop them. Avalon had hugged him tight and he'd promised her everything he had. "I will not let you down. Okay? I will be the very best father I can. Every day. I will protect you and your mommy. I will *never* leave you." He kissed the top of her head. "Everything I have is because you chose me. You won't regret it. I will do a good job. I swear."

"I know. I seen it."

"Thank you for finding me." Midas whispered into her hair. His whole life he'd been lost, until this little girl came looking for him. "And thank you for bringing me your mother." He closed his eyes against her soft curls. "And thank you for being my daughter."

"You's welcome, Daddy."

Then, he'd had to leave the embrace of his perfect baby and walked straight into hell.

All around them, Midas could feel spiteful gazes studying them. Plotting. Predators weighing their chances. Any strangers were bound to draw notice in Celliwig, but Gwen stood out like a beacon in the night. Shiny blonde hair and an expensive wool coat and skin as pristine as her pedigree. Christ, he might as well be throwing red meat to George the kraken.

He should have made her wear the damn invisibility cloak.

The porch wasn't exactly clean, but at least it was above the muddy ground. Midas made his way up to it and carefully set her on the rickety boards. "Stay right here for a second, kitten." He touched her cheek and then walked over, so he was standing at the edge of the steps, looking out over the town.

By this time, half of Celliwig would be watching from their various lairs. He knew that. Since the citizens were all brainless, amoral assholes, they wouldn't understand any complicated threats. Best to be brief and unequivocal in his homecoming speech.

"I'm Midas." He bellowed and his voice echoed over the flat landscape. Everybody in Camelot knew his name, especially here. They knew what it meant to cross him. His gaze swept across the shadows of the hidden men like death, making sure he had their full attention. Then he pointed back at Gwen. "*Mine.*" The challenge in his tone couldn't have been any clearer. He waited for a beat, but no one was stupid enough to take him up on it.

Satisfied, he turned back to his wife.

She arched a brow. "Really?"

"It's not a subtle place." He muttered. "Be careful where you walk." Just in case, Midas tested the sections around the entrance with his foot. They all seemed sturdy enough, but he wasn't taking any chances. "Let me go first."

"Is this the porch?" Gwen asked.

"What?" The front door was unlocked, which was odd. He was sure he'd dead-bolted it before he'd walked away.

"The porch that you talked about last night, when you were so upset. Is this it?"

Midas hesitated. "Yes."

"Why does it scare you?"

"It *doesn't* scare me." He snapped in a harsher voice than he'd intended. "It's just a fucking porch."

"No, I think it's more than that."

He muttered a curse and glanced back at her. Gwen was staring at him with those unfathomable eyes and he found himself telling her more than he'd ever told anyone. "After my parents left, I stayed out here alone for several nights. It was... difficult, for me."

It *had* scared him, but he wasn't admitting it aloud. He still had nightmares about the darkness. It wasn't the porch itself that frightened him, though. It was knowing that he had no place else to go. That he belonged nowhere and to no one.

"You keep saying your parents 'left.'" Gwen squinted, like maybe she was missing something. "Did they die?"

"Eventually, I'm sure they did."

"But where did they go the day you were stuck out here on the porch?"

"I have no idea. I never bothered to look for them."

"You mean they just... *left?* Like vanished?"

"I mean," Midas explained slowly, "when I was nine years old, they packed their stuff, left me a bologna sandwich right over there," he pointed to the railing, "and they didn't come back."

Gwen blinked rapidly. "Well, there has to be a reason." He could see her mind racing for an explanation that made sense through her rosy worldview of parents who turned on pretty nightlights before they tucked their babies into bed. "Maybe your parents had no choice. Maybe they were kidnapped or arrested or lost..."

Midas cut her off. "They *packed*." He repeated. "You don't pack to go get kidnapped, arrested, or lost, Gwen. They just wanted to leave."

Her lips parted, finally understanding. "Oh my God." She whispered. "Oh my *God*."

"It's alright." He said, uncomfortably. "I survived."

"Well, your degenerate parents *won't*." Blue eyes glowed with righteous fury, her innocent confusion burning away in the heat of her anger. "They'd better hope they're far from Camelot. Once I have the throne back, I'm going to track them down and have them both executed. I swear to God, I will."

"As I said, I'm sure they're dead by now. Otherwise, they would have come looking for money. It's a thoughtful offer, though."

"It's not a joke, Midas! How could any mother leave her own son behind on a porch? She must have been evil. Like *completely* evil."

Midas adored her. Gwen thought she was heartless, but nothing could be farther from the truth. She was the most idealistic person in Camelot. "Evil is a strong word."

"No, it's really *not*."

"Black and white answers don't come easy when everything is the color of mud." Midas waved a hand out towards the town. "Right and wrong aren't always clear." Especially not to people like him. "My parents did what many people in their positions would have done." He wasn't sure why he was defending them, except he didn't want to be an object of pity. "They were desperate and I was expendable."

"You are *not* expendable, Midas."

"I'm just saying, they were Good and I was Bad. They did what they had to do to save themselves from this place. That's all."

Gwen crossed her arms over her chest, unsatisfied with that utterly realistic view. "Avalon is Bad."

Midas looked at her sharply, his sanguine façade vanishing.

"You were --what?-- only four years older than Avi is now when your parents left." Her head tilted. "Tell me... Would somebody be *evil* if they abandoned our daughter alone in this town, Midas?"

A sudden and wild rage filled him. Picturing Avalon helpless and scared in this miserable cesspit had the blood pounding in his head. "If some evil bastard left our daughter on this porch," he said very calmly, "I would kill him. And then kill him some more. And *keep* killing him, until we had her back in our arms and his evil insides were smeared all over Camelot."

"Exactly." Gwen nodded. "What your parents did was *wrong*. They were *not* good people. I don't care what their DNA said. It's black and white. Right and wrong. They left their baby to die alone at the hands of murderers and rapists. They were evil."

He thought back to his conversation with Avi. How he'd told her that Arthur was to blame for not loving her and that she was in no way inferior. "I never understood," he said quietly, "why Good people are still called Good, even when they do horrible things."

"Right and wrong are *real*. Good and Bad are *not*. They're just labels we put on people." She caught hold of his arm. "You are a *good person*, Midas. I have seen you do more kind, gallant, *good* things than any knight in this kingdom. There is no one else in the world that I trust as much as I trust you."

"I've done Bad things." He heard himself say. "To you, Gwen. You *shouldn't* trust me. I haven't told you things that I should tell you."

She smiled a strange smile. "Well, I'm sure I'll get them all out of you eventually. I'm pretty clever, you know."

"Just listen, alright? I can't *tell* right from wrong. It's right there in my medical file!"

"Then, it's a lie. You know right from wrong better than any Good folk."

"I still make wrong choices."

"Everyone does. We just keep trying to do better."

"I make them and I'm not sorry, though, Gwen. I made

wrong choices to get you and I'd do it again. You only married me, because I tricked you." There was no other way to say it. "I wanted you and I'm greedy and selfish, so I did whatever it took to have you."

"I was the one who showed up at *your* door and proposed, Midas."

"I had information you don't have. I'm not who you thought I was."

"No, you're *more*." Gwen looked up at him with the purest eyes he'd ever seen, absolute faith in his honor shining in their depths. "I see this horrible place and how you overcame it and I am so *proud* of you. You're the smartest man in Camelot. The strongest fighter. The kindest person. The most supportive partner. The gentlest father. You're so much *more* than I ever expected."

Midas felt like his heart was being ripped right out of his chest. He squeezed his eyes shut, not trusting himself to talk.

"I won't settle, either." She continued, earnestly. "Not ever again. I only want the very, *very* best from my husband. And you're it, Midas."

He let out a shaky breath, his love for her making it hard to breathe. Fuck. He might die on this porch, after all. Gwen was killing him. "I will be whoever you want." He got out hoarsely. There was no other option. "I'll do anything you ask, just so you stay with me."

"Just be yourself." She kept staring at him, like she expected him to live up to all her impossible expectations. "Think about how wrong it is to allow little boys to be abandoned on porches, because someone else decided they were 'expendable.' Think about all the people who suffer, because of blind prejudice. I *know* you see it's wrong."

"Gwen..."

"Just like I know the King of Camelot will save his people. He'll help me bring equality. He'll fight for what's right and he'll win. Because that's just who you are." Gwen touched his face. "The best." She smiled, already convinced he would somehow bring sunshine back to this accursed kingdom.

Midas' insides melted, leaning into her touch. "Alright." He agreed softly, because he would have agreed to anything she asked. Done anything to be the man she saw in him. "I can help you save Camelot."

"I know." She said simply. "You can do anything."

Midas ducked through the front door, before she drove him straight to his knees. He could think of *something* that would drag the kingdom out of the gutter, he supposed. If Gwen wanted it, it could be done. First, they needed to find the wand, though.

He'd half-expected squatters and wild animals to be nesting inside the house. Instead, the interior looked exactly the same. Which was impossible. The whole place should be a crumbling mess, by now. Instead, it was all intact, right down to the artwork and furniture. ...The same artwork and furniture Midas' parents had taken with them when they moved.

Son of a bitch.

Merlyn must have enspelled it. The old bastard's magic had left the outside in disarray, but the inside was warm and clean. Protected. The whole house was recreated exactly as it had been when Midas was a boy. A fucking time capsule of rotten memories. Midas plowed both hands through his hair and struggled to rein in his seething emotions.

"It's very beige." Gwen said from behind him, taking off her coat and dropping it on a neutral chair.

"Yes." Midas didn't bother to remove his muddy boots as he walked across the oatmeal-colored carpet. He'd destroy it all if he could, but the footprints he left were cleaned as soon as he left them. "They liked beige." Everything in his parents' home had always been as tasteful as their limited means could afford. They'd had grand dreams of reclaiming the family's position in society.

It made his skin crawl.

"It's also in very habitable shape, all things considered."

"This is your father's doing and you know it." Midas kicked a perfectly average footstool out of the way. Half a second later, it was right back in its original position. "Merlyn's somehow made it all look the way it did that last time I saw them. And he made it so no one could come in here and mess it all up."

"He wouldn't have wanted anybody else finding the wand. You're probably the only one who could even open the door. It's that way at Merlyn's castle, too. Only family can see it and enter."

Midas's mouth curved. *He'd* been able to see and enter Merlyn's house.

Gwen stopped to look at a photograph on the mantle. His parents were smiling fake smiles. Midas wasn't in the picture. He wasn't in *any* pictures, as far as he knew, except news reports and mugshots. Their surname was on the engraved frame and her thumb brushed over it. "Midas? Is this...?"

"Skycast."

Gwen glanced at him in surprise. "What?"

"Skycast. That's my last name. It was my mother's name."

Her head tilted curiously. "Tell me."

So he did.

"After they left," Midas nodded towards the photo, "a gryphon called Corrah Skycast took care of me. I say I was on my own when I was nine, but that's not really true. Corrah found me. *She* is my mother, the way I am Avalon's father. Because of choice."

"Midas Skycast." Gwen smiled. "That's beautiful."

Some of the tension eased from his shoulders. "So, it's Guinevere and Avalon Skycast." He persisted, wanting to make sure she was serious about sharing a name. "Alright? All three of us." They were a family. *His* family. Taking the same name would tell people that.

"Don't worry." She reassured him softly. "Everyone will know you belong with us."

Midas glanced at her through his lashes, not surprised that she could see right into his deepest anxieties.

"They'd know, no matter what our names are, because I'd tell them. And I know *you'd* tell them. And Avalon tells *everyone*. The Skycasts are not a shy group." She grinned. "And, FYI, 'Gwen Skycast' sounds pretty damn cool."

It definitely had a nice ring to it. Midas nodded. "'Gwen Pendragon' never did sound right, to me." He muttered and looked around the suffocating tan box his parents had created. "So where do you want to start looking for the wand?"

"In the last place you'd *want* to start looking, I suppose."

"That would be everywhere."

The two of them spent the entire day ripping the house apart. Every book was pulled off its shelf, every pillow tossed to the floor, every drawer opened, and every closet ransacked. No matter where they looked, they came up empty.

Midas was getting more and more agitated, especially since the damn house kept cleaning itself as they went. He didn't even have the satisfaction of destroying things. Hours later, he ripped the last floorboard up in the attic, finding nothing. It was the final section of the house they had to check and it was useless.

"*Fuck!*" He barely got his leg out of the way in time, as the wood was all restored into its proper place.

"Cursing's a no-no." Gwen told him archly, sifting through some blankets.

Midas switched to muttered oaths in the gryphons' language.

"You know, I'm going to have to learn how to speak that, just so you and Trystan can't talk about stuff in a secret boy-code and..." She stopped, confused. "What's this?" She held up a sock full of sawdust.

Midas winced, not wanting to distress her. "It's a toy." He admitted.

"It's not a toy. It's an old sock."

Midas stared at her silently.

Gwen's mouth parted. "*This* was your toy?" She demanded, giving the sock a shake. "Did you have any others?" She looked around like maybe there was a train set or roller skates hidden amongst the boxes. "Wait a minute, where's your room? We've been here all day. Why haven't I seen your room?"

"This was my room."

"You slept in the fucking *attic*?"

"Yes. I made that toy to keep me company. I was scared of the dark."

Gwen squeezed her eyes shut. "Goddamn it." Her voice cracked, like she was starting to cry. "God*damn* it."

Goddamn it.

Midas headed over to her, his heart breaking. "Gwen, please don't." He wrapped her in his arms. "I was very content with the sock. I promise."

That made her sob harder. "I had so much and you had *nothing*. It's not fair."

Her tears ate at him. "I would *always* choose for you to be the one who was safe and cared for." He soothed and it was true. "It wouldn't even *be* a choice. I would *always* want you to have everything you need to be happy. That's the most important thing to me."

"I'm sorry. I..." She dried her eyes, like she was worried about upsetting him. "I'm alright." She cleared her throat. "So this sock is why Avalon gets singing wallpaper and I have four hundred and sixty-seven handbags?"

He squinted, not seeing the connection.

"It is." Gwen nodded like it all made sense. "Okay. I get it." She leaned against him. "I finally get it." She kissed his jaw. "It makes you feel secure to buy a whole house full of stuff for your wife and daughter."

"It's my job to provide for you." Avalon and Gwen were *his* family. Midas had worked hard to earn the right to take care of them. He wasn't about to screw it up.

"You do an excellent job of providing for us." She agreed,

hugging him tight. "Not just with money, but with time and attention and affection. And that's *way* more important than dolls and handbags, Midas."

"I just want you both to know you're valued. That you will never be cold. Never be hungry. Never need something that you don't have. …Because I will get it for you."

"We *do* know that."

He nodded and looked around the attic, hating all the fear and sorrow that still lingered within the walls. "I want you to feel… safe." He whispered.

"I know." She gave him a misty smile. "I'm sorry. I was wrong before. You don't have to send me a bill for the things you buy us. We'll change that part of the Contract."

"Really?" That was a huge relief. Gwen was onto his creative bookkeeping and demanding copies of all the receipts. Midas had resorted to just buying the stores, so he could give himself ninety-nine percent markdowns and then provide her with the documentation. Sooner or later, she was bound to notice.

"I want you to be safe and happy, too. The stuff doesn't matter to me. But if buying it makes *you* feel more secure, then I support your ridiculous spending habits."

"Thank you." Midas rested his chin on the top of her head, thinking it all over. "I really bought you four hundred and sixty-seven handbags?" He asked after a long moment.

"Yep. I counted."

Midas considered that. Gwen never even carried a handbag. "That seems like a lot." He frowned. "Maybe I shouldn't buy you anymore of them?" It came out as a question, because he wasn't sure.

Gwen gasped, like he'd just said something amazing. "Yes!" She agreed eagerly. "You shouldn't buy any more. Buying *more* will not make me any happier than I already am."

"I like to buy you things, though."

"I know. I get that, now." Her palm touched his cheek. "Just know that you don't *need* to buy me things. I would still be your wife, even if you never buy me anything else."

"I do know that." He said simply.

"You do?"

"You're not for sale, Gwen. You never have been."

She slowly grinned. "Considering you're *you*… that may be the sweetest thing you've ever said to me."

"Well, I mean it." He lowered his head to nip her earlobe. "But it only makes me want to buy you things."

She swatted his arm, squiggling away from him. "You're a lunatic." She laughed.

Midas chuckled, pleased that she was smiling again.

Gwen shook her head in exasperation. "Look, I'm emotionally drained. Let's eat some of the food your chef packed, get some sleep, and try to find the wand again tomorrow."

Midas' contentment faded. "You want to sleep *here?*" He was aghast at the very idea.

"Where else would we sleep? I don't think Celliwig has many hotels." She moved to peer out the attic window. From their side, the glass was whole. From the outside, it was broken. "Truthfully, even if this place had the most charming B&B in Camelot, I wouldn't want to go looking for it, right now."

Midas headed over to stare out at the street. It was dark, most of the streetlights dead or stolen, but he could see enough. Men were milling around in groups, talking in loud voices. No one was drunk enough or stupid enough to approach the house, but all that might change if they went looking for other lodging. Gwen was too valuable to risk.

"We'll stay here tonight." He muttered. "Let me check on the horses and we'll go to bed. You stay put and lock the door behind me."

Gwen ignored that, craning her neck to look over at the stable, which was two doors down. Every day that Midas had toiled there, he'd had to look at the big house where he'd once lived. "Did your parents own that, as well?"

"No."

"But you own it now?"

"Yes." And fortunately Merlyn had enspelled it, too. There was fresh hay and water for the horses. It seemed like he'd performed his magic on all of Midas' properties in town.

"Why did you buy the stable?" Gwen asked, apparently sensing there was more to the story than his one-word answers.

"I used to work there and I hated it." He shrugged. "I bought every place that had ever made me feel small."

"So... You were a stable boy?"

He frowned, struck by her strange tone. He glanced down at Gwen, wary now. "Yes."

"Really?" Her voice went breathless and she no longer looked tired. "You were really a stable boy. You're not kidding me, right?"

"No, I'm not kidding you. Why the hell would I kid you about being a stable boy...?"

Gwen cut him off, her eyes glowing deep blue. "I want to go with you to the stable. I want to see it." She excitedly declared. "Give me five minutes. I just need to change first."

Change? Midas gave his head a clearing shake. "I don't think it's such a great idea for you to go outside. This town is..."

She interrupted him again, this time by kissing him firmly on the lips. "Trust me. This is the best idea I've ever had."

Chapter Twenty-Seven

Merlyn
Six Years Ago

The video was slanted, because Merlyn couldn't get the camera to sit right on the desk. By and large, wizards were not particularly adept at technology. They liked spells not circuit boards. He was pleased that he could just get the damn thing to turn on. The quality of the recording didn't matter to him, nearly so much as the message he needed to leave for his daughter.

"Guinevere." He cleared his throat, looking directly into the lens. "I've long remembered my death, so I know it approaches. It will not be painful or frightening. I'll simply go to sleep and wake up in another world. Truly, I'm excited to see what wonders await me on the other side, so I do not want you to mourn. You have been the light of my life. Every day with you has..."

He stopped his heartfelt speech, as one of the tripod legs slipped. The camera toppled over, still recording. "Hang on." Merlyn propped it back up, but now it was *really* off-center.

Oh, bothering frogs-legs.

He looked around in irritation and grabbed an ancient scroll detailing stories of the Fountain of Youth from the cluttered desktop. The healing waters would do Merlyn no good, but he enjoyed reading the legends. Also, the text was the perfect width to right the tripod. He wedged it under one side and grunted in satisfaction. Better.

Kind of.

"In any case," he told the cockeyed lens, "I wanted to leave you this message, since I'll be gone soon. I know you only married Arthur, because I convinced you. I know that, in your heart, you're waiting for another. And that man will be the *Right Man*. The one you're dreaming of. I promise you. I've seen him and where he comes from, so I know he will recognize your value. You and your daughter will be everything to him."

Was that red light supposed to be on? Merlyn paused to adjust the tripod again, knocking it even more askew. The little icon on the camera's display said it was still taping, though, so he kept going.

"Arthur is *nothing*." He waved a dismissive hand. "I regret that your life had to intersect with his, at all. But, he is a temporary problem. The child is all that will matter to you, in the end." Merlyn's deepest regret was that he'd miss meeting his granddaughter. "The sorceress you carry now, will make this world a far better place, Guinevere. Always listen to her visions. She will become the Great Queen and you will love her more than you can imagine." He smiled. "As I love you."

The battery began to blink that it was running low on power. How could it be running low on power? It was plugged into the wall. Had it come free somehow? Midas fiddled with the cord, but everything was still connected. Giving up on the tangle of wires, Merlyn decided to complete his message before the camera shut off, all together.

Why in Hecate's name did anyone prefer technology to magic? It was all so baffling.

"The wand," he told Gwen, "I am leaving for you. It has a mind of its own sometimes, as you know. It finds its way into whole other lands and other hands with shocking regularity." He rolled his eyes in exasperation. "It has the best of intentions, of course, so just let it do what it will. I don't see how you can stop it, really. I certainly couldn't."

Merlyn had no doubt that his wand had plenty of plans, for after he was gone. It was more of a pet than an instrument of magic. He'd perhaps put a dollop of extra independence in when he enspelled the thing. Maybe a bit too much optimism, mixed with a touch a sneakiness. The wand wanted to save the world and had its own ideas of how to make it happen.

Hopefully, everyone it wanted to "help" would survive its enchanted assistance.

"It takes a level six talent to control the blasted thing properly and I'm the last of those in Camelot." He warned Gwen. "At least until your daughter comes of age. Until then, just stay out of its way and don't worry. You'll be able to use it to cleanse the kingdom. The wand only wants to do Good."

Wait... had he told her about Dark Science coming? Merlyn squinted a bit, trying to remember in both directions. That was always a challenge. Well, either way, she would figure it all out. His daughter was bright as sunshine. He just needed to explain about his plan.

"When you need the wand, you will be able to find it. I have it sealed up tightly with magic, so it won't wander off. It won't be happy, but at least no one else will be able to steal it." Merlyn nodded, pleased with himself for recalling the details. "So, it will be vital that you retrieve it yourself, just as soon as..." He stopped, tilting his head.

Hang on, had he told her *where* he hid it?

That seemed important. He should probably be sure. "I put the wand in the last place he'd ever want to look. Did I tell you? I think it's quite clever actually. All you have to do is go to the..."

The camera died.

A puff of ominous black smoke emanated from the computerized guts of the gadget, a sure sign that it would never work again. Merlyn had seen the same thing happen with his phone, his toaster oven, and all his ceiling fans.

He made a face. Well, no matter. He'd recorded most of the message. Gwen would figure out the rest. Like him, his daughter was very logical.

Chapter Twenty-Eight

Parties agree to nullify all previously written rules regarding their physical contact, with the exception of the fact that they will remain monogamous. The parties instead agree to engage in any consensual physical activity, at any time and for however long they both wish.

Clothes may come off, as applicable.

Clause 22- Consummation of Marriage
(Containing Nullifications of Clauses 4- Physical Activity Between Parties and 21- Amended Physical Contact Agreement)

"So this is the stable." Midas told Gwen unnecessarily, after making sure the horses were bedded down for the night. "I've got no idea why you wanted to see it, but here it is."

"And you used to work here?" Gwen asked again, leaning against the door. She was watching everything he did with an oddly intent expression.

Midas looked around. "Yes." There were six stalls, only two of them full, but each one was clean and fresh. Merlyn's magic would have made Midas' life a hell of a lot easier, had he possessed it all those years ago. "It was my job to see to the horses."

"So you were *definitely* a stable boy? You're sure you're not making that up?"

"It's hardly something I would lie about to impress you." He muttered, not meeting her eyes. He was wearing thicker work gloves over his regular gloves and he absently stripped them off, slapping them against the width of his thigh in a practiced movement.

Gwen's eyes went wide, a small gasp escaping her.

"Look, I know it's not the most glamorous job." Midas continued, too agitated to notice her response. Working in the stable was always a hot and sweaty business, even in Camelot. His shirtsleeves were already rolled up his forearms, so he tugged open some of the buttons of his shirt, trying to get air. "But I didn't have a lot of options…"

He didn't get to finish that. Her low moan of sexual desire cut him off.

Midas' head snapped around in surprise.

"I'm sorry." She arched her back off the door in a restless, sensual movement that held him transfixed. "I am just *so* turned on right now, Midas. You're making me kind of crazy."

Nothing she possibly could have said would have shocked him more. "Huh?"

Her gaze roamed all over his body. "Would you judge me if I told you my deepest, darkest sexual fantasy?"

Midas had felt overheated in the stable before, but it was nothing to the scorching temperature that burned through him, now. "You can tell me anything, Gwen."

"Even if it's kind of... dirty?"

He was riveted. "Tell me." He commanded, his heart pounding. She was incredibly aroused. He wasn't sure why, but he could see it and his own body went rock-hard in response.

She licked the corner of her mouth. "You know, I've always been a queen, right? Growing up, everyone knew I would marry Arthur, so I was treated like I was already his wife. They said I was his, so they made sure I was untouched by other boys. I told you that." Her eyes drank him in. "I don't think they would have let you near me, back then."

"How the hell could they have kept me away?" Midas stalked towards her, reacting instinctively to the challenge. "They've been trying to hide you from me for years and it didn't work. They threw me in prison and I *still* found my way to you." There was nothing in this kingdom or any other that could stop him from reaching his True Love. Midas stopped directly in front of her, one hand braced on the wood beside her head. "You *weren't* his. You're mine and I will *always* come for you."

Gwen swallowed hard. "Fucking hell." She whispered, unconsciously echoing his favorite oath. "This really is the best idea I've ever had."

Midas' felt his mouth quirk. "Tell me about the dirty stuff, kitten."

Her breathing was chopping. "Well, maybe it's a fantasy all untouched queens have, especially when we've got no interest in the asshole king." She met his eyes. "But, I wanted to be touched by someone bigger and Badder, Midas. So, that was the fantasy I thought of when I touched *myself*. You know?"

Now they were getting somewhere. "Describe it in graphic. fucking. detail." He ordered, breathing in the scent of her. "And I will make it all happen."

She shivered. "Just so you know, I was a very Good girl. I

would *never* actually have done this. Not unless I had met you." Her palms came up to measure the width of his chest, like she just couldn't resist. "Not unless you'd come for me, Midas."

"I *have* come for you." He growled, entranced by the contrast of her small hands against his coarser skin. She was and always would be the classiest thing he'd ever seen. Arthur's hideous ring was gone, so her delicate fingers were long and bare. Too bare, actually. "What do you want me to do, kitten?"

"Well, I have always –*always*-- wanted to seduce a strapping stable boy." She confessed in a rush. "Who is Bad, and kinda rough, and a little dangerous, and a lot hard. And I know it sounds silly, but the fact that you're my fantasy man, is just really, *really* turning me on."

He blinked, trying to form a coherent sentence in his head. "You *like* the fact that I'm a rough, Bad, *stable boy?*" He clarified, making sure he understood. The woman was fantasizing about all the parts of him that he did his best to hide? He didn't know whether to curse in frustration or fall to his knees in gratitude.

"A *strapping* stable boy."

"I have no idea what that even means. It sounds like a word women use to describe men when they don't want the men to understand what they're saying." Which was… intriguing.

"And who's also a little dangerous." Gwen continued, like she didn't even hear his muttering. She nodded earnestly, her attention dropping to the waistband of his pants. "And a lot hard."

"I'm also the richest man in Camelot, you know. Maybe the world. You could probably have a real nice fantasy about that."

"Nope. I just want your strapping body."

If he wasn't so out of his mind with lust, he might have laughed. Goddamn, but he loved this woman. She never failed to interest him.

"So, I was wondering if we could do some renegotiation." Gwen shifted impatiently, brushing against him. Wanting him simply because he was Midas and she was a crazy, beautiful lunatic. "I know that you touched me once already today, but I need you to touch me, again." White teeth chewed on her lower lip. "I'm really… tight."

Midas hadn't known it was even possible to sense your pupils dilating, but he swore he could feel them widen like the lens of a camera, trying to capture this moment forever. Gwen took his stunned silence as a refusal and gave a distressed whimper. The erotic sound shot straight to his groin, nearly doubling him over.

"Please? I'm already so wet. It really shouldn't take much

effort to make me come." She begged. "Please, Midas."

Holy.

Shit.

Breathing didn't used to be hard, but suddenly he'd forgotten how. What the hell did it matter what "strapping" parts of him were turning her on, just so he was turning her on? "Of course, I'll take care of you." He managed to say.

"Really?" She tugged at the edges of his shirt, jerking the final buttons free. They were made of cabochon rubies. Midas didn't even turn his head as they went flying off and were lost forever between the floorboards. Gwen's head dipped to lick across his damp chest and his eyes literally crossed in lust. "You don't mind? I'll stop if you want."

"Don't stop. God, no. Don't stop. I don't need a safe word and I don't want to stop." He somehow managed to step back, desperate to have her. "Where do you want to do this?"

"In the hay." She was already unfastening her long coat. She'd had it on the whole time. "Thank you, Midas. You're always such an accommodating business partner."

Midas walked backwards, not wanting to take his eyes off of her as they headed into the nearest empty stall. "Believe me, this is my supreme pleasure."

The jacket dropped and all she wore beneath it was a short, white negligee. The silk clung to her body, showcasing her beaded nipples. *This* is what she'd changed into, back at the house? Midas was dazzled. She'd been planning to seduce him, all along.

He was the luckiest stable boy in the world.

"It's really very nice of you to give me what I want." She came towards him, like an angel. "You'll always give me what I want, won't you?"

Midas was past talking, so he just nodded. Logically, he must have been the one to pay for that nightgown she wore, so it was now a scientific fact that gold *could* indeed buy happiness. He reached for her, wanting to feel her skin all wrapped in the silk. His gloves were in the way, which just about killed him. All he wanted was that supple flesh beneath his bare hands.

"No, no." She smiled and shifted back, one thin strap sliding off her shoulder. "In my fantasy, I'm the one doing the seducing, remember?" She gave him a light push, wanting him to lay down in the straw.

Fuck yes.

He would do whatever she wanted. Midas sprawled

backwards in the hay, staring up at her in awe. He'd slept in this stall, more nights than he could count, crying and miserable. It was a place he hated like none other. Now, all of the bad memories washed away, leaving only this one magnificent moment. Leaving only her.

"I had fantasies, too." He admitted, yanking off his boots without looking away from the glorious sight standing above him. "When I lived here."

"About a queen seducing you?"

"No. About you, Gwen. About my…" *True Love*. He broke off before he could finish the damning words.

"About your what?" She asked innocently, kicking off her own shoes.

"About my *wife*," he substituted, "who I imagined would be amazingly beautiful. But I never, *ever* imagined she'd be as beautiful as you."

Gwen glided downward, positioning one knee on either side of his body. It was the most perfect experience of his life. "Was I smart and funny and capable, too? Or did you stop the imagining with just my appearance?" She teased.

"You were everything. You *are* everything." Midas watched, transfixed, as she pulled the sinful confection of white silk over her head. The fabric skimmed her body and then she was kneeling above him naked. For the first time, he believed in all the gods Corrah had told him about.

"I really appreciate you helping me out tonight." Gwen assured him, apparently not noticing his reverent expression. "And not laughing about my fantasy. Why, I really don't think you could be any kinder to me, even if I was your True Love."

He flinched, looking away and suddenly hating himself. "Gwen…"

She ignored his interruption, her hands freeing his arms from the unbuttoned shirt. "To show my thanks, let me make sure you're satisfied, too." She murmured, her fingers running from his shoulders to his waist, in obvious appreciation for his size. "I mean, it's kind of pointless to alternate days, now that I think about it. Why can't we *both* be satisfied?"

The muscles in his stomach jumped at the feel of her soft fingers, sliding downward. From out of nowhere he recalled the True Love he'd dreamed of as a young man had smooth, flawless, gentle palms. The opposite of Midas' own hands, which were broken down from scrubbing and shoveling in the stable. In his head, his True Love had possessed the hands of a queen. And he'd imagined that she'd touch him like he was special to her.

...Just like Gwen always did.

"You don't have to do that." Midas offered, but he sure wasn't resisting when she unbuckled his belt. He lifted his body to help her, in fact.

"Oh, it's the least I can do." She gave a mysterious smile and unzipped his pants. "Relax. I know what I'm doing. I've played it all out in my head a thousand times."

Holy *shit*, did she know what she was doing.

Her fingers wrapped around him, stroking at the perfect rhythm, and Midas couldn't breathe. His True Love was sitting on his lap, naked and caressing him, and it was more than he'd ever imagined he could have. "Gwen." His gloved hand came up to cup her cheek and he knew his heart was in his eyes.

Gwen leaned closer to him, face hovering over his. "Tell me you love me." She whispered.

"I love you." The words slipped out and he didn't even try to call them back. "I am so crazy in love with you, there's never been any hiding it. Everyone in Camelot knows I'm yours. I'm already designing the billboards to brag about it."

Her mouth curved. "Neon?"

"I upgraded to the TV ones that show pictures."

"Very not-beige." Her lips brushed his and his whole body jolted. "If you love me enough for billboards, will you give me what I want?"

"Always." Anything she wanted, he would provide.

She adjusted herself over him and he could feel the warm, wet core of her body calling to him. "I'm so empty, Midas. Touching me won't be enough to make the aching stop." She brought the tip of him right to her entrance. "See? I'm soooo ready."

His hips gave an involuntary jerk upward, needing to be inside of the radiating heat. "*Gwen*." A savage hiss escaped him, his hand clenched in the straw.

"Make love to me." She kissed him, like she was frantic. "Say yes. I need you."

His lips met hers wildly, as she slid against him. There was a reason they shouldn't have sex, but, for the life of him, he couldn't recall what it might be. It couldn't be very important. Not nearly as important as Gwen. Being with her. Giving her whatever she asked for. Having her in his arms. "Yes." He groaned.

...And then he remembered.

Midas' eyes shot open in panic, but Gwen was already

moving. She'd been waiting for this. Before he could voice a protest, she was sliding down onto his throbbing shaft. Her body sealed around his and Midas' head went back in ecstasy. "Oh *fuck!*"

Being inside of her was like coming home. Every inch of her body was made for him. Of course it was. She was his True Love.

...And now she realized it, too.

His dazed eyes met her triumphant gaze, knowing she'd just outwitted him. If he wasn't so busy with panic and desire, he would have been impressed. She'd set him up.

"I knew it." Gwen said breathlessly and her dainty fingers dug into his shoulders for support. "I *told* you I'm almost-Bad."

Midas tried to think, but it was hard to focus on anything except the feel of her body. His palms settled at her waist wanting to keep her still so he could form a coherent thought. Wanting to guide her up and down, until his mind was emptied of everything but her. Of his two conflicting intentions, he already knew which one was going to win out. Everything he'd ever owned or desired or possessed meant exactly nothing compared to this woman.

The love he had for her was burned into the very cells of his being.

Gwen pushed up and, for a second, all his worst fears rushed to the surface. She was going to stop. She had what she wanted, so she could just leave, now. She didn't need their deal anymore. She held all the cards and they both knew it.

Desperation filled Midas. That fear of abandonment that lived at the very core of him. "Gwen…" He began, prepared to beg, but his words ended in a blissful groan as she sank back down, her tight channel swallowing more of him.

Her eyes were bright and clear and they stayed locked on his. "Did you really think I wouldn't notice who you were?" She asked, a breathless hitch in her voice.

Midas blinked, his lips instinctively parting as her mouth brushed against his. Why was she still kissing him? Why was she still touching him? He gazed up at her, hypnotized and unsure. "I hoped you wouldn't. I thought it would be safer."

"Why?" Her teeth bit down on her lower lip as she leaned back, trying to take him even deeper. "Don't you trust me?"

For a moment, Midas couldn't speak. She wasn't at the right angle to take him fully, but she wasn't experienced enough with this position to know how to fix it. He was trying to let her set the pace, but his instincts took over and he yanked her hips forward. They both groaned in response.

"I trust you." He got out hoarsely. "God, I trust you like I've never trusted anyone."

"Then why didn't you just tell me you're my True Love?"

His hands slid up to cover her breasts, because he simply couldn't help himself. "I was afraid." There was no sense in denying it. His thumbs brushed the hard points of her nipples, hating that his gloves prevented him from touching her rosy flesh. "I'm still afraid."

"Why?" She asked again. The word was gentle. So were her palms as they came up to cover his, holding them against the soft mounds. Her fingers slid between his, linking them even through the black leather.

"One day you'll see that I'm not who you think I am and you'll leave." Midas gave in and laid himself bare. "And when you send me back into the darkness... I won't recover. I won't even want to. It would be a thousand times worse than being left on the porch. You have more power over me than anyone else could ever have."

"You really think that's my masterplan? To leave you all alone?"

"I never have a fucking clue what you're thinking. I wish I did."

She dipped her head to kiss the side of his jaw. "Well, right now I'm thinking that I've never come with a man inside me." She whispered in his ear. "Want to try and change that for me, husband?"

It was calling him "husband" that did it. Every time she did that, Midas lost whatever remained of his sanity.

He gave a snarl of pure lust, flipping her so she was beneath him. Shiny curls spread across the straw and she laughed in delight. Her cheeks were pink and her hair was blonde and she looked exactly like every dream he'd ever had. Despite everything, the stable boy fantasy was *really* fucking working for him. Maybe because it *wasn't* a fantasy. He *was* a stable boy and he'd somehow gotten his hands on a queen.

Midas stared down at her, breathing hard, as she tugged his pants all the way off. "There is nothing I won't give to keep you and our daughter, Gwen." He wanted her to understand that while he still had the capacity for speech. "*Nothing.*" He planted his hands on either side of her head, caging her in. "Stay with me and I will pay any price you ask."

"You can't buy a family, Midas. It doesn't work that way. If you have to pay for people, they're not really yours."

"I'll take you anyway I can get you."

"You've already *got* me." Her legs came up to clasp his hips, pulling him closer when she should have been pushing him away. "One aspect of this arrangement that you might not have considered: You're *my* True Love, too." Her hand touched his face. "Equal partners."

His eyes slashed up to meet hers, his heartbeat somehow speeding even faster. "You're not sure you even believe in True Love." He reminded her, hoarsely.

"I guess you convinced me."

He blinked. "You're going to accept the bond?" Even in the face of irrefutable evidence, he'd expected her to try and deny the truth. To try and deny *him*. Why wouldn't she?

Gwen gave a strange smile. "Has is occurred to you that I've been the one trying to bring us closer, right from the start? *I'm* the one who proposed. *I'm* the one who insisted that I satisfy you, instead of letting you see other women. *I'm* the one who seduced you tonight and tricked you into admitting that you're my True Love. It's always *me* reaching out. Why do you think that is?"

His brows tugged together in confusion. "I don't... I'm not..."

She leaned up to kiss him as he hunted for words. "Maybe because I am crazy in love with you, too."

Midas froze.

"I *do* see the real you." Blue eyes gleamed, as she continued her revelation. "I see someone who does everything he can, every single day, to take care of me and our child. Who is kind and gentle, even when he tries to hide it. Who lives by the knights' code without anyone at the Academy having to teach him to be gallant. He just *knows*." She smiled up at him. "I see you better than you see yourself. I see the man who was born to save Camelot. I see my husband."

Midas' whole body jerked. "Gwen." It was all he could manage and he said it like a prayer. Her words alone could make him come. They washed over him like rain soothing a parched desert. He would feel his mind soaking them in, needing the life they brought. Combined with the soft warmth of her body, it was nearly impossible to keep his grip.

"I have loved you since before we even met, Midas." She moved against him and it was the closest he would ever get to heaven. "I kind of think you're the reason I had so many stable boy fantasies. Our connection was pulling me to you and I didn't even know it. I have to tell you, it played havoc on my teenage libido. I really did have to touch myself every night, because of you."

"Don't, Gwen." His voice was strangled. "Don't tell me anymore. Not until you're with me. I'm about to lose control."

Gwen grinned impishly, liking that reaction. "I love you." She said again and he could feel himself faltering. "I love everything about you, Midas. I used to do all kinds of naughty things in bed, while I thought about..."

"*Fuck!*" Fun as her games were, he was too close. She was going to come with him deep inside of her, no matter what it took. Midas somehow captured her hands, pinning them above her head with one palm, before her soft touch sent him over the edge. "Stable boy's turn to direct the fantasy."

"What are you...?" She broke off with a keening wail as he pushed deeper and harder inside of her. "*Midas!*"

"This is where I belong." He'd finally found it and he was staking his claim. "Right here, Gwen. With you. Let's negotiate a new contract. I give you whatever you ask and you be my wife. For real. Forever."

"Cheating." She got out, breathlessly. "You always cheat when we negotiate." She didn't seem very upset about his tactics, though. If anything she grew more aroused, her skin flushed with pleasure. "God, you completely outmaneuvered me the night we met. I put in all those clauses and you *still* got everything you wanted. ...Because all you wanted was me."

"All I *ever* want is you, kitten." He lowered his head, his teeth grazing the vulnerable curve of her shoulder. The primitive demand for submission would have shocked any Good folk in Camelot.

...But not as deeply as the fact that Gwen instantly turned her neck to give him access. She always seemed to like his rougher edges and this time was no different. The woman melted into his evil clutches, without the slightest hesitation. "I think you're doing 'strapping,' right now. It kinda means --like-- strong. Muscular. Masculine. *Big*." She gave a soft whimper, as he pressed forward, making her accept even more of him. "God, I love how big you are."

"How *strapping* I am."

"Exactly. Best stable boy *ever*."

Midas kissed her neck, holding her down so he could have his wicked way with her. "Well, the job itself sucks, but it has some *unbelievable* benefits." He was lodged tight inside of her perfect body, her wrists caught in his massive palm, and his teeth by her slim throat. The Queen of Camelot was completely at the Kingpin's mercy. Trapped by a villain. A mongrel from the depths of Celliwig. He could do *anything* to her.

And still she smiled at him like he was a hero.

Midas' eyes glowed, barely holding on in the face of her

unending faith. "I *will* stack the deck to have you." He warned. "I will lie and cheat and kill anyone who tries to steal you away. I'll buy you things you don't need or want. I will do any crazy thing I can think of, if it'll keep you willingly by my side. Because, I really *am* a tawdry, feral animal when it comes to you, Gwen."

And for once he wasn't sorry about it.

Neither was she, apparently.

"I know." Gwen panted, her body completely opened to him. Giving him all of her. "Plus, you're some kind of contract-y genius, so you'll probably use that, too. The way you arranged our deal, so you'd come out on top…? The way you planned everything and got what you wanted…?" Her head went back in blissful surrender. "*No one* else could have done that. Just you, Midas. You are the best businessman I've ever seen. It's *sooooo* hot."

He liked that she'd figured out all the tricks he'd used to acquire her. …And he *really* liked that she was impressed by them. Just like he had a feeling she'd be pleased when he praised her *effusively* for blindsiding him with this stable boy seduction. The two of them apparently enjoyed being outflanked by the other.

"Is the businessman hotter than the stable boy?"

"Thank God I don't have to choose."

"Does this mean you'll stop calling me trusting?"

"No, you're still too trusting." She nipped at his shoulder. "But next time we're in your office, I'll let you take me right on top of your desk and you can brag about how you're the smartest man in the kingdom. That'll be fun for you." Her eyes gleamed. "And me."

"I'm going to take you in every room of our house. And it's a big goddamn house." He suckled her breast. "New contract, kitten." He prompted, wanting to wrap up the details before he died from need. "No more telling me we're 'fake-married.' No more Termination Clause. Just you and me, until death do us part."

Her whole body was quivering, right on the edge. "*Please*."

Midas' tongue rasped her nipple, wishing again he could touch the velvety tip with his hands. "Yes or no: I am your *real* husband and you are my *real* wife."

"Yes." Her glazed eyes locked with his.

"Yes what?"

"It's real. It's always been real."

His strokes grew less controlled. "Who am I? Say it, again. I want to hear it, again."

"*Husband*." It came out as a shriek. "Midas, you're my husband! God, I love you so much."

Yes.

Midas' hips pistoned, driving as deep as he could go and Gwen exploded. "*Oh God.*" Her hips bucked against his. "Oh God, *Midas!*" Her body tightened for an endless moment, rippling around him with strong, erotic, irresistible force.

There was nothing Midas could do but join her. He came so hard the tendons in his neck stood out. "Gwen!" His teeth ground together, not wanting it to end. It was perfect. *She* was perfect. "Love you." He chanted, unable to say anything in that moment except the core truth of his being. "Love you. *Love you.*" He rested his head against hers, his body shuddering. "My wife." He breathed, finally sagging against her. "Love you."

Gwen tilted her face, so she could meet his eyes. "I love you, too." She said, like maybe she suspected he needed to hear it a lot.

She was right.

"Are you sure?" He asked, trying to catch his breath. It still seemed utterly impossible that someone like her would love someone like him. "You won't change your mind?"

"I'm not going to change my mind. But I will find some way to stop you, if *you* ever decide to change *your* mind, so be warned." She kissed him lightly. "It's just you and me and no one else. For ever after."

"That's a deal." He touched her tousled curls, his eyes intense. "You are my True Love. Not because biology *tells* me you are my True Love. But because I am so damn in love with you, I don't know where I stop and you start, Guinevere Skycast."

She gave him a drowsy smile. "Did you know I was your True Love from the first second you looked at me? Just like the internet says you would?"

"Yes."

"Really?"

"I know it every time I look at you."

"I can feel it now, too. I think I always could, I just didn't know what it was." She adjusted her position, like she fully intended to fall asleep right there in the stable. "Our connection is... everywhere."

"I know." He watched in perfect contentment as Gwen settled against him. Her tiny body curved into his like a missing puzzle piece. His lips grazed her temple. "Next time, I get to try out a fantasy."

"Okay." She agreed without even pausing to consider all the immoral thoughts that could lurk in the head of a gangster. Her eyes fluttered shut, with such innocent trust that Midas' throat got tight. "Do I get to wear a leather costume and carry a whip?"

"No, but I like it when you sit on my lap." He admitted, running a hand along her spine. "Every time you do it, I think of Bad things. So, I want you to sit on my lap and I want to be able to do all the Bad things I've been thinking about."

She grinned without opening her eyes. "You could have been doing Bad things to me on your lap for days now, if you weren't so stubborn." She caught hold of his arm and wrapped it around her waist. "But, don't worry. After my nap, I'll show you what you've been missing, husband."

If Midas had magic, he would have frozen the moment forever.

He'd taken his coat off earlier and hung it over the door of the stall. Reaching up, he caught hold of the hem and dragged it down. Expensive fabric ripped. He didn't care. He spread it out over Gwen like a blanket, making sure she'd stay warm. While he was at it, he shifted his large form so he was between Gwen and the door. If anyone was stupid enough to intrude on his happiness, they would be dead before they had a chance to disturb his angelic wife.

Still, a bed made of straw wasn't really the most comfortable place to sleep. He could adjust without difficulty, but he worried about Gwen. "Do you want to go back to the house, kitten?"

"Nope." She yawned, replete and satisfied. "I just want to rest up for a minute before I seduce you, again. I like it here."

"I always hated it." He tenderly picked a strand of green straw from her shiny hair. "In fact this was the exact spot where I had the very worst moment of my life. I was lying here, one night, and I realized that I would never have anything I wanted. Never have anyone who cared about me. I was Bad and poor and dirty and it was all… hopeless."

She opened one eye to look up at him. "And what do you think now, stable boy?"

"I think I just needed my queen to come and find me."

"Good answer."

Midas absently twisted the straw between his fingers until it was braided into a circle. Carefully lifting the edge of his glove, he touched it to his naked palm.

"Straw into gold?" Gwen teased. "Seems too easy for you."

"Kitten, I have worked harder at this than I've ever worked at anything." Readjusting his glove so his skin was safely covered, Midas turned his hand and displayed the golden ring he'd made.

"That's a wedding band." Gwen said softly.

"No."

"No?"

"It's not *a* wedding band. It's *your* wedding band. If you'll take it."

He'd bought her enough jewelry to fill a canyon and she hadn't worn a single piece. Because, none of those gemstones and precious metals had been worth anything. He saw that now. If you wanted the best, you couldn't pay for it with money. You needed to offer something far more valuable or it would slip away from you.

Lake-blue eyes filled with tears. "You're giving me something you didn't buy?"

"It seems fitting. You've given me the only things I can't put a price on. The only things that matter to me, Gwen."

"It's beautiful. *You* are beautiful." Gwen held out her hand, so he could slip the ring in place. "Thank you."

Midas felt the magic sealing it in place and it sent a new, unexpected jolt of desire throbbing through him. The simple gold band glistened and *finally* her finger looked exactly... right.

His wife.

She leaned up to kiss him. "I love you, husband."

Christ, there was no way she was getting that nap. "If you seduce me again *now*, I will turn a whole forest into gold for you." He offered, because --well-- he was still Midas. "Two of them, if you want."

"You know, less is sometimes more..." Gwen began, only to stop and frown suddenly. "Ouch."

"What's wrong?"

She shifted in the hay, doing nothing to alleviate his growing desire. "There's something jabbing into me..." Gwen reached beneath her and came up with a magic wand.

Merlyn's magic wand.

About twelve inches long and silver, it glowed with power. His name was engraved on the side, leaving no doubt whose vast magic it contained.

"So *that's* where he hid it." She said softly.

"The last place I'd ever want to look." Midas murmured, unable to tear his gaze away from the elegant gleam of the wand. "The place I hate the most. ...Until you came along, anyway. You found it, kitten."

"*We* found it." Gwen beamed up at him. "We just saved Camelot, King Midas. All because you're so damn easy to seduce."

"Glad I could help." Midas pressed a kiss to her temple. He didn't give a damn about the kingdom. All that mattered was having Gwen in his arms. "Don't ever leave me." He whispered, because he just couldn't stop himself. "Please."

"I won't." She snuggled into his embrace. "Don't leave me, either."

Midas snorted, holding her tight. "The odds of that happening are absolute zero. You are the only place I belong."

...But when Gwen woke up in the morning, Midas was gone.

Chapter Twenty-Nine

Both parties will promptly share any liabilities that could negatively impact the success of the partnership. (ie- outside deals that would conflict with this Contract, relevant curses/spells, or particularly dangerous enemies.)

When possible, they will deal with these liabilities as a team. If this is not possible, it is up to the effected party to solve the problem quickly, logically, and with as little bloodshed as possible

Clause 15- Liabilities to Partnership

Midas would never leave her alone in Celliwig.
Not ever.
Gwen stood in the middle of the marshy street, her heart pounding as she looked around the horrible town. Her husband was gone. So was the wand. Midas had taken the wand and left her alone in Celliwig. And Midas would never, ever, *ever* leave her alone in Celliwig. Not if he could possibly help it.
There was only one possible explanation for his absence: Dark Science.
The Scarecrow must have finally found a way to put the formula into the air. He'd taken control of all the Bad folk, stealing their freewill. High-jacking their minds. He'd kidnapped her husband. He'd stolen Merlyn's wand. And unless some miracle had occurred, he'd probably abducted Avalon, too.
He was going to use them to enslave Camelot.
That wasn't just Gwen's worst-case-scenario theory of why she'd woken up alone. It was absolute fucking *fact*. She had hard, rational, irrefutable evidence to back it up. All she had to do was look at the blank, marble-eyed stares of the citizens surrounding her.
All the Bad folk in Celliwig --and that was a hell of a lot of people-- were standing shoulder-to-shoulder in a perimeter around the town. Keeping her in. Didn't they have even one Good folk in this dumb village? Apparently not. Or maybe they had fled. Either way only the frozen army remained, trapping her there until the Scarecrow had finished with his vile plans.

Too bad for that birdbrain that Gwen was never, ever, *ever* going to let that happen.

Firming her jaw, she unzipped her knapsack and pulled out the gun she'd packed. She didn't have time for this shit. She had to get to her family and no one was going to stop her. There was probably some simple, awesome, logical plan to defeat this trap without resorting to violence, but Gwen was too frantic to think of it.

She was going with force.

Pushing past the armed felons surrounding her hadn't worked. They'd tossed her back into the center of town like she weighed nothing, at all. Again and again. Trying to find a weak point in their line had wasted several hours of the morning. The Bad folk weren't moving or blinking, but they knew she was there and they weren't letting her by. She couldn't slip between them.

But she could step *over* them.

The last thing Gwen wanted to do was hurt anyone, but she wasn't about to let Midas and Avalon die. A few blown out kneecaps was a small price to pay, in the grand scheme of things. The men holding her would no doubt agree, if they weren't all being remote-controlled by a lunatic. In a way, she was saving their lives. She was going to stop the madman who planned to destroy the kingdom and make them robots. They'd probably even *thank* her later for taking such a practical and Utilitarian worldview.

Probably.

Shit.

"I am *so* sorry about this." Gwen told the man standing in front of her.

Not that he could respond, what with being hypnotized by evil and all. She'd selected a target who looked healthy enough to recover from the injury and kind of like a scumbag. She felt less guilty about shooting someone in the leg, if her victim wore a t-shirt that suggested it was a great idea if a woman copulated with a drunken pig in a trucker hat.

She took aim at the dickhead's shin, chewing her lip nervously. People recovered from bullets to the shin all the time, right? It seemed like a really safe place to get shot. Witch-practitioners could heal non-fatal bullet wounds with a bit of magic and some herbs. This was not a big deal.

"Just so you know, I'm really not a violent person." She assured the guy, steeling herself for what she had to do. There was no choice. Her baby needed her. "Things just keep happening to me."

He didn't respond. Huge surprise.

Even if he wasn't drugged into a fugue state, she almost certainly wouldn't want to hear anything he had to say, anyway. Odds were, it was going to be unpleasant, given what she was about to do to him.

"Sorry." Gwen squeezed her eyes shut and pulled the trigger.

The guy toppled over like a fallen oak, but he was still alive. She could tell by the screaming. That was a really good sign.

"Sorry." She blurted out again and took off running through the space he'd conveniently opened up in the human wall. "It's for the greater good, if that helps, at all!"

It didn't help.

The guy kept shrieking and the sound seemed to awaken all the mean sons of bitches around him.

Heads turned to stare at her in horrible unison. The heads of *everyone,* all at once. It was the creepiest thing she'd ever seen. The creepiest thing she'd ever *heard* soon followed. An unearthly wail rose up from the mindless men. An animalistic blood cry.

Okkkkkayyyy, that was worrisome. She hadn't expected any of the other human statues to even notice that she'd shot someone. They sure hadn't notice anything else she'd done. Even when they'd been tossing her back from their line, it had been with vague robotic movements.

This was so much more. So much worse. The Scarecrow must have programmed in some kind of failsafe, in case Gwen got through his trap.

...And she'd just triggered it.

Moving as one, the entire population of Celliwig lunged after her, like a pack of wild dogs.

"Fucking hell!" Gwen moved faster, already knowing she couldn't possibly outrun them all. Why hadn't she gotten a horse? She should have gotten a horse!

Men were all around her. Dirty hands clawed at her, ripping at her coat, trying to stop her. These people were dangerous and mean, even when they *hadn't* been compelled by a monster. Now they were worse than Henry the monkena. Less civilized. More cunning. It was as if the men's bodies had been awaken, but all their filters had been turned off. Vicious and conscienceless, they fought to bring her down.

"Stop!" Gwen turned to shoot another man in the leg, forcing him to let go of her arm.

He released her so fast that Gwen fell to the ground. Mud

squished beneath her, as she scrambled to her feet. The sticky mire was so deep it made it hard to move and she *had* to move. The men were boxing her in, again. Only this time they weren't just going to stand there. They were going to hurt her.

She looked around trying to find an avenue of escape, but everything looked the same. Filth and angry faces and rundown buildings and…

Midas' house.

Gwen's frantic eyes fell on the hideous structure like it was a lifeboat in the middle of the sea. Midas' house was *Midas'* house which automatically made it feel safer than anyplace else. Plus, it had her father's magic inside. If she could reach it, she might be protected. Gwen headed for it as quickly as she could.

Men kept coming for her. She shot three more, two in the legs and one in the arm, but then her gun clicked empty. Damn it, why hadn't Galahad bought her extra bullets?! He was clearly *not* perfect and she was going to tell him so, if she somehow survived this nightmare.

She'd reached Midas' front lawn when her luck ran out.

A man with a beard and sunken features tackled her, driving her to the ground. Gwen let out a terrified cry as he began tearing at her clothes in a frenzy, his eyes still horrifically blank.

"Stop!" He was stronger than her, but skinny. She managed to kick free, half-stumbling, half-crawling towards the porch. She needed to reach the house. She needed to find some kind of weapon and…

Then Gwen saw *him* and knew she was about to die.

The most dangerous man in Camelot. The person no one alive could beat in a fight. A villain of such grisly renown, that the invincible Kingpin Midas had hired him on as a goddamn bodyguard.

Trystan was here.

She looked up at his emotionless face and froze right there on the ground. Even if she could somehow escape the other Bad folk, she would never get away from him. No one could. The formula was controlling him and so Gwen's life was over.

He stopped directly in front of her. There was a double-bladed axe in his massive hand, already red with blood. He looked like every demonic gryphon stereotype that King Uther had railed against. Death itself, come to collect its final payment.

"It wasn't your fault." Gwen whispered, because King Uther had been an asshole. Gryphons weren't demons. Trystan was a deeply honorable man. He would blame himself if he ever came out of the daze and remembered what he'd done to her. "I hope you can hear that. This *wasn't your fault*, Trystan. You're part of my family and I love you, even if you kill me."

His head tilted to one side.

"If you somehow break through this, please save Midas and Avalon." If Trystan was here without Avi, then the Scarecrow did indeed have her. That was scarier for Gwen than knowing she was about to die. Tears welled in her eyes. "Please find them and keep them safe."

The bearded man was rushing towards her, again. Gwen heard his frantic, excited breathing. She turned her head away, cringing.

...And was promptly showered in something wet.

What the hell?

Her eyes popped open, gaping down at the blood soaking into her coat. Was it hers? No it was the bearded guy's. ...Who no longer *had* a beard, because he no longer had a head. Trystan had just chopped it off.

Gwen blinked at the morbid sight and then looked back up at Trystan.

"You are a terrible fighter." He told her flatly. "I will begin training you, as I train the child. Only slower, because you are far worse than she is."

Gwen's mouth opened, closed, then opened again. "The formula isn't controlling you?" She got out, shocked that she was still alive.

"It does not work on my kind." He reached down to lug her to her feet. "Stay behind me." His axe swung out, killing two more men. Another guy dashed up and was cleaved in half, his torso split right down the middle. More blood splashed out like a fountain.

Gwen's mind was whirling, but she shook her questions aside.

Nothing mattered except finding Midas and Avalon. She barely noticed as bodies hit the ground at her feet. Paying attention to this fight was as pointless as paying attention when Midas played catur with the wizards. The outcome was inevitable. It was Trystan versus the entire town and Gwen had no doubt who would win. She didn't even bother to arm herself. Trystan was taking care of this mess, so she could focus on what really mattered.

"Tell me *exactly* what happened with Avi. I woke up and Midas was gone. Was it like that with her, too?"

"Yes." The word was a snarl. The next man who crossed

Trystan's path served as a fleshy outlet for his frustration. The axe-blade slammed through the guy's body in a series of brutal, angry hacks. "I went to awaken the child and she was missing. Then, the rest of the staff attacked me. It didn't take much deduction to know what was going on."

Gwen covered her face with both hands, trying to hold back her tears. Suspecting it was one thing, but actually *hearing* that Avalon had been kidnapped...

Oh God.

Oh God.

Oh God.

"I have to get my baby back." She couldn't even breathe without Avi. "I have to get Midas back. I *have* to. They're my whole world."

The Scarecrow wouldn't kill them right away. There was still time. She just needed to keep calm, and think it through, and not panic ...and then defeat a megalomaniac who had a magic wand.

She was definitely starting to panic.

All the desperation Gwen had been trying to suppress since she woke up threatened to boil over. She was hanging on by a thread, not sure if she was about to start sobbing or screaming. Her teeth began to chatter, even though she wasn't cold. Her mind played a slideshow of the horrible things the Scarecrow could do to the two people she loved most.

"Trystan." Her voice cracked. "Trystan, I can't think I'm so scared. What if something happens to them? What if he hurts them? I *need* them."

"As do I." For someone without emotions, he was doing a great impression of a man on the edge of a mindless, killing rage. Past the edge, actually. A misty veil was obscuring his face, so his features vaguely resembled an eagle's. "I *will not* lose another clan."

Gwen cringed at the gory mess he made out of the next armed citizen who came flailing at them. The guy ran right into Trystan, bounced off his sheer bulk, and was then basically liquefied. Gryphons weren't really about aiming for the leg. Especially when they were upset.

Gwen patted his arm comfortingly, ignoring the sticky blood coating it. "These men are enthralled, you know." Trystan's obvious turmoil actually helped her to stay in control. He needed her to be strong. Her whole family did. She *had* to do this. "The Scarecrow is controlling them."

"Their motives are immaterial. All who try to kill me, end up on the wrong side of the grass."

"They have no idea what they're even doing."

"They're horrible people, even when they *are* aware!" He roared. "Their lives and deaths mean *nothing*, compared to yours. I need to get you out of this fucking town, as quickly as possible, and they are in my way."

"Just... maybe you could wound them, instead? Fight them in a nonlethal way?"

He rolled his eyes and sliced off an attacker's arm at the shoulder. "Happy?" He demanded, as the guy collapsed into a fetal position, screeching in blood-curdling agony.

She flinched, watching the severed appendage twitch. "Ecstatic."

"Good. If I pick you up, will you fly without hysterics?"

"I've never had hysterics a day in my life, Trystan!" Although she was damn close.

"Many of your kind have hysterics when they fly. You're a strange and earthbound people."

"I'm fine with flying, okay?" She took a deep breath, trying to concentrate. "All I care about is reaching Avalon and Midas, as fast as we can. I don't care if we have to ride a goddamn pegasus, we're finding them. *Now*. They have to be at the Dark Science lab."

"Where is that?"

"It's a separate building, behind the palace. Which has really, really great security, because I burned it down once already. The Scarecrow rebuilt it, better than ever"

Trystan snorted. "Non-lethal battle tactics always reap such futile results."

"Not helping, right now." She snapped. "Just let me think of a plan and we'll go get Midas and Avi. I *know* there's a way."

"*I* will go get them. *You* will stay behind, because you are small and useless."

A redheaded guy tried to grab Gwen. Trystan stabbed him through the stomach, viciously twisting the blade. She'd give his chances of survival a solid 'maybe,' but Gwen had always been kind of an optimist.

"What do you mean 'useless'?" She snapped. "You've been calling me a 'remorseless killer' since we met! What the hell's changed?"

He flashed her a look that suggested she was a staggering moron. "You are now *j'aha.*"

Damn it, she really needed to learn the gryphons' language.

"What does *j'aha* mean?"

"My sister."

A huge, tank of a guy raced at Trystan from behind, trying to seize hold of his wings and wrestle him to the ground. Trystan didn't even bother to turn around to eviscerate him. He somehow chopped the man in half with his back turned.

"I don't think that one will live." He told her without much remorse.

Gwen ignored that, processing his translation of *j'aha* for a beat. "I kind of killed Arthur, you know." She announced, crossing her arms over her chest.

He grunted, unsurprised. "I know. I suspect he threatened the child and you reacted as any worthy mother would."

"He tried to throw her off the balcony."

Trystan's eyes narrowed. "It's a badge of honor to slay such a man. You should boast of it with pride."

"My point is, I'm not a violent person. ...Unless I'm forced to be. And then I'm going to win." It was a promise.

Trystan shot her a speculative look.

"I'm coming with you to save Midas and Avalon. There is nothing you can do to stop me. I know that palace and the lab and the Scarecrow. He wants me to marry him. He'll use them as bargaining chips, against me. I'm sure of it."

"I will gut that birdman with my bare hands, before I let him touch you." It was a snarled vow, made all the more vivid by the body he was tossing aside like a Frisbee.

"I appreciate that. But, my point is, I have cards to play that you don't have." She gestured in the direction of the castle. "Not even you can kill all of the King's Men alone, *and* rescue Avi and Midas, *and* stop the Scarecrow from unleashing God-only-knows what else. You need me."

Trystan gave a growl of aggravation and kicked an attacker hard enough to cause a compound fracture. The guy hit the dirt with a bellow of pain, which Trystan ignored. Instead, he reached back to grab Gwen, lifting her over a slog of deep mud and corpses, without breaking his stride.

"Now, it is *my* husband and *my* baby in danger. I am going to help you kill everyone who threatens them. Brutally and without mercy." She hung onto Trystan's shoulder, her feet not touching the ground. "Actually, you're going to help *me*, because *I'm* in charge."

He arched a brow at that, still looking pissed.

"And thank you for coming to save me," she added a little

belatedly, as he carefully set her down again, "brother. Have I mentioned that I claim you as part of my clan?"

He'd obviously claimed her, too. There was no other reason that Trystan would fly to Celliwig, given the fact he'd seen what the Scarecrow had done. He knew Midas would be gone, just as Avi was. He'd come to the town because he'd realized Gwen would be alone with the worst men in Camelot.

He'd come to rescue her.

Trystan stopped his "nonlethal" carnage long enough to meet her eyes. "I change the pledge I made to you before. I protect Midas and Avalon and *you*. The three of you first and above all else. Keeping my clan safe is all that matters to me."

"Me too. You know that."

"I do. We are the same." He studied her for a beat. "And I know you are a queen and queens are the greatest of all warriors."

"Galahad used to tell me that I was a warrior, too. You remind me of him sometimes." They were men who would sacrifice everything for those around them. Who would walk into danger, heedless of the consequences, just because it was the right thing to do. They were both her brothers.

Trystan didn't seemed thrilled to be compared to a knight, but he pressed onward. "I will not stand in the way of a warrior, when she is intent on saving her people. We go to the palace together."

Gwen hugged him. She couldn't help it. She didn't even mind when he didn't hug her back because he was too busy disemboweling a guy. Battered wings curved, sheltering her, and for the first time all day, she felt real hope. They could do this! They *would* do this.

"I'm going to protect you, too." She promised. "Just like I do with Midas."

"Lyrssa help me."

"I mean it, Trystan." She pulled back and held out a palm to him. "You and I will save our family side-by-side. Is it a deal?"

He didn't shake on the bargain. Instead, he held up a hand in some kind of sacred-oath, team-building, fist-bump. His mouth curved slightly when she responded in kind. "Side-by-side, *j'aha*." He agreed softly.

And then they were flying.

Chapter Thirty

Midas Skycast will formally and legally adopt Avalon Skycast (a minor) and have all the rights and responsibilities of a biological father. He will try not to spoil her too much.

Clause 24- Adoption of Avalon Skycast (a minor)
(Containing Nullification of Clause 3- Care and Protection of Avalon Pendragon (a minor) and Clause 17- Instance of Guinevere's Pendragon's Death)

Midas opened his eyes and saw his daughter …and almost instantly knew he would have to kill himself.

Avalon was sitting across from him in the cell, humming happily as she played with her dolls. The pink backpack was sitting beside her. He had no recollection of how he'd come to be locked in a sterile room with Avi and an army of plastic toys, but he could take a real good guess.

The fucking Scarecrow had finally figured out how to make the fucking formula airborne. He'd brainwashed Midas and Avalon into coming straight to his fucking Dark Science lab.

Son of a fucking *bitch*.

Midas looked around and saw nothing but smooth, beige walls. No furniture or objects he could use as weapons. Above him, there was a mirrored window that he guessed was one-way glass. He instantly thought of the cell Trystan had describe being kept in, back at the WUB Club. Apparently, the Scarecrow had borrowed the basic concept, adapting it to his psychotic needs.

Midas slowly sat up.

He had no idea where Gwen was. The formula only worked on Bad folk, which meant she was probably still in Celliwig. Alone. Shit… His mind caught fire with horrible images of what could happen to her. *Shit*… What was he going to do? *Nothing*. He was locked in a goddamn cage, while his wife was in danger and he couldn't do *anything* to help her.

Trystan.

Midas seized on the name like a lifeline. Trystan would go for Gwen. He would realize what was happening and protect her. That was the only ray of hope Midas could cling to. Trystan would kill half the kingdom to save their family. More than half. He needed Gwen and Avi nearly as much as Midas did. He would make sure no one in Celliwig put their hands on her...

And that's when Midas noticed his gloves were missing.

He stared down at his bare palms. For a moment, he was too astonished to understand. He so rarely saw his fingers uncovered, because they were weapons. They were deadly. Why would anyone be stupid enough to remove his gloves, knowing the damage his touch could do?

Unless they *wanted* him to touch something. To *make* him touch something.

Midas' eyes very slowly traveled over to Avalon. ...And that's when he knew he'd have to kill himself. It was the only path he could take.

"Avi?" He cleared his throat, trying to keep his voice calm. "You okay?"

"Hi, Daddy! I's fine. You be sleeping."

"I know, princess, but I'm awake now. Do you know what happened?"

She nodded earnestly. "Mean men are mean."

"Yes, they fucking are." Midas ran his hands through his hair. His golden touch didn't work on his own body. If it did, this would be a lot easier. How was he going to kill himself without a gun or a knife? "Sorry. Yes, they *p'don* are."

Avalon didn't mind the swearing. "Wanna play?" She held out her favorite doll, wanting to cheer him up. "You can be Lyrssa. She's brave, just like Mommy."

Midas tried a soothing smile, not wanting to upset her. "No, I... " He broke off mid-word, a new idea occurring to him. A solution that would save his daughter. "Do you have Lyrssa's sword in your bag?"

Her head tilted, blue eyes studying him. "Why?"

"I'd just like to see it."

"Why?"

She knew why. Shit. Avalon could read his thoughts, past, present and future. "I need the letter opener, Avi." He'd try to grab it out of the backpack himself, but he was afraid she might try to stop him. Even a tiny touch could be disastrous.

The Scarecrow could control Midas' actions and had taken his gloves. Midas was trapped with his baby four feet away and he could turn her to gold with a single brush of his fingers. There was only one way to keep her safe from his curse and the letter opener would allow him to see it through.

He was going to stab himself right through the heart.

If he was dead, he couldn't be compelled to hurt his daughter. The thought of her little body going still... Every special, perfect thing about her replaced with cold and worthless metal... Her bright, pure spirit gone from the world forever... No. Midas wouldn't risk that. Not for anything.

"Avi?" His tone became more intent when she just silently stared at him.

She popped her thumb in her mouth, distressed. "Love you." Her lower lips trembled. "Don't leave. You promised you wouldn't."

Fuck, fuck, *fuck*.

Midas squeezed his eyes shut, close to tears. Hurting her was the worst torture anyone could devise. "Avalon." He cleared his throat. "Am I your daddy?"

"'Course, Daddy."

"Well, it is a daddy's job to keep his little girl safe, isn't it?"

Another nod.

"So, you need to trust me, now. Give me the letter opener and look that way." He pointed at the wall. "Pretty soon, your mommy and Trystan will come for you." He believed that. He had to. "They are going to take you home and..."

Avalon cut him off, shaking her head so hard her blonde curls swung. "*No!* The Mean Thing will get us if you're not here! I seen it! It's coming. It hurts me and Mommy!"

Midas' insides dropped. "What Mean Thing? The Scarecrow?"

"Nooooo." She was frantic now. "Please, Daddy. Maybe even the birds will eat me, if I'm all alone." She pulled her knees up so they were tucked under her chin, rocking slightly. "I don't see them and I'm scared. Mommy is going to fight them, but you have to keep her safe."

Rage flickered through him, watching his daughter hug herself into a ball. All he wanted to do was pick her up and hold her, but he couldn't. His goddamn curse wouldn't let him.

"You don't need to be afraid, baby. Not ever. I love you *so much* there aren't words for it." Midas tilted his head, so he could meet her damp gaze. "Luckily, I don't need words, because you can look into my head and you *know* what I feel, right? How deep it goes."

She sniffed and nodded again.

"So look into my head, right now. You will see *everything* you need to know." It was a vow. "You will see how far I'm willing to go to keep you and your mommy safe. It's the mean people who need to be afraid, princess. Not you."

Avalon swiped her wrist under her nose. "Stay." She whispered.

She was ripping his goddamn heart out. "Baby, please..."

"You's can't protect me and Mommy if you go away." She interrupted. "You *supposed* to protect me and Mommy from the Mean Thing."

"I *am* protecting you. I will *always* protect you. My curse is dangerous..."

She cut him off again, brightening. "You should fix the curse!" She clapped her hands like she'd just solved all their problems. "Then, you's feel better. Good idea, Daddy. You so smart."

"I can't just break the curse, Avi. If I could, I would've done it long ago."

If she was right about a "Mean Thing" coming (and Avalon was always right), then he also couldn't kill himself, though. His death would leave her all alone there. Midas would *never* leave his baby on a fucking porch, even if it was a science lab. He needed to find a way to rescue her and get to Gwen. His eyes cut around the perimeter of the lab, vainly looking for a way out.

"How come you can't break the curse, Daddy?"

"Because the woman who cast it made sure it would last forever."

"Vivien?"

Midas shot her a quick look and, despite everything, his mouth curved. *His* daughter. "Vivien." He agreed, softly.

"She wouldn't do something so mean. You's mine and she likes me."

"Well, I don't think she liked *me*. She said the curse will last until I have everything. And not even Daddy can buy everything. Believe me, I've tried."

"Oh yeah, you do a real great job of trying!" She praised. "You got *lots* a stuff."

"For all the good it does me." He tried to climb up the smooth wall, towards the window only to fall back down again, cursing graphically in the gryphons' language.

Avalon made a 'tsk' sound. She generally let Midas say whatever he liked, but the vulgarity of that oath was too much even for his 'best friend' to let slide. "I know what that word means, you know."

Fucking hell... so much for his attempts to bypass Clause 3.

Midas shot her an incredulous look. "Trystan taught you *that* word?"

"No, not him." She leaned closer and lowered her voice. "Sometimes I talk to the gone-away gryphons in my dreams. They tells me lots."

Midas wasn't even going to *try* and figure that one out. "Do they?" He asked, not doubting it for a moment.

"Oh yes!" She grinned. "They say I will be the Great Queen and help they's people. They like me, too."

"Well, that's good, baby." The child loved gryphons. If she wanted to discuss them, he was game. Anything was preferable to her crying and scared. Tales of Trystan's people calmed her. "I'm not surprised. Everyone likes you." Midas stared up at the window. How the hell was he going to reach it?

Avalon nodded, like he was speaking deep wisdom. "Trystan was wrong about what '*ha'na*' means, Daddy." She told him importantly. "Did you know that? I don't think the gone-away gryphons taught him it right." She let out a little giggle. "Trystan's silly."

Midas gave up on reaching the window. Unlike Avi's winged heroes, he couldn't fly. There *had* to be another entrance. The Scarecrow hadn't just dropped them into the room from way up there. And if there was another way *in*, there was another way *out*. Unfortunately, it seemed to have been hidden and sealed shut with some kind of locking spell.

"*Ha'na* doesn't *exactly* mean 'light,' he allowed distractedly, "but it's hard to put into our language. I think Trystan wasn't sure how to translate it properly."

"How do *you* say it?"

"Um... I don't know." Midas began looking along the walls for a hidden door. "'True Love,' maybe?"

No, that wasn't quite right.

True Love was two people who were really *one* person. *Ha'na* was more about all the *connections* those two people made. Gryphons were born without emotions, so their bonds with their mates were different. Broader. *Ha'na* was when a male gryphon found his woman and beheld how all the strands of his life that would intertwine with hers. The family they'd build and the future they'd share. The vastness of *everything* he experienced when he saw her, from their very first meeting until he drew his last breath. *Ha'na* was about... everything.

Ha'na meant everything.

Midas went still.

"Daddy?"

"Yes, baby?" His voice sounded faraway in his ears.

"I don't think Vivien cursed you. I think she was *helping* you. Sorceresses is nice."

Midas swallowed hard. He suddenly remembered Gwen sitting on his lap, while they played dolls with Avalon. How he'd known that he'd found *ha'na,* right there in that room.

He'd had it from the moment Gwen walked into his house and upended his entire existence. She'd rearranged every priority he had. She'd given him a daughter. Brought him joy. Drove him crazy. Made him laugh. Dragged Trystan into their fold. There wasn't one piece of his life that didn't intersect with Gwen's and he would die before he ever unbound them. Midas was connected to her and by her and with her.

In his head, Midas heard Vivien's words from twenty years before: *And the magic it will go on and on and on, until you realize the truth. ...Until you finally have* everything.

Gwen and Avalon were everything.

That was the truth. *That* was what he'd been searching for when he went to the lake. Not class or riches or power. He'd wanted a family. A place to belong. It had taken a miniature sorceress and a blunt little queen with a handgun, but he'd finally been granted his wish.

He finally had everything.

Avalon smiled at him. "See, Daddy? I told you Mommy and me'd get you a gift."

"Ah, good. You're awake." A voice echoed from up above, piped in over loudspeakers. "Excellent. It wouldn't be any fun to do this, if you slept right through it."

Percival.

Midas jerked out of his thoughts. His gaze went up to the window, his eyes narrowing. "Aren't you dead yet?"

"Your little baby Baddie is the one about to die, actually. The Scarecrow wants you as leverage, so Guinevere will agree to marry him." He paused. "If you think about it, though. He only needs *one* of you."

"He needs the child." Midas said instantly, his throat going dry. "Keep her alive. I won't fight you, just don't hurt her. Gwen will do anything for Avalon."

"Yes ...and so will you." Percival taunted. "Everyone in the kingdom knows Guinevere and her devil spawn own you, like any other brainless animal. You might as well take out billboards advertising you're theirs."

"I'm already planning several, actually."

"Ooooohhhhh." Avalon exclaimed, liking that idea. "Can one have a robot on it?"

"Shut up!" Percival screamed. "You're both pathetic. Weak. Inferior. You belong with the *gryphon*."

Midas took that part as a compliment. "Yes."

"Gryphons like us." Avalon agreed. "*Everybody* likes me and Daddy, except mean people like you."

"Do you think I'd *ever* allow a soulless savage like you to have Arthur's wife?" Percival ranted at Midas, ignoring Avalon. "To put your dirty hands on a Good woman? Even a bitch like Guinevere? It's a blasphemy against my kind."

"Gwen is *my* wife and no one else's."

"Not for long." Percival informed him smugly. "See, I think it'll be far more satisfying to keep *you* alive and let the child die. In fact, I'm going to make sure you're the one who kills the brat. Then you'll lose them *both*. Guinevere is a stupid slut, but not even she will keep screwing the man who turned her daughter to gold."

A cloud of purple mist was released from hidden vents and floated down. A small dose of the formula, but it would be enough.

Midas' heartrate increased. Even if he was right and Vivien's curse had been lifted, he couldn't prove it. Couldn't be sure. Avalon was the only living thing in the room to test.

"My daddy won't hurt me." Avalon scoffed, not worried about the gas drifting down. "You only get one last chance to fix your behavior, and then you're going to be in *big* trouble. It'll be too late, even if you start to see the truth."

"Shut up!" Percival shrieked again. "God, I'm so sick of you! Midas, shut her up. Touch the little bitch, so I never have to hear her annoying little voice again."

No.

No.

Midas felt the formula seeping into his lungs and fogging his mind. Pulling him towards Avalon, wanting him to tap a finger against her skin. Just one finger. It took everything in him to plant both feet and resist the compulsion. To remember who he was, and who *she* was, and why death was preferable to losing her.

No. No. No.

He chanted the word in his head. Blood began to seep from his nose from the strain of standing still. He wouldn't touch her. No matter what, he wouldn't hurt his baby.

No.no.no.no.no.no.no.no.no.no.no.

"What the fuck...?" Percival sounded angry and confused. "How are you doing that?

Midas fell backwards, hitting against the wall and sliding down it, his hands clamped over his ears like that would somehow help. Or at least stop the blood from oozing out of them. Red filmed his vision, making everything out of focus. Inside his skull, his brain stuttered and began to shut down. The formula didn't like defiance. His head throbbed, threatening to explode, and he knew he would die if he didn't submit.

It didn't matter.

Midas raised his bleeding eyes up to the window, full of hate and triumph. *Nothing* could make him kill his daughter. Nothing at all. No power of man or magic or science went deeper than his love for Avalon.

"You have to obey!" Percival bellowed, like Midas was somehow cheating. "You *have* to touch her. I *order* you to touch her."

Midas' jaw was clenched tight, but he still managed to grind out his simple and unequivocal response. "No."

Chapter Thirty-One

Percival
Now

That gryphon-loving son of a bitch was winning.

Percival had no idea how such a thing could be possible. Midas was *Bad*. Born less and wrong. A criminal, who sided with those disgusting gryphon over his own people. How could he possibly withstand the formula? It was impossible. No one else had *ever* withstood it. He had to be doing something underhanded and evil.

Fucking monster.

Percival's eyes narrowed in fury.

No matter. If Midas wouldn't touch the girl, he would have the girl touch Midas. Avalon was Bad. He could control her easily enough, even if the Kingpin was someone resisting. Percival pressed the intercom button, which was awkward considering his arms were both in casts. "Avalon, go to him and…"

"*No!*" Midas roared knowing what he was about to say.

"Is okay, Daddy." Avalon chirped. "We can touch now. You's all better, so…" She stopped short, her eyes lighting up. "Yay! Trystan's here!"

What?

Percival hesitated, the gryphon's name cutting through his wrath. His hatred of their kind went deeper than his hatred of Midas. So did his fear. A sliver of insecurity sneaked in. Could any gryphon get past the lab's security? Enter the castle's grounds undetected? Could Midas' pet monster have come looking for him?

A sound came from behind Percival, his head whipping around. He didn't see anything, but somehow he knew.

"No." He whispered.

"I like this invisibility cloak." There was a shimmer and the sound of rustling fabric. Then, standing there like he had every right to be walking among the Good folk, Trystan appeared. "I was against the idea, when Midas' woman suggested I use it to sneak in here. It seems like a trick of *your* kind." He shrugged and dropped the unseen garment to the ground. "But, I must admit, it made it simple to slay all your men without detection."

"You won't get away with this." Percival spat out, his mind racing. "Even if you murder me, it won't matter. Your people are still *finished*."

"My people live. They are locked in that room." Trystan pointed to the window. "Except Guinevere, of course. She fights elsewhere."

Percival surreptitiously dug in his pocket for his final weapon. He couldn't defeat the gryphon with two broken arms, but he still had an ace to play. "She'll die, just like the rest of you."

"If you think that, you do not know my sister."

"She is not your sister! Guinevere is one of *my* kind. You are nothing but a goddamn demon! Your whole race is evil and deserves to be wiped from existence. You're a disease, festering on the Good folk of the world!"

Percival lunged forward. Ripping the needle from his pocket, he slammed it into Trystan's arm. A full and concentrated dose of the formula was injected straight into the gryphon's bloodstream.

Trystan stared down at the needle like it confused him.

Percival staggered back in righteous victory. The airborne version of the formula might be malfunctioning, but no one had *ever* withstood a direct shot of it into their veins. The massive dosage Trystan had just received would make him nothing more than a puppet.

"Kill the child *and* Midas *and* yourself." Percival ordered, loving the fact that the gryphon had to obey. That nature was once again in balance and Good folk held dominion over the lesser creatures. "And make it *painful*."

He stood there, breathing hard, waiting for Trystan to submit.

And waiting.
And waiting.
What the hell?

Nothing happened. The gryphon's eyes didn't cloud over with mindless compliance. Instead, he yanked the needle from his arm like it was a harmless splinter. "This *will* be painful." He said calmly. "But not for me and my clan."

Terror came over Percival like an avalanche, chilling him from the inside. "How?" He blurted out, staring up at the monster who would kill him.

"Your godless science is *nothing* to me. As you are nothing to me." Trystan flicked the empty hypodermic at Percival, like a cat taunting a mouse. "It does not work on my kind."

Percival's pulse pounded in his temples. "Of course it works on your kind." His voice was too high. "I've used it on gryphons before. I know it works on gryphons!"

"Yes, but it does not work on *Good folk*." Trystan grabbed him by the front of his chest plate, lifting him right off the ground. "And I was born Good." He smiled. Fucking *smiled*. "How is that not obvious to all?"

With that, he threw Percival backwards, straight through the window. Percival felt the glass crashing around him and then he was pin-wheeling through the air. He impacted the floor with enough force to break most of the bones in his body. Life seeped from him, spilling onto the cement and he made a helpless gasping sound.

"About time you got here!" Midas shouted up at Trystan. "Where's Gwen?"

"She is coming." Trystan casually jumped into the room, his monstrous wings allowing him to glide to the ground. "Is the child alright?" He didn't wait for an answer to that, grabbing Avalon up so he could see her for himself. "Are you safe?" He demanded, scanning her for injuries.

"Hi, Trystan! I was brave like Lyrssa and Mommy!"

He let out a shaky breath, his heathen thumb gently tracing down her face, from her forehead to her chin. "I swear to the gods, I'm going to fucking chain you to my side, Avi."

"Cursing's a no-no, but that's okay," her tiny arms wrapped around his neck in a hug, "'cause I missed you a lot."

The gryphon closed his eyes against her messy blonde curls, whispering words in his primitive language. He cradled her against his chest, his wings curling around her. His massive hands covered most of her back, his bloodstained palms spread wide, as if every part of him wanted to shield Avalon forever.

In his darkening consciousness, Percival suddenly remembered fighting in the Looking Glass Campaigns. Remembered those stupid, senseless, defeated gryphons protecting children of all races in their mountaintop villages. Remembered King Uther laughing at their doomed efforts and asking their captured leader why she bothered. Remembered that one-eyed barbarian sneering like *Uther* was somehow the savage. "The innocent belong to all who would care for them." She'd said with contempt in her voice. "True warriors know this."

And then in Percival's misfiring mind, Galahad stood beside him at the Knights' Academy, once more, his eyes bright with pride and honor. They were young again, reciting the oath that all King's

Men had to take. Saying it for the very first time. Pledging to always fulfill their primary duty:

    A knight protects those weaker than himself.

And there, in his last moments of existence, Percival realized that the gryphons and the knights all vowed to live by the same code. They *all* promised to guard the brightest and most fragile parts of this world they shared, even as they slaughtered each other.

What did that mean?

He wasn't sure and it was too late to figure it out.

The Kingpin marched over to Percival's dying form, intent on finishing him off. The small dose of the airborne formula was dissipating, leaving the maniac's golden gaze clear.

"Still alive? That's convenient." He crouched next to Percival and very deliberately tapped one bare finger to the middle of his forehead. His mouth curved when their skin touched without his curse being triggered. "Well, look at that. You're not gold."

Percival gurgled up at him.

"I'm all cured. ...Too bad you're not." Midas sat back and flexed his uncovered hands. "You have about thirty more seconds to live, asshole. Use them thinking about what a fucking waste your life was." Midas got to his feet. "Where's Gwen?" He asked Trystan again. "Why isn't she here, yet? You said she was here." He looked up at the window, as if he expected to see her.

"She *is* here. At the castle. It is a two-pronged attack." Trystan still wasn't putting Avalon down. "I came here to get you. She will keep our primary enemy at bay, ensuring I can fly you and the child to safety."

Midas didn't like that plan. *"Where the fuck is my wife!"* He bellowed.

Trystan casually shrugged. "She's gone to duel the Scarecrow."

Chapter Thirty-Two

Guinevere Pendragon will, to the best of her abilities, offer Midas (no last name given) protection from her enemies. In the event that her bid to reclaim Camelot is unsuccessful, she will take full responsibility for the hostilities with said enemies and will endeavor to face the consequences alone.

She will at no time allow him to be endangered, if she has the means to prevent it.

Clause 6- Partnership Responsibilities of Guinevere Pendragon

The castle was empty.

Gwen walked through the deserted halls, shocked by how many people *weren't* there. Usually, the palace was teeming with Good citizens and Good staff. The Scarecrow had fired all the Baddies long ago, so no one was missing because they were brainwashed in a corner. They were just *gone*. It seemed that everyone had fled in terror or was hiding from the inevitable showdown.

Who could blame them?

Nobody stopped Gwen as she marched right into the throne room. She knew she'd find the Scarecrow there. There was no place else the egotistical bastard would hang out. Sure enough he was lounging on the eighteen foot golden throne, petting his blackbirds with his twig-y hands. It occurred to her that Midas would really like that chair.

Luckily, she was about to get it for him.

"Guinevere." The Scarecrow's mouth curved into a mocking smile. "I see you managed to escape Celliwig, my dear. I assumed you would, of course." He made a show of checking his pocket watch. Which was *Arthur's* pocket watch that the Scarecrow must have stolen from the dead king's bedroom. "Actually, I thought you be here *long* before now. You weren't quite as anxious to liberate your beloved Baddies as you pretend, eh?"

Gwen ignored the taunt. Trystan was going to rescue Midas and Avalon. She believed that. Her job was to make sure he got them out without interference. Saving her family was all that mattered and she was going to do it if it killed her.

Hopefully, though, it would just kill the Scarecrow.

"You and I are about to have a duel." She told him flatly.

"A duel?" His eyebrows soared, as if that amused him. "Pistols at dawn, perhaps?"

"Not exactly." She stalked over to throw open the huge windows, letting in the misty afternoon.

"Just as well. Bullets won't kill me." He paused meaningfully. "Few things will. I'm grieved to disappoint you, my dear, but face it: I've triumphed." He spread his bundled-stick arms. "Camelot is mine."

Sometimes Midas said things best. "No." Gwen quoted firmly.

The Scarecrow frowned at the simple retort. "You're just being childish. Agree to marry me and I'll consider releasing Midas and Avalon."

"You're lying." There wasn't a doubt in Gwen's mind that he planned to kill her husband and daughter.

"I'm lying." He agreed and his smile grew snide.

Asshole.

Gwen flashed him a glare. "I won't marry you. There is only one way this deal will work. Either you surrender now. ...Or we duel, *then* I kill you, save my family, and get my kingdom back."

He rolled his painted-on eyes. "You really expect *me* to surrender to *you?*"

"No. Honestly, I don't think you're smart enough."

He didn't appreciate that response. "If you require an incentive to acquiesce to my demands, I've no plans to eradicate the rest of the Baddies in the kingdom. Yet." The Scarecrow rose to his feet. His patchwork jacket moved as the birds shifted inside his body. "Admit that *I* am the king of Camelot. Marry me and tell the wizards to provide me with Emerald City's support." He arched a brow. "Refuse and I will have every Bad folk in the kingdom jump from the highest tower they can find."

"Or we have a duel." Gwen waved a "duh" kind of hand. "It seems like I keep repeating myself here. *Repeatedly*. Business negotiations are kind of hard for you, aren't they? No wonder the wizards think you're an idiot."

His taunting smile faded.

Gwen tilted her head, sensing she'd seriously pissed him off. Excellent. "For the life of me, I can't understand how you convinced everyone you were the smartest man in Camelot." She continued, twisting the knife. "Midas is *soooo* much brighter than you."

"I have four doctorates!"

"I know." She agreed in a pitying tone. "Your diplomas were just a *total* waste of money, weren't they? Midas left school when he was just a child and he can *still* outthink you at every turn. He has the crown, power, money, a family who loves him... And he did it all just by being himself." She shrugged. "You can't buy the brainpower Midas has. He was just born the best."

That did it.

"You want a duel, you fucking whore? *Fine.* My babies will stand in for me." The Scarecrow made a clucking sound with his tongue and the blackbirds fluttered free of his straw body. He chuckled indulgently as they flapped around the room like feathered demons. "As you can see, they're prodigiously eager to assist."

"Great. I'll just call my second, too, then." Gwen pulled a dog whistle out of her pocket. "We'll let them battle it out, winner take all." Popping it between her lips, she blew it as hard as she could.

The Scarecrow hadn't been expecting that. "What second?"

Gwen smiled, ignoring his suspicious question. "Did you ever notice how nobody ever asks who the smartest *woman* in the kingdom is? I think it's because we all already know."

"No woman could ever compete with my IQ, so there is no..." The Scarecrow's sexist comment ended in a gasp, when he saw Harriet soaring towards him. "No. *NO!*"

Gwen hadn't been lying to Midas earlier. The firebird *was* learning how to do tricks with her dog whistle. For instance, one long blow and she'd fly right to Gwen's side. Of course, wherever she flew, she left a trail of flames in her wake. On ordinary days, that was a bit of an annoyance.

Today, though, it was kind of awesome.

Harriet glided through the open window, her feathers burning in brilliant oranges and yellows. She kind of looked like a peacock... if a peacock was engulfed in flames. Her plumage was long and thick and endlessly burning. Her glowing wings shot sparks with each flap.

"You remember my pet Harriet, right?" Gwen smiled over at the Scarecrow. "You should. You and Arthur and the White Rabbit are the geniuses who created her. I stopped by my father's house to pick her up. She was dying for a visit."

"Stop her!" The Scarecrow bellowed, waving the blackbirds towards Harriet.

His minions swarmed Harriet, trying to bring her down. Too bad for them, the firebird was about four times their size and made of *fire*. Harriet was a peace-loving creature, who just wanted to follow Gwen around and eat sunflower seeds. The attack shocked her. She squawked in panic as the vicious blackbirds dive-bombed her. She didn't have to worry, though. Her feathers worked as the ultimate self-defense mechanism.

"*I'll kill you and that fucking bird!*" The Scarecrow shrieked, as the blackbirds began to incinerate in midair.

Gwen smirked. "Nobody touches my family, you flammable son of a bitch."

Every time the Scarecrow's "babies" came at Harriet, their own feathers went up in flames. Within ten seconds, the room was filled with dying, flying torches. Harriet was fine, but the opposition forces were falling fast. The blackbirds spun in the air like small cyclones of fire.

"*You stupid bitch!*" Sparks were raining down. They burned Gwen here and there, but the Scarecrow was made of kindling. His whole body started to burn. Screaming in panic, he brought his twiggy arms up to shield his head. "*You stupid fucking bitch!*"

"Don't you wish you'd listened to me about *not* experimenting with animals and Dark Science, right about now?"

"Gwen!" Midas suddenly slammed into the throne room, his eyes scanning for her.

Her head snapped around. He was okay! And just in time to see her victory. "Midas!" She rushed over to his side. The man had never looked more appealing. "Are you alright?" He looked alright. "Do you have Avi? I've been so worried."

"Oh thank God." He started forward, like he didn't even notice the fires blazing around them. "Are you hurt?"

Gwen shook her head impatiently. "I'm fine. Where's Avalon?"

"Trystan has her. She's perfect." He held up Lyrssa's letter opener sword. "She sent me to rescue you with this."

Relief flooded through her. "That's adorable. But, you should be with Avi, someplace safe. Didn't Trystan tell you the plan? I have everything under control here."

His mouth curved, taking in the chaotic scene. "I can see that."

"It's a duel." Gwen leaned up to kiss him lightly. "Stand over there and don't get yourself killed. I'm about to win us a kingdom."

"God, I am just madly in love with you."

"It's fire!" The Scarecrow bellowed, ineffectually swatting at his smoldering body. "I can't be around fire!"

"Midas and I assumed it was the best way to kill you. We had a whole discussion about it, once." Gwen glanced up at him. "Didn't we have a discussion about that?"

"Yes." He nodded like it had been a conversation about the weather.

The last of the blackbirds fell to the floor dead and the Scarecrow gave an anguished howl. "*My babies!*"

Those birds had been winged evil, but Gwen still felt a little guilty witnessing his genuine grief.

Midas didn't share her sentiments. He stomped down on one of the burning carcasses as it twitched, ensuring it was dead. "Damn parasites are *done* scaring my daughter and threatening my wife."

Finally satisfied that nothing else was going to bombard her, Harriet retreated to the windowsill to soothe her long feathers. Luckily, the windowsill was made of stone, so it didn't scorch.

Meanwhile, the Scarecrow's whole body was going up in flames, even as he mourned his beaked goons. Honestly, Gwen was surprised at how quickly the fire was devouring him. If she didn't do something he was going to die.

She frowned. Maybe she should do something.

Accidently killing Arthur had been traumatic. Did she want another life on her conscience, if there was a better way? She wasn't a violent person (no matter what Midas said) and Avalon didn't deserve a mother who'd barbequed a man in the throne room.

"Do you want to surrender, yet?" Gwen offered. There was still time to douse the flames. As much as she hated the man, she was willing to lock him up in jail, rather than cremate him alive. "Give up your plan to enslave the Bad folk and steal Camelot. Then, Midas and I will help you."

Midas sent her a mystified look, crushing another dead bird with his boot heel. "No, we won't."

"We have to."

"Why? I promised to kill him and I'm keeping my word. He kidnapped Avalon and tried to force you to marry him, Gwen. Let the bastard fry."

She began yanking the purple velvet curtains from the windows, intending to use them to smother the flames. "You know, *I'm* supposed to be the heartless one in our marriage."

"Only according to you. Everyone else knows better." Midas was clearly working hard to overcome his kind and gentle nature, but maybe he could practice his new Badass skills *later*.

"Just help me put him out. I won and even he knows it. He doesn't have to die. *We're* not the villains here."

Golden eyes rolled in exasperation. "Fucking hell…"

"You haven't won." The Scarecrow snarled, his burlap face falling apart as his stuffing was consumed. "I won't let you." He crawled towards the throne, his blackening stick fingers grabbing for a remote control devise sitting on the armrest. "I'll die happy, knowing you two will suffer!" He pressed one of the buttons and then slumped onto the floor, the last of his energy expended.

Midas scowled. "What the hell is that thing?"

"I have no idea." Gwen headed for the Scarecrow's still form with the curtains, still intending to help the jackass. "I can't believe you want to keep starting drama, even when you're on fire." She snapped at him. "You could at least *try* to be grateful that, after everything you've done, Midas and I are nice enough people to save your ass."

"Stop blaming me for this idea, Gwen. *You're* the one who wants to save him." None the less, Midas started forward, sticking the letter opener through his belt loop. "And do not burn yourself, helping that idiot. *I* will put him out, if you're so determined to spare his life."

"Then you'd be the one scalding your hands…" Gwen broke off mid-word and her eyebrows shot up, realizing for the first time that he wasn't wearing his gloves. "Midas?"

"Oh. Right." He haphazardly dropped the curtains over the Scarecrow, snuffing out the fire, and then held up his palms. "My curse was cured."

"*Cured?*" She gaped up at him.

"Yes. Wait here for a moment. I need to find an extinguisher." He ducked back into the hall.

"How are you cured?" She shouted after him. "You said it was impossible. You said you had to have *everything* for the spell to be broken."

"I married you." Midas said simply, coming back in with a red canister of fire retardant. "And you gave me everything, Gwen." He shrugged, like it was all obvious.

Harriet warily watched him from the window sill. The Scarecrow gave another sickly moaning threat that sounded like "Camlann Project."

Gwen ignored them, staring at Midas in amazement as he sprayed the entire room down, dousing the flames. "So you can touch me?" She clarified when he was done firefighting.

"Yes."

She grinned, excited and thrilled. "Really?"

"Yes." He set the extinguisher down, moving closer to her.

"Then why aren't you touching me, husband?"

Midas let out a shuddering breath. "I have waited so long." His hand hesitantly came out to brush over her hair, groaning at the feel of her curls against his bare palm. "Jesus." He whispered, sounding awed. "I knew you'd feel better than anything I could imagine."

Gwen was hypnotized by the sensation of his hand touching her with no leather between them. "I am just madly in love with you." She whispered, echoing his earlier words.

Midas slowly smiled, dipping his head down to kiss her.

Before his lips could meet Gwen's, a strange noise came from out in the hall. Both of their heads swiveled towards the door.

...And Gwen immediately knew what the "Camlann Project" was.

What the Scarecrow had been doing with that damn remote control. What Dark Science was capable of at its very worst.

"Arthur." She gasped, horror filling her.

The Scarecrow had reanimated his body. Arthur's smashed, decayed corpse was out of his tomb and walking around. His once handsome face was now a stitched-up quilt of gray skin, held together with bits of thread and metal. He lurched forward, his milky eyes fixed on Gwen. Whatever fragments of Arthur remained in his embalmed brain, he clearly recalled his last few moments of life.

And he was clearly pissed about them.

"Gweeeennnnnnn." It was a hiss of pure hatred.

"Oh *shit*." Gwen retreated a step, her heart hammering, and came up against Midas. His huge arm folded around her protectively and she instantly felt safer. Well, as safe as a girl *could* feel, when her deceased ex had been transformed into a vengeance-seeking monster.

"So that's the Mean Thing." Midas whispered, almost to himself. "No wonder she was scared."

Gwen swallowed hard. "Avi predicted this?"

"She told me he'd hurt you two, if I didn't save you."

Gwen cringed at that news. "Maybe this was not such a great day for you to cure your curse. I'd really, *really* like it if you could golden him still."

"It wouldn't have worked, anyway. He's not alive." Midas nudged her behind him, his attention on Arthur. "Nothing that smells that God-awful is alive."

Arthur seemed to understand that and take offence. His

head tilted in a disturbingly jerky way. His unblinking gaze narrowing at Midas.

"You remember me, don't you, Art?" Midas sounded strangely pleased by that. "You knew I'd be back in Camelot. You *knew* I'd come for what's rightfully mine, you abusive, thieving, lying, cheating cocksucker."

Gwen gave his shoulder a frustrated whack. "Must you antagonize the zombie?"

"He started it."

Yeah... Arthur definitely remembered Midas. His lips pulled back in a snarl, revealing sharpened green teeth dripping with a foul-smelling goo.

"I'm not a dentist, but that doesn't look right." Midas mused, staying in front of her.

"That's one of the White Rabbit's poisons." Gwen caught hold of his arm, not wanting him to get any closer to Arthur. "I recognize the smell. They've dosed his mouth with it. Don't let him bite you."

"Damn, that was my first line of attack, too."

"Is it *really* the best time to be a smartass?"

Arthur emitted a shrill screech of undead rage, his jaw opening to an unnatural angle. Gwen wasn't sure if it was because he was dead or because so much of his face had shattered when he collided with the cobblestones. Either way it was ghastly. She cringed, knowing she'd never forget the eerie width of his mouth or the horrible sound he made.

Arthur staggered at Midas, his arms outstretched. Wanting revenge. Wanting to kill them both. His too-long fingernails were all coated in the green venom, too.

"Get back! Get back!" Gwen dragged Midas out of the way. "We need to rekill him. *Now*."

Midas' laser-fast mind was sorting through ideas. "Do you have that gun?"

"I used all the bullets shooting people in the legs, back in Celliwig."

"In the fucking *legs*? If you're going to shoot, aim for the head, Gwen!"

All the noise and moldering was too much for Harriet. She gave another frantic squawk, wanting to fly away. She really wasn't the brightest bird. Before she found the window that she'd literally been sitting next to, she flailed around the room a few times. Sparks rained down on the Scarecrow's body, lighting the curtain on fire. Just like that, he was cooking, again. Gwen was in no mood to save him, this time. Harriet didn't care, either. She finally figured out how to escape the throne room and took off into the gray sky.

Too bad Gwen and Midas couldn't go with her.

"Arthur?" Gwen tried. "If you're in there, I didn't mean to knock you off the balcony. It was an accident. You didn't give me a choice. Ordinarily, I'm a very nonviolent person."

Arthur responded with another wrathful scream.

"I don't think he believes you about that part, kitten."

"Well he can ask anybody! I hardly ever hurt people, who don't deserve it."

Arthur went for Gwen, again, his body uncoordinated and surprisingly fast. How did he move like that, with so many broken bones? Dark Science was wasted on evil. It should be helping doctors or something.

Midas' pushed her backwards, out of range. "Maybe you should just let me deal with Arthur." He suggested. "I'm the kind and gentle one in our relationship. He might listen to me."

She gave a skeptical scoff, which was a totally fair response considering how "kind and gentle" he'd been so far. "I think you're working hard to hide your sensitivity, today."

"It's actually not that hard to hide." He flashed her a quick look over his shoulder. "Stay right here, okay? I'm going to try something."

"Do *not* die. I'm serious."

"I'm not going to die. When a man has everything, he fights to keep it." He turned back to Arthur, ready to display his innate compassion. "Good news, dickhead. It looks like I get to kill you, after all."

Arthur's attention left Gwen, flicking back to Midas. He snapped his teeth threateningly, sticky poison dripping down his chin and eating through the remaining flesh.

"You should have taken Jill and been happy." Midas told him, his golden gaze intense. "You should have just given me my wife and daughter and left us alone. Nothing could keep me from my family. You *knew* that. Now poor Jill is dead, because you're a greedy fool."

Another infuriated scream, green goo flying like spittle. This one was the most ear-piercing, yet.

"Jill's dead." Midas repeated, as if he understood the meaning behind Arthur's angry noise. In a way, Jill probably would have been happy that her death had effected Arthur so greatly, even in his present cadaverous state. "Your True Love deserved better than you. *So* much better. You killed her, as surely as you killed yourself."

Arthur raced at him, ready to rip him apart.

"*Midas!*" Gwen cried in panic.

But, he'd been waiting for the assault. In one smooth movement, Midas reached down and ripped the burning curtain from the Scarecrow's ashes and hurled it at Arthur. The smoldering fabric enveloped him, lighting his chemical soaked body aflame. Arthur stumbled forward, still yowling. Whether by accident or design, he headed right for Gwen.

She scampered back, terrified that he was going to burn her or eat her or both. "Midas!" She shouted again, coming up against the wall of the throne room. She had nowhere else to retreat.

Her husband responded by slamming Lyrssa's sword straight into Arthur's skull. The letter opener sunk into his head, right up to the handle. Like a puppet who'd had his strings cut, Arthur slumped to the ground dead.

Again.

Gwen stood there for a beat, breathing hard.

"See how much simpler it is if you aim for the head?" Midas demanded.

She gave a nod, staring down at The Mean Thing That Had Once Been Arthur and then up at Midas. "Kind and gentle, huh?" She finally got out.

"You should have seen the tawdry, feral animal option." He shot her a grave look. "Luckily, I'm a king now, so I always go for the gallant alternative. My wife deplores violence."

Gwen straightened away from the wall. "You know, you're not the Right Man, after all."

That seemed to startle him. "Yes, I am." Midas argued. "I know right from wrong and I'm one-hundred percent the *Right* Man."

"Nope." She walked into his arms, leaning against his chest and hugging him tight. "I was thinking way too small, when I made my list. You check off every wish I've ever had for my husband and like a thousand others that I didn't even know I was looking for."

He slowly smiled. "Yeah?"

"Yeah." Gwen leaned up to kiss him. "So you're not the Right Man, Midas Skycast." She met his beautiful eyes. "You're the *Only* Man."

Epilogue

The marriage contract between the parties takes precedent over all clauses of this Contract. All clauses in this Contract will be renegotiated to reflect the changed circumstances of the parties (ie: their status as True Loves) and their desire to stay legally, legitimately, and happily married.

Their wedding vows are therefore considered binding in perpetuity.

Clause 27-Amendment to all Clauses

Six Months Later

Welcome to the Celliwig Animal Sanctuary and Environmental Renewal District!

Gwen smiled, her eyes examining the sign. "That is the classiest billboard I've ever seen. And considering the sheer number of them you've erected recently, that is really saying something."

Midas nodded. "I went with something understated and regal, this time." He gestured to the thirteen foot robotic rocking-horsefly slowly flapping its wings on the top. "Avalon helped me with that part."

"You two are an amazing team." Gwen stood on tiptoe to kiss him. "It's beautiful. Thank you."

Midas' mouth curved. "We just have to hope that Harriet doesn't burn it down."

"Don't worry. I've been working with her with the dog whistle. She's getting *much* better at not starting fires."

Midas shook his head in amused exasperation.

Dragging Celliwig out of the squalor had been Gwen's idea. Not only was it crazy, it was, financially speaking, a dud of a plan. Under her Good little program, the poorest, Baddest citizens of Camelot were put to work replanting trees and caring for all the mutant animals Gwen had adopted. No one in the town seemed to be holding a grudge about Trystan killing quite a few citizens when he saved Gwen. Not when the queen was so very willing to make amends by making Celliwig her pet project. New buildings were going up and food was plentiful for everyone.

Soon, the thick mud would once again nourish a forest and bizarre creatures would populate the landscape. The people who lived in Celliwig would have a new livelihood tending the saplings and running tours for all the visitors who wanted to see the world's only firebird and monkena. On paper, it all seemed nuts and wouldn't show a profit for quite a while, but Midas' had still allocated heaps of gold to the plan.

Parents always had to invest in the future.

Midas' attention slipped over to Avalon. Trystan was teaching her to sword fight and it was adorable. The little wooden blade was painted pink and damn if she wasn't a natural at wielding it. Gwen called him biased, but Midas was pretty sure his daughter was the best at everything she tried.

"More gryphons showed up today." Gwen told him, following his gaze. "That makes nearly fifty."

Midas smiled, pleased. "I didn't know there were fifty of them left in the whole world."

"I think we should give them Mount Baden. No one else lives there, because it's so high, and gryphons love mountains. Trystan says most of his people would be happier if they had their own space." She paused. "By the way, I've made him Camelot's Official Ambassador to Gryphon Affairs."

"Did you tell *him* that?"

"Of course."

"Did he say 'no'?"

"Of course." She smirked. "But, Avi and I will change his mind."

"Of course." Midas had no doubt that poor Trystan would be ambassador-ing all over the kingdom. Gwen and Avalon were an irresistible force. He and Trystan would do anything they wanted, because those two little blondes owned their hearts.

"The gryphons need a place they can fly." Gwen continued, earnestly. "This is the right thing to do."

"I know." He murmured, watching his daughter play. "Give them the mountain. Give them whatever they need to rebuild and thrive."

Everyone deserved a chance to be as happy as he was.

Avi was wearing her favorite outfit, again. The little girl who would one day be the Great Queen had decorated the plain white t-shirt herself. It was studded with random sequins and featured two hand-printed words, with some of the letters backwards: *Lyrssa Lives*. She'd worn it in the official coronation portrait, right over her designer taffeta dress.

That family picture --the first and *best* family picture Midas had ever been in-- had gone viral around the world. Guinevere was in the center of the frame, looking beautiful and proud. Midas had his arm around her, a half-smile on his face as he gazed down at his wife. Beside them, Trystan stood stoically, with Avalon beaming from her perch on his shoulder.

The classiest woman in creation, the former Kingpin of Camelot, a gryphon with battle scarred wings, and a five year old enchantress. Good and Bad, but still a family. Somehow it became *the* picture for the Villains' Rights Movement. Scarlett Riding-Wolf had plastered it on her website, showing people what her crusade for equality was really all about. Midas didn't even complain about her making his family a PSA. He liked everyone knowing the four of them belonged together.

Most surprising, though, had been the gryphons' response to the photograph.

The kingdom that had once led the Looking Glass Campaigns was now headed by a family who bore the name of the Skycast Clan. It contained an actual gryphon and a tiny princess who wore a homemade Lyrssa Highstorm shirt everywhere she went. No other land had ever supported the gryphons so openly. It seemed to give them hope.

The remnants of Trystan's people had begun showing up almost at once and they just kept arriving. Midas was glad. Wherever they had come from and whatever they had faced, everyone could find a new home in Camelot. It was a land for second chances.

"Sometimes the first family you get isn't the right one." He quoted softly.

"I like that. Did you make it up?"

"According to Avalon, I did." He said smugly

She grinned at that. "We really should have more, you know."

"More what? Gryphons?"

"No, *children*." She gave him a playful bat on the arm. "Give Avalon someone new to play with, so poor Trystan can have a moment's peace, every once in a while."

Midas blinked. He hadn't really considered the idea before, but it definitely had some merit. "More is always better." He allowed, thoughtfully.

"So you keep telling me." Gwen leaned against him. "Besides, once you get Camelot whipped into shape, you're going to need something new to occupy your days. I mean you shut down your whole business." She slanted him a quick look. "Are you sure you don't miss it?"

"I'm sure."

Running a kingdom wasn't any different than running his underworld empire, except, obviously, his illegal books had all been in better order. The challenge of getting Camelot organized was fun, though. And he *loved* that he now had a partner to talk to. Midas had no idea how he'd ever gotten anything done without Gwen to offer him her opinion. He thought so much clearer and felt so much surer in his decisions. All in all, being king was head and shoulders better than being the Kingpin.

Plus, he liked the throne.

"You sure?" Gwen pressed. "You don't miss being a notorious criminal?"

"I'm happy with my new job. There's always something to do around this dump."

Gwen elbowed him in small punishment and Midas laughed.

He still enjoyed complaining about Camelot, but most of the kingdom seemed surprisingly willing to accept him as king. It could be because Gwen and the wizards were backing him or maybe because people were just tired of war.

...Or, most likely, because of the bags of money he was dumping into the royal treasury. For the first time in years, Camelot's citizens were getting paid for their work and had access to social programs. Midas' PR firm was sure to mention that on the many commercials he'd commissioned. A little advertising never hurt anything. If it made it easier for Avalon to one day wear her crown, then Midas would do everything he could to help Good folk/Bad folk relations.

Not that everything was perfect, of course. Midas still hadn't found Esmeralda, something Scarlett called to remind him about daily. Likewise, Galahad was still missing. Since Midas had promised his wife he'd find the Great Beige Hope that annoyed him a bit.

Also some members of the Round Table were less than pleased with him cutting all his criminal ties. The Walrus had been especially vocal about Midas' "defection to the Good side" and fled Camelot in protest. Midas wouldn't care, except he heard whispers that the tusked idiot had taken the White Rabbit with him. Midas didn't like the idea of Camelot's foremost Dark Scientist free in the world.

Once they'd had the wand back, they'd been able to erase

Dark Science from Camelot forever, just as Gwen predicted. The formula had been destroyed, along with all the Rabbit's notes on the Camlann Project. Even the lab had been razed. Merlyn's magic had scrubbed Camelot clean, once and for all.

But who knew what other evil thoughts lurked in that bunny's brain? Most Bad folks had bounced back from the formula without any ill effects, but that might not be the case next time. They were going to have to track that cotton-tailed freak down, before he caused more chaos.

Still, Midas could handle all that. The world was only so big. Sooner or later, he would find Esmeralda, Galahad, *and* the White Rabbit. In the meantime, though, he had a job that interested him and a family that brought him joy. His life was blessed.

"I know bailing out Camelot is costing you a lot of money." Gwen told him. "I can't understand any of those budget graphs, but I know you're the one paying the bills."

He shrugged. "I have plenty of money and I like spending it."

"I've noticed that."

Midas arched a brow at her dry tone. "Is this about the diamond sinks in the master bathroom, again?"

"And that really big mattress in our bedroom. It's... *really* big."

"The biggest one ever made." He agreed happily. "I made sure of it."

"I needed a map to find my way off of it this morning, Midas."

"Kitten, keeping you in that bed is kind of my goal in life, so I'm not complaining." He held her hand, because he *loved* holding her hand. "You said I could redecorate the palace any way I wanted. I'm starting by adding a little bit of style to our room."

"The mirrored ceilings *do* make a statement."

Oh yeah. He loved those. He also wanted to make sure that nothing in the royal bedchamber reminded her of Arthur's death. Midas had ripped the wall out separating the king and queen's rooms, making one huge space. He'd also gotten rid of the balcony, replaced all the boring furniture, and added access to a private, rooftop hot tub.

He was pretty pleased with the results.

"People like us can't do beige, Mrs. Skycast." Midas gave her fingers a squeeze. "But I *am* working to be more practical. I didn't build a waterslide for Avalon, or the race track for the senior wizards' home, or the escalator for the kitchen."

Yet.

Gwen eyed him skeptically. "How many trucks of toys drove up to the orphanage yesterday?"

"Only enough to carry the bicycles." He shrugged, unrepentant. "Children need toys."

"You're such a marshmallow."

"Not lackluster, though."

"No, definitely *not* lackluster." Gwen laid her head on his shoulder. "And I like the hospital and school you're building. That's a very practical and worthwhile use of money."

"Well, after a while, even buying diamond sinks and waterslides get boring. You want more."

"No waterslides, Midas. I mean it. Avalon already got the art studio and puppet theater and a whole subdivision of bouncy houses. Clause 24- 'Adoption of Avalon Skycast' says you're not supposed to spoil her."

"It says I'll *try* not to spoil her."

"You're not trying, at all..." Gwen stopped short. "My God. Look at that!" She pointed at the sky.

Midas glanced up, as shocked as she was. The sky was blue. Honest to God *blue*. The clouds were slowly dissipating and the bright sun was shining down. For the first time in years, the weather wasn't gloomy and gray.

Holy shit.

Midas held out his free palm so he could feel the sunlight on his skin. He'd nearly forgotten how warm it was. "Maybe your environmental initiatives are working faster than we thought."

She sent him a brilliant smile. "Maybe Camelot just likes its new king."

He arched a brow at that fanciful thought. "Aren't you supposed to be the practical, logical half of our relationship?"

"I am. Most of the time. But some things go deeper than logic."

"Well, however it happened, sunshine is something money can't buy. Nothing of value is for sale." Midas knew that, now. "I spend a lot, Gwen. I'll probably *always* spend a lot." He kissed her temple. "But, I know you never get the *best* if there's a price tag attached. The best has to be given. You taught me that."

"So you don't wish you could still turn things to gold?" She dragged her attention away from the azure sky. "Not even for a minute?"

"I would go back to living in the stable, before I endured that curse again." Midas smoothed a palm over her hair, reveling in the sensation of the shiny strands against his bare flesh. He would never get used to the magic of it. "Being able to feel you is worth… everything."

Blue eyes gleamed. "I do have a fondness for that stable."

"I know. And since we're in Celliwig anyway…" Midas began herding his wife towards his favorite bed of hay. "We should go take a look at the stable, don't you think? Make sure everything is okay over there."

"It's magically protected." Gwen reminded him archly. She allowed herself to be tugged along, though. "I'm sure it's fine."

"Can't be too careful." His fingers slipped between hers. God, he loved the feel of her skin. He wanted to run his hands over every square inch of her body. Again. The first time they'd made love after his curse was lifted, he'd held her on his lap and come just from touching her. Hell, if he might not do it again.

Gwen's breathing quickened, picking up on his arousal. "I have a feeling this is going to entail more than just a building inspection, your highness."

"Maybe." Midas leaned down so he could whisper into her ear. "On our walk over there, feel free to brainstorm some almost-Bad ways you can thank your gallant True Love for saving this horrible town."

"How about a nice pecan pie? I make a hell of a pecan pie, you know."

"I'm thinking of something sweeter." Midas scooped her up in his arms, carrying her through the mud in front of the stable. "Need some suggestions?"

"I'm pretty sure I can figure it out." Gwen laughed as he maneuvered her through the door and finally deposited her on the ground. "How about this?" She reached into her pocket and came up with a small velvet box.

Midas blinked, surprised. "What's that? A gift? For me?"

"For you." She handed it to him. "Open it."

Inside was a ring. Gold and studded with square cut sapphires, all in his favorite shade of lake-blue. And engraved on the interior were five simple words: *I belong with Guinevere Skycast.*

A wedding band. For him.

"In case you ever forget where you're meant to be." She told him quietly.

Midas' throat got tight. "You are the only place I've ever belonged." He said hoarsely, staring down at his ring with pride. It was better than the billboards. Everyone would know she'd claimed him. That they were connected. "I love it." He met her eyes. "I love *you*."

"I love you, too." She pulled the ring free and slid it onto his finger.

Midas could feel the magic locking it in place and satisfaction filled him. "My wife." He whispered.

"Yours." Gwen stood on tiptoe to kiss him. "Never wear jewelry from anyone else, though." She warned with a mock frown. "I wouldn't like it."

Midas picked her up again and swept her towards the stall where he'd once thought he'd live his entire life with nothing. "All I ever wanted was the best. Now, I've got it. I have *everything*."

"Damn straight." Gwen was already unbuttoning his coat for him. "*My* husband."

"Yours." He always had been. "You and me and no one else, kitten. Equal partners. For ever after."

"It's a deal." She yanked him down for a kiss. "Now strip, stable boy."

Midas chuckled against her lips.

He truly was the richest man in Camelot.

All the Clauses in the Contract

Clause 1- General Purpose of Contract
This Contract is entered into by Guinevere Pendragon and Midas (no last name given) willingly and knowingly. Each party wishes to define their rights and obligations under the arrangement herein discussed and attest that they fully understand all its terms, conditions, clauses, and caveats. The purpose of this Contract is to ensure there will be no misunderstanding in the future and to facilitate a smooth and profitable partnership.

Clause 2- Change of Names
Parties will keep their respective last names. Or lack thereof.

Clause 3- Care and Protection of Avalon Pendragon (a minor)
Midas (no last name given) will do his best to protect Avalon Pendragon (a minor). He will *attempt to* use appropriate language when around her (emphasis his) and refrain from exposing her to unsavory elements. He will provide a suitable bodyguard. He will not harm Avalon Pendragon, endanger her, deliberately hurt her feelings, allow her to be injured by a failure of action on his part, interfere with her upbringing, or instigate unnecessary conversations. When possible, he will simply ignore her.

Clause 4- Physical Activity Between Parties
There is no expectation, implied or stated, that the parties' union will ever be consummated.

Clause 5- Oversight of the Kingdom
Upon reclaiming the kingdom, Guinevere Pendragon promises to make Midas (no last name given) King of Camelot, with the understanding that Avalon Pendragon is to remain, now and forevermore, heir to the throne. He may rule by Guinevere Pendragon's side for as long as he wishes, provided that he does not wantonly oppress, torture, or enslave their subjects.

Clause 6- Partnership Responsibilities of Guinevere Pendragon
Guinevere Pendragon will, to the best of her abilities, offer Midas (no last name given) protection from her enemies. In the event that her bid to reclaim Camelot is unsuccessful, she will take full responsibility for the hostilities with said enemies and will endeavor to face the consequences alone. She will at no time allow him to be endangered, if she has the means to prevent it.

Clause 7- Separate Lives and Other Relationships
The parties agree to lead separate lives. They will do their best not to infringe upon the private business of the other party. Midas (no last name given) is free to pursue outside affairs, so long as he does not bring strangers around Avalon Pendragon (a minor). Guinevere Pendragon will not pursue outside affairs while married to Midas. She will be given her own bedroom, with a lock.

Clause 8- Privacy and Disclosure
Full disclosure need not be given on matters that happened before parties met, do not pertain to the other party, and/or do not violate any other clauses in the agreement. Especially if those matters regard Arthur Pendragon.

Clause 9- Partnership Responsibilities of Midas (no last name given)
Midas (no last name given) will furnish Guinevere Pendragon and her daughter with shelter, food, reasonable support in the face of their enemies, and the supplies necessary to enact her campaign, on the condition that she pay him back for all expenses once Camelot has been returned to her control. He may offer input on the campaign, as he deems necessary, with the understanding that Guinevere Pendragon is in command of the offensive and in charge of *all* strategic planning. (Please note emphasis on the word "all.")

Clause 10- Communication Between Partners
Each day, the parties will meet to frankly discuss new/developing issues that could impact their partnership. Honesty is expected.

Clause 11- Reasons for Nullification and/or Termination of Marriage
The Contract can be voided for any of the following reasons: Abuse, lies, excessive drinking and/or drug use, unseemly behavior around Avalon, general incompatibility, misuse of magic, breaking any clauses in the Contract, and/or a judgment by one or both parties that the

agreement is no longer in the best interest of them, their dependents, or the Kingdom of Camelot for any reason whatsoever, even if it is not specifically listed above. It can also be terminated in case of the discovery of Midas' True Love.

Clause 12- Respect and Cooperation Between Partners
Cooperation is the goal of this partnership. Parties will treat each other with respect and consideration. If need be, they will also provide a sounding board for ideas or offer appropriate support. If an issue is of importance to one party, they can request the second party's assistance, collaboration, or focus on said issue. The second party will do his/her best to accommodate them without whining.

Clause 13- Limitation of Surprises
Guinevere Pendragon agrees to limit surprises to three (3) a day.

Clause 14- Renegotiation of the Contract
At any time, any portion of this Contract may be renegotiated by the parties, to reflect their current and/or changing circumstances. Both parties must agree to the changes, without duress, or the Contract cannot be altered. Once altered it will be binding. Unless they want to alter it again.

Clause 15- Liabilities to Partnership
Both parties will promptly share any liabilities that could negatively impact the success of the partnership. (ie: outside deals that would conflict with this Contract, relevant curses/spells, or particularly dangerous enemies.) When possible, they will deal with these liabilities as a team. If this is not possible, it is up to the effected party to solve the problem quickly, logically, and with as little bloodshed as possible.

Clause 16- Unexpected Situations
If a situation occurs not foreseen by this Contract, but needing action, the parties will mutually agree on an appropriate solution. Guinevere Pendragon will lead the discussion.

Clause 17- Instance of Guinevere Pendragon's Death
In case of the death of Guinevere Pendragon, Sir Galahad is granted guardianship of Avalon Pendragon (a minor) and full control of her estates. If he cannot be found, Midas (no last name given) will assume responsibility. He will try not to screw it up.

Clause 18- Instances of Midas' (no last name given) Death
In the case of Midas' (no last name given) death, his estate and property will be dispersed according to his Last Will and Testament. (Note: As he inexplicably has no Last Will and Testament as of the writing of this Contract, Guinevere Pendragon will help him draft one as soon as possible. Until then, his verbal instructions are that his entire estate pass to Mr. Trystan Airbourne, with the understanding that the man: "Give it all to who I'd want to give it to. He knows who I mean. And --f*ck-- tell him to buy himself a really fancy axe or something fun. Live a little.")

Clause 19- Disposition of Property of Midas (no last name given) in Event of Contract's Termination
In the event that the Contract is terminated or nullified, each party will leave the marriage with the property they brought into it. Therefore, Midas (no last name given) will retain his gold, his castle, his horses, his business, and all material belongings related to any of the above. He agrees to pay Guinevere Pendragon any alimony she wishes, even though she has repeatedly tried to talk him out of it.

Clause 20- Disposition of Property of Guinevere Pendragon in Event of Contract's Termination
In the event that the Contract is terminated or nullified, each party will leave the marriage with the property they brought into it. Therefore, Guinevere Pendragon will retain all estates inherited from her father and/or former husband (provided she can retrieve them from her enemies), her wedding band from Arthur Pendragon, and sole custody of Avalon Pendragon (a minor). She will not pay alimony to Midas (no last name given).

Clause 21- Amended Physical Contact Agreement (Containing Nullification of Clause 7-Separate Lives and Other Relationships)
Parties agree that their partnership is exclusive and monogamous. Additionally, each day, they will alternate mutually agreed on physical contact (ie: third-base behaviors). The purpose of said activity is the satisfaction of needs. Clothes will stay mostly on.

Clause 22- Consummation of Marriage (Containing Nullifications of Clauses 4- Physical Activity Between Parties and 21- Amended Physical Contact Agreement)
Parties agree to nullify all previously written rules regarding their

physical contact, with the exception of the fact that they will remain monogamous. The parties instead agree to engage in any consensual physical activity, at any time and for however long they both wish. Clothes may come off, as applicable.

Clause 23- Sharing a Name (Containing Nullification of Clause 2- Change of Names)
Parties agree that Guinevere, Avalon (a minor), and Midas will share a single, new and permanent last name, just as soon as they find one they like.

Clause 24- Adoption of Avalon Skycast (a minor) (Containing Nullification of Clause 3- Care and Protection of Avalon Pendragon (a minor) and Clause 17- Instance of Guinevere's Pendragon's Death)
Midas Skycast will formally and legally adopt Avalon Skycast (a minor) and have all the rights and responsibilities of a biological father. He will try not to spoil her too much.

Clause 25- Mr. Trystan Airbourne
Parties agree that, in the event of both of their deaths, guardianship of Avalon Skycast (a minor) and control of her estates will pass to Mr. Trystan Airbourne. Mr. Trystan Airbourne responds to this clause (verbally, as he would not sign a "pointless scroll which seeks to explain what is already obvious to all.") that he will not allow Guinevere and Midas Skycast to die. But if they *do*, it's because they were undoubtedly "stupid" and he will endeavor to raise Avalon correctly, so as not to follow their "f*cking stupid examples." Parties agree that this response means he willingly accepts the responsibilities of guardianship.

Clause 26- Jewelry from Other People
Guinevere Skycast agrees not to wear jewelry from other men, so long as Midas Skycast agrees not to wear jewelry from other women and to stop nagging her about this stupid clause.

Clause 27-Amendment to all Clauses
The marriage contract between the parties takes precedent over all clauses of this Contract. All clauses in this Contract will be renegotiated to reflect the changed circumstances of the parties (ie: their status as True Loves) and their desire to stay legally, legitimately, and happily married. Their wedding vows are therefore considered binding in perpetuity.

Author's Note

I almost didn't publish *Wicked Ugly Bad,* the first book in this series. When I finished it, I worried it was a little too strange. A romance novel-y mix of *Prison Break* and *The True Story of the 3 Little Pigs*. I was concerned that no one would get it. It was my sister, Elizabeth, who insisted that people would like it and she ended up being right. It is the bestselling book I've ever written.

Beast in Shining Armor, the second book in the series, was also sort of an accident. I had a dream about what should happen in Avenant's story and that's why he got one. I have never dreamed about any of my other characters, before or since, so I took it as a sign his book needed to be written. I finished the first draft in about six weeks, which is SUPER fast for me, and that book also sold very well.

I was now flushed with success.

Clearly, fairytales were --like-- my new thing. Ideas flowed and fans were telling me I'd done a good job and everything was coming up Cassie. Yay me! I immediately started to write the third book of the series, which would be about Esmeralda, the witch. What could possibly go wrong?

A lot, as it turned out.

Esmeralda hated every single hero I gave her. I am totally, totally serious. I've tried at least six. I have spent tens of thousands of words trying to convince her to pick one, but she's just not that into them. That's okay, though. I'll win her over eventually. And, in the meantime, I found Midas.

One of the many, many, *many* drafts of Ez's book featured her meeting up with a fellow inmate from the WUB Club: A gangster named Midas. Midas is actually mentioned in the first chapter of *Wicked Ugly Bad*, when Avenant is bitching in Tuesday share circle that he wants to join the other, better support group with "that guy who touches things and they turn to gold." Midas didn't actually appear "on screen," but he was there. So it made total sense for me to stick him in Ez's book. Within a chapter, I had scrapped the whole idea of him living in Wonderland, though. I couldn't think of a single reason he'd want to be there. But there was this tiny moment of the two of them walking in a garden, which completely sold me on his character:

Midas glanced at Esmeralda. "I've heard that everyone in

the Enchanted Forest is desperate to find you. Give them time and they'll save you from this nightmarish land. The money Prince Avenant is offering for your return is obscene even by my standards."

That made Ez feel better. "Did he convince Belle to marry him yet?"

"I don't know or care." Midas accidently brushed his hand over a rocking-horsefly that had landed on a leaf. Instantly, the delicate creature turned to gold, forever frozen in mid-flight. For a second, something like regret flashed in Midas' eyes and he yanked his fingers back.

Esmeralda felt bad for him, even though he was a dickhead. It must've been hell never to touch anything living.

Annnnnd… I was pretty much done with that draft of the book.

That rocking-horsefly allowed me to see inside Midas and his *real* story was suddenly right there in front of me. This flashy, misunderstood mobster of a guy had everything except what he most longed for. Almost immediately, I began *The Kingpin of Camelot*.

Guinevere's character was not nearly so clear to me. …Not until the Contract. Once she came up with her plan to create a clause for every aspect of their "fake marriage," she ran with it and dragged poor Midas along for the ride. And he did not resist real hard. Except for vainly trying to edit his constant swearing, Midas couldn't have been more cooperative with my mission to give them a happily ever after. He was just *crazy* in love with Gwen, which made my job simple. Writing their relationship was only difficult in the sense that they talked *a lot*, which is why this is the longest book I've published to date.

Avalon's character was originally added because King Midas has a daughter in the Greek Myth. Trystan came from (surprise) another abandoned draft of Ez's book. Honestly, I'm not sure when I decided to bring him over here, but he liked it and decided to stay. Both of them became *much* bigger parts of the story than I initially intended, as their characters developed. Especially Trystan. He was very pushy about being included.

That is one of the great joys (and sometimes frustrations) of writing. Once the characters start talking on the page, they go their own way and you just have to try and keep up. This is why you sometimes wind up with 112 unacceptable versions of a book about a witch in Wonderland. It is also why you sometimes wind up with a gryphon trying to pass on his culture to a little girl as they play with fashion dolls. Maybe it's because my sister and I used to create epic murder-mystery, action-adventure plays with our bedraggled heaps of Barbies, but that scene is probably my favorite part of the whole book. I always think it's better to let the characters decide how their story will go. They usually have better ideas than I do.

If you were wondering, catur was a real game in sixth century India. It's believed to be the ancestor of chess and it did indeed have elephant pieces. The version Midas played is in no way accurate to the real game, though. It really couldn't be. Apparently, no one knows what the exact rules were or how the elephant pieces moved, but I am intrigued by the whole idea.

The very basic outline for the plot of *The Kingpin of Camelot* came from the *Sing a Song of Sixpence* nursery rhyme:

> Sing a song of sixpence
> A pocket full of rye.
> Four-and-twenty blackbirds.
> Baked in a pie.
> When the pie was opened
> The birds began to sing.
> Wasn't that a dainty dish,
> To set before the king?
>
> The king was in the counting house,
> Counting out his money.
> The queen was in her parlor,
> Eating bread and honey.
> The maid was in the garden,
> Hanging out the clothes,
> When along came a blackbird,
> And pecked off her nose.

Midas = King, Scarecrow = Blackbirds, Gwen = Queen. The other hundred and thirty thousand words are just filling in the blanks. Also, I tossed in some Arthurian legend stuff and pieces of the King Midas myth, obviously. And Dark Science, which I see as the logical antithesis of the natural magic that inhabits this world.

As I've mentioned before, I grew up reading romance novels, most of which were purchased in secondhand bookshops and published in the 1990s. Many of them were Regency Romances, featuring feisty heroines and brooding heroes. (Think of *The Lion's Lady* by Julie Garwood.) I would say the *Kingpin of Camelot* ended up as my funhouse-mirror version of that genre. The couple's marriage comes early in the book, there is an underlying focus on social position, and the real plot is figuring out how two very different people from two very different spheres can make a relationship work.

I would like to write a story for Trystan and figure out where perfect, beige Galahad wound up, but I'm not really sure when that will happen. My next foray into a *Kinda Fairytale* book will almost definitely (probably) be yet another attempt to get Esmeralda to cooperate. Pray for me.

Please drop me a line if you have any questions or comments about this book or any other at: starturtlepublishing@gmail.com. The same email address can be used to sign up for our mailing list for news about our upcoming books. We also have a Facebook page and a webpage, which we update fairly regularly. I hope to see you there!

Be sure to check out *Warrior from the Shadowland*, the first book of the "Elemental-Phases" paranormal romance series also by Cassandra Gannon. Now Available!

Elementals: Water, Earth, Fire and Air are only the beginning. Elementals support everything from Darkness to Time, secretly maintaining the processes of nature. Only now the Elementals are nearly extinct. Two years ago, the Air House released a plague that killed ninety percent of them. With their society in chaos and so many of their kind dead, they can't find their Phase-Matches; the other halves of themselves. Without Matches they can't have any more children and without the Elementals, the world will end. Again.

Cross: Cross, of the Shadow House nearly triggered an apocalypse once before. The last of the Shadow Elementals, the weight of all the Darkness in the universe has fallen on his shoulders. The crushing power of it should have killed him long ago and he would have welcomed an end to the pain. Except Cross knows his Match is out there. The woman he's dreamed of forever. He'll do whatever it takes to find her…even go to the human realm.

Nia: Elemental laws forbid mixing with the humans, but Nia, of the Water House isn't a woman who gives up easily. Nia and her ragtag group of "rebels" believe a small town in Florida holds the secrets to their survival. They head there looking for answers, but everything's going wrong. Other Elementals are out for their blood, human technology is sort of baffling, and now the cops are closing in. When Cross arrives, Nia knows he's her Match. Unfortunately, he's teetering on the edge of crazy and refusing to touch her, because he thinks his powers are dangerous. It's up to Nia to convince him they're meant to be, stage a jailbreak, and evade the bad guys.

Oh, and save the universe.

Printed in Great Britain
by Amazon